"A lu[...]d
and [...]
—[...]y

"This wickedly exciting romance will draw you in and take hold of your heart."
—*USA Today* bestselling author Elizabeth Boyle

"Regency fans will thrill to this superbly sensual tale of an icy widow and two decadent rakes.... Balancing deliciously erotic encounters with compelling romantic tension and populating a convincing historical setting with a strong cast of well-developed characters, prolific romance author Wildes provides a spectacular and skillfully handled story that stands head and shoulders above the average historical romance."
—*Publishers Weekly* (starred review)

"Wickedly delicious and daring, Wildes's tale tantalizes with an erotic fantasy that is also a well-crafted Regency romance. She delivers a page-turner that captures the era, the mores, and the scandalous behavior that lurks beneath the surface."
—*Romantic Times* (4½ stars, top pick)

"Emma Wildes has thoroughly enchanted e-book readers with her emotionally charged story lines.... [A] gem of an author ... Ms. Wildes tells this story with plenty of compassion, humor, and even a bit of suspense to keep readers riveted to each scandalous scene—and everything in between."
—Romance Junkies

continued ...

Also by Emma Wildes

Notorious Bachelors
My Lord Scandal

Seducing the Highlander
Lessons from a Scarlet Lady
An Indecent Proposition

EMMA WILDES

Our Wicked Mistake

NOTORIOUS BACHELORS

A SIGNET ECLIPSE BOOK

SIGNET ECLIPSE
Published by New American Library, a division of
Penguin Group (USA) Inc., 375 Hudson Street,
New York, New York 10014, USA
Penguin Group (Canada), 90 Eglinton Avenue East, Suite 700, Toronto,
Ontario M4P 2Y3, Canada (a division of Pearson Penguin Canada Inc.)
Penguin Books Ltd., 80 Strand, London WC2R 0RL, England
Penguin Ireland, 25 St. Stephen's Green, Dublin 2,
Ireland (a division of Penguin Books Ltd.)
Penguin Group (Australia), 250 Camberwell Road, Camberwell, Victoria 3124,
Australia (a division of Pearson Australia Group Pty. Ltd.)
Penguin Books India Pvt. Ltd., 11 Community Centre, Panchsheel Park,
New Delhi - 110 017, India
Penguin Group (NZ), 67 Apollo Drive, Rosedale, North Shore 0632,
New Zealand (a division of Pearson New Zealand Ltd.)
Penguin Books (South Africa) (Pty.) Ltd., 24 Sturdee Avenue,
Rosebank, Johannesburg 2196, South Africa

Penguin Books Ltd., Registered Offices:
80 Strand, London WC2R 0RL, England

First published by Signet Eclipse, an imprint of New American Library,
a division of Penguin Group (USA) Inc.

First Printing, October 2010
10 9 8 7 6 5 4 3 2 1

To Jon and Jody McMahel, who have been wickedly wonderful friends for years and traveled with me on my author journey.

ACKNOWLEDGMENTS

Many thanks to Barbara Poelle and Laura Cifelli, as always. Your professional guidance aside, you both make me laugh. What a wonderful gift.

Chapter One

London, 1816
Satan's Den

The matter had come down to an old-fashioned duel, no pistols or swords in sight.

It's my own damned fault, Luke Daudet, Viscount Altea, acknowledged to himself, because he'd been more reckless and restless than ever lately, with both women and cards. His reputation, it seemed, had preceded him.

And now he was going to pay for his wicked ways.

"Seven thousand is a sum for boys, not men."

As a challenge, it was made quietly enough, but everyone present seemed to have heard it.

The man across from him smiled. "Let's make this more interesting, my lord. Shall we? Two cards to go in this hand . . . why not up the stakes a bit? If you've the stomach, that is. We play the house, but what about a side bet, you and I, Altea?"

The fire blazing in the opulent marble fireplace was unnecessary, considering the closeness of the shrouded room. Thick velvet draperies contained the smell of cologne, tobacco, and spilled brandy. Silence spread like a graveyard mist, the only sound the crackle of the lively logs spitting in the background. Even the liveried footmen stopped with their ceaseless rounds of drink trays, arrested figures standing almost absurdly still in the shadows as the scene unfolded.

Damnation. I've gotten myself into this.

Was there a politic way out of this untenable situation? He doubted it since, when he thought about it, the whole event was the inevitable product of his recent slide into concentrated debauchery.

Willing himself to not show even the slightest hint of emotion, Luke simply smiled in negligent acknowledgment. His voice pleasant, he asked politely, "How much more interesting?"

"A *lot* more interesting. What say you, my lord?"

Estefan, the croupier, waited, long hands unmoving. The cards were suspended above the tattered baize of the table. Dressed all in black, he was usually nothing but a silent observer, as expressionless as a corpse and about as animated, but suddenly there seemed to be a gleam of interest in those flat black eyes. His thin, dark brows elevated in question.

There was, of course, no limit at Satan's. It was infamous for stakes that would make even rich men take pause. In this place, aristocracy mingled with the merchant class with dissolute ease. All it took to get in was money. Luke *was* a rich man, but then again, he was not alone in that status in this smoky room.

"I'd say I'm curious to know what you consider a sum for men might be, sir." Luke indolently lifted his shoulders. Somewhere, someone laughed in a nervous outburst.

Well dressed and middle-aged, Albert Cayne nodded abruptly. He was thickly built, with keen, dark eyes set in a fleshy face. Other than a deepened color to his already ruddy complexion, he looked bland and self-assured. He murmured, "My lord, you might be a viscount, but there is something to be said for scraping your way out of the gutter. All my money I made meself, and if I choose to hang a goodly portion on a wager, I will. Let's say twenty thousand, *shall we*, on who is the luckier man?"

Twenty thousand? On the turn of a card?

Luke had to admire the man's nerve, if not his good sense. The table behind them playing *rouge et noir* had stopped all pretense of interest in their own game, and the entire room seemed to be suddenly filled with low whispers.

Walk away.

No. Stay. Where's your nerve?

With the barest inclination of his head, he acknowledged the bet.

And when word of this swept through London society, he thought grimly as he lifted a hand in a deliberately languid gesture to signal for a card, he would be struck off half the lists of anxious mamas scouring the fashionable crowd for eligible husbands for their young daughters.

Good. Just as well. He wasn't in the market for a wife. Scandalous, titled, and rich was a fine combination. Subtract *rich* from the equation and suddenly you became nothing but a rake, and a wastrel at that. Any man so flagrantly willing to toss away such a portion of his worldly goods on a game of chance did *not* make good husband material. He could afford to lose, but he had to admit the extravagance of it did give him pause, as did his motivations.

Not that he minded the idea of a few less simpering misses fluttering their fans in his direction. He was just . . . well, quite frankly, worried what his mother and sisters might think. And *that*, he reflected with dry amusement as he picked up the card, glanced at it, and put it back down, was *not* something to confess when in the blackest gaming hell in all of England.

Cayne also took a card, and the collective hiss of indrawn breath as he idly tucked it into his hand sounded like someone had thrown a pail of water on the fire. The man's smile was enigmatic, his gaze steady.

One card to go. Outwardly calm, Luke accepted the last offering from the dealer and the strain of not showing his emotions crawled like fire ants along his skin. The other card had been of such little help that there was no choice but to keep this one, and he hardly spared a look before sliding it into place in his hand.

Cayne shook his head, refusing the last card.

There seemed little doubt the man had confidence in the benign blessings of chance.

Luke's brandy was warm and fragrant, and he swirled it slightly before lifting the glass to his mouth and draining it in one swallow. He was quite impressed that his hand did not tremble even a fraction. The croupier said, "Gentlemen, lay your cards on the table, please." There was a weighty pause. "The wager is twenty thousand pounds."

With a quick flick of his wrist, Luke tossed his hand on the table. Cayne moved more slowly, carefully laying down each card so that the assembled crowd could view it.

For a moment, no one moved.

"By the devil's own luck!" The exclamation came from behind Luke's shoulder, breaking the thick silence. The croupier then gave a grotesque parody of what must have been meant as a smile. He intoned gravely, "The hand to the viscount."

Ignoring the subtle roar of congratulations, Luke got to his feet and offered a stone-faced Cayne a small bow. The older man leaned back in his chair, inclining his head. "The money will be delivered tomorrow, if that is agreeable."

"Of course."

Luke moved with apparent nonchalance toward where a table draped in red velvet held a row of bottles, some in cooling buckets.

Inside, he was still tightly wound from the game, both the tension and the results.

If having a carefully cultivated reputation as one of London's most debauched gentlemen meant more challenges such as this, he was going to have to liquidate more funds in case the hand didn't go his way next time. Picking up a decanter, he sloshed more liquor into his glass and lifted it to his mouth.

"My lord?"

He turned and saw one of the liveried footmen, the young man's pockmarked face carefully dusted with powder, the tray in his hand balanced perfectly. Luke said, "Yes?"

"I've a message for you, delivered to the door just a minute ago. It's urgent, or so I was told."

Luke accepted the envelope and glanced at the seal. "Thank you."

Minutes later he was outside, where a thin drizzle persistently fell from a black sky. His driver, hunched under a slouch cap and cloak, merely nodded when given the address. After he clambered into the carriage, Luke shook out his damp hair and reread the missive. Quickly scanning the scrawled words, he felt a trepidation that had escaped him back in the gaming room when he faced Cayne with a small fortune hanging in the balance.

It really must be urgent, for the sender, last he knew, wasn't even speaking to him.

Why would Madeline write to him, and, more puzzling, why did she need him at once?

She was in trouble.

Madeline May, Lady Brewer, paced across the confines of her drawing room, oblivious to what usually gave her pleasure. The Oriental vase on the small table by the window, which had been a wedding gift, the pale yellow satin on the walls, the portrait of her husband's grandfather that hung over the mantel, the subject's dash-

ing smile and dark hair under his plumed hat achingly
familiar ...

It was dark outside. She hadn't eaten all day, and the
way her stomach churned, maybe it was just as well. The
glass of port she'd downed in a very unladylike gulp
made her head swim a little, but at least it had stopped
her hands from shaking. She eyed the decanter with
longing, but decided a second drink would be a bad idea
all around and would do her empty stomach no favors,
so instead she just jerked back the fine lace curtain once
again to stare at the street. It was empty, with no sign of
life, not even the rattle of a passing hired hack.

Where the devil was the infernal, irritating man?

Don't panic. Stay calm.

A carriage finally rumbled by, but it wasn't his, and
she worried her bottom lip and tapped her fingers on
the sill. The clock in the corner mocked her with each
solemn *tick*.

"To what do I owe the honor of your imperial sum-
mons?"

The sound of the deep voice coming from the doorway made her jump and let out a gasp. Madeline whirled
around to see Luke Daudet in the doorway, one broad
shoulder propped against the doorjamb; his negligent
pose belied by the intensity of his gray eyes. As usual,
Lord Altea was almost too handsome in black, immaculately tailored evening clothes, his cravat pristine and
embellished by a diamond stickpin, his dark blond hair a
shade longer than fashion, the elegance of his masculine
features shadowed because she had only one lamp burn-
ing. He held his gloves in one long-fingered hand.

"How did you get in?" Madeline demanded. "I didn't
see your carriage arrive."

Arched brows went up a fraction at the shrill edge
to her question. "My dear Madge, the tone of your note
gave me pause about simply rolling up to your door, especially at this hour. I'd like to think I am gentleman
enough to at least consider your reputation, so I had my

driver park a block or so away and walked. The servant's entrance was quite convenient and the lock simple."

"You picked the lock?"

He jingled something in his jacket pocket. "Perhaps."

If the circumstances were different, she would be more outraged by his presumption, but then again, she'd sent for him and needed his help. She'd address the issue of the poor security of the house another time, if she managed to not spend the rest of her life in Newgate Prison.

To her disbelief, as if courtesy was applicable to the current situation, she heard herself say, "Would you like a drink, my lord?"

Luke's eyes narrowed. "I doubt you asked me here for a social glass of wine, and I can best describe your face as well beyond pale, and maybe even ashen. Why don't you sit down, take a deep breath, and explain to me why you need my help? I thought we were not on cordial terms."

"We aren't." She usually managed marginal ice-cold courtesy in public, but she detested the notorious Viscount Altea with every fiber of her being. Yet, as mortifying as it was to admit it, he was the one man she knew who could help her, and never had she needed help more.

"Ah ... well, then, I am perishing with curiosity as to why you sent a servant running around London looking for me."

Maybe he was right. She was decidedly light-headed, and sitting down was probably a good idea. The humiliation of fainting in front of him was not something she wanted to suffer. She chose a delicate silk-covered Louis Quatorze chair and sank down, telling herself fiercely that if there was one thing that was *not* going to happen, it was crying. Absolutely not, and especially not in front of Luke Daudet.

It was difficult to summon up her composure, but she managed to lock her hands together as he dropped into an opposite chair and stared at her in open question. "Madge?"

"I hate that nickname." To her alarm, her voice was nearly unrecognizable, and her eyes stung despite her resolve.

"I know." His smile had nothing to do with humor. "Why do you think I use it? I can only imagine what *you* call *me* when I am not around. Nothing flattering, I presume. Now, then, all that aside, I have to admit I am becoming alarmed. You are usually the epitome of the poised, sophisticated aristocratic lady of the *ton*, but quite frankly, darling, this evening you seem about to go into a fit of hysterics, which I prefer to avoid. Most men hate displays of female emotion, myself included. It will be easier if you just tell me what's wrong, and we can go from there."

Though she reminded herself on a daily basis how much she loathed the incredibly attractive but notoriously fickle Altea, his matter-of-fact tone did help her hold on to at least a modicum of her dignity. She fought a small sob, won the battle, and then told him the awful truth.

"This evening I killed someone."

Chapter Two

He wasn't often rendered speechless, but Luke had to admit, as he gazed across the elegant, civilized drawing room at the beautiful woman he thought about far too often, he couldn't think of a single thing to say.

Madeline sat, ghostly pale, her slender shoulders visibly trembling, only a few paces away. No simpering ingenue, at twenty-six she was a mature widow with her own fortune, a reputation for wit and impeccable taste, and a darling of society, much sought after by any hostess of consequence.

Sought after by quite a few gentlemen also, himself included. As far as he knew, he was the only one who had ever succeeded coaxing the delectable Lady Brewer into his bed, that one night indelibly preserved in his memory.

For her to be shaken out of her serene self-possession told him even more than her words had. Normally she was all poise and sophistication.

Except, an errant voice in his head reminded him, *when she is trembling and breathless in my arms.*

Luke finally found his voice. "I'd stake my life you aren't capable of deliberate malice, so maybe you'd better just start at the beginning and explain what happened. Please include where the incident happened. Who, why, and how might also be useful."

Midnight blue eyes, with a shimmer of hovering tears, gazed at him. "I am not even sure why I sent you that note."

"You know perfectly well why you sent it." It wasn't the easiest task on earth to keep his tone even and reasonable. "Because you realize, despite our differences, that I will help you. So just tell me."

"It was Lord Fitch."

This just got worse. Fitch was a prominent figure in British politics, with influence and money, and he was an earl in the bargain. Luke never liked the swaggering bastard, but that was neither here nor there. His lordship's demise was unlikely to go unnoticed. If the man was dead, there would be inquiries. "He's annoyed me once or twice, but never enough for me to murder him. What happened?"

"I didn't *murder* him," Madeline shot back, and he was happy to see her square her shaking shoulders and some color come back into her face, even if it was due to outrage. "I accidentally killed him and it is quite different, thank you."

"I stand corrected." He felt a flash of amusement over her reaction despite the grim revelation she'd just made. "But keep in mind you have yet to tell me the sequence of events."

Her knuckles whitened as her hands clasped together tighter in her lap. "He's been making improper suggestions for quite some time. It has gone well beyond the stage where it is an annoyance and into downright harassment. I loathe the very sight of him."

The blackguard. Luke wished with savage intensity the man weren't dead so he could strangle him himself. "I am not a female and have never been subject to that sort of persecution, but I don't blame you for your aversion to his lordship. In fact, I wish you'd come to me sooner."

"I didn't want to ask for *your* help even in my current circumstances."

The trembling of her shapely body made him want to rise, go to her, and take her in his arms, cradle her close and promise all would be well. But he knew she wouldn't appreciate it, so he stayed where he was, though it took some effort. "Very well, perhaps I deserve that, but let's get back to the matter at hand. Fitch was lascivious and inappropriate. Go on."

"I've tried to avoid him." Her lower lip, so lush and full, quivered. "At every function, in public venues . . . *everywhere*."

"Madge, I am sure you have."

"It didn't work. He deliberately put himself in my path as often as possible."

Luke silently waited for her to continue, stifling futile fury at a man who was already dead.

"He . . ." she trailed off, looking forlorn and very young suddenly, with her pure, averted profile and tendrils of hair escaping from her chignon and caressing her neck. "He has something of Colin's."

Of her deceased husband's? Luke wasn't sure how that was possible, when Lord Brewer had died at least five years ago . . . perhaps even six.

With a tremor in her voice, she went on. "I very much want it back and endeavored to bargain with his lordship, but there is one price I am not willing to pay."

Price? His jaw locked. The use of her luscious body. She didn't even have to say it out loud. Luke felt the angry beat of his pulse in his temple and actually flexed his hands to keep from reaching for her when the crystalline line of a tear streaked down her smooth cheek. Even his jaded sophistication was no match for her genuine distress. "He's been blackmailing you?"

"No." She stared at the patterned rug. "Not precisely."

Not precisely. What in the hell did that mean? The gravity of the moment precluded him from muttering *women*, but he had to acknowledge a rising sense of frustration over the lack of a clear explanation. "I don't understand. It seems to me a person is being blackmailed or they are not."

She made a small hopeless gesture with her hand. "He . . . he knew things. And would mention them at inappropriate times. I began to suspect . . ."

By nature he wasn't a patient man anyway, and when she trailed off again, Luke prompted curtly, "Suspect what? Devil take it, my dear. Perhaps I am obtuse, but right now I have little more idea what has happened than when I walked in the door. Just explain it to me so we can deal with this."

"It's mortifying."

"Good God, woman, you just told me you killed a man. If it is mortifying, so be it, but get to the point. With my reputation, I am unlikely to judge you."

For a moment, she just stared at him, as if seeing him for the first time, her beautiful eyes wide. Then she nodded, just the barest tilt of her head.

"Colin kept a journal." She took a deep, shuddering breath but went on. "He was always scribbling something in it. Apparently, he wrote down everything, even details about our . . . our married life. Lord Fitch got a hold of it, though I can't really imagine how. After enough lewd but accurate comments and suggestions, I began to realize the odious man *must* have the journal. They weren't friends, and Colin would never tell him anything so private. I can't imagine he'd tell *anyone*. It was the only explanation. *I* hadn't even read it because it seemed like too much of an invasion of Colin's privacy, so I'd locked it away. Sure enough, it is missing."

And, it went without saying, it was certainly an invasion of Madeline's privacy as well. Luke knew she'd loved her husband with all the depth of a woman's first passion, and his death had been a devastating blow to her. He could only imagine the sense of violation she felt over his personal notes and thoughts being read by a stranger.

"I almost had him buried with it." Her voice was choked. "But I suppose I thought one day I might want to read it for comfort."

Instead a heartless toad like Fitch had made a travesty of the intimate writings of the man she loved. If the earl hadn't already met his untimely end, Luke could have killed the worthless scoundrel himself. He said with forced coolness, "Whatever happened to his lordship, it sounds to me like he quite deserved it. Where is he now?"

"In Colin's study."

The answer was said in such a low whisper he almost didn't catch it. Madeline looked blindly at the wall, her expression so remote it worried him. One slender hand plucked restively at her skirt. "Here?" Luke asked.

She nodded, the movement jerky. "I requested a meeting to discuss the journal. It seemed prudent and more to my advantage to conduct business in a way a man would do so, and Colin's study was a logical location. I had Lord Fitch escorted there when he called in response to my note."

At least they were getting somewhere. Luke rose. "Take me there and we'll sort this out."

As if one could sort out having a dead lord in a man's study. But he was willing to do his best.

For her. Because, though he didn't wish to admit it even to himself, Luke had an admiration for Lady Brewer that extended quite beyond her matchless passion and undeniable beauty. Since defining it meant examining his own feelings, he'd avoided too much introspection on the matter, but he certainly had come running when she asked.

That was telling. Knight in shining armor was normally a role he disdained.

Woodenly, with the movements of a person who had suffered quite a shock, she got up and without speaking walked out of the drawing room and led the way down the hall.

Her hope that it had all been some sort of bizarre dream was dashed when, unfortunately, Lord Fitch still lay in the same lax sprawl on the floor by the fireplace in a pool of his own blood. It was a pity, Madeline thought, because she'd always rather liked that rug, even if it was faded on one side from the sunlight that streamed in through the window in the late afternoon. Since Colin's death she had often come in and sat at his desk, the aroma of his tobacco in the jar on the desk familiar and poignant, his pipe just where he had left it the day he first complained about the headache that eventually blossomed into a fever, aches, chills, and, within two days, death. The room, with its paneled walls and worn books, was a comfort. Or it had been until now.

"I take it the fireplace poker was the method of dispatching his lordship to where, even now, I imagine he is shaking Satan's hand." Luke gazed dispassionately at the dead man, his tone cool and calm. "Not an original choice, but perhaps it is so popular because it is so effective."

"Yes." Lord Fitch had been taunting her . . . enjoying it. She could still hear his oily voice. *So, Lady Brewer, is it true you once, at the opera, behind a curtain, let your husband lift your skirts and . . .*

It had been impossible to reason with the gloating old goat, and certainly appealing to his nonexistent sense of honor hadn't been effective.

"When a request for him to return the journal didn't work, I offered him money for it. He merely laughed at me and said it was far too entertaining and wasn't for sale." Her voice was low and dull, but the awfulness of the evening had begun to take its toll. "I pointed out that it was mine in the first place, and returning it was the least any gentleman would do. He refused and continued to make the most disgusting, insulting suggestions you can think of."

"My imagination is excellent," Luke said in a tone that was pleasant, yet it sent a shiver up her spine. "For instance, I would have chosen a much more painful manner of execution for this piece of refuse right now soiling a perfectly good rug. Finish the story."

"He threatened to publish it."

Damn it all. Another tear ran down her cheek and she swiped it away with the back of her hand, like a child might. While the last thing she wanted to do was weep in front of Luke Daudet, of all people, in the light of this current disaster, she didn't care all that much.

"So you conked him with a poker. Excellent decision."

"I didn't conk him with a poker, as you put it," Madeline said defensively, "just because of that, though I was appalled. Men settle things with violence. Women are more civilized."

With irritating logic, he pointed out, "Ah, perhaps, but I am not the one with a dead man in my study."

Ignoring that comment, she explained haltingly, "I—I had by then realized any further discussion was useless and disliked the way he looked at me, so I got up to go fetch Hubert to escort the man out. When I came around the desk, Lord Fitch . . . he, well, grabbed me and whispered an extremely repulsive suggestion. He'd obviously been drinking, for his breath reeked. I was close to the fireplace, and as I struggled to get away, I must have grabbed the poker, for next I knew he was lying on the floor."

"Clearly self-defense." Luke reached into the pocket of his perfectly tailored jacket and took out a snowy handkerchief embroidered with his initials in one corner and handed it to her.

"Thank you." She wiped away another wayward tear.

Luke knelt by the body and took up one limp arm. "He's still warm, so I take it you sent for me immediately. Where's his carriage?"

"That's the one blessing in all this. He must have walked, as he lives only a block or so away."

"What did you tell your staff? Obviously everyone is in bed."

"That his lordship dropped off due to too much drink and that I sent for you to see him home."

"Good thinking." He frowned, his handsome face in profile showing the first true expression of chagrin of the evening. "Only we have one enormous problem, my dear."

One? She'd just killed an earl in her husband's study. She had countless troubles ahead, as far as she could tell.

"The bastard is still alive."

"What? There's so much blood!" Madeline stared, not sure if she even believed him, crumpling the fine piece of linen in her hand. "He wasn't breathing—I'd swear it. I checked."

"You were understandably distraught, I am going to suspect, but I can feel a pulse. I'm no physician, but as irksome as it might be, it seems quite strong and steady. Head wounds, also, bleed with notorious profusion. I saw my fair share during the war."

She experienced a wash of relief so acute her knees nearly buckled. "Thank God. While I am not an admirer of Lord Fitch, I did not wish to be the cause of his death."

"You are kinder than I am, obviously. I'd gladly meet him on the field, and if he survives, I just might call him out. However, I can't countenance killing an unconscious man, no matter how much he deserves it, so I suppose our first order of business is getting him home and some medical attention. If you'll just open the door for me, we'll be on our way."

Call him out? Madeline was startled by the lethal vehemence of Luke's tone, not to mention the grim expression on his fine-boned face, but too distraught to address it.

Though Fitch was portly, he was much shorter, and Luke heaved his lordship's body over his shoulder with what seemed like little exertion.

"He's bleeding on your jacket," Madeline whispered, leaning limply against the desk.

"I have more clothing."

"I . . ."

Lifting Lord Fitch's plump posterior in the air, Luke looked at her, his brows elevated in sardonic question. "Just help me get this horse's arse out of here, then have a glass of wine and forget it all happened."

How easy he made it all sound.

"Luke," she started in protest, for truly, though she wanted his help, she hadn't counted on him shouldering the entire problem.

"Open the door. I'm going to take care of everything. You needn't give it another thought." His voice was full of quiet, purposeful promise and completely unlike his usual flippant tone.

She moved to comply, preceding him through the quiet town house, helping with opening doors. When he slipped out the servant's exit, she watched his shrouded figure disappear into the darkened alley, only to hear the rattle of wheels a few moments later.

If locking the door was effective, she didn't know— not as effortlessly as Viscount Altea had accessed her house—but she did it anyway. Then she wandered back to Colin's study. The ghastly stain on the rug wasn't going to be dealt with easily, and she supposed the whole thing would have to be discarded.

And how to explain it . . .

Nosebleed, she pondered, wandering over to stare at the horrible spot, wishing she'd wake up and find it all a nightmare. Could she claim Lord Fitch had a dreadful nosebleed and had ruined the carpet?

Maybe. Until the selfsame lord told the true story. While she was glad she hadn't actually killed him, she wasn't all that delighted he was still going to be able to torment her. Madeline stood there, trying to imagine the rumors that would surface if Fitch spread the word that she'd invited him to come to her home, and twisted the reason why. He'd been smart enough to not actually blackmail her, so no real crime had been committed except some repugnant comments. All he had to do was deny he had the journal and accuse her of attacking him without cause.

The facts were the facts. If he'd been spiteful and sly before, he'd be tenfold worse now if he recovered.

If.

She took in a shuddering breath, clenching her hands into fists at her sides. Luke had sworn he'd take care of it.

That was another matter entirely.

Of all people, she'd called on Luke Daudet, the notorious and sinful Viscount Altea, sending her footman haring first to his club, and then apparently to one of the most shameful gaming halls in England.

Which was worse? Held captive by Lord Fitch's malicious amusement, or being beholden to Luke?

She wasn't sure, but certainly counted *this* as one of the worst evenings of her life.

Chapter Three

"Any thoughts?"

Michael Hepburn, the Marquess of Longhaven, gazed at his companion across the breakfast table. Luke smeared jam on a piece of toast, his brows lifted in question, his pose seemingly casual, but Michael wasn't fooled. He said, "Well, for one, any time you write down words you'd prefer others besides the intended recipient not see, you take a chance something exactly like this might happen. I burn all private correspondence."

"I feel certain you do." It was a dry observation. "I agree also that jotting down intimate details of your sexual moments with your wife is a poor idea, but a private journal is just that: private. I am sure Lord Brewer did not expect to expire at such a young age. Besides, he is not the first person who chronicled the experiences of his life on paper each day. Many people keep diaries."

"True," Michael admitted, though if he happened to be so inclined, it would be a breach in security that would make the Crown very unhappy indeed. He thought Lord Brewer foolishly sentimental, but refrained from saying so. Luke didn't open up easily, and he had a reason for arriving on the doorstep at such an early hour. "It was an error in judgment, but not everyone anticipates such a contingency as someone with low moral values prying into your life."

"I couldn't agree more." Luke seemed absorbed in taking a bite of sausage, chewing carefully and swallowing before asking, "If you were me, what would you do next?"

"About Lady Brewer's dilemma?"

Or, Michael thought privately, *about the lady herself?*

"Something has to be done about Fitch."

"Are you asking me for advice, or do you wish me to step in?" Michael picked up his coffee cup and looked pointedly at his old friend.

"I'm not sure. You are much more versed in matters of this sort."

"Bloodied, senseless gentlemen in the house of one of my paramours? No, I have to say that is out of the realm of my experience."

"She isn't my paramour." The words were clipped. "Madeline is an acquaintance—that's all."

The beautiful Lady Brewer felt free to call on Luke in a moment of dire need, and considering his prickly attitude about the woman in question, Michael somehow doubted *acquaintance* was the right word, but he let it go. Lately Luke had been touchy and more restless than usual, and maybe it had something to do with her. He kept late hours, and this morning in particular looked urbane and collected as usual, but there was a tired line to his mouth.

The morning was bright and clear, the sky outside the windows of the informal breakfast room showing a sea of cloudless blue. After a sip of coffee, Michael set down his cup with deliberate care. "You say you returned him to his town house and told his majordomo you'd found him unconscious in an alley outside our club?"

"I thought it sounded like a plausible explanation."

Luke's lean body held a subtle but discernable tension. "He summoned the physician, who pronounced the wound superficial and said he thought Fitch was more foxed than anything, if the smell of brandy was an indication. I can confirm the man reeked of it, and when I put him in the carriage an empty flask fell from his pocket, though I doubt his excesses of the evening were confined to that one container."

"But we are still left with the dilemma of Lord Brewer's private writings somehow in the possession of the nefarious Fitch, whether he recovers or not, correct?"

"Correct."

"I believe I can probably take care of that."

For the first time since his arrival, Luke smiled, and while it didn't have the same effect on him as it did on the susceptible ladies of society, Michael was glad to see the normally careless Viscount Altea resurface for a moment.

Luke murmured, "I thought you might be able to help."

"For Lady Brewer's sake?" The question was delicately put.

Luke ignored the insinuation. "It seems prudent to take steps now."

"Fitch was unpleasant before last evening's incident, so it is a logical assumption that his mood isn't going to be improved with the addition of what I have to assume is a colossal headache this morning."

"The doctor said between the liquor and the blow to his thick skull, he might not remember how he came to be injured."

"That would be best for everyone, but until we know, you should take care to protect her one way or the other."

"It's hardly my responsibility." Luke shrugged, but Michael thought it didn't reflect a true indifference.

"No," Michael said mildly, "but yet you are here, enlisting my aid on her behalf."

Luke tossed down his napkin and rose with his usual nonchalance. "Speaking of which, let me know when the journal is rescued and I will return it to its rightful owner. I'd promise to give you due credit, but I doubt Madeline would appreciate that I told you about it in the first place."

In his profession, credit was not advisable, so that was for the best. Michael elevated his brows. "I will be in touch."

"Thank you for breakfast."

"Of course." He paused and said neutrally, "Did you really wager twenty thousand last night on one hand?"

Luke lifted his brows in a sardonic arch. "Gossip travels quickly as ever, I see."

"In our circles, most certainly. I knew by midnight."

"I'm not quite sure why I took Cayne's challenge."

"I think I can take a guess." They'd been together in Spain during the war, and as a result, their demons were not a secret to one another.

"Don't." The single word was clipped. "I don't need a father confessor, Michael, but I would appreciate that journal."

After his friend departed, Michael sat and stared thoughtfully at the doorway. He knew, of course, the beauteous Lady Brewer. Pale gold hair, exotic dark eyes, a body that any healthy male would appreciate, but she'd been devoted to her husband and withdrew from society for an unfashionably long time after his death. She was reputed to be uninterested in any type of attachment, casual or permanent.

He had to admit he found it worthy of note that the lady turned to Luke for aid. He wasn't aware they knew each other well, and certainly Luke had never as much as mentioned her in his presence. The only time he'd ever seen them even exchange a word was at their mutual friend Joshua's wedding to Lady Brewer's cousin. Come to think of it, Michael mused as he leaned back in his chair, coffee in hand, at the time he remembered noticing the stilted chilliness in Madeline May's voice when she greeted Luke. With his looks, fortune, and facile charm, most women fell at his feet.

Or into his bed.

But Luke said she was not one of his lovers, and she certainly did not have a reputation as a woman who indulged in casual liaisons. Luke didn't believe in any other kind, so it was probably the truth. All that taken into consideration, they didn't make likely friends either.

It was interesting but immaterial to the problem at hand. Michael finished his coffee and left the breakfast room for his study.

He needed to send a message. He had connections that could handle this sticky little matter with ease. Either Antonia or Lawrence would take care of it quickly and discreetly.

He was never indecisive, and it irritated him when, with his hand lifted to knock, Luke dropped it and considered leaving. Logically it made perfect sense if after the events of last evening, he called to see how Madeline was feeling and to tell her he hoped to have her husband's journal returned to her soon. But there was a certain part of him that reminded him Lady Brewer was dangerous to his peace of mind.

He didn't *have* to see her. A brief letter would do.

Had the door not opened he might have remained there on her front step, waffling like a nervous adolescent for God alone knew how long, but it did open and Madeline herself appeared, a startled look on her face as she saw him standing right there. "Oh. Lord Altea."

It slammed into him. He should have sent the letter.

The sunny day, the busy street, the neat bricked steps, any possible watching eyes . . . it all faded away. This morning she wore a soft lemon yellow day gown with short, ruffled sleeves and lace shirred underneath the bodice, which drew the eyes to the curve of those full, firm breasts. Her shining hair was pinned back, and in her hand she had a reticule, which made sense, for she was obviously on her way out.

As beautiful as she looked, all delicate, fascinating female, it was the faint dark circles under her eyes that moved him the most. Those telltale, fragile smudges were a reminder of what she'd been enduring alone. How much had she cried . . . alone? Lain awake and wondered if she was about to be humiliated by having the most private part of her life put on display?

That was why a note wasn't sufficient.

"Good morning, Lady Brewer," he said formally, in case there was a footman within hearing or her butler was near the still-open front door of her town house. "I thought I might call, but I can see you have an errand or appointment. Perhaps I can escort you or offer my carriage."

She was composed and her smile merely polite, but her gaze searching. "That's very kind of you, my lord. I was going to walk over to visit my sister-in-law, as the weather is so pleasant, but we could use your carriage instead so you are not forced to walk back."

Her dark eyes, so unusual in contrast to her blond beauty, gazed at him in open, unhappy question. He said, "It would be my pleasure to give you a ride."

Instantly he wished he'd used different wording, for his anything-but-innocent mind envisioned giving her a different sort of ride than a polite jaunt in his carriage, the kind of journey that began with slow, melting kisses, then involved discarded clothing, and ended with her straddling his hips as they moved together toward a common erotic destination. . . .

One night. They'd shared one night together almost a year ago, and his body traitorously remembered it whenever she was nearby. A whiff of her perfume, a chance glimpse of her profile at a crowded event, the sound of her low, musical laugh, and his cock begged him to forget why he'd declined to pursue an affair. Madeline was one of those rare women who was refined, sophisticated, and glib in public, and deeply passionate in the bedroom. Moreover, he admired her intelligence and sense of humor as much as he did her physical allure, and the combination filled him with the deepest sense of alarm.

This was a woman men fell in love with, not one they casually bedded and left behind. He wasn't all that surprised that the literary-minded Lord Brewer had rhapsodized over his wife's charms, for they were well worth recalling.

Having once loved and lost, Luke knew he wasn't interested in such emotional pain again. Back in Spain, amidst war and all the hell that accompanied it, he had met the woman of his dreams. It remained just that, an illusion, and he woke each morning aching for the loss. The ordeal was too agonizing to risk a repeat performance. In obligation to his title, he would probably marry eventually, but at thirty, he wasn't interested at all in that change in his life right now. When he did decide it was time, he had every intention of selecting his wife in the most dispassionate way possible. He might even— God help him—let his mother give him advice on whom to select as a suitable bride.

"I expect if anyone sees me getting in or out of your carriage," Madeline murmured as he politely assisted her inside the vehicle, "there will be gossip."

"Your virtuous reputation can probably withstand a few whispers," Luke replied in cynical amusement at her prim tone, though he did understand her reservations. No one would care if he was seen with her, but the other way around *did* matter. "Now, then, where does your sister-in-law live, so I can give my driver instructions?"

"Brook Street."

"Ah, that *is* close by. I'll tell him to take a turn around the block first so we have a few minutes to talk."

Without waiting for her to agree, he gave Harold the address, and then clambered in to settle opposite. As they pulled away, he said without preamble, "It was the doctor's opinion Fitch wasn't even seriously injured, and his unconscious state might just as easily have been liquor induced as anything."

"I am relieved. At the same time, he might be more vindictive than ever now. I'd like to say it doesn't worry me, but of course it does." Her mouth trembled just enough that it unfortunately drew his attention to her soft lips, and he recalled a little too clearly how they felt crushed beneath his in a fiery kiss.

"I am going to venture a guess he might not even remember the incident, and even if he does recollect it, he won't possess the journal much longer." Luke smiled without humor. "And if he approaches you in any way, in private or in public, he won't possess his *life* much longer. Don't worry, my dear. If he decides to cause you any more grief, just let me know and he will understand clearly he is dealing with me now."

"Why are you doing this?" Her fingers were clenched white where they clasped the reticule in her lap.

"Doing what, precisely?"

"Helping me so generously."

"Why do you think?" An evasive and unfair answer, mostly given because he didn't quite know what to say.

Because I can't forget you. No, that would never do.

Dark eyes regarded him intently and she said nothing for a moment, the carriage rumbling along the street fast enough her slender form swayed just a little on the seat. Then she said, "Do not ask me why, because I can speak from experience that you are not always gallant or reliable, but I knew you would aid me."

The reference was, of course, to how after spending that one memorable night making love to her over and over with an unleashed hunger she seemed to share, he had just simply walked away. "I had reasons to be ungallant," he said coolly.

She arranged her skirts with an idle hand, but there was nothing nonchalant in the poignant expression on her lovely face. "Besides Colin, you have been my only lover." The confession was hushed.

He suspected as much, and having it confirmed didn't make him feel better about what had happened—and then not happened—between them. There was little question he'd been less than honorable, and while he wasn't a saint, he didn't normally involve himself with anyone like Madeline. She didn't resemble in the least the jaded *ton* beauties who played at intrigue and pleasure like practiced courtesans.

Her voice just above a whisper, she continued, "When you never called upon me afterward, acted so distant in public, as if it had never taken place, and declined to answer the note I had swallowed my pride to write and send, I had to assume that I somehow disappointed you. Was the passion I remember only one-sided?"

Hell and blast, he had wanted to talk to her, but not about *this*, though it probably needed to be said. "Far from it," he admitted. "Which I think you know, whatever you've told yourself. My considerable enthusiasm for your charms was hardly feigned."

"Then . . . why?"

"Because you are not the type of woman who becomes a man's mistress, and I have no intention of marrying you. I thought it best ended quickly."

Madeline stared at him in clear bewilderment, and he had the impression he had perhaps hurt her more at this moment than he had with his deliberate indifference a year ago.

He felt like a scoundrel. A bounder. A callous rakehell. All, and probably even more unattractive descriptions, applied.

"If I interpret what you just said correctly, you enjoyed my body, but my company is distasteful. Is that it?" Her voice was carefully devoid of emotion.

"Not at all. You are intelligent, articulate, and charming in every way." He owed her that much, and it was the truth. "When you remarry, your husband will be an extremely lucky man. I hope you choose well."

"Is it marriage, then, that is the issue?"

"I will marry someday. I need an heir."

Her chin lifted a fraction, but her face had taken on color, as if he'd insulted her. "I gave Colin a son."

Luke knew she hadn't come to his bed lightly, and that in itself was part of the problem. "I am aware of that. What is he now, six?"

"Trevor is seven," she supplied, looking more confused than ever. "Luke—"

He couldn't possibly do this, hurting her even though it wasn't his intention. It might be ill-advised, but he bit out, "You are beautiful, generous, desirable. I desire you still." The carriage was slowing, and he was relieved the conversation he'd avoided so diligently for the past year was nearly over. "But we don't suit for one important reason, my dear Madge, and it is an insurmountable one."

"Enlighten me."

They rolled to a halt and he lost no time opening the door, alighting and offering his hand to help her out.

Madeline refused to take it, sitting stubbornly in the froth of her yellow skirts, her mouth set. "You have come this far, Altea. Enlighten me as to this insurmountable reason."

God help him. She was so very beautiful.

"Can you promise me you won't die?"

Her eyes widened and her lips parted.

Gently he said, "No, of course you can't. Now, then, I hope you have a pleasant visit with your sister-in-law, and don't worry further about the little matter with Fitch. It is well in hand."

Chapter Four

The symphony of whispers rose and fell and rose again with the arrival of each guest, and particularly, Elizabeth Daudet noted, when her brother was announced. Something had happened she wasn't aware of, and whatever it might be, it certainly had tongues wagging. Asking her mother was out of the question. If it involved a female, Elizabeth was supposed to pretend she didn't know gentlemen like Luke entertained themselves *that* way.

Luckily, she knew precisely how to find out what was going on.

Elegant in dark evening wear, Luke strolled to the edge of the crowd, his height giving him the advantage as he scanned the milling throng. He smiled in acknowledgment when he spotted her sipping champagne and standing with a small group of her friends, and then a beautiful woman with red-gold hair and a daring décolletage swooped in and coquettishly took his arm, and his attention was diverted.

The notorious Lord Altea was Elizabeth's guardian,

and she was not unaware it amused the *ton* to no end to see him diligently monitoring her social life. She found it a bit funny herself, but doubted Luke enjoyed the role of chaperone imposed on him. It wasn't at all that he neglected to fulfill his role as viscount and, subsequently, head of the family, but since his return from Spain he was . . . distant.

He didn't talk about it, but something had happened to change him. Maybe it was just the war itself; it was beyond her realm of experience and she couldn't begin to understand, but it was *there*.

There didn't seem to be a better way to describe it, though how *was* a man supposed to act after spending half a decade away from his home and enduring bloodshed and danger and whatever else returning soldiers refused to mention in polite company?

It could hardly be Lady Hart's blatant interest in Luke causing the current furor, Elizabeth knew, for the lady in question had been in full, unabashed pursuit for weeks now. There was no scandal in someone flirting with her handsome older brother. Women did it quite frequently.

"Excuse me." Her smile was perfunctory, for the small group of young ladies around her were more acquaintances than close confidants. "I promised his lordship a dance."

Suitably vague. The reference could apply to most any male in the ballroom, for there were plenty of titled gentlemen in attendance. Elizabeth handed her glass to a passing footman with a tray and scanned the crowd as she circled the swirling dancers. *There.* She caught a glimpse of a familiar profile, her quarry's partner a young woman she recognized as the daughter of one of Parliament's more influential lords, which could possibly be why Miles was now swirling her across the floor.

The music ended, and as the polite exchanges and exodus off the floor began, Miles spotted Elizabeth standing close by, and lifted his brows in unspoken question.

She waited as he bowed over the hand of the—simpering, in her opinion—young woman, and then joined her by the open terrace doors. "What?" he asked without preamble, adjusting his cuffs in an affectation that annoyed her, which was probably why he did it in the first place. He'd been antagonizing her since childhood. "And before you tell me why you are loitering here, pinning me with that penetrating stare I know so well, may I say I like that shade of rose much better on you than that insipid pink gown you wore the other night that made you look both sallow and about twelve years old?"

She regarded her cousin with a withering look. "What a lovely, well-worded compliment. I might swoon in gratitude."

Miles, as always, was unfazed by the sarcasm. "At least I didn't mention you are no longer quite as flat-chested, and those occasional, unfortunate spots seem to be a thing of the past. A porcelain complexion is quite the fashion right now. My compliments."

In a saccharine tone, she retorted, "In the spirit of generosity, I'll say your longer hairstyle somewhat distracts one from noticing the length of your nose. Perhaps you are growing into it after all. I despaired to see it happen."

"My nose isn't long." He had the nerve to look offended, as if he hadn't started the argument.

"My chest isn't flat."

"Isn't that what I just said?"

"You shouldn't be looking, either way."

"Men happen to do that once they reach a certain age." He merely grinned, clearly unrepentant. "I also have to shave quite often now too."

When had *he gotten so tall*, she wondered in pure irritation, since she came up only to his chin at best, and once upon a time, she had been able to look him in the eye. His shoulders too had broadened, and his features, which had once been almost girlishly pretty, had done some sort of inexplicable metamorphosis into masculine angles and clean lines that her friends actually thought attractive. They even whispered over him.

Just imagine, whispering over *Miles*.

In fact, her cousin was fast gaining a reputation as a rake, and no one was more surprised than she was that the awkward, irritating companion of her youth was becoming so popular with the beau monde.

Elizabeth took his arm in a firm grip. "I want to talk to you."

"Apparently so," he said dryly, but didn't resist when she tugged him toward the corner by the already disordered and almost empty canapé table. "What's so urgent?"

"What did Luke do?" she asked bluntly when they were relatively alone, sandwiched between the abandoned tables and a potted plant. "I can tell something has happened, but no one wants to mention it to me, apparently."

Her cousin regarded her with his usual lazy insouciance. "You wish me to repeat common gossip?"

"Absolutely, if it concerns my brother."

"He might not thank me for it." Miles propped a shoulder against the wall and shrugged. "Look, El, it isn't anything truly scandalous, so just forget it. Reckless, maybe, but he can afford it."

"Afford what?" she asked. Truth was, she was worried about Luke. The joie de vivre exterior he sometimes presented was at odds with the long hours he spent brooding in his study. Though she hadn't mentioned it, she knew their mother also disapproved of his overnight absences and distractions. It wasn't like him.

"Luke might have my head for telling you. We have a gentlemen's code."

"Code?" she echoed with a small snort that might even be interpreted as unladylike. "Aren't you the same *gentleman* who once slipped a frog into my bed?"

"I was ten." But he laughed.

Actually, Elizabeth realized, when he laughed like that, he did look quite handsome. His dark brown hair and his eyes, so light a brown as to seem almost gold in color, were not quite as nondescript as she'd once thought. Maybe the giggling young ingenues weren't completely daft. Despite his maddening tendencies to be deliberately obtuse and tease her relentlessly, he had a certain charisma. As children, it had served them well. His clever explanations had gotten them out of more than one scrape that might have proved uncomfortable.

She said acerbically, "Luke might have *my* head for poking my nose into his affairs, but I'm asking anyway. So tell me, what did he do he could afford, but shouldn't have?"

"Wagered twenty thousand on one hand of cards."

Elizabeth blinked. "Twenty thousand *pounds*?" It was an enormous sum. She might not be privy to her brother's finances, but that didn't matter. Twenty thousand was a significant amount.

Miles gave her a supercilious look. "Right."

"Oh." Elizabeth stared at the crowd for a moment, digesting this information. "It doesn't seem like Luke," she said eventually. "He might not act like he cares about being responsible and beholden to his duties, but I know he does. Look how he has squired me around when I know he'd much rather be doing something else. I don't understand his actions."

"I don't either." To her amazement, Miles didn't sound infuriatingly superior for having more information than she did, which was out of character. Usually he gloated over it. It had started when she was about five and he was eight. But right now, he was frowning, rubbing his jaw. "Something is wrong. He's moody and distant."

Distant. There was that word again, repeated by Miles, no less.

She could count on one hand the times the two of them had agreed on anything lately, and wished this wasn't one of those rare instances. "You've noticed it too?"

"Occasionally," he drawled in a dry tone, "contrary to your disparaging opinion of my character, I do manage to divert my attention from my own interests. Yes, I've noticed. He's preoccupied, though he's doing his best to be perceived as enjoying himself with the usual pursuits available to wealthy, aristocratic gentlemen. If I had to guess, he had no intention of entering into that bet. It just happened because it was assumed he'd relish such a staggering wager."

That was insightful enough that Elizabeth was startled. "You've given this some thought. And when put that way, at least it makes some sense."

"Now *that's* frightening." Her cousin's mouth quirked at one corner, and his thick lashes dropped a little over those unusual amber eyes. "The last time we were thinking along the same lines, we decided to take your father's brand-new phaeton for a spin in the country. If I remember the disaster correctly, I couldn't sit down for three days afterward when we were caught upon our return. My father was furious with me."

She'd always felt a bit guilty he'd gotten the caning for that little misadventure, while she'd merely been confined to her room. "You shouldn't have claimed it was all your idea. We both knew I was just as guilty."

"My idea of chivalry at the time." He shrugged. "I'm older and wiser now, as the saying goes, so the answer to your question is a firm no."

The music swelled again, filling the room with the strain of the latest popular waltz. "I haven't asked anything," she muttered, studiously adjusting her glove.

Miles straightened from the wall in a lithe movement. "You were just about to suggest that I try to find out what is bedeviling Luke."

She *had* been. Damn him. "Not at all," Elizabeth said coolly.

"Liar." His grin flashed, and then faded. He shook his head. "Women just don't understand men."

"Why the devil would we want to?" she muttered. "But could you be more specific as to what I don't understand in this instance?"

"I'm not going to pry. Sorry, El. If he wished to discuss it, he would bring it up himself. It isn't my business, or yours, for that matter, if something is awry."

"Pardon me if I am concerned about my brother."

He knew that stubborn set to her soft mouth. Miles Hawthorne uttered an inner curse and resisted the urge to grab Elizabeth's slender shoulders and drag her out through the French doors to the terrace and explain in the plainest terms possible how little the average male liked an interfering female trying to order his life.

Or drag her out there and do something else entirely. A passionate kiss came to mind. It came to mind quite often, in fact, when he was around Elizabeth.

If they *were* really cousins, this would never have happened, but he'd known since he was old enough to understand the complexities of the situation that they weren't related. His widowed mother had married Elizabeth's father's cousin only a few years after Miles was born, and they had moved to the Daudet estate. There wasn't a drop of shared blood between him and Elizabeth. He was so conscious of it, the knowledge disordered his life.

She disordered his life.

This evening she was striking in deep rose tulle that bared the creamy upper swells of her breasts, the low cut of the bodice emphasizing the graceful column of her neck. Her shining hair was upswept, and at the moment her eyes, the signature striking Daudet silver, regarded him with haughty disdain. High cheekbones held a hint of outraged color.

She wasn't classically beautiful, but was still considered a beauty. It was hard to define, and he'd love to spend a lifetime trying to analyze it. Those luminous, long-lashed eyes dominated her delicate face, and her chin was a shade square, her nose tilted up at the tip in a piquant angle. . . . When she was younger the combination lent her an elfin look, all eyes and long, curling hair, but as a woman, it lent her distinction from the perfect, blond, incomparable ideal of the *ton*. The color of her hair was impossible to define, waves of dark chestnut with a touch of gold in the light, and a hint of auburn as well.

Part of the allure, he knew, was her vitality. Elizabeth rarely did anything halfway. Some poor, unsuspecting man was going to have a devil of a time keeping her out of trouble once she was wed.

Some very lucky man, sod him.

She was glaring at him now with unconcealed irritation. Nothing new in *that*.

"Luke managed to stay alive during a war in Spain," Miles pointed out, returning her look with unperturbed steadiness. "He's titled, wealthy, and thirty years of age. He doesn't need you fretting over him. I daresay he'd be annoyed just to learn we'd had this conversation."

She crossed her arms under her breasts in a militant fashion. "Well, he won't ever *know* we had this conversation, will he? And I still say you could at least talk to him. For whatever reason, he likes you."

Elizabeth could needle him like no one else. Miles took a moment and then replied, "Your gift at bestowing compliments rivals my own. I could list a goodly amount of reasons he *would* like me, first and foremost being I have no inclination to interfere in his life."

"I'm merely asking you to—"

"No." A few familiar strains floated out from the orchestra. Miles arched his brows and looked at his cousin. "The subject is dropped, El. Shall we dance? Unless you are, of course, eager to have the next waltz with Porter, who is determinedly heading this way."

The diversion worked. A look of panic crossed her face. "I'd even rather dance with *you* than him. Hurry."

"I'm flattered, of course." He caught her hand and led her toward the floor. "Porter being a dead bore and all."

Elizabeth had the grace to laugh. She was graceful in other ways too as she swirled into his arms, though a polite distance naturally separated them, and her hand rested primly on his shoulder.

They'd danced together countless times, since they'd both had the same dancing master and essentially learned together. It was instinct to move in perfect accord to the lilting music, the patterns predictable, her body swaying against his in provocative motion.

Unconscious provocative motion, he knew, as her full skirts brushed his legs. *He* found it provocative, though it was perfectly proper. Those dancing lessons had been heaven mixed with a liberal dose of hell.

Damn all.

When, precisely, had he fallen in love with her? He couldn't recall. There hadn't been a brilliant flash of recognition of the moment, no trumpets had sounded, nor had he caught sight of Cupid poised anywhere with a quiver of arrows strapped to his back. As they matured he'd just become aware of it, like noticing the sky is blue, or the verdant color of a country pasture coming into focus. It was just *there*.

She'd still been so innocent, so unconsciously lovely as she'd begun the transition from a girl to a woman. It was only a few years ago—she was just nineteen now—but he'd done his best to keep his distance, and it hadn't been too difficult during the years he was at Eton and then Cambridge. He'd finished university early and gone home to Berkshire, his natural aptitude for academics putting him back in her sphere right about the time she was preparing for her bow. It was upon his return that he was forced to acknowledge the reality of his position.

She didn't look at him the same way.

It wasn't the only obstacle in courting her either. He was merely the stepson of a baronet, with nothing but a modest portion from his inheritance. No title, no fortune, no aristocratic lineage, except that his grandfather had been an earl, but his father had been the youngest son out of four before his death when Miles was two years old.

In contrast, Elizabeth's brother was a wealthy viscount, her dowry generous, and she was both lovely and intelligent. In short, she could, and no doubt would, do much better than him.

It was just the cold, unpalatable truth. He'd kept his role as brotherly childhood friend because it was *something*, and no matter his thwarted passion, she was still, and forever would be, his best friend. So they bickered as always, and his secret was safe.

"Uncle Chas said you persuaded him to invest in your shipping company." As they danced, Elizabeth gazed up at him from under the veil of her lush lashes. "Luke is considering it also, I understand."

The company was his idea, but though Miles was sure enough of the venture, he wasn't quite willing to claim it as his very own. "There are multiple investors," he said evasively, swinging her into a turn, one hand at her slim waist. "It isn't mine alone."

"Hmm."

"What does that mean?"

Her eyes narrowed. "It means when you get that particular shuttered look, you have something to hide. I know you."

He wished she knew him. In the biblical sense. He'd taught her to swim, to ride her pony, to climb a tree . . . how he'd love to enlighten her on how to make slow, long, lingering love, initiating her into the joys of the flesh with a thoroughness that would leave them both gasping and sated afterward . . .

He wasn't at liberty to tell her that the royal family had also decided to invest. If this endeavor was successful, and he was as certain as he could be that it had potential, he might someday be a rich man.

Someday would be too late. Elizabeth would marry this season.

To change the subject and needle her, instead he said with a wicked smile, "Lord Porter is hovering, waiting for this dance to be over. I don't think you're going to escape so easily, El."

She muttered an unladylike word that he'd taught her long ago, and he stifled a laugh.

And got to waltz with her for the next dance.

Chapter Five

He woke—it happened all too often—sweating, disoriented, trapped in the misty moonlight that spilled across the bed. Luke sat up, shivering as the sheets fell away, even though it was full summer and the air was warm, sticky even. He swallowed against the protestation of a dry-as-dust throat, and stumbled out of the bed.

"Damnation," he muttered, "when will it stop?"

Naked, he walked to the window, shoved up the sash so he could catch the hint of a breeze, and braced his hands on the sill, taking a deep lungful of air. Looking out, he didn't see the neat, shadowed paths and cultivated flower beds of the formal back garden, but instead a rocky slope, icy cold in the grip of a Spanish winter, a ruined convent silhouetted against a lurid sky, and the licking flames leaping upward, devouring without mercy. . . .

In his nightmares, he heard the screams. In truth, that hellish night had been quiet except for the demonic crackle of the fire.

*She'd looked so beautiful that day in her mother's man-
tilla, her dark hair shining as she knelt before the altar
and placed her hand in his, the candles flickering around
them. He barely remembered the ceremony, simply re-
peating the words, and then it was done.*

She was his wife.

*What a pity that same day he discovered only fools fall
in love during a war. . . .*

His face was wet. *Perspiration, not tears*, he told himself, and went to the basin to dip a cloth in the tepid water and wipe his sticky skin. He dressed quickly, because
he knew from experience he would not be able to go
back to sleep. Breeches buttoned hastily, shirt tucked in
haphazardly, boots pulled on, no coat . . . it was too warm
to need one. Raking his fingers carelessly through his
hair, he went down the stairs of the Mayfair mansion in
the dark, knowing the way so well he didn't need more
than the obscure moonlight slanting through the gallery
windows to negotiate the long, quiet hallways.

The walk to St. James Street was dark, his restless
footsteps echoing, his pace exacting as he tried to erase
the dream through physical exertion. He went up the
steps of the elegant town house, used his personal key,
and let himself into a foyer that carried a hint of lily
of the valley perfume. Once upon a time—what seemed
like a distant life—he had bought the town house for
himself. When his father died and Luke inherited the title, he'd been in Spain. On his return, he had moved into
the viscount's apartments in the sprawling family home,
albeit with reluctance, because of his sense of duty.

A lamp was still lit down the hallway, but he wasn't
surprised. Regina kept odd hours. He'd rather counted
on it. She also always had a decanter of his favorite whiskey on hand for his visits, and he'd counted on that too.

She was in the library in her dressing gown, frowning
over a series of drawings scattered all over the floor, her
long hair in a veil over her face until she glanced up as
he entered the room. The tall bookcases were shrouded,

the furniture pushed to the side to give more space for the informal display of her work. "I thought I heard someone open the door. What time is it?"

"Late." Luke smiled wryly. "Or early, depending on how you look at it." Her unconcern for an unknown person entering her home was all too typical. Luckily she had a competent housekeeper who looked after mundane matters such as locking the doors at night.

"I don't look at it at all." Regina rose gracefully from the floor and smoothed her indigo silk dressing gown, a faint smile on her face. "My eclectic psyche doesn't register the movements of the sun, you know that."

She was only half joking. His half sister was an artist, and a free spirit extraordinaire. "I've noticed. Is this a new project?" He gestured at the charcoal sketches. "Usually you work in colors."

"I'm always experimenting." She walked over to a small table, lifted the crystal top of a decanter, dashed amber liquid into a faceted cut glass tumbler, and came over to hand it to him.

"I didn't say I wanted a drink." He looked around for a place to sit, since the chairs were arranged in a disordered manner.

"You didn't have to." She sat down on a velvet-covered chair at right angles to the collection of drawings, compensating by draping her legs over the arm. "You only get that singularly hollow-eyed look occasionally, and this seems to be one of those nights. Considering the time, I can't imagine it takes great powers of deduction to figure out you can't sleep."

"Sleeping," he muttered, and took a drink of the sharp beverage, "is part of the problem." He decided to just go over and prop a shoulder against the closest bookcase.

Considering they'd had different mothers, Regina looked uncannily like Elizabeth, with the same large gray eyes and fragile features. However, their older sister had a statuesque build, unlike Elizabeth's slender form, and had also inherited her mother's disdain for convention. In her midthirties, she was unmarried and had shown no inclination to change that status. If she had lovers, she was discreet enough that Luke knew nothing about it.

"Bad dreams again?" She crossed her elegant bare ankles and regarded him with an unwavering, questioning gaze.

"Bad dream in the singular. It doesn't vary." His head ached, and the whiskey wasn't likely to help, but he drank again anyway, the warmth curling in his stomach.

"Someday you'll tell me?"

"No." His voice was harsher than he'd intended, the memory of the dream hauntingly vivid. She had no idea what she was asking of him, nor did he want to involve her. It was best for his family, he'd decided before he ever set foot back on English soil, if they didn't know.

"It might help." Regina was unfazed by his curt response.

His smile was devoid of humor. "It might give *you* nightmares. I've enough on my conscience as it is without adding to the burden."

"It strikes me you should worry a little more about yourself and a little less about the rest of us."

"I'm Altea, remember?" One brow lifted in an ironic arch. "It is my duty to concern myself with my family."

"Is it also your duty to inspire young rakehells to risk their entire portions on a single hand of cards?"

Luke rubbed his throbbing temple. "That single reckless moment is being vastly exaggerated."

"Is it?" Regina lounged in her chair, her dark, silky hair in careless disarray. "Are you telling me you didn't accept that wager and the entire affair is being romanticized for the benefit of gossip?"

After a moment, he said with resignation, "I should never have gone to that questionable establishment in the first place. I was just restless, I suppose, that evening, and somehow I found myself in an untenable position."

"You could have declined to wager such an outrageous sum."

"I thought you understood the male of our species better than that." Luke brooded at his glass for a moment. Then he sighed. "I've been playing deep lately, bringing the whole incident on my own head, I admit it. Can we change the subject?"

"If you wish." Regina adjusted the folds of her dressing gown. "What would you like to discuss in the wee hours before dawn?"

"Tell me about your newest work." It wasn't an original ploy, but it always worked. His half sister's enthusiasm for art bordered on single-minded obsession.

She did, and he listened, admiring her passion for her calling as her lilting voice rose and fell with fervor, regaling him with the virtues of Leonardo da Vinci's studies of the human form, and how she derived inspiration from them when traveling in Italy recently and viewing not only the museums, but also private collections. The new sketches, Regina informed him while he negligently sipped his drink and the first glimmer of light appeared outside the tall windows of the town house he'd given her on the day he'd inherited his father's estate, were still life impressions: a single flower, the Greek cyclamen, the buds just beginning to unfurl; a waterfall, the veil of water gliding over a cascade of ancient rocks, she'd seen in Cyprus; the facade of the Pantheon on a hot summer day, magnificent and timeless. Her talent was undeniable, and he was proud of her, just as he had never denied their relationship, even if she was the illegitimate daughter of his father's former mistress. The affair had been before he'd married, and Luke didn't fault his father's indiscretion.

He'd made a wicked mistake or two of his own.

And he hadn't been alone.

Madeline's stricken face the other day wasn't easy to banish. Maybe it had even brought on the dream. "I always envy you your passion," he told his sister when she showed him her depiction of the Bridge of Sighs in Venice at night. The drawing captured perfectly the glint of moonlight on the water.

"And I envy you your detachment," she replied as she let the picture drift back to the pile on the floor. "But when are you going to abandon it?"

"Abandon it?"

"Luke." Her tone held gentle remonstration. "You are running away from something."

If only he could. Still, he dissembled. "Running away? It seems to me I am right here."

"Don't be obtuse on purpose. I mean in a symbolic way." She laughed, the sound as light as the coming dawn.

Unfortunately, he couldn't run away. Not from his obligations to his family and fortune, and not from the memories that kept him frozen in the past. "Perhaps," he said with a mirthless smile, "since you have my acquiescence on that point, tell me, what are you going to draw next? Have you thought about Hailes Abbey in Gloucestershire? Or Whitby? England has some splendor also in her countryside."

His sister wasn't fooled, but she was also distracted by the notion of transepts and flying buttresses, and his discontent was quickly forgotten as they discussed monastic ruins and dramatic settings while the sun rose slowly, bathing the horizon in a pale wash of rose laced with streaks of gray.

"As I understand it," Lady Hendricks said, sotto voce, "his lordship was brutally assaulted right in the street by footpads."

Madeline kept a calm expression, difficult as it was, idly drinking her tea. "The story changes constantly. I do believe much of it is exaggerated."

And, thanks be to God, the odious man doesn't seem to remember what really happened.

Luke had extracted the note she'd sent from Lord

Fitch's pocket, so his lordship wouldn't have that to
jog his foggy recollection of the evening, but even if
he didn't know who hit him or where he'd been at the
time, he still had the journal. And until she got it back,
he could continue to make his disgusting innuendos and
vile suggestions.

Why, oh, why, hadn't she followed her first inclination
and had Colin's precious scribbling buried with him? Of
course, she'd had no inkling he'd been so *specific* in his
writings either. Who would think he'd write down details of such personal moments anyway? A part of her
was angry with him, but she knew he would be horrified
to cause her distress or embarrassment, much less spur
on the unsavory attentions of a man she detested, especially since he wasn't there to protect her.

Luckily, she could call on Luke. Or was it lucky? Yes,
for he'd certainly helped her, but she would have been
better off keeping her distance.

The obligatory Tuesday-afternoon tea in her mother's
elegant drawing room was particularly trying this day, in
light of recent events. Usually Madeline didn't mind being decades or more younger than the other women in
attendance, because she found their endless tittle-tattle
amusing, but despite the golden sun coming through the
windows and the cloudless sky outside, she felt a little
cold.

Mrs. Pearce, who was a close friend of Madeline's
grandmother, wore her gray hair in a tidy bun, her ami-
able face reflecting a thoughtful frown. She said, "Quite
frankly, Fitch isn't my favorite person. Not that I would
wish ill upon him, but he has a most grating manner at
times. Too forward by half, if you ask me."

Grate. Fireplace. Poker. There was an ironic connection there, Madeline had to acknowledge with a cynical
inner wince. "I don't care for him," she admitted, hoping
her expression was bland. "But neither did I—er—do I
wish him ill. Perhaps it was all an accident."

"Brave of Altea to run off the footpads and take his lordship home." Lady Hendricks reached for another éclair. "His heroics aren't confined to the war, apparently."

Now, there was a variation on the story Madeline hadn't heard yet. "I thought he found him lying there in an alley close to his club."

That version was dismissed with an airy wave of plump fingers as not as interesting as a gang of murderous ruffians. "Either way, going into a deserted, sordid pathway in the middle of the night cannot be a pleasant experience."

If the infuriatingly nonchalant and detached Viscount Altea emerged from this debacle some sort of hero, and it looked like matters were going that way, it would just be salt on the wound. Madeline fought the urge to grind her teeth and acknowledged silently with cold common sense that if he truly retrieved the journal, he *was* a hero.

He'd come at once at her request, she had to grudgingly admit. And effectively hauled off the unscrupulous Fitch like so much baggage. It stung to owe the man who had once spurned her, but she *did* owe Luke, and his confidence in regaining the journal meant the debt might be deepened even more.

How would she repay it?

Madeline's mother, who presided over tea like a queen, looked serene as she refilled her cup. "It isn't unlike a Daudet to stumble headfirst into some sort of intrigue, and the viscount in particular. I remember his father. He was extremely dashing. Women adored him."

Since all of this had to do with her and a possible scandal that was at the least mortifying, Madeline tried to change the subject. "I hear the Baltimore ball has been changed to next week."

"Yes." Lady Hendricks wasn't impressed with the announcement, and unswervingly returned to a more salacious topic. "I remember too the viscount's father. He was almost as beautiful as his son." Her smile was smug and feline. "Almost."

Luke. Tall, so handsome, with those intense silver eyes and his dark blond hair . . .

That one night was imprinted so clearly on her mind that Madeline could almost taste his kiss, feel the hardness of muscle and sinew under her questing fingertips, not to mention the delicious erotic friction as he moved with seductive expertise between her legs. . . .

That was a memory better banished to a distant part of her mind that wouldn't recall it when in a room full of matronly ladies. She delved into her cup, hiding her expression. Lately, she'd been thinking a great deal about the emptiness in her personal life, and the entire unpleasantness with Fitch had dredged up the past. Not just the intimacies she'd once shared with Colin, but also the combustible passion she'd experienced with the cynical but undeniably attractive Lord Altea. The strange ending to their conversation the other day in his carriage had fretted at the edge of her mind ever since, but what she remembered most was his admission that he still wanted her.

I desire you still. . . .

And as outrageous as the idea might be, she was starting to think she needed a lover. Perhaps a husband, but she'd been a widow for a while now, and no one had in the least appealed to her for such a permanent arrangement. Was it necessary she marry again to taste passion? The social whirl of society was entertaining, her son was the center of her world, and her family was warm and caring, but in the end, Madeline was beginning to realize that as each day passed, she was losing more and more of the woman inside her. She was Lady Brewer, she was a mother, she was a daughter and sister, but she didn't feel like a *woman*.

As a married lady, she'd discovered she had a sensual nature. When Colin died, she had dismissed that part of her life, thinking it could be put aside and forever ignored. Obviously that wasn't true, or the one night with Luke would never have happened in the first place. Now, having seen him again, spoken with him, looked once more into those mesmerizing gray eyes, she couldn't stop thinking about that wanton, delicious night . . . about *him*.

Mrs. Pearson said blithely, "I've heard some wicked rumors about Altea, I admit it."

"Do tell." Lady Hendricks stopped in the act of taking another sweet.

"He's as reckless in the boudoir as he is in the gaming rooms."

"Where there's a Daudet male, there will always be women," Mrs. Pearce agreed sagely.

"Brazenly willing women, no doubt. I was afraid Lady Hart was going to ravish him on the ballroom floor the other evening. She's positively shameless in her quest to snare his interest."

"Well, I heard—"

Oh, no. This was the last scenario Madeline wanted. Older ladies exchanging intimate gossip about Luke. She rose abruptly. "I just noticed the time. My apologies, but I forgot I have an appointment. Please excuse me."

"Darling . . ." her mother began to say, her eyes wide and startled.

There was no question of explaining her precipitous departure. Madeline smiled at the room at large and murmured a hasty farewell, exiting the house to find her driver waiting by the carriage, idly talking to a tall young man in a nondescript coat and threadbare hat, his lean jaw showing a straggle of dark whiskers. An interesting scar bisected one eyebrow and lent him the air of a down-on-his-luck pirate. He politely tugged on the brim of the disreputable hat when she approached. "My lady."

Her questioning look was met with a small smile. He bowed and produced a small packet from his jacket. "I was instructed to wait and hand this to you personally, Lady Brewer."

It was oblong and heavy, and a small thrill of relief went through as she realized just what it was. Colin's journal, no doubt. Luke had come through as promised. "Thank you," she said with as much dignity as possible.

The man's eyes showed a certain keen level of intelligence at odds with his threadbare clothing. "Not at all. A pleasure to serve such a lovely lady."

She watched him walk away, a little bemused, and then let her driver help her into her carriage. Once inside, she unwrapped the delivery as they pulled into the street, her hands not quite steady.

Luke's note was brief. *For you, as promised.*

For you. As promised.

Madeline held the journal in her hands and gazed out the window, not seeing the passing houses or hearing the street hawkers on the corners. Touched, moved, relieved . . . she was all of those things and more.

Unfortunately, so much more.

What to do about it was the question.

Chapter Six

"I can't."

"Why?"

"Because." Elizabeth gazed at her companion with exasperated consternation. "Miles won't court someone just because I tell him I think he should do so. He might, in fact, form a distaste for Miss Meyer if I encourage him to consider a romance. He likes nothing more than to irritate me. We are always squabbling over something or another."

"You told me you and he were inseparable as children."

"We've grown up and it isn't the same." That was an understatement. The Miles she remembered had changed. It was hard to define how, but it was *there*.

"Yet you waltzed with him twice the other evening." Walking next to her, Amelia St. James seemed to consider a group of playing children with their watchful nannies, but her mouth twitched.

"He's my cousin." Elizabeth shrugged, enjoying the warmth of the beautiful afternoon. The park was predictably crowded with both fashionably dressed gentlemen and ladies, and the horse paths were also busy. They walked side by side, parasols above their heads. "We grew up together. Quite frankly, I am not sure why he is garnering so much attention. He's just . . . Miles."

Her friend laughed. "To you, perhaps. To the rest of the young females of this season he is rather deliciously handsome. He also reputedly possesses a decided skill for flirtation and has that singular lazy smile. Trust me, I know the power of a wicked smile quite well."

Considering Amelia's recent marriage to one of London's most celebrated rakehells, Lord Alexander St. James, youngest son of the Duke of Berkeley, she probably did know. "Hmm. Well, Miles isn't half—no, even a third—as charming as your husband," Elizabeth muttered. "He's abrasive and annoyingly smug at times. Not to mention his sometimes questionable sense of humor."

"He's considered *quite* charming."

"If they knew him, they might change their minds."

"That is precisely what Susanna wants. To get a chance to know him. Miles Hawthorne isn't titled or rich, but she has enough money for the both of them and her father indulges her."

Oddly enough, the summary of Miles's shortcomings as a suitor made Elizabeth bristle. "His family, even aside from the Daudets, is perfectly respectable."

"My very point." Amelia raised her brows slightly. "Can I tell Susanna you will give your cousin a gentle nudge in her direction? She's a friend."

The flicker of irritation was illogical. Elizabeth couldn't care less what young woman Miles chose to consider in a romantic fashion. She nodded once. "For what it is worth, I will mention her name the next time I am in his company."

"Thank you."

Elizabeth glanced sideways. "Perhaps you can return the favor."

Blond, stunning in lemon muslin this warm afternoon, her parasol held in slim fingers, Amelia was the personification of the true English beauty: pale, perfect skin, shining hair caught at her nape, azure eyes framed by long lashes. No wonder St. James had fallen for her. And Alex St. James just happened to be one of Luke's closest friends.

"How so?" Amelia's eyebrows rose in question. "Is there someone who has caught your interest? Does Alex know him?"

"That isn't the kind of favor I mean. I'm worried about my brother," Elizabeth said bluntly. Amelia was trustworthy; of that she had no doubt. "I know you've heard about the wager of the other evening. As I understand it, all of London is agog."

A small child raced after a puppy in front of them, both delightfully clumsy, an observant nanny trailing behind with an indulgent expression on her face. Amelia smiled as both puppy and child collided in a heap of chubby legs and wagging tail and the little boy shrieked with laughter. She acquiesced, "Yes, I heard."

Green grass brushed their skirts and the breeze was gentle. "Will you ask Alex if he has noticed anything wrong with Luke lately? They know each other well, and if Alex would confide in anyone, it would be him or Lord Longhaven. I cannot quite imagine asking the formidable marquess anything, but *you*," she said pointedly, "also know *Alex* very well."

Mirth surfaced in Amelia's voice. "I suppose you could say that, as he is my husband."

The word *husband* conjured obscure images of dark bedrooms and secretive touches, and Elizabeth had to acknowledge that her lack of information on just what marriage entailed became more and more the subject of her thoughts as the season progressed. "You always smile a certain way when his name is mentioned. Is it really that . . ." She trailed off, not sure how to finish.

"Magical?" Amelia supplied, her voice hushed. "I

cannot speak for everyone, naturally, but for us . . . Yes."

"I really can't imagine it." So far, the whirl of society had been entertaining enough, but Elizabeth wasn't impressed with any specific gentleman. They varied from foppish and eager to smooth and sophisticated, but with none of them had there been any certain sense of elevated interest on her part. A few she liked quite well, some she thought pleasant, but her attitude in general was ambiguous.

She wanted to fall in love, which was a hopelessly romantic view of the entire process, she knew, but it had happened to Amelia, so why couldn't it happen to *her*?

A mischievous smile curved her friend's mouth. "You mean you can't imagine it *yet*. There's a distinction. When you meet the right gentleman, it could all change."

"I want to share your confidence." Elizabeth gave a rueful grimace. "But so far, marriage doesn't seem all that appealing."

"I completely shared your views until one evening, when a mysterious stranger appeared on my balcony."

"Balcony?"

"Never mind." Amelia waved at a friend, her expression as sunny as the sky. "My point is you should be open-minded about the possibilities ahead."

"I'll accept your word on it." Disappointed, Elizabeth murmured, "In the meantime, as we wait for me to discover my gallant prince, can you please ask Alex to talk to Luke? I am not sure how to describe it. He's restless, distant."

There was a pause. Then Amelia nodded once. "I'll ask. Though I can't promise Alex will be in favor of complying with my request. Men are such strange creatures at times."

Thinking of Miles's infuriating refusal to interfere, Elizabeth said darkly, "I agree."

Quiet settled between them, except for the chatter

of the children and the people strolling in the park. The slanting sun added to the bucolic feel of the afternoon, even in the middle of the city.

She might be an ingenue, and she might be a debutante with little experience, but it suddenly struck Elizabeth that her friend seemed extraordinarily absorbed and had been since they set out on their stroll, their maids a suitable distance behind them. The direction of Amelia's gaze was definitely fastened on a baby in his pram.

A light dawned. Elizabeth was uninformed, not completely ignorant, and Amelia had so precipitously married the notorious St. James. Her eyes widened. "Oh."

Amelia blushed.

The banks of the Serpentine were crowded, and they walked parallel through the grass instead of on one of the winding paths. Elizabeth observed neutrally, "I am not a mystic, but also not without some intuition."

"Like?"

"You've been quite absorbed in the children ever since we started this walk."

"Have I?"

"Indeed, you have." The remonstration was gentle but direct. "Can I guess the reason?"

"You always have been able to be perceptive about the emotions of others, with the exception of your own." Her friend was composed and amused, her cheeks still a becoming pink. "Well, yes, then. Alex and I are expecting a baby."

This was, Elizabeth realized, why Lady Amelia had called on her and suggested the walk in the park in the first place. She smiled warmly. "Congratulations."

"Thank you. We're delighted, of course. I—"

"Good afternoon, ladies."

The interruption of a deep voice made Elizabeth jerk her attention back to the path. A man stood there, bareheaded, his ironic smile all too familiar. He was dressed casually in buff breeches and a white shirt, his cravat looped in a simple tie, a well-cut dark brown coat completing the informal ensemble.

Miles.

What an inconvenient coincidence.

At what point had he lost any semblance of dignity and begun to drift into a life of humiliating covert surveillance?

Probably when I was about ten, Miles decided sardonically, inclining his head politely and taking Lady Amelia's hand. It was the first time he remembered following Elizabeth and her governess. Then it had been harmless enough; he'd hated Latin and wanted to avoid his lessons and tutor. Whatever his spritely young cousin had been doing was surely more interesting than Marcus Aurelius.

Now it was a bit less innocent.

Silver eyes with a hint of disdain regarded him from under the rim of a parasol that exactly matched her moss-green gown, and the richness of her hair was even more vivid in the sunshine. For whatever reason, both Elizabeth and her companion were blushing, and as they'd just spotted him, it must have to do with the conversation they had been absorbed in before he stepped into their path. He said, as pleasantly as possible, "May I say you are both extraordinarily lovely this afternoon?"

"And you are very gallant, Mr. Hawthorne." Amelia St. James was undeniably one of society's loveliest jewels, and her recent marriage to the Duke of Berkeley's infamous youngest son was still referred to in scandalized whispers. Personally, Miles didn't blame St. James in the least for her seduction and the elopement, whatever the order of occurrence. The young lady was breathtaking.

Elizabeth made a small, derisive noise over the allusion to his possible gallantry, which he ignored.

"Mind if I join you?"

"If I said yes, I do mind, would it stop you?" Elizabeth asked, her tone lofty, but there was a hint of a smile in her eyes.

At least she is glad to see me. It is something, if I can't have anything else. Always we are aware of each other. Will she ever realize it?

"Stop me? Probably not," he responded with an irreverent grin.

"That is exactly what I thought, so I suppose we have little choice. Do we?"

Lady Amelia looked amused at the byplay. "I, for one, am delighted at your arrival, Mr. Hawthorne, because I think I see my husband coming this way. He is developing a tendency to hover, which I assume will pass as soon as he adjusts to the situation. In the meantime, however, I think my walk is being cut short. At least Elizabeth can continue."

Sure enough, Alex St. James was walking toward them with long strides. "Lady Elizabeth, good afternoon. Hawthorne." Bareheaded, his dark hair and eyes a contrast to his wife's delicate fairness, he took Lady Amelia's hand, touched it to his mouth, and announced, "I've decided we're going to Berkeley Hall. The country air will be pleasant."

"Now?" The lady looked bemused.

"Your maid is packing for you." He smiled in apology at Miles and Elizabeth. "I'm afraid I am going to steal her away from you. Will you excuse us?"

They watched as he steered Lady Amelia immediately toward a waiting curricle.

Mystified, Miles turned to Elizabeth. "What situation?"

"Oh, please, Miles, think about it for a minute." His cousin didn't take his proffered arm, but she did fall into step next to him. "Why would he want to whisk her off for some fresh country air?"

He dropped the arm with an inner resignation and frowned. "She's newly married, of course."

"Precisely." Elizabeth looked at him, the corner of her mouth lifting.

He was a man, after all, and the first topic on his mind was not the specific results of the act of procreation, though the process of it did consume a lot of his attention. He caught on quickly enough, more from her high color than anything else. "Oh, I see. Good for St. James."

"*That* is your reaction?" She made what could only be described as a snort of disgust. "I cannot see why he gets the credit for the conception."

"I certainly hope the credit goes to him, as she is his wife."

"You are deliberately missing my point."

"If it is on the end of your barbed tongue, I've been cut by it often enough, thank you."

"Miles." She blew out a breath in a huff of outrage, but it was also a half laugh.

Was it perverse of him to love the way she said his name, especially when he'd needled her into that certain tone? Elizabeth was delectable when angry. Actually, to his frustrated misfortune, she was delectable all the time.

He elevated his brows. "I doubt we should be discussing this indelicate topic."

"I have never understood how having a baby is indelicate." She twirled her parasol and her brow furrowed as they strolled along. With unswerving logic, she pointed out, "It is how we all got here, after all."

"Is that how it works?" he murmured dryly.

"As if *you* don't know." Her gaze was accusing. "Word has it you are becoming quite an expert on the subject."

The acerbic tone of her voice held a note he wasn't sure he recognized, and he could swear he knew every inflection and nuance. "What does *that* mean?"

"Your"—she obviously groped for a suitable word—"licentious ways have been noticed."

He did his best to keep a neutral expression, but he wanted to laugh at her censorious observation. Besides, he didn't have licentious ways. Occasionally he flirted a little, mostly to see if she was paying any attention to what he did at all. Until now, he didn't know she had. "I see. I am surprised I am worthy of any gossip."

"Worthy? No, I agree. Yet others aren't quite so perceptive. I am supposed to bring Susanna Meyer to your attention."

If she had been able to keep her voice even, he wouldn't have experienced a small thrill of hope, which was something he usually denied himself with ruthless practicality.

He should deny it now.

But Elizabeth sounded . . . jealous.

Or was it his hopeful imagination?

Undoubtedly. *Jealous* was too strong a word. *Miffed* might work better.

"Who?" he asked with feigned perplexity, though he remembered the young woman well enough from their recent introduction and subsequent dance. Wide-eyed, breathless ingenues were not his preference, no matter the opulence of their bosom or father's fortune.

No, for whatever reason, he was captivated by a silver-eyed, childish hoyden who had grown into a very provocative woman.

The slight breeze drifted a loose tendril of glossy hair across her smooth cheek in a languorous caress. "I am sure you recall her," she said, her face just slightly averted as they walked. "She certainly remembers *you*."

"Maybe," he admitted, just to tease her. "Or at least one part of her . . . er . . . abundant anatomy."

"It is just like you to say something so tasteless." She stopped, rounding on him in derisive confrontation.

"I'm appalling," he agreed softly, gazing into her remarkable eyes, at the moment the shade of a stormy summer sky. "A veritable scoundrel. How did you put it? Oh, yes, licentious."

"Your female admirers don't seem to know that yet."

"I have female admirers?" Dangerous ground always, to taunt her, but he liked the reaction. It was *something*.

"It seems so. Do not ask *me* to explain it." Her voice was lofty, and she resumed their leisurely pace.

A few steps behind, he indulged himself by admiring the gentle sway of her hips. Then he grinned and followed. He wouldn't miss the rest of this fascinating argument for the world.

Chapter Seven

The dinner was a long, boring affair full of political debates and social gossip, and as Luke finished his roast beef, expertly cooked and served with a luxurious sauce of wine and braised shallots, he reflected that at least the food was excellent. Masters had a decent wine cellar also; Luke had probably drunk a bottle of claret just himself.

Ill-advised, considering his mood.

It didn't help to have Madeline sitting across the table, albeit four chairs down, next to a handsome blade named Morrow. She was dazzling this evening in a teal gown that complemented her flawless complexion and showcased her firm, high breasts.

He didn't miss a detail, from the lace sewn strategically along the neckline of her gown to the simple pearl earrings and gold bracelet she wore. The lace, he thought in sardonic contemplation, hinted at silken, bared skin in a teasing way, and made the gown more modest—and at the same time more risqué—than it actually was. He guessed her taste was too refined to wear a gown that low-cut without the suggestive lace, but enjoyed the illusion of scandalous adventure.

Her dinner companion hadn't missed that comparison either. The impudent young man alternated between surreptitiously ogling her décolletage and leaning over to whisper in her ear. Not that Luke particularly cared whom she chose to flirt with, but surely she could do better than that young cub.

Or he thought he didn't care. After a few glasses of wine, he found perhaps he did.

The entire evening annoyed him. If it wasn't for Elizabeth, he wouldn't have agreed to come in the first place.

"Such pleasant weather we've been having, isn't it, Lord Altea?"

He managed to wrest his attention from his wineglass long enough to look politely at the plump matron seated next to him. "Yes," he said abstractly. "Very pleasant."

Ye gods, had he really just said something so inane?

Lady Bunton, or Button, or whatever her deuced name might be—he'd been introduced, but couldn't remember—leaned forward a conspiratorial distance. "So very brave of you to rescue Lord Fitch the other evening. I understand you single-handedly ran off an entire mob of footpads."

He almost choked on his wine.

The ridiculous story was out of hand, but luckily, since the nefarious Fitch really didn't seem to remember what happened and they now had the journal, thanks to Michael, Madeline was kept out of it. He risked another swift glance across the table, saw her gazing his direction, and quickly looked back at Lady B. "I'm afraid that's an exaggeration, madam. I merely happened to notice him lying in the alley unconscious and took him home. No bravery involved."

She beamed at him. "You are being too modest."

Heaven help him. He gestured to have his wineglass refilled. To his relief, the dessert course arrived and

Lady B was effectively diverted by chocolate pudding with hard sauce.

When their hostess announced it was time to retire to the drawing room for a round of charades, Luke knew with every fiber of his being that he could not endure an insipid moment of it. As the exodus began from the dining room, he quietly pulled Miles aside into a corner by the pedimented doorway. "Will you please escort my mother and Elizabeth home?"

"I take it the idea of watching Lady Helton act out parts of *Macbeth* doesn't hold much appeal?" Miles grinned, but it turned into a grimace. "That was a rhetorical question, of course. Not for me either, if you want the truth. But I'll be happy to see the ladies home safely." Then in a very diplomatic, casual voice, his stepcousin asked, "Is anything wrong?"

"Nothing." A lie, but Luke wasn't about to explain. "I'd just appreciate a reprieve from having to be social this evening. If I stayed, I feel certain I would put my fist through a wall. Bloody bad manners in polite company."

"You have seemed a bit grim lately." Miles's gaze was not openly inquisitive, but Luke could feel the unsaid question.

"Ennui," Luke said curtly.

"I see." His cousin hesitated, and then said bluntly, "Oh, hell. I refused to meddle, and I still have no intention of prying, but just know Elizabeth is worried about you. To tell the truth, *I've* wondered what might be bothering you."

He'd always liked Miles. Even when as children he and Elizabeth were running amok, causing havoc all over the estate, Luke had thought Miles basically a levelheaded individual, a foil for his somewhat impulsive younger sister. At twenty-two, Miles was venturing into business with a sound concept that had intrigued investors, Luke among them. He had no doubt his stepcousin was astute enough to be successful.

But he wasn't at all in the mood for confidences, no matter how much he liked and trusted Miles. "The mood will pass," he murmured negligently. "Tell her to worry instead about her own life. I am glad she's enjoying the season, but she needs to eventually select a husband out of her many admirers. I haven't noticed a preference yet for any of those eager gentlemen."

A change in expression crossed Miles's face. It was a flash, masked a moment later: a slight tightening of the mouth, a muscle twitch in his jaw. He said carefully, "With all the interested suitors, I am sure she will, but if *I* tell her to do so, keep in mind, it will be her inclination to do just the opposite."

Luke might be battling his own demons, but he had started to wonder about Miles and Elizabeth. As far as he could tell, she was as of yet oblivious to the possibility that her cousin—who was not at all a cousin in any form except a distant connection by marriage—was no longer the rambunctious childhood companion, but a grown man who might not look at her with platonic indifference. In turn, she was no longer the mischievous hoyden with a tendency to drag him into all sorts of trouble.

As her guardian, Luke hoped *those* days were past. It wasn't that he didn't trust Miles or Elizabeth, but together . . .

He might need to pay a little more attention.

But not tonight. His mother was there. She could play duenna. He needed to get away as soon as possible. Away from playacting and charades, away from matrons with an inflated and false sense of his heroic antics, away from temptation . . .

In regards to the latter, away from Madeline.

"You could be right. I'll talk to Elizabeth myself." His smile was wry. "Now, if you will excuse me, I am going to make my farewells to our host and gratefully slip away."

Moments later he made his escape, going down the steps into the warm evening air, mercifully free of the dubious theatrical talents of the assembled party. He'd walked, as the evening was pleasant, and no sooner had he reached the street when he heard a breathless call.

"Luke. Wait, please."

Madeline. *Damnation.* He knew her soft, lilting voice.

He halted, uttered an even more foul curse, and turned. He'd hoped to make it through the evening without actually having to speak to her, and with a little effort and because the hovering Morrow monopolized her, he'd managed it.

Until now.

Her beauty always struck him in a unique way—it had the first time he'd seen her and never failed since. It wasn't quite so much her form and face, though both were exquisite, as it was the air of sensual sensitivity, so feminine, and those luminous dark eyes, tilted at the corners to give her an unusual, striking loveliness. . . .

Those glorious eyes that seemed to see right through him.

She came down the steps, her silk skirts gathered in her hands, her expression difficult to discern in the dim glow of the starlit sky. "You've avoided me all evening."

The edge of reproach in her voice did nothing to soothe his restive mood. "If you noticed it, may I ask why you just chased out the door after me?"

She flinched, but then squared her shoulders. "Do not use that acerbic tone with me, Altea. I am sure you are aware I wish to thank you for the return of Colin's journal."

"You are welcome." His bow was slightly mocking, because it was the only way to deal with it—to deal with her. "Now, then, that being settled, I am sure Morrow is in there pining for your company. Best not keep him waiting."

"Are you jealous?" One arched brow lifted an infuriating fraction.

Was he? *Maybe*, he silently acknowledged. He certainly had no right to be, but life didn't always follow along logical lines. "I don't believe in that unproductive emotion."

"You *sound* jealous."

He definitely didn't want to have this conversation. "At the risk of being rude, I was taking my leave, Lady Brewer."

"You aren't going to call me Madge?"

Her smile was deliberately provocative. A slight curve of those soft, full lips, her eyes shadowed by long, lush lashes, her sumptuous bosom just gently rising from her precipitous flight down the stairs.

"You dislike the name." He knew he should turn and put as much distance as possible between them.

Just walk away, you blasted fool.

"I believe I like it from *you.*"

The soft, sexual innuendo in her words might not be intentional, but as his gaze narrowed on her face, he wondered if it might be exactly that.

She took a single, crucial step toward him. "You also said you didn't believe I was the kind of woman who would ever consent to become your mistress."

Now she was too close, too tempting, her evocative scent reminiscent of exotic gardens and forbidden passion. Distracted, it took him a moment to register her words.

He *had* said that, of course.

"Well," she murmured, looking directly into his eyes, "I have been thinking about it, and you were wrong."

Playing with fire was too tame a phrase.

Madeline gazed up at the tall man standing so still next to her, the star-studded, velvety night sky lending shadows to the chiseled planes and angles of his face and his enigmatic expression. His dark blond hair, entirely a different shade from hers—a tawny color shot with streaks of lighter gold—and curling over his collar, suited him, suited that aura of leashed wildness under his studied civility. At dinner he'd been moody, noticeably lacking in the suave niceties, and he'd even eaten his food with an almost impatient irritation, and drunk wine with little restraint, though his capacity must be formidable, for he didn't appear the least impaired.

Or maybe he was, at least a little, for he'd watched her almost the entire time, and if she was guilty of flirting at least a little with the handsome young Charles Morrow to see if Luke reacted, she was unrepentant.

At one point, when the man next to her had leaned forward too much for propriety, she'd wondered if Luke might come across the table in a single, lethal lunge. The realization had at first startled and then intrigued her. His glittering stare had been noticeable. She needed adventure in her very respectable life, and who better than Altea to take her on the journey?

That moment with Morrow leering at her and Luke silently watching with a primal look in his eyes in response had been a decisive turning point. Luke was a gambler—all of London knew that after the infamous reckless wager. Perhaps she was one too.

He *had* been jealous. She'd known it then and she certainly knew it now. He could coolly win a wager with twenty thousand at stake, and yet he couldn't convincingly bluff her on that fine point.

How ... satisfying. How very empowering.

"Madeline," he drawled in a deceptively soft voice, "go back inside and finish the evening entertainments, and I will forget you ever said that."

She shook her head. "Let's go somewhere and discuss it. The street seems a rather public venue."

"It?"

"Us," she said firmly, though her heart was pounding and her palms damp. *Am I really going to do this?*

Yes, she was. Why not? She was not an ingenue angling for an advantageous marriage. She'd had that already and it was gone. When Colin died, she'd been devastated, but while the pain would never completely fade, it was blunted by time, the sharp edges softened now by memories. He'd also left her both wealthy and independent. If she wanted to take a lover, there was no reason she couldn't. The scandalous implications of a relationship with Viscount Altea were a little daunting, but widows had infinitely more freedom than unmarried women, and she was, after all, nearing thirty and hardly in the first bloom of youth. It wasn't like she was looking for another husband, so why not a virile, handsome lover whom she knew firsthand could acquit himself with tender, wicked skill in the bedroom, was witty and charming when he chose to be, and, though she sensed he held a dark side of himself at bay, would treat her well?

There was a combustible attraction between them. She was tired of trying to deny it, and he had even admitted he wanted her.

He didn't move, and his eyes held a singular glitter. "There is no *us*, darling Madge."

"Have you forgotten that night?" Acutely aware of the attendants at the carriages lining the street and possible curious eyes from inside the house, she didn't touch him—though she wanted to—but her voice dropped to a husky murmur. "I haven't."

"A mistake," he said shortly, but he still didn't walk away.

"*Our* mistake, then." Madeline smiled. It was a vixen's smile, her best attempt to sway him, for though he still seemed impervious, she could sense an inner battle. "Shall we," she said delicately, softly, "discuss our mutual imprudence elsewhere? Like my bedroom?"

Maybe it was the considerable amount of claret, or maybe it was simply male capitulation to an offer of erotic carte blanche, but Luke swore under his breath—an oath she didn't quite catch, though a shocking word or two came through.

Yet the look in his eyes took on a searing heat.

Exactly what she wanted.

"That you followed me outside will be all over London by dawn," he told her, but he'd already lifted his hand to her driver to summon the carriage. Since they were the focus of all curious eyes, he was instantly obeyed.

A daunting thought, but she believed she was prepared for the whispers behind gloved hands. He was right, of course. Her abrupt departure in his wake would be noted, and she was sure their conversation on the street before the Masterses' fashionable town house also would draw both comment and interest.

"Rather like your reckless wager. I didn't think notoriety bothered you," she pointed out dryly. For the past year she'd thought about him every single day, and if this was what it took . . .

Then so be it.

"It doesn't," he admitted, "which is exactly my point. And you know my stand on the issue of permanence." One elegant brow arched upward. "I am considering your reputation, not mine. Still wish to continue this discussion in your boudoir, Lady Brewer? Think of the risks."

This was where she could point out that she knew his stand on the issue of permanence with *her*, because he'd stated quite plainly he intended to marry eventually. But Madeline didn't want him to examine the topic at length at the moment and change his mind. To that challenge, she said simply, "Yes."

"If I'm considering this it's because I've had too much wine." His voice was restive and edgy.

"Not too much, I hope." Her voice was arch with amusement as the carriage rattled up and her young driver jumped from the seat to open the door for her.

Was this her? Playing the pursuer, inviting a man into her bedroom?

"Don't worry. That isn't what I meant." Luke waved the driver off and did it himself, handing her into the vehicle and pausing for so long a moment in the open door as she settled on the seat that she thought he might at the last moment change his mind. His gaze held hers. "I'm tempted," he said softly. "Damn you."

"I want you tempted," she replied, her voice just as quiet.

"You're too beautiful." The words were more an accusation than a compliment. He stood there, not shutting the door of the carriage, his tall form shadowy.

Yes, if anyone was watching them, there would be talk.

"According to popular opinion among the female populace, so are you."

His smile was faint. "How flattering."

Like he wasn't aware of it. She said tartly, "The pointed advances of Lady Hart in front of all society come to mind as proof."

"Is it now my turn to ask if *you* are jealous?" The amusement in his voice was unmistakable.

Yes. But she refused to say it. The only way this would work was if she matched his detached sophistication. "I noticed," she murmured. "I am sure that admission will sufficiently add to your arrogance."

"You're certain?" His voice was suddenly hushed, and there was no doubt about the actual meaning in that simple question.

"Yes, Altea, I'm sure." Her voice was infinitely more composed than her feelings, which were scattered to the four winds.

"I'm concerned the inevitable outcome of this will hurt you." He still didn't close the door of the carriage, but neither did he get in.

"Let me worry about myself," Madeline said with more aplomb than she felt. She was worried about it as well, but not enough to change her mind. That *he* worried about it was touching—and a good start. In life, all the things worth having involved some risk. Childbirth was not without its hazards, but she wouldn't trade her son for anything on earth—or in the heavens, for that matter. "Come in through the servant's entrance again. I won't bother to make sure it is unlocked, as I know firsthand that's hardly a hindrance for you anyway. My suite is the second door on the right at the top of the stairs."

He grinned then, a flash of straight white teeth. "I like a woman with command in her voice." His gaze drifted down her body, stopped for a moment at her bosom in open admiration, then traveled back up to her face, and his smile could only be described as sinfully seductive. "Are you going to order me about in bed as well, my lady?"

His palpable charm, when he chose to exercise it, was more disconcerting than his dark, deliberate distance. She adjusted her skirts in an attempt to delay her response, and then looked him in the eye. "I might. Will you obey?"

The smile widened. "I might. Or I might not. Either way, I think you'll enjoy yourself."

No, she was no match for his careless approach to seduction, but she was willing to learn. "I'm counting on it," she said with what she hoped sounded like serene self-assurance.

Then he closed the door, and a moment or two later the carriage jerked forward and pulled onto the street.

Chapter Eight

The alley was shadowed, deserted, and the picklock worked sweetly. Two clicks, and he was letting himself into the darkened, silent house.

This is indiscreet, ill-advised, Luke thought as he slipped down the hallway, and had he not sat through the teeth-gritting ordeal of that dinner, he would never have agreed to Madeline's invitation. Maybe it *was* the amount of claret he'd drunk, but he doubted it. He felt clearheaded enough, though it appeared his judgment was cloudy at best. No, it wasn't the wine.

It was *her*. In teal silk with lace at the bodice, those dark, slightly almond-shaped eyes meeting his gaze directly, and worse yet, the hint of a blush on her cheeks as she made her ridiculously reckless offer.

He should shake some sense into her.

Or make love to her.

There had been women, of course, since that one night a year ago when he'd taken her to bed. He wasn't a monk any more than he was a saint, and had never aspired to either calling, but none of those liaisons since—none of them—had erased the memory of her.

One night. Only the one. He should have forgotten her. God knew he'd tried. He'd walked away easily enough from the others since then, but then again, they had been bored, spoiled aristocratic ladies who wanted nothing more than a night or two of lighthearted pleasure without strings, much like himself. The encounters were physically satisfying, but did nothing for his soul.

She was different. Not a woman who gave herself lightly.

Bloody hell. No true gentleman would consciously risk ruining her reputation this way. Maybe this said something he'd suspected all along about his character.

Up the stairs with swift stealth, he passed the first doorway, and then he saw the line of light under her door. The knob turned quietly in his hand.

The soft glow of a single lamp illuminated her lush form, clad in a rich blue silk dressing gown, her fair hair shining and loose now, a silvery fall down her back to the womanly curve of her hips. She was standing at the window, and the curtain dropped from her hand as she whirled around with a gasp when the door clicked shut. "I didn't hear you coming."

"Five years in Spain fighting the French gives you certain unique talents." His gaze swept over the feminine furnishings of pale yellow silk covering walls, the floral pastel hues repeated in the thick patterned rug, the ornate bed hung with velvet, a Queen Anne armoire in the corner. Her dressing table was remarkably uncluttered, just a brush and several crystal bottles of perfume, but then again, someone of her fascinating beauty did not need an assortment of cosmetics. He turned and said bluntly, "I could still leave."

"Do you want to leave?"

"No."

"Good. For a celebrated rake, you are considerably

too polite." Madeline's smile was languorous and, unfortunately, far too alluring. "I'm finding this conversation redundant, my lord. I am not an innocent maiden. No irate father will seek satisfaction, and there is no outraged husband in the background. I don't understand your reservations."

No, she didn't. They weren't entirely selfless either. Her reputation wasn't the only issue. His reservations were not only about the inevitable notoriety an affair with him would bring her, but also his ability to stay detached. *I needn't bare my soul*, he reminded himself sharply, her closeness and undressed state bombarding his senses and causing a primal masculine response as old as time.

She was his for the taking, and God knew he wanted her.

"Very well," he agreed with a wolfish smile, walking slowly across the soft, expensive rug, predatory and willing to accept her assurances. *Maybe*, he thought, *she is more worldly than my impression of her. . . .*

No, he immediately corrected as he noted the small tremble of her soft lips. He was excusing himself so he could make love to her without the requisite repercussions of a chafing conscience. But at the moment he didn't care.

"It's been so long," she whispered as he stopped before her and caught her waist with both hands, pulling her close.

"Since me?" Damn all, he *was* jealous.

"Since anyone. Kiss me."

A year. Why the idea of her abstinence inflamed him, he wasn't sure, but a small voice in his brain acknowledged part of it was a sense of male possession. That was too disturbing to address when his erection was already swelling from just her proximity and the scent of flowers drifting from her hair. "Is that my first order?" he said with lazy insouciance, one finger lifting to trace the delicate curve of her cheek. "If so, I am your obedient servant."

He lowered his head, his mouth first just brushing hers, touching, seeking, before he settled into a long, sultry kiss. The clasp of her hands drifted up to his shoulders, and he felt the pressure with pure pleasure, his cock stiffening against the confining material of his breeches.

If I am a fool—and he was certain that was the case—*so be it*, he thought as he kissed her, their mouths melding with a sensual intensity that managed to sweep the breath from his lungs.

Madeline made a small sound of protest when he broke away, but it slid into a sigh when he abruptly lifted her in his arms, took three long strides across to the bed, and deposited her on the fine linen sheets, already turned back for the night. His fingers flew to his cravat. "Forgive the impatience, but please tell me you have nothing on beneath that robe."

"Nothing." She tugged at the sash and the material parted.

While not an inexperienced man, his breath still caught. Madeline was the epitome of sensuous female allure, with her tumbled fair hair, ivory skin, and provocative curves. Opulent, rose-tipped breasts; long, supple limbs; the dainty patch of pale hair between her thighs; her face slightly flushed with evident desire—it all caused his hands to momentarily halt in the haste of ridding himself of the impediment of his clothing. The way she looked at him also cast a spell, as if she was wanton and wanting, but also still somehow an uncertain young woman risking a great deal. The implied trust was humbling.

He didn't deserve it, but then again, he wouldn't betray it either. During the war he'd learned honor wasn't as nearly black-and-white as modern society portrayed it to be. The blurred boundaries of that elusive commodity surprised him, but in the end he thought it came down to making choices a man—or a woman, for that matter—could live with. He'd also learned that gender did not define courage or intelligence.

There was no question of asking her again if she was sure she wanted this. The repeated question implied she didn't know her own mind, and he was sure now she most certainly did.

How fortuitous that they desired the exact same thing.

His coat dropped to the floor. Boots went next, and then his shirt, so hastily unbuttoned he lost patience at the end of the process and just jerked it over his head. When he unfastened his breeches and pushed them down, her gaze was riveted to the surging length of his erection as he moved to the bed and joined her. He propped himself up on one elbow and trailed his hand over the curve of her shoulder, looking into her eyes. "I think my enthusiasm for your invitation is undisguised, my lady."

"Despite all your hedging," she teased, her glorious eyes holding him captive. "Who would think a notorious rogue so difficult to seduce?"

"I didn't notice it took much effort on your part." He leaned forward and brushed her hair aside to nibble on her earlobe. She smelled like heaven and woman, which was a heady combination.

"On the contrary, it took a full year." She tentatively ran her fingers over his bare shoulder and down his back. Her eyes drifted shut as his mouth drifted across her temple. "I thought I'd forgotten . . . but seeing you the other night—"

The genuine emotion in her voice made him stop her speech with a searing kiss. *Neither* of them had forgotten, unfortunately. *But for once, I am going to concern myself with that tomorrow*, he thought, drowning in the pleasure of tasting her, drawing her close so their naked bodies touched, his erect cock hot against her thigh. He was tired of being so guarded, so . . . jaded. Some part of her needed him, and, God help him, he needed her.

All night, his mind reminded him. *Now*, his body answered, the force of his need causing sweat to prickle over his skin. "Forgotten what?" he murmured against her mouth. "This?" he teasingly licked her lower lip.

"You. All of you. I tried, but I couldn't." A sigh brushed his cheek.

Her words arrested him, albeit momentarily, his fingers brushing the swelling fullness of her bared breast, measuring the erotic weight of the pliant flesh, his thumb caressing one perfect rosy nipple. The implication was he was different, special, that she'd not taken another lover in all that time because *he* was the only one she wanted enough to invite into her bed.

Disquieting to a man who preferred detached, sophisticated lovers.

Or do I, he wondered, as she tentatively traced the line of his jaw and then rose to follow the path of her hand with small, artless butterfly kisses. Obviously she had enjoyed a healthy sexual relationship with her husband and she wasn't shy in bed.

It was useless to keep trying to analyze the situation, he decided as she arched into the intimate possession of his hands, her nipples peaking against his palms. Nuzzling the valley between her breasts, he began to titillate her senses with practiced purpose, licking, tasting, gently sucking until he heard the telltale increase in the cadence of her breathing. Then he kissed a sinful trail down the delicate curve of her rib cage, across the plane of her stomach and lower, first cupping her hips with his hands before spreading her legs with the pressure of his palms.

"An entire year?" he murmured against the silken skin of her inner thigh. "I think I am obligated to make it worth your wait, my lady."

Her answer was a shudder as his practiced fingers gently parted the folds of her sex and he pressed his mouth to the most strategic spot to inflame female arousal. Madeline moaned, her hands flying into his hair as he teased with the tip of his tongue and at the same time slid one finger into the heated satin of her vaginal passage.

"Luke."

It was gratifying to hear his name said in that throaty tone, unlike her usual cool contralto.

It took very little time to coax her into a satisfyingly vocal climax, her soft cries echoing through the darkened bedchamber, her slender body quivering against the ministrations of his mouth. With a triumphant grin he rose, positioning himself between her open thighs, the tip of his rigid cock testing the receptive give of her female entrance. "Let me know when you are recovered enough for this." He pushed in a fraction, sucking in a breath at the exquisite warmth and tightness of her body. "Would it be ungentlemanly of me to hope it's soon?"

There was no question of it: she'd denied herself too long, tried to put aside secret desire for the practicality of everyday life. Languid in the aftermath of exultant sensation, Madeline rubbed the muscular shoulders of the man poised over her and whispered, "I'm ready whenever you are, my lord, and it seems to me you are very"—she reached down and stroked his erection lightly—"ready."

The inward hiss of his breath at her touch was telling, as was the hot-blooded look in the storm-gray depths of his eyes. Luke leaned down, took her mouth in a tempestuous kiss, and surged forward to full penetration.

She gasped at the forceful invasion, and he instantly went still. "I didn't hurt you?"

"No." It was true. The last thing she was feeling was pain. He impaled her so thoroughly she was stretched, filled, possessed, but it was deliciously pleasurable. Almost as delicious as Luke himself, his nude body hard and lean under her questing fingertips, his skin just touched with a sheen of perspiration, the amber silk of his hair brushing his shoulders. Those sculpted, handsome features so many—*too* many, she thought with illogical jealousy—women admired were taut now as he peered down at her. "You're sure?"

"You just feel . . . enormous." Her smile was deliberately enticing and she lifted her hips, taking him a crucial fraction deeper.

"Now, that's something a man hates to hear." His laugh was a small burst of breath.

She didn't have enough experience to know the variations of male endowment, but she thought he was probably larger than most. Certainly he was bigger than Colin, though he was also inches taller and wider in the shoulders. . . . Not that it mattered; her husband had given her pleasure in bed even on her wedding night, when she'd been nervous and awkward. . . .

No, she wasn't going to think about what she'd lost *now*. This night was for her—the selfishness assuaged by the growing conviction over the past few years that she was not interested, in a personal sense, in making a second dynastic marriage just so she could belong to another man. Colin had been wonderful. She had been lucky. Luke Daudet could fill the void in her life and he wouldn't demand more from her.

It was very different from her marriage, but, in short, a perfect arrangement.

Wasn't it?

With playful enticement she grazed her nails across his firm buttocks. "Hmm . . . Altea, if you wouldn't mind . . ." She wiggled just a little.

He made a low sound deep in his throat and began to move. Slowly at first, with control, his warm breath fanning her cheek, his eyes half closed in concentrated pleasure. It was sleek, it was glorious, and the friction of sex into sex so decadent Madeline couldn't suppress small pants of enjoyment that were probably unladylike in extreme.

She didn't care.

Pleasure gripped her body, holding it prisoner. Each

inward glide was exhilarating, each withdrawal made her inner muscles clench in protest, and the brush of his hair against her hands where they clutched his shoulders added another layer of sensation.

Her already aroused body surrendered first, the orgasmic tide a drowning flood. Her thighs tightened around his lean hips and every muscle went rigid in the pulsing splendor of the moment. Luke responded with a low, telling groan as his tall body stiffened, and at the very last moment he withdrew, the hot, liquid rush of his ejaculation spilling across her thigh as he shuddered in her arms.

Breathless, entwined, his face buried in her outspread hair and his weight balanced just enough on his forearms so he didn't crush her, neither of them spoke for several long moments, until he lifted his head and gifted her with his mesmerizing smile. One eyebrow lifted in a lazy arch. "I hope that was worth waiting for."

"Don't look so arrogant, Altea," she retorted, but her laugh was breathless and her fingertips drifted down his spine.

"I'm always arrogant." He kissed the side of her neck, his lips lingering. "I thought you knew."

"I might have noticed." She arched back to give him better access to the point where her pulse still fluttered.

"Don't women like confident men?"

"It depends on the level of the confidence and how it is expressed."

"I see." He nibbled his way up to her mouth, murmuring against her lips, "What if I told you I am confident I can keep you up all night?"

It could be true. He was still hard, the long length of his cock rigid between them, as if he hadn't just spent himself. Madeline kissed him, a long, leisurely meeting of their mouths and tongues, the play more delicate and teasing now that the first burst of passion was past. "Uhm . . . I'd say you would have to prove that to me."

"It would be my pleasure to do so." He lifted the edge

of the sheet and wiped the residue of his seed from her skin.

"And mine." She drifted her fingers through the silk of his hair.

"I'll do my best, my darling Madge."

She gave him a light, exasperated slap on the shoulder, though the disapproval was feigned. When he spoke that way, with the heavy intonation in his voice, her entire body tingled. "No one calls me that but you."

There was no sign of repentance in his grin, and his silver eyes glimmered. "Good. Madge belongs to me alone, then."

Had he not begun to take her again, in subtle, slow strokes of withdrawal and invasion, she might have pondered that possessive statement more, but the beguiling rhythm disordered all cognizant thought, and later—hours later, as he promised—when she drifted asleep in his arms in exhausted contentment, she dreamed of romantic, sunlit glades and crystalline seas, and soft, warm summer breezes.

Luke dressed quietly, sitting down on an embroidered chair to pull on his boots, his gaze fastened on the woman in the disordered chaos of the bed. Madeline slept on her side, her face peaceful, the glory of her luxuriant hair cascading over her slender, bared shoulders. Her maid, he knew, as he stood to button his shirt and tuck it into his breeches, would know someone had been with her mistress, but the least he could do was spare Madeline the embarrassment of having him still in her bed in the morning.

She was enchanting.

Sensual, artlessly responsive, intelligent enough to challenge him as an equal, but secure enough to not feel the need.

Her intellect not in question, he still wondered if she was experienced enough with public censure to realize what came next. Had she truly thought about the repercussions of this night? When the whispers started . . . how would she feel then? She had a son to consider also.

Regret was a commodity he usually disdained, but not everyone felt that way. A beautiful young widow with dozens of potential suitors eager for her favor had a lot of options. She didn't have to settle for illicit passion with a man who had no intention of doing more than offer transient pleasure.

He wished he could, he realized as he stood there in the semigloom, just watching her sleep, his throat curiously tight.

He very much wished he could.

And that was a disturbing revelation.

Chapter Nine

Her brother might have shaved and changed his clothes, but Elizabeth wasn't fooled when Luke strolled into the sunny breakfast room. She was a light sleeper and she'd heard him come in just as the first streaks of light touched the horizon. Her suite of rooms was opposite his, and she had most definitely heard the sleepy voice of his valet and his answer, and then the closing of the door. It was now midmorning, but if he'd slept more than a few hours she'd be surprised.

"You look cheerful for someone who was out carousing all night," she observed in a dry tone, since it was just the two of them. Miles had risen early to meet with solicitors and bankers over his precious shipping company. Uncle Chas and Aunt Gloria had returned to the country estate in Berkshire, and their mother rarely rose before noon.

Arched brows rose, clear amusement in his eyes, as he chose a seat opposite. "I wasn't aware my arrivals and departures were so closely monitored."

She passed him the rack of toast. "You left the Masterses' gathering quite early but didn't come home. Miles said you weren't at your club either." Elizabeth studied him openly. He did look somewhat tired, but not quite as . . . distant. Or *abstracted* might be the right word. No, that wasn't right either. He didn't look as *shuttered*. That fit better.

A window had opened somewhere, and she was curious as to how and, more importantly, *by whom*, though she had a fair idea.

"Ah, your spies are everywhere, I see." He helped himself to the rasher of sausages, and a footman unobtrusively brought in a fresh, steaming platter of eggs. "Unfortunately for you, London is a rather large city. I could have been anywhere. Perhaps you could hire a Bow Street runner to investigate my absences."

"Very amusing. And I am not spying on you. Count it as sisterly concern."

"Elizabeth, I survived a war. I think I am capable of managing my own life, thank you." He stirred sugar into his coffee. "I'm *your* guardian, not the opposite."

"*Did* you survive it?" She said the words quietly. "You are quite different from when you left."

"I imagine all soldiers are." He carefully set aside his spoon. "You were a child when I joined Wellington on the Peninsula. I was younger then too, and, yes, I think enduring a bloody war would change anyone."

"I'd like to see you happy again." She paused delicately. "Did Lady Brewer inspire that particular smile you wore when you strolled in here?"

"I was afraid there would be gossip," he muttered and shook his head. "If anyone noted, she left alone in her own carriage."

It was interesting he hadn't answered her question. "She's very beautiful," Elizabeth murmured as casually as possible. "I assume you've noticed."

"I am still breathing, I believe. Yes, I've noticed. Can we change the subject? For instance, can you tell me why Lord Fawcett sent me a missive requesting an audience this afternoon?"

It was her turn to be discomforted. She concentrated on smearing marmalade on her toast. "He's been very attentive."

"Yes," her older brother confirmed dryly. "The fragrance of roses has become rather cloying lately if one passes the drawing room. Your feelings on his lordship, should he wish to offer a proposal?"

She wasn't sure. The marquess was charming and handsome enough, she supposed, and she'd never heard rumors that indicated he was a scoundrel or gambled and drank excessively. Of the eligible bachelors openly looking for wives this season, he was certainly considered to be a catch.

"He did not confide his purpose to me." She took a bite of eggs. "I was unaware he was going to call until this moment."

"Well, I assume he will state his business to me." Luke touched his napkin to his mouth. "Care to be a bit more clear on the matter? What if he should suggest a marriage between you?"

She shrugged. "I think he is nice enough."

"And what does that mean?"

"No," she admitted, dumping more cream—too much—in her coffee.

"No, you do not wish to marry him?"

"No, I do not wish to marry anyone whom I just think is nice." With a certain gloom she stared into the swirling liquid in her cup. "Surely I can do better than *nice*."

"Or worse," Luke pointed out.

"I am not interested in settling for a man who inspires nothing but ambivalent feelings of casual friendship."

"Then I will tell him you are not yet ready to make a decision."

Elizabeth gazed at her brother in exasperation. "I just said I was not interested."

"And I heard you quite clearly. But make no mistake; males have just as delicate feelings as females." His smile was wry. "I will put him off, he will understand eventually, and no one will be hurt."

She drummed the fine Irish linen tablecloth with her fingertips, mouth slightly pursed. The brightly shining sun laid long blocks of light on the rich, patterned indigo-and-ivory rug. "That is better than the truth?"

Luke nodded, his eyes suddenly holding an odd weariness. "At this stage, yes. You've not passed flirtation. I assume you've done nothing to lead him to believe a deeper bond exists, correct?"

At least she could honestly say she hadn't. "No."

"Then he is better off not knowing you don't fancy his attentions. I like him well enough, so I'll just diplomatically deflect his offer."

"Humph." Thoughtfully she eyed her brother across the table. "Do you reserve such solicitude for just your gender? I ask because rumor has it you've broken hearts all across England."

"Rumor is an extremely fallible medium for information."

"Is it, now?" She clearly recalled Lady Brewer abruptly excusing herself and leaving the dinner party the evening before, and, or so she heard later, having a rather impassioned discussion with Luke before getting in her carriage. Elizabeth rather liked the viscountess, with her gracious charm and lack of pretention. The question was, *how much does Luke like her?*

"It is." His defensive tone was tempered by a slight smile. "So, if we are done debating my possible foibles and Fawcett's unwelcome suit, can we move on? Where is Miles?"

Like she kept a diary of her cousin's movements. "Something about his solicitors," she muttered, picking up her toast.

"Perhaps it would be best if you two didn't go out alone again." Her brother said it in a nonchalant tone, spearing another sausage.

What?

"What on earth are you talking about?" Elizabeth didn't intend to sound so abrupt, but quite honestly, the suggestion took her off guard.

"I just said to not go alone. The other day I believe he took you to the milliner."

He had, quite naturally, because his favorite tobacco shop was on the same street. "We ran an errand. How ridiculous to take two carriages if we are bound in the same direction."

"Yes, well, though I agree, society sees it quite differently."

"We've caught eels alone also. Would society whisper about it if they found out we'd engaged in that activity together? One is about as romantic as the other. I picked out a hat, and he purchased a new pipe."

Luke was irritatingly unperturbed at her acerbic tone. "I am assuming that you, as a proper young lady, have left your eel-catching days behind you. Miles is a grown man, and he is not really our cousin. I hope you do realize it."

It was true, of course, but what the devil did it matter? Elizabeth set down her knife on the tablecloth accidentally, heedless of the marmalade, and stared at her brother. "I hadn't ever really considered it, to be honest. Why does it matter?"

"Trust me. It does."

So? She and Miles were not related. Set aside all those childhood larks, the peccadilloes that landed them in so much trouble, the endless fights, but also the way they'd stood with each other in every instance of trouble, and it was true: they were not related by blood, but by a much closer bond, actually. She had first cousins on her mother's side she'd never even met.

What an odd revelation. More slowly, she said, "Surely you don't mean I have to take a chaperone when I am with *Miles*."

"For the sake of your reputation, I would prefer it."

"But—" She stopped, not sure how to feel about this . . . this ridiculous new restriction.

"You were also seen walking with him in the park the other day."

"Of course." For whatever reason, her cheeks heated. Why would she blush? This might be the most inane conversation of her life. "I was with Amelia, and he happened to be there as well. What was I supposed to do, pretend I don't know him? I think he and I have taken a bath together."

"When you were two years old." Luke looked bland, and he could do bland very, very well. "You aren't two any longer."

"This is absurd."

"This is London society, Elizabeth. The censure exists. Take my word for it. I trust Miles, you know that. I am as fond of him as you are. I'm merely pointing out that your association needs to be entirely appropriate."

"Take *my* word," she muttered. "There are times I am not all that fond of him."

Luke lifted a brow. "Perhaps, but for all your constant quarreling, you were inseparable as children. I know it seems very natural to continue the habit of a lifetime, but in this case, I caution you to be aware of how others might see it."

Inseparable. Hmm. Yes, she supposed it was accurate, but they weren't that much apart in age, after all. She and Miles had specialized in being wild and daring: pirates, taking over a mythical ship that was really a beached float on the lake on the estate; highwaymen who accosted innocent travelers . . . in their case, the gamekeeper who always pretended to be properly terrified when they popped out of the bushes, and offered up his nonexistent purse on a regular basis. . . .

She missed old Liam Sullivan, who after the holdup inevitably offered them bannock cakes. They ate them greedily, usually with honey, their fingers sticky. She missed the country estate in general, but Luke was probably right. Life had changed. Soon she would be a wife, and eventually, like Amelia, a mother.

Perhaps it was time to grow up.

Well, it wasn't like she'd *miss* Miles. Besides, she'd still see him every day. They lived, after all, in the same house.

She took a bite of toast. The marmalade seemed a little oversweet for some reason, maybe even cloying. "Fine."

"Fine?" Luke had a certain way of betraying his amusement. It was subtle, just a unique lift of the corner of his mouth, but it was also hard to miss. "I never win an argument with you so easily."

"It isn't like it will be a hardship," she said coolly. "Miles has his life and I have mine."

"He has such remarkable energy, doesn't he?"

Madeline smiled, watching Trevor chase a butterfly through the garden. Her son had inherited his father's coloring, dark hair and olive skin, and also the same easygoing, almost naive appreciation of the world around him. "He loves being outdoors. I feel a bit guilty when I come down for the season, because I know he misses the freedom of the country. But that huge house and just the two of us . . . It was different, of course, when Colin was alive, but now I find it oppressive quickly."

Marta Langley adjusted the skirt of her elegant day gown, the sun shining on the heavy coil of brunet hair at her nape, her parasol closed and set aside on the stone bench, which was probably not a wise decision, since she had a tendency to freckle. "You need some gaiety in your life, darling. Guilt is a self-destructive emotion most of the time. Besides, you adore Trevor, and he can always come to the country with us. For however long you can bear to be apart from him. You are a wonderful mother, but begin to live your life again for you and not just your son."

I have. Yes, Madeline needed something, and last night certainly came to mind.

Luke knew how to arouse a woman's passions, how to touch in a particular way, to tempt, to taunt, and the exquisite timing of exactly when to give her what she craved. He moved with a carnal precision that spoke of experience and sensual skill, as if he were tuned in to the tingling of her nerve endings, the cravings of her body, the escalation of erotic need. His self-control was as flawless as his execution when making love, and when he finally allowed himself to join her, even then she sensed, at the moment of explosive climax, that he held something back.

Whatever happened between them, she did know this: one day she would like to have all of him.

Colin had been an enthusiastic, considerate lover, but there was little question that the rakish Viscount Altea was vastly more experienced. More sensitive too. Though that was a paradox, because no one had been more idealistic than her husband, while Luke Daudet appeared cynical and worldly in the extreme.

There was definitely more to him than met the eye, but ferreting out his secrets was no doubt impossible.

All she knew, she thought as she tilted her face to the beautiful azure sky above and smiled, was that her decision to coax him into her bed again had been reckless perhaps, but . . . there were no regrets.

Madeline murmured, "I don't know if gaiety was precisely what I needed, but I *am* glad I came to London."

"Yes," her sister-in-law said after a moment, surveying her with narrowed eyes. "I can see that. I thought when I arrived this morning you seemed inordinately cheerful. May I ask why?"

"You may ask." Madeline did her best to sound serene and detached. "But I doubt I'll respond. How's David?"

"What a very pointed and not-so-subtle change in subject."

"You noticed."

Marta sighed theatrically. "Fine, then. I will hope you will tell me eventually. David is fine. We're staying another week so he can meet with the prime minister."

Eventually, perhaps, Madeline thought as she listened to Colin's sister's recital of their journey from Kent and plans for the week, she might tell Marta about this change in her life. But for now, Luke was her own wicked secret.

"Mama! Auntie Marta!" Trevor walked at a very circumspect pace toward them on the stone path through the garden, his hands carefully cupped together. He might look like Colin, but his eyes were hers, the same shape and the exact same color. "Look."

He opened his hands like a flower in the morning sun, and a small, pale yellow butterfly with black spots sat in the cradle of his palms for a moment before it fluttered away.

Madeline leaned forward and gently brushed his dark curls in a light caress. "How clever of you to catch but not hurt it. What a lovely one too."

"It was very fine," Marta told him with a smile.

He grinned and dashed away, intent on yet another capture.

With two healthy sons of her own, Marta was no stranger to young male exuberance. "Ah, to be so fascinated by an insect. I fear we lose that sort of innocence all too fast."

"I suppose so." Madeline watched her son dart through the flower beds. "Though he's far too young for me to worry over it yet."

"You shouldn't have to worry alone. He needs a father."

Those last four quiet words were unwelcome and Madeline frowned, tucking an errant tendril of hair behind her ear. "I've already told you I don't believe I wish to marry again. I miss Colin terribly. If he hadn't died so unexpectedly, I know we would still be happily wed. But to be honest, though I adore my son, I will not marry again just for his sake. Before I blink an eye he will be off to Eton, then Cambridge, and come into his majority. He'll embark on his own life, and yet I would still be stuck with a husband. No thank you. I did not wish for widowhood, but since fate has put me in this position, I am determined to enjoy the benefits of my freedom."

"I doubt my brother would want you to live like a nun the rest of your life."

Since her behavior the night before was hardly chaste—quite the opposite—Madeline strived to seem nonchalant, but she could feel the inconvenient rush of heat to her face. Marta wanted her to remarry, not form a scandalous liaison with the notorious Viscount Altea. "It would require just the right man and considerable persuasion to make me change my mind."

"And in the meantime, you are alone. You are entirely too young and beautiful to pine for Colin."

You are too beautiful. . . .

Luke had said the same words with a restive edge of resentment.

"I am not pining for him." Madeline chose her words carefully, because it was important. "I am just unwilling to settle for less. If anything, I want more. We had barely been married more than two years before he died. Our relationship was budding, not in full bloom. I was happy with our beginning, so naturally, I wonder what the fragrant garden would have been like."

Marta looked pensive for a moment, but then smiled and reached over to clasp her hand. "Poetic, my dear, but you must realize that reality is much different than our idealized view of the world."

Oh, she did. Reality was a silver-eyed lover who held his secrets like a miser and dispersed pleasure like a magician.

In the years since Colin died, Luke was the only man to even tempt her to consider a future.

A futile dream, since he wasn't interested in offering one.

She squeezed Marta's hand in reassurance. "Please stop worrying about me."

"That I can't promise, but I will say if you retain this special glow you have this morning, I will stop the lectures." Her sister-in-law's gaze was appraising.

Would she retain it? It was hard to say. She'd woken alone, the only sign of Luke's presence the rumpled other half of the bed. The last time they'd shared a night of passion, he'd avoided her afterward.

This time she was determined that it would be different.

Chapter Ten

He'd really hoped to avoid running into Lord Fitch indefinitely, but logic told Luke it wasn't possible to dodge the man forever. After all, they did patronize the same club, not to mention attend many of the same social engagements.

"Altea."

The booming greeting made him glance up from his newspaper, and he gave Fitch a cool nod that hopefully concealed his dislike. "Good afternoon, my lord."

You sodding lecherous bastard.

It was somewhat satisfying to see the earl sported a gigantic bruise, the purplish discoloration from temple to the line of his jaw a tribute to Madeline's accuracy with a fireplace poker.

The low hum of voices and the scent of tobacco and brandy filled the air. Usually it was evident if a man was enjoying a quiet moment reading in solitude, but Fitch had never been attuned to subtlety. He pulled out a chair and sat down uninvited, his florid face congenial.

Except Luke didn't much care for the gleam in the man's eye.

"It seems I owe you thanks. Can I buy you a drink?"

"I have one." Luke pointed at the glass of whiskey in front of him. "And if you are talking about the other evening, it was nothing, rest assured. Whatever they are saying, there were no heroics involved."

Especially since he'd just as soon have dumped his lordship in the filthy waters of the Thames and let him drown.

But, unfortunately, Luke still had *some* scruples, despite the war. He'd killed men in fair combat, but never murdered one.

Fitch lifted his hand to summon a waiter and ordered a brandy. He was almost two decades older, in his late forties, going slightly to fat around the middle, his features handsome enough but showing signs of dissipation in the reddish veins visible by his nose and his hair lightly streaked with gray. His deep-set eyes were hooded, and his expression at the moment was speculative. "I have no idea how I came to be in that alley, if you want the truth. Can you tell me exactly how you found me?"

Luke shrugged, setting aside his paper, since good manners insisted he do so. "I just happened to be passing by and spotted you lying there."

"I wasn't robbed."

"Perhaps my arrival scared off your assailant." In retrospect, he should have relieved his lordship of his purse and given it to a worthy charity. His mistake, but then again, he didn't know at the time that Fitch wouldn't remember the incident.

"Did you see anyone?"

"Actually, no."

"The steward here said he didn't remember my arrival or departure." His lordship leaned back, his heavy face enigmatic. "You're certain I was in the alley almost a block away?"

He evaded the direct question. "Maybe you were on your way here. If that was the case, how could the steward remember you?"

"On foot? That's unlikely. It's too far, and my driver didn't take me anywhere."

The last scenario Luke wanted was for Fitch to eventually recall what really happened, but then again, the implication that he could be lying—though he *wasn't* telling the truth, but all in a good cause—was intensely irritating. "My lord, are you thanking me for taking you home and summoning the physician, or questioning my rendition of what happened that night?"

Fitch's hooded eyes narrowed. "I'm missing something and wondering if it is tied to the vicious, unprovoked attack on my person."

Unprovoked? Luke pictured the man across from him cornering Madeline and fought to keep his face from showing his fury. "I thought you just said you weren't robbed."

"Perhaps I should have been more clear. My pockets weren't picked. I find that most curious, don't you?"

"No."

"No?"

"I find it exceptional good luck. So you escaped with your purse *and* your life." Luke picked up his drink and finished it before setting the glass back down with a definite *click*. "It sounds to me like you should count yourself quite a fortunate man."

How subtle was he required to be? Should he just go ahead and warn off the blackguard? Fitch was fishing around because it was obvious the doctor was right and he didn't really remember much, and it was logical to assume that Luke would know more than anyone else. As long as the immoral ass didn't tie the incident directly back to Madeline . . .

That was, apparently, a dashed hope.

"Not as lucky as you, or so I hear." Fitch adjusted his cuff with a languid hand, but his flat eyes were watchful. "I understand you left Masters's last night with Lady Brewer. She's a pretty piece, if there ever was one. Isn't she?"

The urge to pick up the man by his collar and shove him against the wall before beating him to a bloody pulp was suppressed, but only barely. That would cause a scandal extraordinaire. One did not rescue a man one day, and then assault him a few days later without drawing comment. "What the devil are you talking about?" he asked, hoping the murderous flare in his eyes wasn't too obvious. Normally he had better self-control.

"There's a bit of gossip. Concerning you and Madeline May."

"Are you being disrespectful to the lady?" Luke asked through his teeth.

"Not at all. I'm merely pointing out the allure of her undeniable charms." Fitch spread his hands in a self-deprecating manner, but he looked annoyingly smug, like he'd just learned something from Luke's reaction. "Who could blame you, Altea? I'm merely offering my congratulations at breaching the impenetrable guard of her all-too-proper distance. Don't be so testy."

Once again, he reminded himself it would be noticed if he put his fist solidly in Fitch's face in such a respectable establishment, so he took in a steadying breath. When Luke thought about Madeline enduring the man's tormenting comments and threats, the urge to protect her was definitely there.

Luke stood up, folding his paper in half and tucking it under his arm. "You are misinformed," he said with lethal emphasis. "Lady Brewer left in her own carriage, quite alone. The lady's honor is undisputed. Now if you will excuse me, I have an appointment."

"Of course." Fitch inclined his head, his smile more of a faint smirk. "Thank you again for your . . . *assistance*, Altea."

As he strode from the room, Luke pondered darkly if he should tell Madeline about the exchange. Quite obviously Fitch had made the connection between the missing journal—now in the hands of its rightful owner—and Luke's supposed rescue. Maybe the earl didn't remember clearly, and it didn't seem he did, but he still suspected the disappearance of the journal and the attack were linked.

Damnation. Why couldn't it be all clean and neat? The obnoxious Fitch was no fool, which didn't help matters. Depraved and conscienceless, yes, but a fool, apparently not.

He should definitely warn Madeline that this business wasn't over.

And, a small voice told him as he nodded at the footman at the door and gained the street, *you wouldn't mind seeing the beauteous Lady Brewer again anyway.*

The meeting had seemed endless, but when Miles rose and shook the hand of Henry Goad, Esq., and exited the small but prestigious establishment, it was with a sense of inner accomplishment. The sheaf of papers in his hands represented a promising future, and he needed to concentrate on that and put out of his mind what wasn't quite so promising.

Like, he'd discovered when he arrived at the palatial Daudet mansion, where his family had their own set of apartments, Lord Fawcett's carriage prominently sitting out front, the gilded crest on the side of the equipage unmistakable.

The joy of the day vanished.

Fawcett's interest in Elizabeth had been blatant enough. Miles ascended the steps and sternly reminded himself that the marquess was a decent sort and would no doubt make an admirable husband.

Small consolation there, damn all.

He had every intention of heading directly toward the private section of the house, but unfortunately, Lord Fawcett had apparently just arrived and was still in the polished splendor of the foyer, ostensibly admiring an ornate Oriental lacquer table as he was announced, his hands clasped behind his back.

Yes, the day had started well enough, but this was a definite deterioration.

"Hawthorne," the marquess said pleasantly, turning as Miles came in, an affable smile on his face. "I always forget you live here also. How are you?"

Nice to be so unmemorable, Miles thought wryly, but he nodded politely. "Well, thank you."

"I'm calling for Lady Elizabeth," Fawcett confided, as if it weren't easily deduced. He was dressed immaculately in a bottle green coat with an embroidered matching waistcoat, doeskin breeches, and polished boots, the elegance of his attire striking, with lace at his cuffs and a tasteful diamond stickpin in his intricately tied cravat. To make it worse, though he didn't usually waste much time contemplating the looks of other men, Miles had to grudgingly acknowledge that Fawcett was handsome enough, if you favored fair-haired men with white, straight teeth.

Most women, at a guess, did. Especially when the man was also titled and wealthy, and, as loathe as he was to admit it, a good sort as well.

"So I gathered." Miles did his best to maintain a facade of cordiality.

"She doesn't appear to be home, but it is Lord Altea I wish to see anyway."

The purpose for a call on her older brother and guardian was clear enough. Though it took some effort, Miles said, "Best of luck, then, with gaining Luke's approval."

"A moment, Hawthorne, if you would."

Miles, about to walk past the other man and escape, halted with reluctance. The marquess hesitated and then asked, "Has she mentioned me? I know the two of you are quite close, and I wondered if Elizabeth had ever expressed her feelings on my courtship to you."

It was one matter to secretly pine for a woman you couldn't have, Miles decided, and quite another to en-

courage your competitor, even if said competitor had
no idea he was metaphorically stepping on your toes.
"She'd be unlikely to discuss her preferences in suitors
with me," he murmured, his tone deliberately blasé. "We
tend to argue more than converse."

"I do admire her spirited approach to life."

"*Headstrong* would be more my take on it."

His lordship laughed. "She did mention the two of
you were somewhat of scapegraces when you were children. In fact, she mentions you quite often. That is why I
asked if she'd ever mentioned *me*."

She hadn't. She hadn't talked about any of the ardent
pursuers that flocked around her at every ball and rout.
Which, now that Miles thought about it, was a little curious. Or maybe not. Three sentences into a conversation
and they were already quarreling with each other, so her
reticence was not exactly a surprise.

Elizabeth mentioned him quite often? In the most
scathing of terms, no doubt.

"I'm afraid we haven't discussed you," he admitted.
"But as I said, that really means very little. She actually
doesn't share her personal thoughts with me."

"If she should say something . . . I'd appreciate a good
word. You and I have known each other since university,
haven't we?"

Yes, they had. Fawcett was a few years older, but it
was true. In a loose sense, they were friends.

Dammit. If Miles could properly detest him, it would
be easier.

Luckily, they were interrupted just as Miles opened
his mouth to vow to help the blasted man.

"Lord Altea asked me to show you to his study, my
lord marquess." The butler bowed formally and allowed
a grateful Miles an expeditious escape. Fawcett was led
off toward Luke's study, and Miles headed across the
main reception area toward the graceful dual staircase,
trying to suppress his chaotic emotions. This would not
be the first real offer for Elizabeth's hand, but he had a

feeling it was the first one that might get sincere consideration. Fawcett was a very respectable candidate.

When she marries, he reminded himself as he gained the top of the stairs and stalked down the hallway, *I'll lose her*. It wasn't a new revelation, but Lord Fawcett's presence certainly made it more immediate.

With his gloves clenched tightly in his hand as he climbed the steps, Miles decided he could leave for Brussels with the shipping contracts, orchestrating an escape, should a betrothal be announced. He'd planned on sending an emissary in the name of the new company, but if he absented himself from the country for several months, he could skip the engagement party, the rounds of congratulations. . . .

Yes, that would work. It wasn't the best time, in a business sense, for him to leave London, but certainly better than staying. . . .

"You've been gone long enough."

He froze in the doorway of his bedroom, his hand still on the glass knob. The object of his thoughts stood by the window, which was open to the late-afternoon breeze. She wore a day gown in a pale yellow color, a demure lacy froth on the puffy short sleeves and around the neckline, and her glossy hair was held back simply with a white ribbon.

"What are you doing here?" he asked, his traitorous mind conceptualizing the proximity of her presence and the most prominent object in the same space.

Elizabeth. My bed.

The latter, a Louis Quatorze piece, the elegant carved posts hung with simple dark green silk, the coverlet the same color, was only a few feet from where she stood. His sole contribution to the decoration of the room was a miniature of his father on the mantel; the rest of the elegant furnishings—an armoire, a writing desk, two chairs by the fireplace—were all his mother's selection. He could actually care less about the decor, because although he considered this his home in London, it was his goal to someday purchase a country house of his own.

"I'm spying." Elizabeth looked unfazed by his ungracious greeting. "Your window overlooks the street." She turned to peer out the window again. "It appears Lord Fawcett has arrived."

"Yes." It took some effort to not grit his teeth. "I ran into him in the foyer."

"He wishes to speak with Luke."

"I received that impression myself." In retrospect, Miles should have accepted the offer of a drink with Mr. Goad and avoided this excruciating situation.

Elizabeth sighed and did the unthinkable. She went over and sat on the edge of the bed—his bed—with an uncharacteristically pensive look on her face. "I hope you do not mind if I hide here until he's gone."

He did mind, but then again the word *hide* struck him enough he could only stare at her. The house was huge. Of all places to choose . . .

"Why would you hide, pray tell? I thought young ladies about to become engaged to an exalted marquess were all giggles and simpering smiles."

"I've never simpered in my life," she informed him, her chin coming up and a look of annoyance crossing her delicate features. "You know that. I am not in the mood to be teased, Miles."

That was the Elizabeth he knew.

He finally moved into the room, feeling a little foolish hovering in the doorway. "Very well. You have your flaws, but I concede I haven't seen a simper, for which I am eternally grateful, and you haven't giggled since you were in pigtails." He set the sheaf of precious papers on the desk and turned around, lifting a brow. His next question was oh so carefully nonchalant. "May I ask again why you are hiding?"

"Don't sneer at me, but the answer is simple cowardice."

"I don't sneer any more than you simper." Miles

propped one shoulder against the wall and crossed his arms over his chest, studying her averted profile. "What are you afraid of, El?"

"After Luke rejects his offer, I am afraid Lord Fawcett will ask to see me. Knowing my brother, he will send someone for me, of course, if his lordship requests it. If they can't find me . . ." She trailed off with a rueful smile and spread her slim hands. "So, you see, pure cowardice."

Rejects his offer.

The phrase had a nice ring to it. Suddenly Brussels didn't seem nearly as appealing.

"I doubt anyone would look for you in my bedroom, true," Miles said dryly, hoping the impractical elation of his reaction didn't show. "And you can rest easy, for Fawcett is under the impression you are out. May I ask why you are so confident Luke is rejecting his lordship's proposal?"

"Because I don't want to marry him, of course." She rubbed her temple. "Don't be a dolt, Miles. Luke asked me what he should say and I told him that I am not interested in the marquess."

The warning was useless. He *was* a dolt, because he was delighted she wasn't wedding the handsome, rich Lord Fawcett. It was nothing but a reprieve before she chose someone else, but he was still irrationally grateful. "I am genuinely curious as to why Fawcett doesn't suit. He's titled, has a respectable fortune, and I haven't noticed his ears are green or that he has a repulsive wart on the end of his nose. He is, in short, a decent catch. Isn't he?"

"Catching," Elizabeth said firmly, "is for fish. And if, in your roundabout way, you are trying to say his lordship is good-looking, he is, I agree—green ears aside."

"I doubt I'm a good judge of whether a man is appealing in looks."

"That is so ridiculous. Women know if other women are pretty or not."

She had a point, but he wasn't going to argue it. He said stiffly, "I merely meant *I* wouldn't be attracted to him."

Now, that came out all wrong. *Hell and blast.*

Elizabeth burst out in a peal of laughter. "I should hope not."

His face reddened. She often had this effect on him. He clarified, "If I were a woman."

If I were a woman? Oh, Lord, even worse. Why had he said *that*? He amended quickly, "And wanting to find a wealthy, titled husband."

She evidently found that image even more amusing.

He really, really should shut his mouth and perhaps not open it again in his lifetime.

To his relief she stopped laughing finally and instead looked at her hands. "You make it sound as if something as permanent as marriage shouldn't be based on more than pedigree and wealth. It isn't fair. *You* get to take your time, deciding when to take a wife. *I* have no such luxury."

A much safer discussion. More than once they had debated the inequity between male privilege and female subservience, and he shifted to this middle ground with relief. "Men run the world. We both know it."

"Perhaps that's why there are so many wars." Her silver eyes took on a militant glint.

He could look into those stormy depths until eternity. "You don't find it admirable we are willing to die in the cause of defending our countries? Our families?"

"I find it stupid in the first place you force the situation upon each other. Women would never do so."

"They prefer their embroidery and gossip. Much more productive."

Elizabeth loathed anything that involved cloth and a needle, and she wasn't petty enough to whisper over anyone. Her haughty look could have melted a lesser man into a puddle of apology, but he was used to it, and executed a small, mocking bow with a wicked grin, grateful to have at least a little equilibrium restored. "Present company excluded, of course."

"I am not sure why I ever confide in you."

"I thought you were here because of my strategic view of the street."

Elizabeth thrust herself to her feet and paced back to the window. "That is part of it," she admitted, "but I can't discuss this with Luke . . . he would simply look right through me in that way he has. I certainly cannot broach the subject of marriage with my mother, for she turns an unbecoming shade of red if I begin to truly ask questions."

Lord, if she thinks for a minute that I am going to answer questions about the intimacy between men and women . . .

A demonstration, perhaps, complete with heated sighs and blissful pleasure, but that was out of the question, and so was the discussion.

"I'm hardly qualified," he said carefully, still propped against the paneled wall, his pose deliberately negligent. "I am as unmarried as you are."

"But not half as sheltered." Lush lashes lowered over her beautiful eyes. "However, I am not asking you about anything except about your attitude on the subject. Am I wrong?"

"Wrong in what way?" he inquired cautiously.

"I realize this isn't a fairy tale, with mythical princes and unicorns floating across lush meadows, but certainly it isn't too much to want to fall desperately in love, is it?" She swallowed visibly, the muscles in her throat rippling. "Or am I being a hopeless, naive idiot?"

Falling desperately in love, in his experience, was a little bit of hell.

"A little naive maybe, considering your position in society, El." It was as honest as he could be, as the subject was poignantly painful. Miles didn't want her marrying for position and stature, and, perversely, he didn't want her falling in love either. That would be worse than having her settled down in contentment with a nice fellow like Fawcett.

Unless, of course, she fell madly in love with *him*.

The clatter of wheels turned her back toward the window, one hand coming up to grasp the drapery. The silhouette of her slender body in the lemon silk gown, her face reflective as she stood there, might be etched forever in his memory. "Lord Fawcett is leaving," she said in evident relief.

"So you are spared the explanation of your refusal," he murmured, straightening. "And now might be a good time to exit my bedroom before anyone knows you were here in the first place."

"Sound advice." She made a small face. "I've already received the lecture from my brother about how you and I aren't actually related."

Miles had wondered once or twice if he wasn't fooling Luke about his feelings for Elizabeth. "Did you?"

"Luke said something about us going out alone. I pointed out he was being overprotective and ridiculous."

"Did you?" Miles repeated with a cynical smile.

She moved toward the doorway in a graceful swirl of silk skirts and lilac perfume. "I told him our relationship hadn't changed just because we'd gotten a little older."

"Did you?" he said softly for the third time as she left the room.

Chapter Eleven

The journal sat on the desk, and Madeline eyed it like one might gaze at a coiled serpent.

It had caused her considerable trouble, and in the course of that said trouble, changed her life. She couldn't help but wonder how Colin would react if he knew what had happened just because he'd felt the need to jot down his private thoughts.

When it was delivered back into her hands she had immediately locked it in the strongbox for safety, as opposed to where she'd put it before, merely in a drawer. She assumed where she kept the cash for the household expenses would be safer, but it spoke volumes that she was relieved to find it there. Maybe a better hiding spot was prudent.

Truth was, she'd attempted to forget about it, but had been compelled to take it out now and at least think about reading it.

What puzzled her most was how Lord Fitch had gotten a hold of it in the first place. If he'd done it once, what was there to say he couldn't do it again?

The study was quiet, Colin's leather chair comfortably worn from much use, since he'd loved to sequester himself away and work. Madeline had always indulgently suspected that a lot of his time was spent daydreaming, solving word puzzles, reading, and obviously writing in his journal. The bookcases lining the oak-paneled walls were full of his beloved books, his rack of pipes and tobacco jar exactly as he'd left them.

How different her new lover was in every way.

Her husband's romantic nature had evidenced itself in gifts of flowers, moonlit picnics, and bits of composed verse.

Luke was more suited to disposing of unwanted bleeding men in her house and retrieving stolen property. There was little question that they were very disparate men, but, she sharply reminded herself, she wasn't looking for a substitute for Colin anyway.

From the poetry he'd written to her, she could only imagine what her husband might have scribbled down when he thought no one would see it. Invading his personal thoughts still seemed wrong, but confidentiality had already been violated by Fitch, and perhaps she could deal better with his lordship's lewd looks and lascivious suggestions if she knew exactly what the man had read.

Still, it took some courage to open the leather-bound volume, the cover soft and creased from years of being opened and closed. The familiar, careless sprawl of her husband's handwriting made a lump rise in her throat, but she forced herself to read on.

It wasn't until a half hour later that she stumbled on the first truly personal passage, as she found the book wasn't written like a diary; Colin had instead just picked it up sporadically and written if suddenly inspired about small snippets of his life, including, Madeline noted with amused interest, the women he had considered courting before they met. Truly, this was a personal journey, and she was *absorbed*.

At one point she sank down farther in the chair, her slippered feet extended under the desk, and muttered, "Carole Faulks—really?"

It appeared he hadn't touched the journal for a while, until the morning after their wedding night.

> *... more nervous than my bride. I tried to not be too eager and frighten her, and I suppose there was a certain clumsiness to my seduction, but then again, her virginity was upon my mind the entire time. Madeline proved to be delightfully receptive to the act of intercourse, gloriously embracing the sensation of our joining, and she didn't insist I douse the lights, which I was perfectly willing to do if she requested it. I was pleased to note she is one of those women with very sensitive breasts, so when I suckled her she made it plain she enjoyed it, running her fingers repetitively through my hair. I wished to take all due care to hurt her as little as possible when I ruptured her maidenhead, but she urged me on with breathless sighs and the urgent motion of her hips, and I was glad to realize the pain was negligible in comparison to her evident enjoyment of the sexual act itself.*
>
> *I believe I have married a very passionate woman. . . .*

Alone, the journal in her hands, she still blushed furiously, recalling that evening. Colin was wrong; she had been quite nervous, but it was tempered by her knowledge that he would do his best to make it all as pleasant as possible, and, indeed, it had been a matter of touch, soft kisses, and, finally, a revelation in the unexpected pleasure. She hadn't climaxed, but she had loved the feel of his hands and mouth on her body, and knowing she gave him such pleasure was a startling lesson in both power and intimacy.

That night she had realized her potential as not just

a wife, but a woman, and she would be ever grateful to
Colin for his care in initiating her into the joys that man
and woman could share in the bedroom.

However, she *loathed* that Fitch had a window to the
events of her wedding night.

The soft knock on the door made her start, as if she
were doing something wrong, and she had to stifle a ridiculous urge to shove the journal into a drawer in the
desk. "Yes?"

Hubert eased the door open, his expression apolo-
getic. "I know you said you planned to stay in and have a
quiet evening, my lady, but you have a visitor who asked
to be announced."

Madeline glanced at the case clock in the corner, saw
it was nearly ten o'clock—not such a late hour in terms
of fashionable circles; many events didn't even start until midnight—but still a late time for a social call. "Who
is it?"

"Viscount Altea."

Luke. It was impossible to not experience a rush of
satisfaction and excitement. Part of the reason she chose
to not attend any of the entertainments she'd been invited to this evening was a reluctance to face him in public just yet. She wasn't at all convinced she could control
her emotions enough if he avoided her like the last time
after they had shared a night of lovemaking. A determination to make sure he didn't ignore what had happened
was very different from success. Luke was not easily
managed—she had no illusions over that point. That
he'd chosen to call on her was a coup. With as much dignity and detachment as possible, she murmured, "Please
show his lordship in here and bring some claret."

What would Colin think of this? It was the first time
she'd asked herself the question. A part of her thought
Marta was correct; he'd want her to be happy. Another
part wondered if he'd be jealous, possessive, territorial—
though with Luke, that would be futile. Her lover didn't
want a claim, just a casual distraction.

But yet he wished to see her.

"Of course, my lady."

She now wished she wasn't wearing her day gown of sprigged muslin at this late hour—she hadn't wanted to bother with changing for dinner when she was going to dine alone, so she'd taken a tray instead in her sitting room upstairs. After her son's bath, she read a book to him, his warm little body snuggled close as he began to doze. Trevor roused only for the part where the dragon swooped down to carry off the maiden in peril. He had a fascination with dragons, not beautiful maidens, but no doubt *that* would change.

"You aren't going out." The four words were a statement, not a question, and Luke strolled in, overpoweringly elegant in dark evening wear, his gaze sweeping over her much more casual attire without either censure or approval. "Is this an avoidance of the possible whispers?"

"No," she was able to say truthfully. "*Are* there whispers?"

"A few." He glanced meaningfully at the new rug. "I see all evidence of Lord Fitch's unfortunate mishap has been removed."

"Well, I'd hardly leave it here, would I?" Madeline looked pointedly at a chair. "Please have a seat. I've ordered wine."

His mouth quirked in amusement, but he did take a wing chair opposite the desk. "What makes you think I'll be staying?"

Despite the question, she knew he would be. It was there in the intensity of his eyes, and Luke Daudet didn't casually drop by. "You rarely do anything that does not involve a definitive purpose, my lord."

"I try not to." He leveled a lazy grin her way. "And you know me so well?"

"Very well in some ways." Madeline smiled back, glad of his presence, so large and male, of his rangy body settling in the chair like he belonged in her house, of the way the lamplight lit his dark blond hair.

She added softly, "Not so well in others, but I am beginning to learn."

Luke leaned back and casually crossed his booted feet. "What am I thinking now, then?"

"I don't claim that kind of expertise."

"You might know," he said with quiet emphasis, "better than I do."

In a moment, the tone of the conversation had changed.

In other words, he wasn't sure why he'd come, but there he was, unable to stay away. Her heart did an interesting flutter. "Can I venture a guess the same impulse brought you here as the one that sent me flying out the door in front of the Masterses' last evening?"

"You can venture—" He stopped speaking as Hubert came through the door with a silver tray bearing glasses and a decanter.

Once the wine was poured and the servant departed, he finished as if he hadn't been interrupted. "—anything you wish. I am open to all interpretations of our actions, Madge."

The way he said *our* pleased her, as if they shared something more than a transitory passion. "I am unsure of a diagnosis of our particular malady, my lord, but can I say I am very glad you decided to call this evening?"

"I like it when the tone of your voice lowers that distinctive notch," he murmured, but then his gaze shifted to rest on the journal on the desktop. "I see you decided to read it."

She was luscious in plain ivory muslin with green ribbons, tendrils of her pale hair escaping from the pins in wayward wisps, a hint of fragile shadows under her eyes because he'd kept her up most of the night. Madeline followed the direction of his look to her husband's journal and the smile faded from her soft lips. "I thought I should."

"Because knowledge is power," he agreed. "And

while I am sure your husband was a good man or otherwise you would not have loved him so deeply, it might be better to know at least as much as Fitch of his private writings."

She must have sensed something in his tone for there was a glimmer of dismay in her dark eyes. "That's why you're here, isn't it?"

"In part." Luke studied her, his wineglass dangling in his hand. The heavy, square desk dwarfed her slender form, the simple gown she wore making her seem younger than she was, as did the vulnerability in her expression.

"He remembers." There was resignation in her tone, but also a slight tremble. "I didn't think you'd casually call this time of evening unless there was a good reason."

"No, he doesn't remember precisely, and Fitch aside, a perfectly sound reason would be to see you. After all, we are embroiled in a liaison, are we not, Lady Brewer?" He deliberately kept his tone light and teasing because he truly didn't want to distress her.

"And something has evidently happened to make you believe we cannot keep it discreet and just between us."

He had never honestly thought they could, especially after her precipitous exit from the party in his wake. Before his conversation with Fitch he'd been willing to try, though, for her sake. Widows had more freedom than unmarried ingenues, true, but the *haut ton* paid attention to every possible scandalous nuance. However virtuous her past, an association with him would bring a certain notoriety.

So, if there were going to be whispers anyway, perhaps it was best if it was understood that Madeline was protected by his honor. Luke regarded her for a moment before he decided to just be forthright. "Our mutual departure last night was noticed, even if you left alone in your carriage. I knew it would be. I've been thinking about this most of the day, and in light of Fitch's barely veiled insinuations that he knows somehow we retrieved the journal and were involved in his mishap, I think it best if everyone understood you are under my protection. At the least, it will spare you the approach of other men who before now considered you immune to their advances."

Until, of course, they went their separate ways. Then she would be fair game and no longer insulated by a reputation for virtuous distance.

"Define *protection*. I don't need your financial support, Altea." Madeline's beautiful eyes held outrage and her slender fingers tightened on the rim of her wineglass. "I hardly—"

He interrupted with calm amusement, "I wasn't offering that kind of protection, Madge, so don't don that haughty look of dismissal. I meant if we appear in public openly together; if I squire you around to social events with a proprietary air, then Fitch will leave you alone, or at the least understand he is dealing with me."

And so would all the other supposed gentlemen who admired her.

Damn them. He had to admit to a certain restive jealousy. It meant Madeline was different, but he'd known that all along. It was why a year ago, he'd just walked away.

Unfortunately, it changed nothing as far as his stance on marriage.

But at least he could offer her some measure of safety, if not from gossip—he'd come to the conclusion that they were already past that point—then from a conscienceless villain like Fitch.

"I suppose I should bow to your expertise in matters of licentious behavior," Madeline murmured, her smile resigned. "And as I believe *I* brazenly propositioned *you*, I should shoulder the responsibility for the gossip, but I am willing to accept your help over this change in my life."

There were aspects of their relationship he didn't

clearly understand, and that was one of them. "You could marry again."

"I married for love once," Madeline said, her gaze drifting to her husband's journal, the leather cover soft as butter from being opened so frequently. "I was lucky also, for he returned my feelings in full measure. I do not believe I'd enjoy a different sort of arrangement. Selfish of me, I suppose, for Trevor could use a father. But then again, how many men are anxious to raise another man's son?"

Luke sat silent, not certain what to say. His refusal to consider marriage had nothing to do with her child. Were his position different, the idea of a child in his life held an appeal he hadn't considered at length before, but maybe his responsibilities to Elizabeth and her future had given him a new perspective on parenthood. Madeline was raising a child alone, and he admired her for it.

"You are a personal indulgence, my lord." A small smile—womanly and seductive—curved her mouth, and he remembered what it was like to taste those soft lips, to savor her sigh as he kissed her, to run his fingers across heated, satin skin.

"I can say the same about you." His predatory stare raked her body, the evening ahead holding a promise of sensual reward once they'd made a perfunctory appearance or two. "Now, then, since we seem to have the same goal in mind, why don't you go upstairs and change? I am sure we were both invited to the same events this evening. It might be the opportune time to informally satisfy the gossips and warn off Fitch before he does something foolish enough to accuse one of us of the attack on his person." He added with lethal casualness, "I don't *wish* to have to kill him."

That barbaric declaration made her eyes widen. "Would you really issue a challenge?"

"My dear Madge, I have already said I would. Does he deserve your concern?"

She rose in a flurry of crumpled muslin, her lashes slightly lowered. "Does it occur to you, Altea, my concern might be on your behalf?"

"No," he said honestly, politely getting to his feet. He was a dead shot and nearly twenty years younger than Lord Fitch.

"Men," she muttered, coming around the desk.

"Women," he countered, lazily lifting his glass to his mouth but holding her gaze. "Don't be too long with your toilette, please. We'll just attend an event or two, so society notices our arrival together. I am much more looking forward to *afterward*."

Chapter Twelve

Not since she reentered society, a good four years after Colin's death, had Madeline experienced a twinge of nervousness while entering a ballroom. This was entirely different, of course, because then she had, for the first time, faced the treacherous waters of society alone as a single woman who no longer needed constant chaperones, and this time Luke's muscular arm was under her fingertips as they were announced.

He bent his head close in an unmistakable gesture of intimacy. "It's quite a crush. I think our point will be made very easily."

His breath fanned her cheek, warm and tantalizing, his mouth very close to her ear, the fringe of his dark lashes shading a wicked gleam of amusement in his silver eyes.

"I'd say you are correct, my lord," she murmured. They were already the object of dozens of interested stares, their arrival together sparking a subtle rise in the volume of voices around them as they reached the bottom of the staircase and gained the crowded floor. The consequences bothered her—Marta and her husband's possible censure was a consideration, and her own mother might take issue with an association with someone like Viscount Altea, who was well-known enough for his fleeting romantic attachments—but not enough to deny herself completely.

"Lady Brewer." Their hostess, the Duchess of Debonne, came forward, a smile on her face, her dark hair upswept in an intricate twist, diamonds at her wrist and neck, one pendant the size of a quail egg nestled in her generous décolletage. "And Lord Altea. How lovely you could attend also."

"Your Grace." Luke's bow was perfection over the duchess's hand, his lazy refinement matched by the charisma of his deliberate smile. "We are delighted to be here."

So now he speaks for *me*, Madeline thought with a twinge of humorous annoyance, though she found, to her surprise, she didn't really mind. "The viscount was kind enough to escort me."

"If it is kindness, which I doubt, it is of the most self-serving kind." Luke lifted his brows just a fraction in charming denial. "You look particularly dazzling this evening, Bess. The Debonne diamonds suit you."

The familiarity of address didn't escape Madeline, and she controlled the impulse to shoot him an accusing look. The duchess was older, maybe in her early forties, but she had a regal beauty, and even after four children, a figure any woman would envy.

Apparently they knew each other quite well. *How* well was the question.

The compliment drew an indulgent smile from the recipient. "And you are extraordinarily handsome, as usual, my lord."

"How's George?"

The duke was dismissed with a small, graceful wave of the duchess's hand. "Well, and at his club, I imagine. You know he detests social events like this."

"Looks to be a smashing success, though, and appears a coveted invitation. Is everyone in London here?" Luke surveyed the crowd.

"It feels like it, doesn't it?" Her smile was brilliant. "If one must put on this sort of event, I'm glad it is well attended. We must waltz later if Lady Brewer doesn't mind my borrowing you for a few minutes."

That easily. Madeline wasn't quite sure how to feel. All she had to do was walk into a ballroom on Luke's arm, and everyone assumed they were having an affair. Which they *were*, but it was still disconcerting. She'd been without a single taint on her reputation before this evening.

"As if I could keep him from doing exactly as he wishes," Madeline said with what she hoped was a serene smile. "Since you seem to be well acquainted, I am sure you agree he's somewhat intractable."

"How true." The duchess laughed and playfully tapped Luke on the shoulder with her fan. "At least she understands you, darling. I had some of George's best brandy set out in case you and Longhaven decided to make an appearance."

"You are too gracious, as always, Bess."

"And you have a surfeit of wicked charm, Altea."

Yes, he *could* be charming. He could be intensely sensual and seductive. He could also be evasive and distant. Always he was urbane and handsome.

The duchess circled away to other guests, and Madeline gave her tall companion a pointed glance. "Do all women flirt with you?"

He shrugged. "I've never really paid attention."

"I'm just asking in case her grace isn't the only woman in attendance who knows what kind of brandy you prefer."

"And knows Michael's preference as well, as you heard. George, her husband, is a friend." His height enabled him to see over the milling crowd, and he nodded to one corner of the vast room. "Lord, it's hot in here.

Shall we see if we can make our way toward the drinks table? Maybe a glass of cool champagne would help."

Sparkling wine for her, she guessed, allowing him to guide her through the throng, his hand at her waist, and the duke's brandy for him. She'd never doubted her sophistication before, but suddenly she did on the arm of the notorious Altea. Jealousy was an unfamiliar emotion.

"I would never touch George's wife," he murmured, low enough only she could hear it. "So you needn't think less of the duchess, because we truly are just friends."

How the devil did he know what she was thinking so easily? Madeline schooled her expression. "You needn't defend yourself to me."

"I wasn't. I was defending her."

"That's even more irritating." And gauche of her to admit the irritation.

"You'd prefer less chivalry?" There was a laugh in his voice.

Did she? No, and she was being ridiculous anyway, because she had no claim on Luke. He'd helped her, and though her inexperience with casual love affairs was a problem in their relationship, she was intelligent enough—if she saw the situation clearly—to know it was *her* problem.

They edged past a group of matrons who didn't even bother to hide their interest, a few with quizzing glasses boldly raised. "I'm sorry," she said haltingly, her voice equally as quiet. "I haven't your sangfroid over our . . . circumstances."

His expression softened. "My dear Madge, I know. I'd like you a great deal less if you did."

He liked her. Well, she supposed lovers should *like* each other. Anything more would complicate matters.

The next two hours passed in a blur. She danced, drank champagne, and listened to the hum of voices that consistently rose above the music, alternately wondering how many people were talking about her and thinking it was vanity to assume her life was of such interest. Luke did dance with the duchess, his blond good looks a foil for her dark elegance, and when they passed each other amid the swirl of couples, Luke smiled at Madeline in a sinful curve of his mouth that made the evening's tension melt away. It was as if they shared a special secret, a promise of what would come later when they were alone and in each other's arms.

Like I used to feel with Colin, she realized wistfully, her hand on the shoulder of some young man whose name she couldn't remember, swirling to the music.

Only what she had with Luke was *nothing* like her marriage.

"And here I thought reclaiming the journal was the end of it." Michael spoke in his usual neutral tone, his hazel eyes speculative. "Or so you said."

Madeline was dancing still, her blond hair unmistakable, as was the fluid movement of her body, and Luke watched her waltz with meditative attention. She'd chosen a gown of indigo taffeta, a foil for her ivory complexion. "I thought it was. Fitch is still a complication. I don't want him causing trouble for her."

"So you decided to gallantly ruin her reputation instead?"

It wasn't censure. Michael never judged. The way he looked at life was always oblique, never based on straightforward concepts like moral judgment. That aside, the observation was accurate enough, if all the avid attention they'd received this evening was an indication. Luke's smile was rueful. "I admit to mitigating circumstances."

"Like her undeniable charms, which apparently you find irresistible."

"I believe most healthy males would be tempted."

"She is lovely." Michael's gaze followed her progress across the dance floor. "But that has never been enough for you. I've never seen you publicly escort anyone except your mother and sister."

They stood by a Grecian pillar that rose magnificently upward, the column at least five feet in diameter, to support the arched, frescoed ceiling. Painted cherubs cavorted above their heads as Luke rubbed his jaw. "It wasn't an impetuous decision. We are both adults and free. We can do as we please. She's aware of my thoughts on a more permanent arrangement."

"Is she, now?"

He transferred his gaze to his friend's face. "I don't have the luxury of it being any other way. Madeline is a passionate, lovely woman who happens to need my protection at the moment. It's a mutually satisfying relationship. Trust me."

"I'd trust you with my life," the Marquess of Longhaven murmured. "That is undisputed and has been proven, I believe."

They'd trusted each other back in Spain, and neither of them would be standing there if that trust wasn't merited.

"But?" Luke's negligent pose was feigned. He always valued Michael's opinion.

"Have you ever read *The Merchant of Venice*?"

Had he not been used to the leaps necessary to follow Michael's thought processes, he would have blinked at the sudden change in subject. "Shakespeare? Of course."

"'To do a great right, do a little wrong,'" Michael quoted softly.

"Is this a lecture?" Luke grimaced. "If so, stop quoting literature and just speak plainly."

"I never lecture."

Then the enigmatic Marquess of Longhaven straightened from his negligent pose by the pillar and strolled away into the crowd.

What the devil was that all about?

Damnation. Luke refused to feel guilty about all this. If Madeline hadn't pursued him out of the dinner party, he'd have been perfectly willing to keep his distance.

More than willing—he'd done his best to stay clear of her, for both their sakes. If memory served, *she'd* propositioned *him*, and . . .

"I take it I am the appointed male of the evening again to see Elizabeth and Aunt Suzette safely home in the wee hours." The droll voice interrupting his silent rationalization belonged to Miles, dressed similarly in tailored, dark evening wear, his eyes holding a certain muted curiosity.

"Did you have other plans?" Luke asked, realizing to his chagrin that for the first time all season, he hadn't taken his sister's social schedule into consideration when he decided to visit Madeline and suggest they attend the ball together.

His young cousin shook his head and leaned against the pillar in Michael's place, idly lifting his champagne flute to his mouth. "Nothing more pressing than a visit to Brookes. I can do that anytime."

Luke didn't relish his duties as chaperone, but normally he didn't shirk them either. There was no rule to say he had to accompany his mother and sister on the round of *ton* activities, but he'd made it a point since Elizabeth's coming-out in the spring. His sister's future was important to him. Miles, however, was trustworthy. The lecture he'd given Elizabeth on not being alone with him had been based on what others might think, not any personal doubts. Besides, his mother would be with them, and that was perfectly acceptable. "I'd appreciate it, then. I'm otherwise engaged this evening."

"So I gathered."

He no doubt deserved that dry inflection, but he'd never made apologies for how he lived his life and wasn't about to start now. Besides, Miles was unlikely to say anything more. Other than Luke's concerns for Elizabeth's carefree, innocent assumption that she and Miles could enjoy the same camaraderie as they had when they were children, Luke was pleased to have another male family member in London. "Speaking of which, I think if I can capture Lady Brewer's attention, it might be time to take our leave."

His passage through the crowd was delayed by greetings from friends, and another waltz was in full swing by the time he got to the edge of the dance floor. Luke waited patiently enough, but the minute the music ended, he purposefully edged through the dancers before another partner could claim Madeline for the next dance, intercepting with a scathing glance a young man he didn't recognize. Only barely did he resist the impulse to possessively put his arm around her waist and guide her off the floor, instead choosing to offer his arm at the last moment. "I thought you look tired."

"And you're bored," she said with gracious understanding.

"Considering the alternative to being around all these people, yes. Our point has been made, and I'd rather be alone with you."

Slender fingers settled on his sleeve, and though she was already flushed from dancing every turn since their arrival, he thought her color deepened. "I am ready to depart if you are."

"With all of London watching, I warn you." He fixed his gaze on the doorway and the gauntlet of guests between them and their quick escape.

"So it appears." She sounded quite composed as they navigated the crowd. "You needn't act as if you are exercising seigneurial rights just to intimidate Lord Fitch, though. I am more than willing to leave. If I trip over my skirts, I believe that will draw even more attention, and we have enough already. Must we exit at a dead run?"

She was right, of course; he was being unforgivably presumptuous and in an undeniable hurry. Luke shortened his stride, amused at himself, and yet at the same time, unaccountably disconcerted. "My apologies."

Moments later, when they were able to gain the doorway and his request for his carriage brought the conveyance around, he handed her in with a bit more restraint, though he couldn't answer for the rest of the night. Luke settled on the opposite seat and rapped on the ceiling of the vehicle to signal his driver. "Maybe tomorrow I should look for neutral ground."

Madeline, striking even in the muted light, dangling sapphire earrings complementing her gown, sounded baffled. "I beg your pardon?"

The luscious swell of her bosom was infinitely distracting. His gaze traveled back up to her face and he clarified. "A place where we can meet and stay together that does not involve our normal household staff or our neighbors."

Lush lashes lowered a fraction over her beautiful eyes. "No. While I appreciate the offer—since I know it is for my sake, as I believe you abandoned the notion of propriety and embarrassment years ago—it isn't necessary."

He wanted to promise her the world would forget their indiscretion or not label it as such, but the world—their world—wasn't so forgiving. Still, he'd make sure he was gone in the morning. Many illicit romances were twittered over, and servants often knew more than the most accomplished gossipmonger, but the urge to protect her wasn't just limited to foiling Fitch's nefarious advances.

"We'd have more privacy."

"I very rarely spend the night away from Trevor. We always breakfast together. As he gets older it isn't as often, but sometimes he needs me at night if he has a bad dream or feels ill. Please understand."

"That hadn't occurred to me." His smile was almost involuntary. She was close, warm, all scented, opulent flesh with her bared shoulders and lustrous hair. He didn't think of her as a mother, but as an alluring woman. "I made arrangements for someone to see Elizabeth home, but my responsibility for a nineteen-year-old woman is not at all the same as yours for a little boy. Forgive my ignorance."

"There's nothing to forgive. When you have children of your own, perhaps you'll understand how . . ." She trailed off, averting her gaze for a moment.

She couldn't know that would cut through him. Luke merely said, "The measure of his need for you is magnified, I would guess also, by your independent state." He did his best to smooth over the awkward moment. Did she want more children? That hadn't occurred to him either. She'd given her husband his heir, but perhaps she desired a larger family. Did women desire daughters the way men wanted sons?

He didn't know. The image of Madeline, lush and ripe with his babe, invaded his mind before he obliterated it as quickly as possible. He'd lost the woman he loved and the child she carried once before. There was a part of him that knew he couldn't endure it again. At least Madeline had her son.

"Yes." The reply was one word, firm and with conviction. "He doesn't remember losing his father because he was too young."

"It might be just my own experience, but it isn't much easier when you are older and do remember." Luke moodily contemplated the passing houses, the shade raised on the carriage window since the night was pleasant. "I was in Spain when I received the letter. We'd just fought a bloody skirmish and hundreds had died, and that I could understand, because it was war, but I couldn't comprehend how a perfectly healthy man like my father could suddenly succumb to what the doctors thought was little more than a slight cough."

"I'm sorry."

"So was I. Imagine a grown man—one who was used to dealing with the destruction of war—so struck he retired to his tent and wept like a bereft child. I suppose nothing can prepare you for it."

"No one expects you to be made of stone, my lord." She spoke very softly.

Perhaps not, but there were times when he wished he

didn't feel so deeply. The brittle facade did not match the inner man. "However we appear, we all have our demons."

"I agree." Madeline hesitated for a moment and then added, "I disliked being manipulated by Lord Fitch in the extreme. I kept asking myself what was the worst he could do to me besides humiliate me publicly, and then I discovered, when he accosted me, there *was* something worse he could do."

"And you handily conked him over the head with a poker," Luke pointed out with a straight face, relieved the discussion had moved on. Besides their foolhardy mutual attraction, both he and Madeline had experienced too much loss too young. There was no need to dwell on it.

Her answering look was reproving, but her mouth twitched. "I was going to say the debacle made me reassess my life."

"How so?"

The cobblestone streets were loud under the wheels of the vehicle, the night air warm, the moment poignant. He'd been in that definitive place—where circumstance met fate, and yet he didn't say so. He wasn't ready to explain himself. He might never be ready.

Madeline adjusted her skirts with a languid hand, her face averted again just enough so he could see the clean outline of her profile. She cleared her throat. "Like I said before, Altea, you are a personal indulgence, and though I hate to admit it, maybe even a necessity against Lord Fitch. I am not worried about hiding our affair if it protects me, and in due course, my son as well. I refuse to give in to blackmail just to avoid a scandal. "

There was enough about her to admire already without adding in her quiet dignity and courage. Luke said with a sinful smile, "Don't worry, my lady. I will make the scandal worth your while."

Chapter Thirteen

*H*ow far, Miles asked himself grimly, *does my duty as chaperone extend?*

When he missed a step and nearly trod on his partner's toes, he did his best to jerk his attention back to the matter at hand, which was finishing a dance with the daughter of one of his stepfather's friends. Miss Furnish was blond, pretty, but unfortunately insipid, and, as far as he could tell, giggled after each word she spoke, God help him. Not even for the benefit of having another investor in his fledgling company could he endure a second waltz.

He was grateful when the music ended, for a myriad of reasons, and not all of them to do with his unappealing current partner.

What the devil was Elizabeth doing?

The answer was, of course, that she had no idea Peter Thomas was fast growing into his father's reputation for vice and extravagance, and what little fortune was left in the family coffers, he was studiously frittering away as fast as possible at gaming and in brothels. At the latter, rumor had it, he was known as Naughty Peter, for a propensity for enjoying being spanked. All Elizabeth saw, unfortunately, were blond curls, blue eyes, and a courtly manner.

To say Miles detested the man was putting it mildly, and if Luke had still been in attendance, Miles was sure there would be discreet interference on a *third* dance with the winsome Lord Peter. But Luke wasn't still there, and the problem was, if Miles showed the smallest trace of disapproval, he was worried Elizabeth would find the young scoundrel even more appealing.

Lady Altea, whom he always referred to informally as Aunt Suzette, was with her usual retinue of friends. He managed to shoulder his way through the milling guests to her corner, plastering his most charming smile on his face as he greeted the somewhat intimidating phalanx of matrons, and drew his aunt aside. "Do you really think Elizabeth should be so conspicuously in the company of Peter Thomas this evening?"

"He's the son of a duke," she replied, as if that absolved the subject of Miles's concern from his considerable sins.

"The debauched son of a duke," Miles explained, knowing he couldn't go into detail. It wasn't gentlemanly to explain about another man's gambling habit, and he wasn't about to mention Thomas's penchant for whores and his peculiar fetishes to his aunt, no less.

Still, *something* had to be done.

Suzette Daudet was still a beauty even in middle age, and Luke had inherited his coloring from her, while Elizabeth more resembled the late viscount. Miles thought his aunt frivolous at times, but from long acquaintance knew she was more astute than she appeared. Her eyes narrowed slightly and then she sighed. "I recognize that look. Men are all alike. You know something not in his favor you are reluctant to tell me."

"You could say that." He wished he could be frank, but he just couldn't. "At the least his family fortunes are depleted. That is common enough knowledge. Elizabeth shouldn't be married for her dowry. She would realize it eventually and be furious."

And hurt. He knew well that would hurt her gravely. If Miles couldn't have her, at least she should marry someone who deserved her, damn all. He wanted her, but he also wanted her happy.

"I'll go interfere." Aunt Suzette patted his arm. "It is very dear of you to worry over Elizabeth."

"I'm not worried," he said defensively, quite certain no male enjoyed being called dear. "I'm just . . ."

She waited with a small lift of her brows for him to finish.

Oh, hell, yes, he *was* worried. The idea of Elizabeth fulfilling her fondest wish and falling desperately in love kept him awake at night. Naturally, he wished he would be the object of her plunge into romantic devotion, but so far he was fairly sure she was oblivious to his true feelings.

It was *not* going to be a depraved twit like Peter Thomas.

"Last I saw, they were over there." He discreetly pointed. "I admit to some concern he was going to try to convince her to step out onto the terrace with him."

That raised alarm, and Suzette hurried off in a rustle of lavender silk. He followed at a more leisurely pace, covertly observing as his aunt neatly linked her arm through Elizabeth's, murmured something undoubtedly much more polite than Thomas deserved, and drew her daughter away.

Vigilant but trying to stay unobtrusive, Miles didn't dance again. Instead he loitered on the edge of the crowd until their departure. He watched Elizabeth smile and flirt, and by the time his aunt asked him to summon the carriage, his jaw hurt because he'd clenched it most of the evening and he almost trampled a hapless footman that accidentally stepped in his way through the foyer, his muttered apology more of a curse over his distraction.

Therefore, the rousing argument once they all got in the carriage was probably not a huge surprise, given his fractious mood.

Elizabeth had a certain way of bestowing a withering look that Miles was fairly sure was reserved for him alone, a sort of cross between a scowl and a glare. "I understand Lord Peter doesn't meet with your royal approval," she said, settling into the seat across, her tone sweetly accusing. A vision in a low-cut gown of ivory lace over a peach underskirt, her glossy hair artfully arranged so several long, dark ringlets fell over the curve of her bare shoulder from her chignon, it was no wonder she'd been swamped with partners all evening.

"That isn't at all what I said," his aunt protested, looking at her daughter in reproof as they pulled away from the ducal mansion in Mayfair. "I merely stated that Miles felt it prudent you not allow yourself to be monopolized by Lord Peter Thomas."

"Since when is Miles's judgment of what is prudent the standard against which polite behavior is measured?" Elizabeth leveled another scathing look in his direction. "Last I knew, *his* name was attached to some questionable females. Like, for instance, a certain very young countess married to a very old earl, who likes to entertain herself with unattached young men."

His aunt gasped outright. "Elizabeth!"

Immediately Elizabeth's face took on high color, but her gaze was unwavering. "It *is* what I heard, and if he is criticizing my behavior, perhaps we can examine his."

The charge was close enough to the truth that an infuriating heat filled his face too. He'd been more pursued than pursuer, but he wasn't aware so much of the gossip was widespread enough that it had reached her innocent ears. Still he hadn't taken the countess to bed, and not because the lady wasn't willing either. He found his love for Elizabeth a detriment to casual affairs, and all he was guilty of was harmless flirtation. "My reputation isn't the issue," he said stiffly. "And this is hardly a contest."

"I danced with a man in plain sight of hundreds of people. My reputation isn't an issue either."

"Ask Luke if he doesn't agree with me on the suitability of Peter Thomas as a possible suitor." Let her brother formulate the diplomatic answer. If Miles was certain of anything in this life, he knew Luke would agree with him in this case.

"A sound reason for your suggesting my mother drag me away in front of everyone would be nice."

She was right, but he was right also, and the impasse was an irritant. "I know things about him you don't."

There was the usual challenge in her eyes. "Then tell me."

He'd used an unfortunate explanation. She detested him knowing anything she didn't. Besides, the gossip truly wasn't something he would repeat to her. "No."

"Then forgive me if I don't lend a lot of weight to your objections, not that what you think makes much of a difference anyway."

"Elizabeth," Suzette said in firm admonishment, her outraged gaze having gone back and forth as the volley of exchanges began. "Miles has no motive at all to object to anyone who shows interest in you except your well-being. I think you are being singularly ungracious about this."

Hopefully his inward flinch wasn't visible. He had the most compelling motive of all to object to any man who might court Elizabeth, but then again, he *was* trying to protect her, he reminded himself quickly. Hands down, Thomas was an objectionable man.

"Ask Luke about Peter Thomas," he said shortly. "I refuse to discuss it any further."

He *refused*.

Male arrogance made her want to scream. Elizabeth

stared at Miles, wondering if she wrapped his cravat around his throat and strangled him, if it would make her feel better.

Probably, she guessed.

The truth was, she had come to the conclusion herself that Lord Peter was being rather too deliberately charming. Maybe she was young and her experience with society limited to the few months since her debut, but she possessed a perfectly functioning brain and could separate real interest from calculated flirtation. The only reason she'd danced with him three times was that he happened to be amusing company and an excellent partner. There was nothing more to it.

She hardly needed *Miles* to interfere. "Very well. But let me say this—"

The man sitting across from her, his long legs extended, thick lashes half lowered over his eyes, gave a low, theatrical groan and interrupted, "I knew you wouldn't let it go, El. Lord, do we have to continue this? We disagree yet again. I said my piece. Now let us set it aside."

"I'm not an empty-headed doll, Miles," she snapped, ignoring his suggestion. "I am perfectly capable of making my own decisions, and that includes whom I wish to dance with and how many times."

"You may think so, but this evening doesn't exactly bear out that supposition." His voice was infuriatingly mild. "Tell me: did he try to persuade you to go outside with him?"

The man in question had. Twice, with an offer of fresh air and a starlit sky. At her hesitation, Miles muttered, "Aha. I thought so."

"I refused." Elizabeth quelled the unladylike impulse to slap the smug look off his handsome face. "So don't act as if butting your nose in made any difference in my evening, except to humiliate me by having my mother so pointedly drag me off."

"I'd hardly call that humiliation." One of his dark brows lifted and the corner of his mouth twitched.

"Rest assured, the next time you dance with someone *I* dislike, I'll be sure to let you know."

"You are terribly defensive about this, aren't you?"

"And you are terribly presumptuous, aren't *you*?"

"Good heavens," her mother interjected firmly in unconcealed exasperation. "That's enough. Miles is a grown man and he may dance with whomever he wishes without your comments, Elizabeth. I, for one, appreciate his concerned interest."

Meddling was more the appropriate term, but Elizabeth bit back another sarcastic comment out of deference for her mother, and sat in silence the rest of the way home, listening to the clatter of the wheels on the street. A wry sense of inner amusement began to assert itself by the time they rocked to a halt and a footman hastened to open the door of the carriage. Perhaps her reaction *had* been a bit childish for someone so convinced she was mature enough to judge a man's character on short acquaintance, but then again, Miles had a tendency to ignite combustible reactions when they argued, which happened to be often.

Not that she hadn't sensed Peter Thomas might have ulterior motives to go along with his flattering attentions, so she was right about being able to discern for herself—in his case anyway—the nature of his pursuit. But, she grudgingly admitted as she allowed Miles to politely lift her from the carriage, that meant he was right, too.

It was odd, but even when they quarreled over something, they usually basically agreed. It had always been that way between them.

"Truce?" he asked softly, his hands lingering at her waist as he looked down into her face.

How many times have we said that word to each other? she wondered. However, he wasn't that young boy who had tripped her in the mud, or suggested they sneak off to wade in the river when their nanny had specifically forbidden it. The starlight showed off the nicely shaped line of jaw and the arch of his brows, and though his golden eyes didn't hold a hint of apology, she usually found it impossible to stay angry with him anyway.

"Truce." Elizabeth nodded, suddenly aware of the warmth of his palms through the material of her gown. "If you'll tell me why Lord Peter is such an undesirable match."

"Never." He dropped his hands, his expression suddenly closed. "Not for your ears, El, trust me."

"You aren't even three years older than I am." The exasperation was evident in her tone. "Why is it you get to know this obviously defamatory information, and I don't?"

"Men gossip just like women." His wide shoulders lifted slightly in a negligent shrug. "I think we just talk about different matters. And don't act as if the closed ranks among men are any different than between women. I feel confident you know certain things no one will ever tell me."

"Maybe we could trade information." She was joking, of course. She would never tell him that the females of her acquaintance twittered over him. It annoyed her enough without *him* knowing it as well.

"I'm not protecting Peter Thomas. I am protecting you."

An odd notion—Miles protecting her. But, reflecting back, he always had in his own way. "I'll avoid him," she acquiesced in quiet retreat from the argument, her smile wry. "Perhaps you should provide me with a list of disreputable gentlemen with sordid secrets currently on the prowl in our social circle. It would make matters much simpler."

His laugh showed a gleam of white teeth. "And, in turn, you could warn me with some sort of special signal if a female fastens her sights on my bachelorhood as a matrimonial prize."

"I warned you about Susanna Meyer." She walked up the steps next to him, her lace skirts slightly lifted in her hands. "But I suppose I could whistle like you taught me if one walks past."

"Now, *that* would be ladylike."

"Wouldn't it?" She shot him a teasing smile.

"I'm sure you'd make quite an impact in fashionable circles." The remark was dry. "And, yes, you did warn me about Miss Meyer. So now we are even." He paused to let her enter the foyer first. "And I am grateful, for while she has some admirable . . . er . . . qualities, she makes me want to run the other direction as fast as possible."

It was easy enough to guess what qualities he found admirable. "Like a true rake," Elizabeth murmured.

"No," he corrected, following her down the polished hallway, "like a man with a modicum of self-preservation."

"Define the difference." She passed by a painting by Bernini that hung in the vaulted space that accessed the public rooms and idly tugged off her gloves, but remained acutely tuned in to Miles's answer. The hem of her gown whispered over the polished marble floor.

Had they just quarreled? As usual, it was over like a fleeting summer storm.

"Avoiding the predatory advances of eager young women is not at all the same as seducing them," he said with a twitch of his mouth.

"I never said those were the ones you seduced."

"Are you keeping track of my private life? If so, mayhap you should ask me for the details and make sure your information is accurate."

"I could give a fig about your private *affairs*." Her wave was deliberately dismissive.

"Yet you seem to bring it up in conversation often enough."

They crossed the huge, imposing main hall and gained the staircase. Elizabeth was in front as they went up the graceful curve of the steps. "Only because you annoyed me this evening."

"That's unusual," he muttered so low she almost didn't catch it.

She turned halfway up the staircase and looked him in the eyes, as he was only a step behind. His dark brown hair, glossy in the lamplight, was a little disordered, and he halted with one foot on the next step, his gaze inquiring. For some reason, a flush spread over her skin, the scent of his cologne subtle but tangible at this close proximity, and she was very aware of his height, the athletic, muscled power of his body, and, even more, of how he looked at her.

Miles.

Elizabeth all of a sudden couldn't recall the withering retort in response to his sardonic observation. They stood there for a moment, until his brows lifted in subtle question and she realized her heart had begun to pound.

For absolutely no reason.

Then she turned and hurried up the stairs toward her room without saying another word.

Chapter Fourteen

It was very late, and the room hung with muted shadows. Madeline's fingertips drifted down his spine. "Hmm."

"Is that a compliment?" Luke laughed, his breath stirring her tumbled tresses, content with his pulse slowing now in the aftermath of such strenuous lovemaking. The woman beneath him was soft, perfumed perfection, all heated sighs and sensuous warmth, and he kissed the hollow of her throat in a lingering gesture of affection.

"When I can think again, I'll answer." Madeline arched beneath him, her eyes still closed, the dark length of her lashes against her cheekbones.

He eased himself away from her body and rolled over, nude and covered in a sheen of perspiration, his chest still lifting rapidly. "And maybe when the roaring in my ears subsides, I'll hear you."

"Is *that* a compliment?" She stirred and curled closer, the provocative scent of sex in the air.

It was—she undoubtedly knew it, despite the teasing way she'd phrased the question—and he deliberately didn't glance at the ormolu clock ticking on the mantel. There was no question he should go—and, surprisingly, no doubt that he didn't wish to go. Wanting to wake in her bed and arms was a dangerous indulgence. "It might be," Luke replied with studied casualness when he didn't actually feel casual at all about the situation.

"We complement each other." She touched his jaw in a tentative exploration and then quickly added, "Here anyway."

She meant in bed. The equivocation made him wince inwardly, not that he would let her see it. Luke caught her hand and pressed his lips to the pad of each finger in turn in a lingering kiss. "Yes, we do."

She frowned then, just the slightest furrow of her smooth brow. "Or maybe I am being naive. Perhaps all of the women you have bedded feel this way."

What way? He actually almost asked the question.

The realm of feelings was dangerous. He smiled and rose on one elbow, lightly running a questing finger down her torso, navigating between her breasts, over the flat plane of her stomach, and lower. "I think you are analyzing what can't be defined. How much a man and a woman enjoy each other's company is always a subjective experience. I can assure you I am enjoying myself very much indeed."

"You *seem* sincere. . . ." She arched as he brushed her thigh with his fingertips.

He was. He also wished he could have forgotten the magical sweetness of her kiss, her unique sigh as he entered her supple body, the warm, fragrant silk of her skin . . . but he hadn't. He found he couldn't, and however all this ended, Luke had the fateful sense she would haunt him as much as his past.

In other words, he hadn't learned from his mistakes, but compounded them.

This was not at all what he sought when he succumbed to his base impulses and took her to bed again.

A summer night, a chance encounter, a beautiful lady

*in the gardens when he'd been oh so vulnerable and sus-
ceptible, because Spain was like a lifetime away, he was
in his new role as viscount, and the jumble of his feelings
resulted in a less than polished exchange of commonplace pleasantries. . . . and then—and then—Madeline
had looked at him with those gorgeous eyes, and for the
first time since Maria's death, he'd felt a flicker of desire
for another woman. She had acquiesced when he'd suggested he might escort her home, and it was only later,
after a night of unforgettable passion, that he'd learned
the beautiful woman he'd seduced was actually a virtuous young widow who had just recently reentered society. He hadn't wanted that, had desired just a casual
tumble . . .*

Or, an insidious voice in his brain hinted, *maybe it was*
exactly *what you wanted.* A casual liaison wouldn't have
left him so shaken. Maybe he was being granted heaven
on earth *now* without having to don angel wings. "Neither of us forgot that night long ago," he said in compelled honesty, "or we wouldn't be here together. Don't
make the mistake of thinking you aren't different."

He wanted to give her that much—the knowledge he
had kept his distance from her at some personal cost.

"Am I?" The uncertainty in her eyes told him she was
unsure how much to pursue his statement. "Different
how?"

He'd said leagues and miles and fathoms deep too
much already. Deliberately he twitched his mouth into
a smoldering smile. "Where shall I begin? No one has
breasts like yours. Womanly, full, but not so abundant
as to be too much for my hand." He cradled her warm,
pliant flesh in his palm. "Every man tonight at the ball
envied me."

"And every *ton* beauty must be jealous of me after
our arrival and departure this evening together." Madeline said it lightly, but her voice held a very slight but
discernable edge.

He made a derisive sound. "As if every young buck

wouldn't want to carve out my heart because I am here with you."

"But I wouldn't." She looked into his eyes, her voice hushed. "Be with any of them, I mean."

The trouble was, he believed her. Not that he had enough of a claim to pass judgment, but he *believed* her and was arrogant enough to ask in return, "Why am *I* different?"

"I don't know."

Luke ran his fingers through the iridescent runnels of semen on her inner thigh where he'd spilled his seed, the evidence of his desire for her slick on her smooth skin. "I don't know why I'm here either." Then he grinned, not wanting seriousness to interfere with his current state of contentment. "Though too much analysis at this time of the morning is dangerous. Let's just say I find you slightly hazardous to my peace of mind and yet still can't quite control my carnal urges."

"That makes two of us. Logic doesn't apply to our situation, so let's not waste our time trying." She smiled back, a hint of mischief in her eyes. "May I add that I like what you are doing with your fingers now, but a few inches higher might be preferable?"

Her willingness to dismiss the discussion was a relief, especially since pragmatic dissection of motives and consequences was impossible when she reclined, lush and available for erotic play, against the fine linen sheets. Her long blond hair, thick and lustrous, reminded him of Chinese silk, the color not gold, not platinum, but an illusive shade between the two, and the unusual shape of her eyes conjured images of harems and exotic, forbidden evenings far away from the world. It was a fantasy, and he was more than willing to indulge her—and himself.

"Like this?" He touched her lightly, stroking the dainty triangle of hair between her thighs before slipping a finger inside her passage in gentle exploration. Naturally, she was slick with the lubricating fluids of her own desire, and so hot and tight that he began to harden once again.

Even he was amazed, for while he'd never considered virility a problem, he would have thought he'd be sated by now.

Supine and languorous, she let her lashes drift downward, relaxing her thighs and opening her legs. "Do you never tire?"

"I am a little tired." He kissed the underside of her breast, tasting the essence of her skin, the salty tang of it like the most powerful aphrodisiac. "And yet not quite ready to leave, apparently."

"I can tell." She gazed at his returning erection through heavy-lidded eyes.

"Are you too fatigued for me to stay a little longer?"

"Absolutely not." The slumberous tone of her voice supported her sincerity.

"That's what I thought." Propped on one elbow next to her, Luke began to mimic the act of love, teasing her, sliding his finger deep into her vaginal passage and then withdrawing slowly, adding a second finger to make her take in a shuddering breath.

"Yes." Her hips lifted to the rhythm of his penetrating fingers.

"Did I ask a question?"

"I have no idea." The answer was a gasp as he rotated his thumb between the damp folds of her sex with provocative, slow pressure.

"Do you want me to fuck you again?"

She glanced up at him, startled and obviously shocked at the crude word, uncertain enough that Luke discerned she and her husband had never played games in bed. His grin was slow as he again aroused her. "Forgive the language, but my choirboy status was revoked a long time ago."

"I'm not surprised. You don't qualify for anything remotely related to divine works...." Madeline might have said more, but he moved his thumb again and instead she inhaled on a swift breath and began to tremble, her skin exquisitely flushed. "Oh . . . God."

"Ask me nicely and I'll finish this for you."

"Luke . . ."

"A simple *please* will do." He knew she was close—very close.

"Fine . . . yes, please . . ."

He obliged her, and felt the tightening around his invading fingers with satisfaction. When she climaxed, he kept her there for long, lingering moments until she pushed his hand away and lay in panting dishabille, her luscious form quivering. "Beast," she said succinctly.

He laughed and stretched out next to her, his erection at full mast again. "*You* asked *me*."

"Perhaps two can participate in your little diversions, Altea." Madeline rolled to her knees, shaking back her hair.

It was gratifying to see the surprise in his eyes when his usual cool sophistication so often made her feel like an ingenue again. She was well aware he could resist at any time and she could do nothing about it, but when she placed her hands on his shoulders and ordered him to lie back, he complied with no more objection than a quirk of a brow.

The beauty of his body was enough to make her stop to admire the hard, muscled contours of his torso, the long length of his legs, the trim, flat plane of his stomach, and, of course, the splendid, rigid length of his penis, smooth and erect, the swollen tip glistening. She wasn't bold by nature, but this sexual sparring with Luke was different. She was not a submissive wife learning about sexuality in small, subtle ways; she was a *mistress*.

Odd, it gave her a special sense of enlightenment and power. This was her choice—all of it. And if she wished to walk away tomorrow, she could. He would let her—she knew that—and maybe that was part of why embarking on this journey felt . . . safe.

Power was a heady intoxicant.

Reaching over, she slid her hand up the unyielding length of his erection, surprised that the pulse of his heartbeat was discernable under her exploring fingers. Luke said in a strangled voice, "What if I apologize now for being autocratic?"

"You don't like this?" She glided her grip down the impressive, springing length of stiff, heated flesh, squeezing gently at the base.

"I absolutely like it, but I have a feeling you are intent on exacting some revenge." His heavy-lidded eyes regarded her warily. "And I am in a somewhat vulnerable position at the moment."

He was too extraordinarily handsome, she thought, with his tousled hair and patrician features, not to mention that fleeting smile that rarely surfaced unless he was being deliberately charming. Propped against the lace-trimmed pillows on her bed, he looked more masculine than ever. "I won't hurt you," she promised in a low purr.

Then she lowered her head. Only once had she pleasured Colin with her mouth, and that was after they'd been married for well over a year, when he whispered the suggestion in her ear and shocked her to her core. Yet, if she remembered correctly, he'd enjoyed it immensely, and Luke certainly deserved to be rendered as positively shameless as she had been by his wicked manual manipulation.

The swollen head of his cock slid past her lips and she licked gently, hearing a satisfying groan. His skin was satin over steel flesh, and the essence of his sexual fluids salty against her tongue. He whispered huskily, "Madge . . ."

Brawny thighs were taut under the pressure of her palms, and she moved her tongue carefully up his shaft, cognizant that she wasn't particularly skilled at what she was doing, but improvising as she went along. If his erratic breathing was any indication, her lack of practice didn't matter.

"You . . . shouldn't." His fingers threaded into her hair in contrast to the words, his cock pushing a little more into her mouth.

Did he mean no real lady would ever do such a thing? Perhaps, but in bed, she was finding being a lady had no real advantages, while doing as you pleased—and what pleased your partner—was much more enjoyable. For instance, at the moment, Luke was entirely at her mercy, his neck arched back against the pillows, his chest lifting rapidly, the outward hiss of his breathing audible.

How nice to bring a man of his impressive control to his knees, even if only in a figurative sense.

"I'm almost . . . there . . . stop." His voice was choppy but his hands insistent as he tugged her head up, then toppled her over to her back, his eyes gleaming in the lamplight. "Minx," he muttered, and kissed her as he adjusted his position, using his knees to push her thighs apart. His entry was heated and forceful enough to make her gasp, but not in pain; more like sublime sensation as he sank deep and forged their bodies together.

"This won't take long," he whispered in her ear, his breath hot, his skin also on fire beneath the press of her hands.

It was feverish, wild, and erotically satisfying, and, as he promised, over quickly. Both of them were so aroused they expired in mutual intense pleasure, shuddering together, and lay in the panting aftermath, slick against each other.

"I blame you entirely for my adolescent impetuousness just now," Luke finally murmured, his voice full of amusement. He brushed her hair back from her brow, his smile a glimmer. The gesture was tender and gentle in contrast to his insistent possession.

"Do you?" She laughed, loving the feel of him, so large and sleek, his weight balanced enough so that he wasn't crushing her. "Should I apologize?"

"For being gloriously sensual and uninhibited? I should think not."

"You are a bit reckless yourself, my lord." She ran a hand over the muscled curve of his shoulder.

"Speaking of which, I should go." He turned his head and glanced at the window, where through the parted curtain the first faint, reddish streaks of dawn were visible. "Let me correct myself: I should have left an hour ago."

Madeline would have objected . . . she wanted to drift to sleep in his arms again, but he was right. Trevor rose early enough that at most she'd get a few hours of sleep. She refused to miss breakfast with her son.

So she merely nodded and watched as Luke rose from the bed, washed quickly with the water in the basin by her dressing room, and, with deft, efficient movements, donned his clothing. A tall figure in the shrouded bedroom, he hesitated a moment and then walked over to give her a swift kiss good-bye. A delicious one, too, with the lingering pressure of his lips bringing forth a telling sigh.

And then he was gone. No promises, she thought, physically content and pleasantly exhausted, but emotionally not so stable. Luke didn't give promises. He'd made a point of saying there would *be* no promises.

I knew it all along, she chided herself, lying there with his scent still on her skin.

This journey had been her choice, and if at the end, the journey itself was her only reward, that had to be enough. Luke might protect her, he might desire her, but his self-proclaimed disinterest in marriage was something she'd known before she'd invited him into her bed.

Yet she knew some perverse part of her wondered if she couldn't change his mind.

Chapter Fifteen

More flowers. It made him want to put his fist through a wall. Miles plucked the card from one of the new arrivals and saw it was from an earl nearly twice Elizabeth's age. "Letch," he muttered.

"Do you always read other people's private communications?" The voice behind him was cool.

He turned, chagrined, not even sure why he'd ventured into the drawing room in the first place, and certainly not willing to admit he did it every day to see what new suitors were vying for Elizabeth's attention. "It's a particularly ostentatious bouquet," he drawled with as much aplomb as possible for someone so fairly caught. "It smells like an overblown garden even out in the hall."

Elizabeth crossed her arms over her chest and arched a brow upward. "I am sorry if the floral odor offended you. So, tell me. Who is it from?"

"Let's just say he's old enough to be your father and leave it there. Shall we?" He tucked the card back in among the blooms and took out his handkerchief to studiously wipe some yellow pollen from his fingers.

It was the best ploy he could think of to keep from looking at her. It was only moderately successful, he found, when he was forced to glance up for the sake of politesse. In a simple white gown, she stared at him with those eyes that haunted his dreams—erotic dreams no innocent young maid should ever guess existed—and said, "I can't imagine you care who sends me notes and flowers."

Evasion was easy enough. He was becoming practiced at it. "Perhaps you should open your own conservatory, or better yet, a shop for unwanted arrangements. I'll even help you think up a name. Let's call it El's Discarded Bouquet Boutique, or perhaps The Rejected Roses Repository, or—"

"I advise you to stop trying to be amusing, Miles, as you are sadly failing." She moved into the room, not looking at him, seemingly intent on the sprays of chrysanthemums and various other blooms in crystal vases. One fingertip touched a yellow rose. "You don't approve of gentlemen sending ladies flowers, I take it. What do *you* do?"

Her profile was pure, perfect, and so familiar he could close his eyes and see it. Miles couldn't remember his life before her, and certainly couldn't imagine it when they went their separate ways. Distracted, he forgot to answer her question.

Actually, what the devil *was* her question?

"What do I do about what?" he asked stupidly, admiring the slender ivory column of her neck. The hollow between her collarbones was delicate and perfect, and he could so easily imagine pressing his mouth to that very spot. . . .

Silver eyes flashed amused annoyance. "Don't be obtuse. When you are courting a lady, how do you go about it?"

He didn't court them, of course, not in the sense she meant. Oh, he wasn't celibate, or at least he'd had his share of sexual encounters on the most casual level possible, but he didn't *court* anyone. He'd been in love with Elizabeth so long he really couldn't imagine being serious about anyone else, but maybe, he'd told himself, once she was married and irrevocably out of his reach, then he would forget her.

Forget? No, not possible. Then he'd adjust to her absence in his life.

Probably not possible either. All in all, the looming experience promised a lesson in pure misery.

"I don't waste my money on pots of posies. That is for certain. Very unoriginal." He pointed at a small silver vase full of delicate violets. "Lord Peter doesn't agree."

"Are we going to argue over that tiresome subject again? Besides, you are avoiding answering my question."

In profile he could see the lacy fan of her lashes and the charming—or it was to him—slightly elfin shape of her nose. He summoned an answer. "I haven't exerted myself to attempt to win one specific lady yet. I'm only twenty-two."

"I'm only nineteen," she pointed out accurately, turning to glance at him. "Yet I am supposed to race to find a husband like the hounds of hell are nipping at my heels."

He couldn't help it—his mouth twitched at her acerbic tone and the less than divine comparison. "I thought all young women wanted nothing more than to ensnare some unsuspecting male into a lifetime of carping at him for his bad habits and spending his hard-won money on female fripperies."

"If that is what happens," Elizabeth retorted with her predictable fire, "it is because we are forced into it. Quite frankly, I envy Lady Brewer. If she and Luke are lovers, it is her choice, and she is not required to marry him."

The word *lovers* evoked a predictable fantasy, and Miles eyed the doorway with longing, though Elizabeth stood closer to it than he did and he would have to brush by her to exit the room. "I don't think we should speculate on their relationship. It is their business and their business only."

"Is that how you think of your liaisons?"

Was she jealous, or was she just jealous of his greater freedom as a male in a society where men held the power? "I decline to comment."

Even as he started to walk to the door—damn her for looking provocative somehow in that virginal, pale gown—Elizabeth asked in a completely different tone, "What is it like?"

"Can you be more specific?" He stopped involuntarily, for what he wished most was to leave her presence as soon as possible.

And, perversely, to stay with her always.

A damned dilemma.

She shifted so she leaned back on a mahogany library table, her arms crossed over her chest. "Let's not dissemble. You are beginning to acquire a certain reputation as a rakish sort. I admit I found it disconcerting at first, because . . . well—let's face it—you're *you*. But now I wonder if I shouldn't just ask you all the questions I can't seem to get my mother to answer."

Apparently the hounds of hell were also interested in his heels, for he couldn't imagine wanting to run any faster. The Pyrenees were probably delightful this time of year. If he emigrated there . . .

His voice sounded oddly strangled. "May I ask what prompted this sudden combative attitude?"

"No."

Perhaps it was from dealing with their mothers, but most males instinctively knew when they were in trouble with a female. Miles stood there with his hands at his sides, wondering just what he could have done to provoke her sudden antagonism. It wasn't that Elizabeth had never been angry with him before—quite the contrary—but he didn't think it had anything to do with him reading a simple card on a bouquet of flowers.

He refused to ask the simple but deadly question: *what did I do?*

"I loathe being ignorant about anything, but especially so if you know more than I do, Miles." There was a hint of color in Elizabeth's cheeks, but her gaze was direct. "After all, we've known each other forever . . . our forever anyway. I don't see why you can't be forthcoming with a few details."

Our forever. She couldn't have more casually selected a knife with which to cleave out his heart. "What the devil do you want to know?" he asked with hoarse brusqueness.

"What, exactly, *happens.*"

Unfortunately, he understood the request. He even understood the inquiring look in her lovely eyes, the innate curiosity that made her demand he teach her to swim, to learn how to bowl a cricket ball, how to climb a tree . . .

Not the usual interests of well-bred young ladies, which might be why so many of them bored him. Elizabeth had never been a dull companion, even in the days when he was a superior eleven-year-old and she was merely *a girl.*

What she was asking now was certainly not an inquiry a well-bred young lady might make. "I'm not," he ground out, "going to give you some sort of a tutorial on licentious behavior. I think you have gone well beyond the pale to ask. Now, if you'll excuse me . . ."

"Since when do you care about propriety, especially between us?"

"Are you being deliberately argumentative? If so, I think I'll decline the discussion." He was leaving, no doubt about it.

She actually stepped forward and blocked his way, "All I want is a simple technical explanation of what happens between a man and a woman in the bedroom. Why is it such a secret?"

*   *   *

There was a certain part of her that wondered what she was doing. It stemmed from last night, when she'd been so disordered, her world set askew, and she wanted . . . revenge.

Well, maybe not revenge. Wrong word.

Retribution? No, that wasn't right either. She just wanted to make him pay somehow for the sleepless night when she'd sat and stared out the window for hours, trying to reconcile that singular moment on the stairs when she'd looked at Miles and really *seen* him.

The man. The one looking at her now as if she'd lost her mind, his dark brows drawn together, his tall body tense.

Perhaps she *had* gone mad. She was attracted to Miles, of all people.

For that disquieting revelation alone, he should pay. How dare he—he who had always been so insufferable—be so handsome in his own way, with his slightly disheveled hair and amber eyes. And now he had the audacity to look at her as if *he* were wary.

The entire situation was untenable.

All those eligible gentlemen vying for her hand, and she was thinking about Miles. In the backwash of that disquieting realization, she wanted him to pay somehow, and maybe demanding something personal from him was a sort of revenge. Petty, perhaps, but then again, she reminded herself, she actually wanted to know.

"What?" he asked, disbelief comically etched on his features.

It was a bit rewarding to see him discomforted. Elizabeth raised her brows slightly. "I assume you have first-hand knowledge of what I'm asking?"

He flushed. It was barely discernable under the bronze of his skin, but she knew him, and his embarrassment fueled her determination to put him as off balance as he currently had her. He said unsteadily, "If . . . you think for a moment I am actually going to tell you anything on this subject—"

"Why not?" She didn't move, standing firmly in his path, wondering how she'd never noticed there were darker flecks in his eyes, or that the sensual curve of his lower lip was slightly fuller than the upper, and that when he shoved his hand carelessly, impatiently through his hair, his fingers were masculine and graceful.

"Your mother wouldn't appreciate it, for one." He stared down at her, but didn't move to walk around her and leave. "Luke might have my head."

"I wasn't suggesting you call them in to listen. We've kept secrets before."

"What the devil kind of logic is that?" he muttered.

How many women have there been? She wondered, the twinge of jealousy unwanted but definitely there. *How many had smoothed back that wayward lock of hair from his brow and . . . ?*

And what? Lain with him naked, gazing into his eyes as they touched and kissed?

It was her turn to blush at the direction of her thoughts, remembering how recently she'd been in his bedroom, dodging Lord Fawcett. "How am I not being logical? I have a few questions and you should know the answers. That is a straight path from beginning to end, as far as I can tell." Whatever her reasons, she wasn't going to give him the satisfaction of backing down. She played what might be an unfair card. "At least I know you'll be honest with me."

"Will I?" His gaze was veiled. "Don't be too sure. Ask Luke instead."

"I'm hardly going to ask my *brother.*"

"How am I so different? I'm your cousin."

"No, you're not."

Three simple words. So much meaning.

He was right about the sweet smell of the flowers. It was cloying, the room stuffy in the warmth of the afternoon, the elegance of the rich furniture bathed in a somnolent glow through the sheer curtains drawn against the heat. She caught her breath, and wasn't sure why.

"No, I'm not," he repeated finally, so softly the words were almost inaudible. "So with that acknowledged, shall we cease this ridiculous debate? I have an appointment anyway. Excuse me."

She watched him go, unsettled, embarrassed a little over her insistence and request, and still not sure what, exactly, prompted her irrational behavior.

When her mother came in a few minutes later, she was still there, pensively studying the empty doorway.

"I just passed Miles. He seemed a little preoccupied."

"Did he?" Elizabeth watched her mother fuss around the flowers and glance at the cards. She added wryly, "He did leave a bit abruptly."

"He's busy now with his new business venture."

"I suppose so. Fawcett will be there tonight, I imagine, darling. What will you wear?"

"Luke understands that I am not interested right now in an agreement with his lordship." Elizabeth plucked a rose from an arrangement and idly twirled it in her fingers. Her hand shook slightly from the recent confrontation. What *was* she interested in? She wasn't sure, but it didn't include flowers and poetry and meaningless compliments.

She *was* worried it might include Miles.

Her mother carefully set down one of the vases and turned. "I understand the season is a whirlwind, believe me. I remember my bow. Importunate gentlemen and salacious gossip and all the staring eyes. It can be daunting."

"It's not precisely overwhelming, but I admit to a certain degree of confusion." The declaration seemed appropriately neutral, though confusion took on a whole new meaning after the night before and the telling moment on the stairs. "Most of my friends seem to know what they want. I am not as certain. Lord Fawcett, for all his fortune and pleasing looks, is not what I envisioned in a husband."

"By the fortuitous circumstance of your brother's fortune and his open mind, I am sure you are not going to be coerced to accept a proposal you don't want. Now, then," her mother said with elegant aplomb, crossing to sit in a chair and reach for the bellpull, "shall we sit and have tea and wait for the callers? You can entertain me by telling me what you've heard about Lady Brewer. I know little about her except for the remarkable display she and Luke put on the other evening. It isn't like him to flaunt his private life. Do you have an indication why he would? What does Miles have to say about it?"

The sequence of rapid questions was a relief, as the subject wasn't *her* social life, but the reference to Miles made Elizabeth swallow and wait a minute before answering. "How would I know what Miles is thinking?"

"You always do, darling," her mother said simply.

Not any longer, Elizabeth thought grimly, recalling the look on his face when she'd impetuously challenged him earlier.

Not any longer.

"I think it all could be rather more complicated than you imagine," she murmured.

Chapter Sixteen

He wasn't given to romantic gestures.

Then again, maybe he should at least acknowledge he was tempted to make one and get it off his mind, though Luke wasn't sure how much he could presume. He eyed the glittering case, the contents showing all colors from the palest aquamarine to the deepest scarlet. One of London's most fashionable stores, the establishment had an understated opulence, with velvet-lined cases and a discreet storefront on a popular street. Here, gentlemen could purchase gifts for their wives or their current paramours, depending on the depth of their purses. It was a very *expensive* and exclusive shop, and a man needed deep pockets to afford it.

His reasons for choosing it were even unclear to himself.

The topaz earrings, he decided, to match the elusive hint of darker gold strands in Madeline's hair. They were extravagant in price, yet tastefully elegant. And undeniably unusual—like the beautiful woman currently occupying his thoughts to an unsettling degree. He turned to his companion. "What do you think?"

"I think I have never seen you contemplate a jewelry case before as if it were actually a weighty life decision." Regina lifted a brow in an amused arch. "And I do adore the topaz eardrops, if that is what you are asking. What woman wouldn't? They are exquisite. And very old, if I am to judge. Elegant. I like the phallic shape of the stones."

Phallic shape. Only Regina would say that particular phrase in such a blasé tone.

The hovering clerk, sensing a sale, smiled ingratiatingly. "They are antique, my lord. I am told they once belonged to an Etruscan princess."

Luke didn't precisely trust the story, but the gold filigree was superb enough it might be true, and to him the stone simply had a lovely cylindrical symmetry. Italian goldsmiths were rare artisans back to antiquity, and he wanted to surprise Madeline. He'd address that impulse later. For now he told himself he was Madeline's lover and was duty bound to bestow a gift or two. "I'll take them. Please have it delivered to this address, with my compliments."

"Yes, my lord." The delighted clerk took the slip of vellum.

"And that," Regina said, tucking her arm in his as they went toward the door, "will be fodder for the gossip mill for days. You are usually more discreet. She must be special."

She was. Unfortunately, she *was*. He didn't need the complication.

"Since when do you pay attention to gossip?"

"Since you started seducing pretty young widows. Which I happen to know is against your principles."

"You have a quaint interest in my social life for someone so secretive about her own." He shot Regina a wry glance. "I make it a point not to ask you. Can't you extend me the same courtesy?"

"I am secretive for a very good reason. Besides, I'm older, you don't order my life, and we aren't talking about me. Viscount Altea is just a name. You mean more to me in another role, that of Luke Daudet, and I want to know what *he* is thinking."

He was a worldly man and guessed Regina had had lovers in the past, but she didn't choose them from the *haut ton*. Since he was her brother and loved her unconditionally, whatever made her happy was fine with him. Her private life was her own. They had always existed in a state of mutual camaraderie because they allowed each other distance. "Hmm," he said noncommittally.

"Is she?" Regina gazed up at him as they stepped outside the shop onto the busy thoroughfare. Bond Street was always full of pedestrians, and today was no exception.

He deliberately misunderstood, putting off his answer. "Is she what?"

"Special."

Yes, a voice in his head unequivocally answered. *No*, his pragmatic soul argued back. She was captivating and sensuous, and in Madeline's arms he experienced a unique sense of luxurious pleasure. Maybe it was because though she wasn't an innocent, she was definitely not experienced at dalliance either—far from it. A fatalistic sense that he was going to hurt her had existed from the first moment they met. "Since you are so persistent, I admit she's different."

"How?"

He chose evasion rather than answering the question. "Madeline is hardly in the first bloom of a debutante season. She is widowed and has a son. You know our relationship is perfectly acceptable. Why are you asking?"

"At what point did I sound censorious? I merely wondered if the unprecedented request for me to accompany you to select a present for the lady had some significance. You never have asked my opinion before, so I assign some special importance to this shopping trip."

She had a point, of course, and he had to concede it, albeit reluctantly. "Significance? Only that if I was going to extend the effort and expense, I'd prefer she like the gift."

"I see." She laughed. "Though may I say I doubt a man who would wager twenty thousand on a hand of cards is worried about the expense of one gift?"

His inward wince was reflected in his wry smile. "How long do you suppose it will take for me to live that down?"

Regina teasingly patted his arm, strolling along next to him, heedless of the misting rain gathering in crystal-line beads on her glossy hair. "Don't worry. Just a decade or two, I'd guess." Her gaze was speculative. "Care to tell me why you did it in the first place?"

"Accept the wager? Are we back to that tedious subject again?"

"One does wonder, Luke. You have your faults, but acting irresponsibly usually isn't one of them."

"Am I obligated to explain?"

"Ah, the Lord of the Manor tone. I wondered when you would trot it out. Yes, you are obligated, because I am your sister and I am asking with all due concern."

Pedestrians streamed by, hurrying in the late-afternoon drizzle. Luke guided his older sister around a puddle, trying to decide if he was annoyed or found her interest humorous. Regina tended to think about her work to the exclusion of the human beings around her. "Lord of the Manor? Are you implying I am arrogant upon occasion?" He did his best to ignore the warm summer mist settling on his hair and jacket.

"I wasn't clear?" She laughed, a light, melodic sound. "And here I thought I was putting you so neatly in your place. Actually, you sounded rather like Father when he was irritated with my incessant questions." There was a short pause, and she said simply, "I miss him."

To his credit, though Regina was illegitimate and female, their father had always treated her as his firstborn and made sure she was well educated and included in the family circle. Hence her militant—and sometimes inconvenient—independence. She'd inherited a nice portion of her own, and because she disdained convention of almost any kind, had declared flatly she was uninterested in sharing it with any high-handed male.

It seemed he was acting like one.

"I miss him too." Luke meant it. His affection for his parent aside, inheriting the title wasn't without drawbacks. He was now responsible for a great deal more than just his own actions.

"Is it possible you might settle into a permanent arrangement with the winsome Lady Brewer and produce the next Viscount Altea? He would be pleased. Socially I've heard she's most acceptable."

"No."

"No?" Regina said the word with an exploratory philosophical contemplation. "No, she's not acceptable, or no to the permanent arrangement?"

"The latter."

"Why?"

"Do I interrogate you about your future plans?"

"Will I like her?" Regina smiled serenely, ignoring the testy tone of his voice.

Would she? "Probably," he muttered, "but the two of you are unlikely to meet."

"We're alike, then." She waited for him to open the carriage door. "Good choice. You need someone independent enough to not be offended by your tendency to hide your feelings."

That sweeping assessment gave him pause, but before he could respond, she accepted his hand into the vehicle and settled into the seat, saying, "Now tell me about Elizabeth. Since this is her bow, I've been wondering how it is all progressing."

There was almost twenty years of difference in age

between his two sisters, so it was no wonder that they didn't interact more—notwithstanding that they looked uncannily alike and exhibited some of the same willful traits. "She's not showing a preference for anyone in particular." He clambered into the equipage and knocked to signal the driver. "Which might sound familiar. In some ways, she is very much like you."

"I never did have a strong belief in the sanctity of marriage for the sake of pleasing others."

"We all noticed." He suppressed a grin. Her eclectic nature was infamous.

"I'm glad our younger sister doesn't either. It is nice to know Elizabeth has her own mind."

"Oh, yes, she has that." Luke hesitated, but then shook himself out of it, for if he could confide in anyone, it was Regina. Privacy was sacrosanct to her. "I think Miles has other-than-cousinly feelings for her. He hasn't said anything, and I don't believe she's aware, but I've . . . noticed."

"It took you long enough." His sister's smile was indulgent and superior at the same time. "I wondered when it might occur to you."

Her attitude was no surprise. That was just Regina. He asked with an edge of exasperation, "Did you ever consider telling me?"

"No." Her mouth twitched. "What would be the enjoyment in that, may I ask? I love the delicious scenario of rakish viscount supervising the innocent ingenue. You commanded the attention of Wellington, but one nineteen-year-old girl—"

"Woman," he interrupted. "She's old enough to be courted, won, and wed, so I am doing my best to not think of her as a child."

"And yet failing. Your protective hackles are raised. Why?"

"What do you mean, *why*? We are talking about her future. Naturally I'm protective."

"Naturally," she repeated.

The urge to argue her open amusement was only barely suppressed and she knew it. "So, that aside, what should I do about Miles? I told Elizabeth it wasn't advisable to spend time alone with him. It isn't a matter of trust, but more of propriety."

Regina grinned, shaking out her damp cloak. "Ah, the wicked Viscount Altea preaching propriety . . . How did *that* settle with our younger sister?"

"I was more diplomatic than to put it that way."

"Darling Luke, how *did* you put it? Please tell me it wasn't an autocratic ultimatum."

Had it been? At the time he hadn't thought so, but now, with Regina's face alight with laughter, he wasn't sure. Elizabeth had certainly been put out, but had agreed readily enough. Too readily, if he recalled the conversation. He muttered, "Of course not."

The garters were crimson, the stockings black, and Madeline had no doubt as to the identity of the sender.

Fitch. That despicable villain.

Proving it, of course, would be somewhat more of a problem. There was no card, the box had been delivered anonymously, and she hardly wanted to rush out and tell Hubert what was enclosed in the package or emphasize her interest in who sent it.

Damn his salacious lordship.

With fingers that trembled, she lifted the note. It read: *I may not know with utmost certainty, but I can guess what happened.*

Getting the journal back was not going to be the end of it; she'd known it all along, despite Luke's assurance that flaunting their relationship would make Fitch take pause before he did anything else. There was one problem with ethical men when faced with their contemptible counterparts. The honorable side did not understand the depths of the black souls of the truly despicable. This was not a fairly waged war; it was something else entirely. Luke could not fathom harassing a woman in the way Fitch could. And it put him—both of them—at a disadvantage.

Yet Luke had retrieved the journal for her, though it was clear Fitch recalled some of the details all too well.

Yes, Colin had bought her black stockings and red garters and encouraged her to wear them now and again. It was a game they'd shared—a fantasy her husband had enjoyed, and that anyone was privy to the details made her furious.

Not ashamed. A bit mortified and angry, but not ashamed.

She'd found the passage just a few days before as she read through her husband's writings, so it was quite fresh in her mind:

Monday, April 16, this year 1808

Last evening when I retired I was gratified to find my lovely wife had embraced my gift. The sight of her waiting in her room for me, on the bed, clad in nothing but the stockings and garters was so arousing I fairly tore off my clothing. I fear I might have been too impetuous, but she seemed to enjoy it as much as I when I mounted her. She is so fair, the contrast between the black silk and her pale skin was tantalizing in a way I cannot explain. Though I know she is virtuous and demure, the suggestive image pleased me, for though I would never stray now that I have married, in the past I have always enjoyed variety in my bedmates. Madeline's allure is, as always, incomparable. I am a supremely lucky man. . . . I am already contemplating my next purchase . . .

The sound of someone clearing his throat brought her abruptly back into the moment. Madeline glanced up.

"This just arrived, my lady." Hubert hovered in the

doorway, this time extending a small box wrapped in silver paper. "It appears it is a day for deliveries and visitors."

Visitors? She was glad she'd just replaced the silk stockings back in the box. "Who is calling, Hubert?"

"Your mother and aunt, my lady."

Hardly fortuitous timing, but she summoned a smile as she accepted the elaborately wrapped gift, noting there was at least a card this time, whereas Fitch's gift had arrived unadorned. She set the package aside on a small table. "Please show them in and have some tea brought at once."

"Yes, madam."

With deliberation she took a calming breath and unobtrusively put the lid on Lord Fitch's obnoxious present, set the box on the floor by her chair, and braced herself. When her mother and Aunt Ida sailed through the doorway, she was smiling and hopefully composed. Madeline rose and dutifully went over to give them each a kiss on the cheek. "How lovely of you to stop by."

Her aunt was older than her mother, with pale hair tightly wound into a bun and a perpetually disapproving air that was particularly grating considering the circumstances. Of all the people Madeline didn't need to see at the moment, Ida was one of them. Though she'd expected the visit when rumors about Luke surfaced, she wasn't ready for it *now*. The disquieting gift had her admittedly rattled. Poise was needed when dealing with censure, and hers was currently hanging by a thread.

When her aunt raised her quizzing glass to examine her in an affectation she found quite annoying, Madeline suggested, striving for as much graciousness as possible, that they all have a seat.

For the first few minutes her mother attempted to make idle small talk, until Ida said bluntly, "Be quiet, Jane. You're chattering. We're here, Madeline, to find out why you have embarked on this ruinous course. Are you mad?"

The confines of the very civilized room grew very quiet. If it hadn't been for the arrival of the stockings, she would have been able to respond in the manner she'd rehearsed. As it was, she irrationally wished for Luke to be present, though that would cause even more of a furor.

Immediately she rejected that longing. She didn't, she reminded herself, need a man to take care of her. Up until Lord Fitch's unwanted and unsettling advances, she had done well enough on her own. "Ruinous course?" she asked, folding her hands.

"Your association with Altea has not been overlooked." Ida intoned the words with appropriate weighty condemnation, the starched lace of the collar of her gray gown matching the stiffness of her voice. "People are talking."

"I'm a widow." She did her best to keep any hint of defensiveness at bay. "And there is no reason for anyone to pay attention to whether or not I allow the viscount to escort me to a social event now and then."

"Darling, I know you are not that naive. He's very eligible, of course." Her mother smiled, but it was a bit tight. "Yet his reputation is hardly pristine. What are your plans?"

"I am not sure we have any." Madeline smiled back, hoping her expression didn't show that she knew beyond a doubt they absolutely had *none*.

Can you promise me you won't die . . .

She'd still not asked him about that disturbing remark. They were lovers, but she had yet to breach his considerable wall of emotional reserve. As far as she could tell, she'd not even managed to put a ladder against it. "Lord Altea is not prone to making plans, nor is there any call for it. We're . . . acquaintances. There's no need for alarm, Mother."

Aunt Ida made a derisive sound that could possibly qualify as a snort, though she would deny making such an undignified noise until her dying day. "It is not what *I* heard."

"People are talking, naturally." Madeline's mother could regally ignore anyone, even her sister. She had a specific purpose herself, or she wouldn't have agreed to the visit. "He's a conspicuous personage in the highest circles. He counts the Duke of Berkeley's son as one of his best friends, and also Lord Longhaven, who tends to be elusive at best."

"I am aware of who his friends are." Madeline sat back against the settee, doing her best to not overreact or become too combative. "I'm getting the impression their notoriety is the point of this conversation. Despite his less than pristine reputation, may I point out Lord Alexander recently married and married well?"

"Good for the Earl of Hathaway's daughter, but do you think *you* can bring Altea up to scratch?" Ida asked bluntly. "He's not known for his fondness of permanence. Quite the opposite, in fact."

It took a great deal of restraint to not point out that she was twenty-six years old and her life—and what she did with it—was entirely her affair. Part of the purpose of this visit was concern, no doubt, but part of it was just plain interference. She'd known what it would be like the very instant she dashed out the door the evening Luke so restively abandoned the dinner party, so this wasn't a surprise precisely; it was just irritating.

But she did have a family, not to mention a child, and though her own happiness should count for something, she did have a certain responsibility to them all. "Have you considered I might not *wish* to bring him up to scratch? All he's done is escort me to one social event, and as you pointed out, he's not exactly known for his monkish habits. I was happily married once. I don't know I am convinced Lord Altea would make an admirable husband."

"Perhaps you should have thought of that before you appeared in public on his arm."

"I did," she said calmly.

Her mother and aunt exchanged outraged glances,

but the arrival of a maid with the tea trolley halted the conversation. After she'd poured, Madeline deliberately steered the topic in another direction and sent for Trevor, who was delighted to get out of his lessons, as lemon tarts were infinitely preferable to mathematics. He was well behaved for a seven-year-old boy, but his exuberant antics were still distracting enough to quell further interrogation.

When her mother and aunt left, she was relieved and introspective, her cup of tepid tea forgotten on the table. To her surprise, she was just relieved the discussion was over. While she wasn't indifferent to their opinion or the gossip, neither bothered her as much as she had expected.

"Aren't you going to open it, Mama?"

"Open what, darling?"

"That." With a small child's fascination for shiny, wrapped boxes, her son pointed to the small package on the table beside the settee where she sat.

Madeline had all but forgotten it, preoccupied with her conflicted feelings and the first true repercussions of her relationship with the notorious Viscount Altea. "I suppose I should." She smiled and let him hand her the box with a small flourish, his expression intensely curious.

The card was written in an unfamiliar hand, the impersonal message only announcing the identity of the sender, yet her pulse quickened predictably. Pulling the ribbon free, she slipped off the paper and found a jewelers box, the stamped insignia of the exclusive shop making her raise her brows. Inside, against white velvet, the amber stones took her breath away. And when she lifted one of the earrings, the exquisite gold work of the setting and uniqueness of the piece brought a soft smile that had nothing to do with the undoubted value of the gift, but the thoughtfulness that had gone into the selection.

Luke Daudet was many things. Resourceful, confident, undeniably dangerous, with a touch of arrogant male, emotionally distant but utterly charming when he chose to be . . . and, apparently, he had a thoughtful side she had yet to glimpse before this moment.

The gift was . . . *perfect*. Baubles didn't impress her in particular. She had jewelry. This was different and pleased her very much.

And he'd bothered. She knew Luke well enough to recognize that the act itself was out of character for a man of his supreme detachment.

"Pretty," Trevor said, touching the dangling stone with a fingertip, and lost interest. "May I please have another cake?"

He shouldn't, of course. As it was, she doubted he would eat his dinner.

"Just one," she said with a smile, because happiness should be shared and she was unreasonably, foolishly happy at the moment.

The vindictive Lord Fitch be damned.

Chapter Seventeen

"**I** hope he knows what he's doing." Alex St. James sat on the terrace of the stately home a Duke of Berkeley had built six centuries ago, his gaze on the smooth expanse of the green park, a pond shimmering in the distance. A pair of swans floated on the surface, serene in the afternoon sunshine.

Michael contemplated the question. After a moment, he sighed and turned his face into the breeze, relishing the clean scent of grass and water after weeks in the city. "Luke wants to protect her, and I think the way he is going about it would be a good tactic, except for two very salient points."

"And those are?" Alex's eyes held concern. His dark hair was ruffled, his attire the epitome of country gentleman. In a white, full-sleeved shirt and dark breeches, his boots well-worn, he looked deceptively relaxed.

There were times when Michael wondered if any of them would truly recover from the war. Though he could speak only for himself, contentment was a capricious illusion and emotional involvement like a match to gunpowder. Even Alex, happily married, with fatherhood looming in the not-so-distant future, held his guarded edge.

"It's clear to an observant eye—and believe me, all of society is agog—that he is spending time with the beauteous Lady Brewer, not just in public, but in her bed as well. I am sure he justifies it by saying it will dissuade Fitch from bothering the lady, but as far as I can tell he has lost sight of the initial problem."

"And that is?"

"How the devil did the blackguard get the journal of a titled gentleman who has been dead nearly five years anyway? A friend of mine relieved Lord Fitch of the pilfered property and gave it back to Lady Brewer, but I have been asking myself ever since then . . . how did Fitch come by it in the first place? He's an amoral rodent, but hardly a canny thief."

Alex leveled a look his way. "I know you well enough to realize you never speculate this way. Did you actually come out to the country to tell me Luke is squiring around a lady that might have finally thawed his frozen stance on marriage? It is unusual, I admit, but then again, I'm not sure why you'd rush over to tell me. You tend to keep secrets, not reveal them."

"Actually, I don't believe his stance on marriage has been thawed at all. But I did come here to discuss that aspect of the matter."

"You never interfere unless asked, or unless there is an alarm raised. Clarification would be welcome."

Friends who knew you well could be advantageous allies or be annoyingly astute. Michael smiled, but it didn't reach his eyes. "What if I told you Lady Brewer's husband was related to someone the Crown suspects of collaboration with the French for most of the war?"

There was a pause. His friend gazed at him across the table with an open air of consternation. "I'd say," Alex said finally, "you have, as usual, more trickery in your right pocket than the average conjuror. Who is it?"

"Lord Brewer's cousin."

"I . . . see. When did you learn this?"

"Two years ago. At the time we were all in Spain and it meant little more to me than a name on a piece of paper. Now it takes on a singular significance."

"Two years ago? Does Luke know?"

"I haven't mentioned it yet because I have no idea if it means anything." Michael abstractly watched a butterfly land on a small, decorative bush with tiny yellow flowers. "My theory is the journal must have been stolen in case there was some damning mention of Brewer's cousin in the text. Maybe a visit that would put our suspect in the wrong place and ruin an alibi, or show this person had access to certain information. Any number of scenarios could apply."

"Do you suspect Lord Brewer of being party to treasonous activity?"

He didn't. Michael had sat and thought about it and come to the conclusion that Colin May had been an unwitting accomplice, if he were one at all. He shook his head. "No. There's nothing in the journal whatsoever that is suspicious. I read it carefully. I even wondered if there might be an embedded code, but as far as I could tell it was just ramblings of a man with an ordinary life, and a contented man, at that."

"You *read* the nefarious journal?"

"Of course."

Alex stared at him, laughed, and then shook his head. "I forget sometimes the very definition of what you do means you know things that perhaps you shouldn't. Go on."

"Take my word. I passed over the details of his amorous encounters with his beautiful wife. I gather intelligence, but I am not a voyeur." Michael crossed his booted feet negligently at the ankle. He had a conscience; he just reserved its admonishments for the important moments in life. He had only invaded Lady Brewer's intimate world in his quest to decipher questionable possibilities in her husband's journal—and he wouldn't have unless it was his duty to do so. He wasn't Fitch. The journal had been interesting, but not on a salacious level.

He went on with a wry smile, "Besides, I've known how the sexual act is done for quite some time, and as we both know, participation is much more satisfying than reading about it. Lord Brewer's ill-advised, detailed descriptions of how much he enjoyed his wife's bountiful charms aside, I found nothing incriminating in the journal. Neither did whoever took it, for the culprit gave it away or sold it to Fitch or maybe even passed it to a third party we don't know about yet. At some point the lascivious earl came into possession of it, but he isn't the catalyst, or even truly involved, if I had to take a stand on the matter. The journal itself isn't the issue. This is about motive."

A frown furrowed Alex's brow. "I suppose you are right. I see now your dilemma. Why was the journal stolen so recently?"

"We don't know when precisely it was taken. From what Luke told me, Lady Brewer didn't even look for it until some of Fitch's comments were so detailed, she wondered where he could possibly be getting his information. That was when she found the item in question was gone from a locked drawer. So you are right. It's more a puzzle of why has it resurfaced so recently."

"Why not just ask Fitch how the devil he got a hold of it?"

Michael shook his head. "Once a soldier, always a soldier, apparently. March straight on the most direct course. My approach is somewhat more oblique. Besides, I am confident his lordship will simply deny he ever had it, and I dislike the idea of him making a connection between the disappearance of the journal and me. Not that I mind him knowing I was responsible for the burglary of his home—he had stolen property and was using it for blackmail, and therefore forfeited his right to privacy—but there are a few loose ends for the

Crown to clean up, even with Bonaparte disposed." He paused, and then murmured, "There was espionage on both sides, naturally. In a war, there are always secrets being traded. England has its share of traitors we haven't caught yet. It rankles to think of them walking free."

"Is that your capacity for the king at the moment? Unearthing elusive, disloyal spies?"

The butterfly flitted off on a flutter of brilliant wings. Michael said nothing, and just lounged in his chair.

His friend gave a wry laugh. "I don't know why I even asked. Dismiss the question. Now, then, what is it you want from me? God knows I owe you. Your special skills, as it were, helped me immensely in clearing up that little matter between my family and Amelia's."

"It was my pleasure." And it *was* a pleasure to see Alex so deeply in love with his beautiful young wife. Michael's role in helping to settle the dispute between their quarreling families had been a reward unto itself. "And it seems to me the debt at the time was mine. You did haul me out of that French prison."

St. James waved that feat away with a casual lift of a long-fingered hand. "That was war. I was doing my duty."

It *had* been war, but it had also been an example of the depth of their friendship. Michael knew full well if both Luke and Alex hadn't insisted on a push for action to mobilize a rescue, he would be dead. Spies operating miles behind French lines were considered expendable when captured. Alex's tenacity and Luke's influence with Wellington were the reason he was still alive.

What was odd was that though he remembered the capture—there had been a double operative in their midst, and to this day he still didn't know which of his comrades had betrayed him—he recalled very little of the torture, though the scars were a very real reminder. What he remembered most was the cold, gray day and the thin sunlight as Alex carried him outside, the icy wind penetrating through the shredded layers of his bloody shirt, and Alex staggering under the burden of his weight. Michael had lost consciousness, but when he woke in the tent with the surgeon hovering over him, he'd known that despite the pain, he was alive due to the perseverance of his friends.

Alex St. James owed him nothing. Yes, he'd helped straighten out a small misunderstanding between Lady Amelia's family and the St. Jameses, but in his mind, it was little enough compared to his debt.

"I was thinking of John," Michael said neutrally. "I think he might be in a unique position to help me with a delicate matter."

Alex looked amused. "My notorious older brother, at work for the Crown? I am sure the idea would appeal to his adventurous spirit. What can he do that you can't? After all, you are also a marquess. How is his assistance needed?"

"He can talk to Baroness Schaefer on a personal level I cannot, for I believe they were once good friends."

"That's a polite way of saying she was once his lover."

"I am polite to a fault, as you know."

"Especially when it serves your purposes." Alex grinned. "So, tell me, what should he ask of his former light o' love? I'm trying to imagine what the lady might know that could help you."

The envelope was in the pocket of his tailored jacket, and Michael reached in to retrieve it and hand it over. "Just give him this, if you will."

"Of course." Alex eyed it curiously but didn't ask questions. "Can you stay for dinner? Amelia would love to play hostess, even if she is napping at the moment. I'm afraid the pregnancy makes her sleepy in the afternoons."

"I'd like to stay." Michael rose. "But can I accept the invitation for another time?"

"Urgent business?"

"You might say so."

"I'll get this to John right away." Alex tapped a forefinger on the envelope lying on the table, his gaze inquiring. "But before you dash off, you said there were two salient points that made you wonder if Luke's involvement with Madeline May was wise. The first is obviously there is more to the theft of the journal than meets the eye. What's the second?"

Michael considered for a moment and then said quietly, "He isn't free."

"Because of what happened in Spain." Alex's dark eyes held a troubled glint.

"Because of what happened in Spain, yes."

"I knew he was involved with Maria, of course, and she was killed sometime after Badajoz."

"Involved? Yes, he married her." Michael's smile was bleak.

Alex was shocked. It was clear in the way his eyes widened and the sudden stillness of his posture. "He *married* her?"

Was this his story to tell? Michael wasn't sure, but this was Alex, and Michael thought that though Luke hadn't spoken of it himself, he wouldn't mind. "They found a small church with a priest who would perform the ceremony, but it was dangerously close to the French lines. On their way back to the convent where she had taken refuge, they ran into a small French patrol. Maria was killed and Luke wounded badly enough he was left for dead. The Frogs burned the convent to the ground."

"Good God." Alex sat back, his dark eyes bleak. "On their wedding day. He never told me."

"He never told me either." Michael had learned about it through intelligence channels. Luke had not ever mentioned it, so neither had he.

"I knew it had happened," Alex slowly said. "I knew she'd died, but not about the wedding. No wonder he is so . . . closed. She was killed on their wedding day. How does a man recover from that? As one who dearly loves his wife, it makes me rethink my preoccupations with insignificant matters. How could I not know this?"

"He doesn't want to discuss it. Can you blame him?"

"No," Alex agreed softly. "No. Why revisit that pain? I wouldn't be able to bear it. How does he cope with it?"

"I've never been married, so I can't answer with any accuracy," Michael said grimly, "but I am going to venture a guess and say he doesn't. But perhaps Lady Brewer can help him."

"I thought we were going to the opera." Madeline peered out the window of the carriage, her shadowed features showing surprise, the length of the journey finally registering.

Luke smiled with bland reassurance. "I thought I'd surprise you with something more entertaining than doomed lovers and pathos. Perhaps it sounds less than cosmopolitan to admit it, but I have never cared all that much for Italian drama. It overshadows my enjoyment of the music, however superb it might be."

"What do you have in mind instead?" She sounded suitably wary, and so she should be. Tonight she was dazzling in white satin with a deep gold trim at the neckline and hem, the sleeves ending at the elbow in a froth of lace, her fan a work of art with ivory carvings on the handle and an exotic motif of leopards and charging elephants. The earrings he'd given her dangled in an enticing sway against the slender column of her neck as the carriage moved along the cobbled street, and her eyes were large and dark as she gazed at him in open, charming confusion.

Good. She had *him* fairly confused as well, and seeing her wearing those earrings had sparked a certain unreasonable possessiveness, as if they were a symbol of a bond he wanted to ignore but couldn't.

The facts were actually quite simple. He was deeply attracted to her and he had never tried to deny it. He knew she was absolutely the wrong woman to become involved with, because with Madeline the word *involved* took on a frightening significance.

And yet he'd done it anyway.

"I wanted you to myself tonight," he said with uncharacteristic candor, trying to gauge her reaction. "I'm following an unprecedented whim."

"You are never whimsical, Altea."

"Try me," he said softly to her challenge.

Her fan snapped open, ostensibly to remedy the lack of fresh air. "Oh, I've *tried* you," Madeline murmured, her lashes lowering provocatively. "I believe that is what got us both in trouble in the first place."

"*Are* we in trouble?" The moment he said it, he wished he hadn't.

"I don't know. Are we?"

There was no question of him answering that volatile inquiry. Instead, he chose to return to sexual repartee. "If we are speaking in innuendo, my lady, may I say I enjoyed that initial sampling immensely?" Comfortably sprawled on the seat, he regarded her with heavy-lidded eyes. "Too much so, as I was unable to resist a repeat performance. I had no intention of seeing you again after that night last year."

That was honest.

"Can I express how delighted I am you changed your mind?"

There and then, she silenced him, and it was ironic that *he* was delighted too. And he had every intention of being particularly delighted *this* night. If sybaritic pleasure was all they had . . . then he wanted to make the most of it.

"I think we are in accord there."

"Will you tell me, then, where we are going?"

"No." He smiled to lighten the denial. "Don't you like surprises?"

"Only pleasant ones, Altea."

He stifled a laugh. The austere tone of her voice was balanced by the speculative look in her eyes. He said, "I always strive to be infinitely pleasant to you. Have I not succeeded?"

She didn't answer at once but continued to examine him before she finally murmured, "You have succeeded to an unsettling degree."

"Is that a compliment or a criticism?"

"Both, I suppose. I don't know."

He debated the finer points of addressing the ambiguous nature of her response, but she looked too young and uncertain in contrast to the sophisticated cut of her gown, so his reaction was more of tender indulgence.

A revelation in and of itself, as he was more a passionate lover than a sentimental one. With Madeline he was both. "I'd say, then, that I wish you would trust me in this instance, and if I disappoint, feel free to be as vocal as you wish. How is that?"

"It isn't a secret," she said quietly. "I have gone this far. So it is clear I trust you."

I have gone this far ...

The inn was outside Mayfair, discreetly so, and as he'd made all the arrangements ahead of time, they were expected. Luke got out and helped Madeline alight. The unprepossessing exterior made her glance uncertainly at him, but he took her elbow and guided her toward the doorway, leaning close to whisper, "You can trust me."

He meant it. All four of those usually simple words.

In this case, they weren't simple at all.

Inside the establishment was quiet, the delicious smell of food in the air, and as he'd requested the best parlor for their meal, they were seated in a small room with low ceilings and an unlit, massive stone fireplace. Tapers burned and the windows were open to the small walled garden, making the flames flicker. The courses were to his specification: chilled cucumber soup, Dover sole, a rich duck confit with port wine, beefsteak, and, from his own pastry chef, a beautiful concoction of custard, caramel, and whipped cream for dessert. He'd also had a variety of wines brought in, and champagne was served after the last course by one of his staff, a young footman who was the grandson of the butler who had served the

Daudet family for decades, his silence guaranteed by both loyalty and a healthy monetary incentive.

Renting out the entire homey inn for the night was a stroke of genius, he decided as he watched Madeline daintily lick her spoon after devouring her dessert. The neighborhood was out of the way of the beau monde; the elderly proprietor unlikely to gossip, considering what he'd been paid; and, for once, they could spend the entire night together. He'd planned this the moment Madeline had mentioned her sister-in-law was taking Trevor along with his cousins to the country for several days. Once the idea had occurred to him, it wouldn't let him be until he'd made the arrangements.

Perfect. He wouldn't ask her to take time away from her son, but with the opportunity right in front of him to get her entirely alone, how could he resist?

That's the trouble, he thought. *I can't.*

"There's no one else here," she observed, setting aside her glass. "I know there is staff in the kitchen, but otherwise it is very quiet."

"The walls are thick."

"But I am not." Madeline's observation was dry. "We are the only guests, aren't we? Why go to all this trouble and expense when we could simply stay at my town house?"

"A quiet dinner together cannot be given a price. Besides, I don't want to have to watch for the dawn."

"My maid already knows." Her dark eyes were more exotic than ever in the candlelight. "She hasn't said anything to me, but I have been the recipient of more than a few sly smiles."

"But she has never seen me in your bed." He was more worldly, more in tune with the subtleties of the razor teeth of the *ton*. "It matters. A guess is different. If she caught us fair out, imagine that scandal."

"You are too gallant."

"I'm a damn fool," he said out loud, which he didn't intend, but to be in this moment, looking into the depths of her eyes and knowing—knowing—what was to come in the hours ahead when he had her alone and all to himself, made him reckless when he was rarely out of control. He wanted her and wanted her freely, and as sentimental and absurd and simple as it was, he had a fantasy of waking next to her.

"Aren't we both fools?" Madeline laughed, the light sound stirring him, and not just his passion, but his heart.

Good God, his heart.

No, not so. He didn't have one any longer. It was in a grave on a Spanish hillside. When Maria had died, he was so sure he had figuratively died along with her.

Maybe you were wrong.

God help him, maybe he *was* wrong.

"Yes," he said in dark agreement, and stood, extending his hand. "Shall we go upstairs? This surprise has just begun."

Chapter Eighteen

It was a fairy-tale scene, albeit a somewhat humble one. Lit candles on the mantel, a comfortable tester bed taking up most of the space of the room, mullioned windows letting in a soft night breeze, and rose petals liberally scattered . . . everywhere. Across the linens of the bed, the floor, even on the windowsills. The scent of the crushed flowers was heady.

Madeline had to stifle a laugh at Luke's expression. He muttered, "I believe I said *romantic*. I didn't realize that included decimating innocent flowers."

He said romantic. That, she found, was romantic enough in itself. Not to mention the closeness of his tall body in the small room, his height such that his head was just below the beams of the timbered ceiling, his elegant evening wear an accent for the classic, fine-bone structure of his features.

"All this effort is worth a reward, I think." Madeline heard the husky undertone in her voice, and knew a man of his sophistication wouldn't miss it either. She took the step necessary to be close enough to reach up and touch him, lightly running a questing fingertip along the curve of his lower lip. "Can you think of anything you fancy?"

"I might be able to come up with an idea or two." Luke pulled her into the circle of his arms and lowered his head, his mouth finding hers with gentle urgency, his hands spanning her waist.

Perhaps this truly is a brilliant idea, she thought, luxuriating in the feel of him against her, and the slow, heated possession of his kiss. It *was* different, not quite so rushed, so secretive, so forbidden. . . .

"Shall we undress?" Luke murmured against her lips. "We can discuss the remainder of our evening more comfortably."

She'd been bereft, as she always was, when Trevor had departed with Marta and his rambunctious cousins for the countryside, but she trusted and loved her sister-in-law, and Colin's family deserved to be part of his son's life. Normally she endured the quiet house and the emptiness his absence left in her life, even if it was for a short while, and she wondered now if she should feel guilty for her inner glow of happiness that developed from this time with Luke.

No, she decided a moment later, because her life was important too, and though she would die for her son and put him before her own needs without hesitation, she didn't love him less for loving someone else.

Love. Though it was probably not the best lesson in self-preservation or a prudent course, she was afraid it was all too true. Her feelings went far beyond infatuation and she'd known it all along, if she cared to be honest with herself. Why had she never been tempted by anyone else? His physical attractiveness aside, in Luke she sensed a kindred soul . . . a man she liked for what he was, not just a lover, but someone who could also be a friend, a partner, a lifelong companion . . .

Not that acknowledging she was in love with the un-attainable Lord Altea was reasonable or prudent, but in his presence she'd proved to be neither of those and she'd probably known a year ago it had happened or she never would have gone back into his arms in the first place. So, to put the evening in perspective, she mused as Luke turned her by the shoulders and began to unfasten her gown, they deserved this time together.

She needed it, and she had an intuitive sense so did he.

A second chance at love was surely a rare gift, and if he didn't return her affection, he still had gone out of his way to make a special time for them together. It filled her with a quiet joy.

Together.

His mouth grazed her nape as his fingers were busy with slipping buttons loose one by one, and then warm palms slid over her bared shoulders. "You enchant me."

Madeline leaned her head back against his chest, taking in a long, slow breath. Warmth spread through her limbs as his lips tickled her collarbone. The scent of his hair was woodsy and masculine where it brushed her cheek. "Are you implying I cast a wicked spell on you, my lord?"

He laughed in a low, intoxicating exhale across her throat. "*Something* has happened to my good sense."

To both of our good sense, she thought hazily, resting her head against his shoulder, delicious sensation holding her prisoner. Her nipples peaked both from what he was doing at the moment and what she knew was to come, and a soft sound echoed in the room as he slid her dress downward. The whisper of the silk across her sensitive skin wrung a second telling sigh as it pooled around her feet.

"You're exquisitely distracting." His hands slipped up to cup her breasts through the thin lace of her chemise. "Ask my steward. I paid very little attention to his report on the estate today. Instead I was thinking about this." His thumb made a slow, tantalizing circle around her nipple. "When he asked me the same question three times in a row, I rescheduled the appointment with my apologies."

"I don't know if I am distracting, but I am certainly distracted." His touch elicited tiny pulses of pleasure. "You are far too practiced at what you are doing at the moment, but I can't summon sufficient outrage."

"Because of my undeniable charm?" His thumb moved again in a sensuous curving motion, as teasing as his voice.

"That must be it," she murmured, pliant against him.

When he lifted her onto the bed, she closed her eyes, the moment overwhelming because she knew she *loved* him. This time, when he'd divested himself of his clothing and stripped away her shift and they lay skin to skin, their mouths softly touching, hands exploring, the room silent except for the chorus of insects in the garden and the occasional cry of a night bird, she could imagine not just the pleasure, but . . . so much more.

How dangerous. She shouldn't.

"The earrings suit you," he told her, his smile sinful, "Especially now, when they are your only adornment, besides your incomparable beauty."

"That's somewhat flowery for you, my lord." She reached between them and stroked the velvet-smooth length of his arousal. "Especially when I can tell you are interested in an activity other than conversation."

"Astute and beautiful." He licked her lower lip. "What a delightful combination."

Luke touched and aroused her with skillful ease, and when he lowered himself between her thighs, it was his tongue, not his cock, that teased her to the trembling edge of release. Her climax was swift and vivid and vocal enough that she was glad the inn was nearly deserted. Dropping a light kiss on her thigh and smiling, Luke rose and smoothly joined their bodies in a slow, measured thrust of sex into sex, male into female.

If only joining our lives could be as easy, she thought through her sensual haze, adjusting her pelvis instinctively to accept the deepest penetration of his erotic movements, her hands on his tense shoulders.

At this moment, when they were so intimately one, it was too easy to be caught up in the glorious pleasure, the strong feel of him over and inside her, the rhythmic communion of their bodies....

The white-hot pinnacle came again, and this time he made an inarticulate sound from deep in his chest and dropped his head, his eyes tightly shut as he stiffened, the pulse of his ejaculation hot and forceful. Madeline clung to him, the hot, liquid rush of his release in conjunction with the wash of scorching ecstasy....

And inside her. Deep inside, as close as two human beings could be, with his hips hard against her open thighs and her hands at the small of his back.

He hadn't withdrawn, and she could tell the moment he realized it, for he went very still, his breathing arrested for a moment before he released it in a rush of ... what? Frustration, fear, or anger at himself?

Don't, she pleaded silently. *Don't ruin this beautiful moment with an apology.* An unplanned pregnancy would be a life-altering event—she knew this and he had been careful so far—but what had just happened would be utterly spoiled if he regretted it with such swift immediacy.

"Open your eyes," he said softly.

Slowly her lashes lifted and she found him staring down at her, his weight lightly braced on his elbows, their bodies still intimately joined, his tousled hair brushing the clean line of his jaw.

To her surprise, he asked in the same low tone, "What are you feeling right now? Tell me."

That I love you. That I'd want your child, if you just gave me one.

No, neither of those would do. It was what she wanted to say, but was too afraid it was not what he wanted to hear.

"Life takes us along a winding path," Madeline whis-

pered, smoothing her fingertips along one of his downy
brows, a smile hovering on her mouth. "We cannot control everything, try as we might. As trite as it may sound,
what will be will be."

His silver eyes were unreadable, but at least they
weren't filled with regret. "*You* have an unfortunate effect on my self-control."

Not exactly a flowery declaration of love, but it was
a concession. She heard it in his voice. Madeline murmured, "I think it is obvious you affect my judgment
also."

"I'm trying to be careful with you."

What did that mean? Careful in that he didn't want
to impregnate her, or was there caution for another reason? "I am not a delicate flower, my lord."

He grinned then, looking younger and lighter. "No,
indeed. You are very much a passionate, independent
woman, Lady Brewer. I simply meant I'm trying to
not make this complicated, but I fear it is happening
anyway."

"My very point." She smiled, loving him more for his
concern for her, for what had to be a difficult admission
from a man who had wealth and power and was used to
getting what he wanted and walking away from what he
didn't.

His gaze was searching and intent. "The damage is
done, you are saying. If there is a child, we will deal with
that situation as it happens?"

Careful to seem unruffled by the possibility, she said,
"A woman does not conceive every time. It took Colin
and me nearly half a year before I was pregnant with
Trevor."

"Very well. I will concur it would ruin the tenor of the
evening to worry about it now." With a muffled laugh, he
withdrew and rolled to his back. "Anticipation is apparently an aphrodisiac. That was over quickly. Should I be
embarrassed?"

"In my opinion, there is something to be said for all

due speed in some cases." Madeline opted for the same light tone, doing her best to keep the tumult of her feelings under control, but not quite able to summon fashionable detachment, not after making love with such fevered enjoyment.

"In some cases, the choice is taken from you," he said in wry amusement. "I shall have to assuage the blow to my manly pride on such a quick performance. Any objections to long and slow and . . . wicked?"

"I am sure with you any pace will be an unforgettable experience."

Something flickered in his eyes that told her she'd said the words too softly and with too much sincerity. His reaction didn't escape her, and quickly she said with teasing inflection, "Though you haven't impressed me too much with your wickedness yet, Altea."

"Haven't I?" The corner of his mouth lifted lazily. Arms folded behind his head, he lounged in unselfconscious nudity, the light defining the ridges of hard muscle on his torso and the bulge of his biceps. His softened cock nestled between powerful thighs, and she couldn't help but compare him to what she envisioned of Spartan warriors: smooth, sleek, all dangerous male. "I'll have to rectify that oversight."

"I look forward to it." There, she'd regained some of her feigned insouciance. Madeline stretched, gratified when his gaze went immediately to her uplifted bare breasts and then drifted lower, to the juncture of her thighs.

"I doubt it will take long," he murmured, reaching out to touch the damp triangle of her pubic hair. "You could tempt an angel from heaven, and I think we both know I am not an angel. And you are so conveniently close. . . ."

This position, Luke thought as primal, delirious pleasure saturated his senses, was intensely satisfying physically, but he found he missed watching the flush rise under skin and the way her eyelashes fluttered just before she surrendered to orgasmic release, and from behind he also didn't experience the telltale frantic bite of her nails on his shoulders. On his knees, he grasped Madeline's hips, drove even more insistently into her contracting passage, and lost the battle to withhold his own climax when he heard her breathless scream.

What the hell am I doing? He wondered in the chaotic aftermath as his heart finally stopped trying to beat out of his chest. They were both covered in perspiration, twined together, his cheek resting on the silk of her hair.

Fucking her into a state of exhaustion isn't going to solve anything.

Almost the moment the thought intruded, he mentally corrected himself. The crude euphemism for what he experienced when he touched Madeline didn't apply. He made love to her. Unfortunately, he knew the difference between casual sexual congress with a woman and something deeper.

Hence the problem, dammit.

Earlier she'd looked at him. . . . and, well, he recognized that soft light in her eyes. It was indelibly etched in his psyche, as if without speaking she had given him a gift he couldn't return or forget. There was a very good reason he'd avoided her for the past year, and now that he certainly wasn't holding on to his resolve to keep himself as distant as possible, he needed to deal with the possible consequences of his actions.

He could easily have gotten her with child. After that first fiery joining, he had yielded to both the temptation of it and the knowledge that he'd already been unforgivably reckless and made love to her without reservation or restraint. Had the impulse been entirely unconscious and prompted by exquisite pleasure, or had he gambled on fate deciding the future for him?

Tomorrow, he promised himself, too content, too

aware of her soft, tempting body gathered against his, cognizant that happiness could be a fleeting emotion. In the morning he'd address his disquiet, but for now ...

"Lord Fitch sent me something."

The small declaration jarred into the moment. Luke raised his head and peered at Madeline's averted face, his reaction visceral. "What?"

"In his disgusting manner." She made a face. "Stockings and garters. Colin used to ... well, he used to like me to wear stockings and garters and nothing else. I haven't read all the journal quite yet ... I can't bear to now, but that is in there. It must be Fitch. No one else would know."

Michael might know, but Michael was the last person who would torture Madeline, quite the contrary. Without reservation he'd retrieved the journal for her, not to mention his criticism over the destruction of her chaste reputation. Luke's hand, where it rested possessively against her stomach, flattened involuntarily, pulling her closer in instinctive protectiveness. He said with lethal softness, "The earl apparently has no desire to live to a ripe old age. I've tired of his antics."

"He isn't worth rising at dawn." She touched his hand, smoothed her fingers over the back of it, and then twined their fingers together. "But you are touchingly gallant."

The charge of gallantry was dubious to his mind, but was he infuriated at the idea of Fitch continuing to torment her? Absolutely. "Fitch's vicious tendencies need to be corrected, and the pleasure all mine."

"Don't, for my sake." Madeline turned in his arms, small and warm against him, her voice holding an edge of sleepiness because he had kept her up very, very late. "I just told you because I can't really tell anyone else and it upset me."

All the more reason for him to annihilate the man responsible for her distress. "Don't think about it—about him—again," he told her, kissing the small, delicate hollow beneath her ear. "He's finished with his little, nasty jokes. You have my word."

"Hmm . . ."

That was hardly an answer, and Luke saw she'd slipped into sleep so quickly he wondered if she had slept at all the night before. In the moonlight, her hair was gilded to a pale glimmer, and he held her carefully, a contrast to their explosive passion.

If he could only erase the past . . .

But he couldn't. No. It was emotional suicide to even try, and he was done with the idea of sacrificing oneself on the altar of bleak memory. Bitter experience existed—to an extent, every human being had to deal with it, because life by definition involved loss and betrayal—and to face it made him pragmatic, not a dreamer.

Maria had trusted him with the same sweet, giving generosity. She'd carried his child, and he had married her, and then she had died. . . .

The pattern terrified him.

In Spain, on one chill spring night, he'd learned not to dream.

So, he pointed out to himself in the darkness as the candles began to gutter, *I might not be able to offer love on bended knee, but I can protect Madeline from the machinations of her current nemesis.*

As magical as the evening had been, in the light of day, their parting took on the clarity of practicality.

They'd eaten breakfast in the same small, intimate dining room, the ordinary trappings of coffee, currant scones, country ham, and shirred eggs somehow different with Luke across the table, casual in just a white, full-sleeved shirt unbuttoned at the neck, his smile quicksilver as he glanced up and caught her watching him over the rim of her cup. The conversation had been commonplace, with careful avoidance of future plans, and he'd managed the transition from passionate lover to polite acquaintance with unsettling ease.

For her it was not nearly as easy to dismiss their closeness, the intimacies they'd shared, the possibility she might have conceived his child.

Actually, she wondered if it was easy for him either, for he was remarkably quiet when they got into his carriage, and didn't speak until they arrived at her door in the midmorning.

Her neighbors would not miss *that*, she was sure.

"Thank you," she said with simple sincerity when he lifted her out of the vehicle. "You went through a great deal of trouble."

The sunlight picked up the highlights in his hair and cast his face in chiseled angles. "Thank *you*," he said softly, "for being very much worth it."

"I imagine that if before there was speculation we are lovers, it is no longer conjecture, as you are bringing me home in my formal gown." Madeline was resigned enough she managed to smile.

His hands dropped from her waist, his smile rueful. "I suppose I only planned carefully enough to ensure I could awaken in the morning with you in my arms. Men don't have society watching their every movement with such avid concentration. But our association is hardly in question anyway. Do you mind?"

Did she?

No. Not considering she'd just experienced the night of her dreams. Wicked dreams, perhaps, but if a dream involved Viscount Altea, that went without saying.

"I'm not as indifferent as you are, my lord," she said, smiling demurely, "but I am learning quickly enough."

He nodded, his expression changing. "I'm leaving London tomorrow for a few days. I'll call on you upon my return."

She truly was too involved, for the very idea of him leaving made her heart tighten. "Have a safe journey, then."

He nodded, his expression impassive, and then he clambered back into his carriage and it pulled away.

Madeline shook herself mentally, realizing she was standing there in front of her town house, and quickly went up the steps. She didn't want to watch his carriage go down the street, leaving her. She wanted nothing to tarnish the memory of what they had shared.

The elusive Lord Altea had planned a romantic tryst.

Surely that was some sort of triumph.

Chapter Nineteen

The sound of the small fountain was quiet, the musical fall of the water reminiscent of the country, even in a walled city garden. There were birds also, finches that flittered among the ornamental bushes and more melodic songbirds, a background to the noise of the street and the passing of an unseen vehicle.

Elizabeth sat down on the marble edge of the pool and pensively trailed her fingers through the water. It was clear, the air warm with the sultry edge of a summer day, the fine azure sky above streaked with wisps of white clouds.

Normally she reveled in this kind of weather. Today she was as bleak as a Yorkshire winter.

Miles was avoiding her. It was clear enough, as pointed as a cut direct at an exclusive soiree, and she wasn't the only one aware of it either. Her mother had certainly noticed and commented, and even Luke, in his current state of self-absorption, had asked her if something might be wrong.

The answer was simple. *Everything.*

The fountain tumbled the water downward, the statuary, a stone fish with its mouth open, gurgling a never-ending cascade. It was tempting enough she leaned down, lifted her skirts, and kicked off her slippers before unfastening her stockings and rolling them down her legs. She turned back and dabbled her toes in the water before sinking in to midcalf. It felt marvelous, but inside she was still extremely unsettled.

She'd made a complete idiot of herself, and now she was doing penance for it. Why had she found it so necessary to challenge Miles, to be so confrontational and bloody forward?

"You know, you shouldn't have left this in my bedroom."

The calm voice made her jerk around. The subject of her thoughts—that wasn't so remarkable, as he was frequently the subject of her thoughts for the past week—stood there, her note in his hand. To her relief, he looked . . . ordinary. Well, like Miles anyway, with his dark brown hair and amber eyes, his expression mildly inquiring.

"It wasn't like I could hand it to you in person." She eyed the note in his hand. "You've been pouting."

His brows shot up. He stood there on the garden path in his shirtsleeves, his coat no doubt removed because of the warmth of the day. "Pouting? While I might risk being perceived as rude by disagreeing with a lady, I'm afraid you are mistaken. Grown men do not pout. We might brood or grow surly, but *pouting* does not apply." He waved the piece of vellum. "Now, then, what's this about?"

It had irked her enough to write it. She really didn't wish to *discuss* it. Only he seemed very normal, and maybe . . . it was possible that the emotional unrest of the past days had no basis in anything but her imagination. She shook crystalline droplets of water from her fingertips and smiled in what she hoped was a very collected fashion. "I was attempting to express my regrets for our misunderstanding the other day."

His mouth did an interesting quirk at the corner, almost as if he couldn't control it. "There was no misunderstanding. I just refused to cooperate, and it irritated you. But," he added with cheeky arrogance, "I found your note most moving, believe me. In the extended course of our mutual acquaintance, I have never known you to apologize for anything."

"I most certainly have," she denied heatedly.

"Name once."

Well, maybe she *was* obstinate when it came to admitting she was wrong. Not that *he* was any better, but he had a point. No particular instance came to mind.

Before now.

"Ah, I thought you might be unable to come up with a certain circumstance if pressed," he said.

That very expression on his face had been irritating her since she was five years old. Before that, probably, if she could remember further back.

It retrospect, she *shouldn't* have placed the note on his pillow. That someone might have discovered she'd been in his bedroom aside, she shouldn't have written it in the first place if he was going to be smug about it. Elizabeth snapped out, "We live in the same household. I made an effort so we might be on speaking terms."

"I didn't know we weren't."

"When is the last time we did?" she asked frankly.

"I'm busy."

"You *aren't* avoiding me?" she asked, the sun hot on her shoulders through the thin muslin of her day gown, the air unmoving.

If there was one aspect of his personality she knew well existed—and she thought she knew most of them—it was honesty. That was why he'd endured a great deal more punishment when they were children, because when their transgressions were discovered and charm didn't work, when asked a direct question, he told the truth.

His hesitation was palpable and he didn't meet her eyes.

"See," she said accusingly.

Interestingly enough, his gaze seemed riveted on the fountain. No, actually—where her legs must be visible through the clear water under the gathered froth of her skirts.

He's seen my ankles more times than I can count, she reminded herself as she waited for him to answer. But . . . not lately.

"It seemed best." He jerked his gaze back up to her face.

She kicked her feet in the water, sending a silvery spray. "Why?"

"I accept the apology." His expression was polite and studiously indifferent as he deftly sidestepped her question.

To say her frustration with the situation was interfering with every aspect of her life hardly did the chaotic state of her emotions justice. Besides, he was being so very . . . *Miles.* Without thinking, Elizabeth bent and scooped a handful of water from the fountain and flung it at him in exasperation.

He was close enough that it splattered across his white shirt in a satisfactory manner, and a few droplets ran down his lean cheek. "What the devil was that for?" he muttered, tugging a handkerchief from his pocket and wiping at his face.

Instead of answering, she splashed him again, this time with more vigor.

"El!"

The nickname only he used and said in outrage didn't soothe her riotous mood. Elizabeth would have splashed him again, except he stepped forward and caught her around the waist, hauling her up and setting her on her wet feet to jerk her around to face him, his hands hard on her shoulders.

"We aren't children any longer, so don't act like one," he bit out.

When he'd arrived home and removed his coat, he'd

also taken off his cravat and his shirt was open, showing just a glimpse of his chest and the strong column of his throat. A bead of water ran down his neck and disappeared under the fine linen of his collar, and Elizabeth watched the journey with a disturbing fascination. They stood very close, and she caught the scent of sandalwood and clean linen, intriguing and masculine.

"No, we aren't children any longer," she agreed softly, and made the mistake of looking up into his eyes.

He wanted to kiss her. The realization wasn't a shock either. She just understood it, as if there was a silent communication in the way his hands clasped her shoulders, in the slight lowering of his lashes, and the quick, audible inhale of his breath.

The surprise was that though she and Miles rarely agreed, at the moment they were in complete accord. It was exactly what she wanted too.

The sunshine must be responsible for the flush in her cheeks, Miles told himself. Or maybe her little burst of temper, but neither could be responsible for the way she looked at him, half inquisitive, half knowing, as if she somehow understood despite her innocence exactly what predatory male thoughts were crossing his mind at this definitive moment.

Damned women's intuition.

Yet if she knew what he so desperately wanted— and he was fairly certain she did—Elizabeth didn't pull away. Quite the contrary, she stared up at him expectantly, those enticing rose lips just slightly parted. She was delicious in plain sprigged muslin, her hair gathered back simply with a white satin ribbon. His heart had all but stopped beating when he'd walked out onto the brick terrace and seen her in the center of the sunlit garden, her skirts hiked up to her knees, slender calves immersed in the sparkling water.

Part of it too had been the pensive expression on her face.

For the rift currently between them?

His hands slid down from her shoulders and settled at her waist as they stared at each other, not speaking, the light cascade of the water and the birds the only sounds.

I love you.

The whisper hung on his lips unsaid but echoed in his mind like an incantation. *I've always loved you, even when you laugh at me, when we disagree, especially when you point out my flaws with that special smile I know I own. . . .*

"Miles—"

Recklessly, he lowered his head and caught the sound of his name on her lips, his mouth seeking the sweetness of hers, finding, tasting . . .

And then she was kissing him back, her hands flattening against his chest, her uncertainty when she felt the gentle insistence of his tongue giving way to compliance as she parted her lips and he swept inside her mouth, exploring every crevice, skimming her teeth, licking the corners of her lips. He broke away and then kissed her again, and this time his arms tightened around her so they were pressed together like lovers.

Maybe too much so. His body reacted predictably to her proximity, his cock hardening, and he wondered if she could feel his growing arousal.

Apparently so, for her palms suddenly exerted panicked pressure, and he finally loosened his hold so she could push away. Breathless, they stood and stared at each other, a foot or so apart, close enough he could reach out again and—

"Don't," she said shakily, stepping back, her gray eyes huge. "What are we doing?"

"That was a kiss." Miles was probably more shaken than she was, but did his best to look bland. Or perhaps his face was just frozen along with the rest of him.

"I know what it was—I mean—I know it was a kiss, damn you, but I don't know what it *was.*"

True ladies didn't swear, but since he'd taught her the word himself, he didn't think it was prudent to mention the slip. Elizabeth stood in flushed, disheveled, barefoot outrage in front of him, her hands clenched in the material of her skirts. Very quietly, because he'd had so much longer to adjust to how he felt about her, he said, "It is whatever you want it to be."

"Pardon the intrusion, but may I have a word, Miles?"

The clipped, cold voice broke the moment, shattering it into the return of reality. Miles turned his head, registered Luke's presence a few feet away, and took in a deep, much-needed breath. What did he expect? The garden was in full view of the back of the house and Luke's study was on this side, and on a day like this one the windows would undoubtedly be open.

Elizabeth looked confused, as if she hadn't heard her brother, and still stared up at Miles as if she were seeing him for the first time in her life.

Even with Luke's disapproving presence, Miles had to consciously keep from dragging her back into his arms. "Of course."

Luke walked past them to where Elizabeth's discarded stockings and slippers lay by the fountain, and he picked them up and held them out to her. "You might want to take these with you."

"I'm staying." She ignored the offering, gazing defiantly at her brother, though her cheeks were stained with crimson splotches. "If you are about to launch into some kind of outraged-guardian lecture, shouldn't I hear it too?"

"No." Her brother merely inclined his head toward the house and pushed the items into her hands. "Not unless you know absolutely how you feel about what I just saw, and I sense you don't."

At a guess, any other argument would not have worked, but that one did. Elizabeth hesitated for a moment, shot Miles an unfathomable look, and left, hurrying up the terrace and into the house.

Tense, not sure if he should be apprehensive or exhilarated, Miles waited. No doubt he deserved a dressing-down for what had just happened, but then again, he wasn't going to apologize for falling in love with Elizabeth either. He might as well say he was sorry he was still breathing.

"So, now that it's happened, where do you think you stand?" Luke regarded him with cool, dispassionate appraisal. "For that matter, maybe you should declare your intentions before we even begin this conversation."

"Blast it, Luke, you know I would never treat Elizabeth in any way except honorably." Miles set his jaw and met the other man's stare without flinching. "I love her."

"Yes," his cousin said dryly, "we've all noticed. Except her. Now, after that rather dramatic embrace, I assume she's noticed as well."

That shook him. He'd thought he'd hidden his feelings well. "All?"

"Anyone remotely paying attention, excluding my sister, who is far too close to the situation. What are you going to do next?"

It was reassuring to not be facing Luke's formidable wrath, but answering the question was not a simple matter either. He shoved his fingers through his hair. "I have no idea. I'm not . . ."

Luke answered for him when he trailed off. "Lord Fawcett? No, and apparently that is a point in your favor. Elizabeth informed me very firmly she wasn't interested in an engagement to the marquess."

"I received that impression myself, but has she said anything about *me*?" Miles had never been sure how Luke would react if he knew that *cousinly affection* didn't accurately describe his feelings toward Elizabeth.

"No, at least not in the terms you mean."

That was disappointing, but then again, the kiss had been quite—*very*—satisfying. She'd responded to him. *It could have just been curiosity*, he quickly reminded himself. He was intelligent enough to realize that young women were as sexually curious as young men, and she had even *asked* him about the subject.

This was *hell*.

"She could do better," Miles pointed out with painful, searing honesty.

"Socially, yes, I agree," Luke said with equanimity. "But, quite frankly, I'm more interested in her happiness than wedding her to the man with the most illustrious title and fortune who presses a suit. The real question is, what does *she* want?"

Miles stared at where she'd disappeared into the house and asked hoarsely, "What do you think I should do? If I tell her how I feel, it might ruin everything. At least how it is now, I have a special place in her life. If I declare myself, however it turns out, I'll lose that."

"I hate to point this out, but I think you rather effectively lost it already," Luke drawled with ironic sympathy. "As for what you should do, I haven't the slightest idea. You are asking me to predict how a female is going to react to a situation, and even an inveterate gambler like myself will not wager on the incomprehensible workings of a woman's mind. You are on your own, Miles."

"With your blessing?" It might be a mistake to ask, but then again, it would be nice to know where he stood.

Luke's silver eyes were unreadable, but that wasn't new. "I think I made it clear I want her to be happy. I've business out of town for a few days. I'm going to trust the two of you to behave yourselves. If not, Miles, I will hold you accountable."

Not exactly encouragement, but not discouragement either. Miles watched his tall cousin walk back toward the house, and then went to sit down in the same spot where Elizabeth had been on the edge of the fountain when he'd come outside to find her. It was wet from where he'd hauled her out of the pool, but he didn't care about the water soaking his breeches.

He needed to think.

The birds still sang, the water still flowed in a melodious gurgle, the sky above was still a cerulean blue, but the world—his world—felt different.

It *was* different.

Everything had changed.

Elizabeth dropped onto the bed and clasped her trembling hands together, and tried to bring the whirl of her chaotic thoughts into some semblance of order. The breeze she'd enjoyed outside moved the lace curtains at her window, but did little to cool the warmth in her face.

God in heaven, she'd kissed Miles.

No, correction: *he'd* kissed *her*, but she had undeniably kissed him right back.

The experience was not at all what she'd expected, but entirely more intimate, more intriguing, more . . . she wasn't sure what, but the reality proved much different from her imaginings, not to mention that Miles hadn't been the shadowy figure in those girlish daydreams either.

He'd tasted her. There seemed no other way to describe the exploration of his tongue, the heated possession of his mouth slanted over hers. He'd felt hard, muscled, overwhelming, as he'd urged her closer and closer. . . .

It might be next week before she stopped blushing.

She plucked at the coverlet with a restive hand, the galvanic turmoil inside requiring movement of some kind. Luke had seen them, which was mortifying, but then again, it took away the need to explain that something had happened.

Catastrophe or revelation?

She wasn't at all sure.

Chapter Twenty

They collided in the doorway. Lord Fitch muttered an apology. Luke, on the other hand, had waited deliberately for the moment, and he merely looked at him with unconcealed contempt. "We can discuss our business here, or you can discreetly accompany me. Which shall it be?"

Bath was as busy as usual with the elite of British society, and Pulteney Bridge was especially crowded on this pleasant morning. As soon as his lordship recovered from the shock of the encounter, he cleared his throat and apparently recognized the threat in Luke's tone. "No time for it, I'm afraid. Good day, milord."

"Our business," Luke said in clear enunciation between his teeth, "is Lord Brewer's journal. The one you stole or bought covertly. The one you were attempting to use to blackmail his widow."

"I haven't the slightest what you are about, Altea." He tried to walk on past.

Luke's hand shot out and grasped his arm in a steely grip that boded no argument. "Don't you? Down the street there's a small tavern, but if you'd prefer we go someplace more isolated—"

"No." The idea of solitude didn't seem to appeal to the earl, who had turned an unflattering shade of green all of a sudden, but he still attempted a blustery outrage. "A drink is fine, since you seem intent on speaking with me, Altea. I wasn't aware you were in Bath."

"I wasn't aware you'd left London," Luke told him with a thin-lipped smile. "Though it wasn't a bad decision, for at least I had all the hours of travel to get here to decide it wasn't worth it to kill you. Not that"—his smile widened grimly—"I wouldn't get great satisfaction from it, but someone I hold in great esteem might make the connection between your untimely demise and my current state of irritation and become distressed. She's experienced enough angst lately, in my opinion, for the most part due to you."

"W-what are you talking about?" Fitch's voice sputtered, and he wrenched his arm free but fell into step.

Pedestrians streamed by, and perhaps it was the way Luke held his shoulders and his unswerving stride, but their path down the walk across the bridge was unimpeded as the strolling masses parted, though a few curious looks were sent their way. Probably because Lord Fitch looked a tad pasty.

So he should.

"I thought I'd made my position quite clear," Luke said pleasantly enough, walking with his hands behind his back, the epitome of the English gentleman, in direct contrast to his barbaric urge to toss his companion off the bridge into the water below. "And yet you decided to continue your games."

"I have no notion at all what you are insinuating."

"Lady Brewer did not appreciate your gift."

"What gift?"

If that self-righteous expression on the man's sallow face was meant to convey sincerity, it didn't succeed, in Luke's opinion. Instead of answering the question, he walked determinedly to where a small establishment sat at the edge of the shops across the street. It was early enough not many of the tables were occupied, and he selected one at the back, the surface of the table clean but scarred, the ale-scented air a bit close for his tastes. Then again, he didn't intend to remain any longer than it took to make his message crystalline clear.

When the barmaid hurried over, Luke told her crisply, "My friend will need a whiskey. I'm not drinking."

He waited, knowing the value of making an opponent squirm, until the girl came back with a glass and a bottle. Wise beyond her years or maybe experienced enough at a young age given her profession and the weight of a certain tone of voice in a customer, she left the bottle.

Fitch's hand wasn't quite steady as he poured some of the amber liquid into the thick tumbler.

Good. If the man understood his danger, all the better.

"I cannot believe you'd be surprised that I would ever allow you to send Madeline such an inappropriate communication without retaliation." Luke folded his hands on the table deliberately and watched the other man take a convulsive swallow of his drink, unconcealed enmity in his eyes. "Not only did you insult the lady, but you insulted my sense of honor."

"You're mistaken, Altea." Glass clattered against his lordship's teeth as he took another gulp of whiskey.

"No, I am not," Luke informed him, leaning forward just a little. "Don't continue to annoy me. It's tempting to call you out as things stand, but that always creates a nasty fuss, and, quite frankly, you aren't worth the trouble. I can see you thought it would be fine to send off the gift and duck out of town. Maybe you gambled I would never know. After all, it is a bit embarrassing for her to explain. Did you think she wouldn't tell me?"

Fitch shook his head, whether it was in denial of the whole debacle or an answer, Luke didn't much care. It was a warm day, but the earl seemed to be sweating perhaps a little more than the weather warranted, drops of perspiration on his pallid brow.

"Lady Brewer is inviolate. Do you understand? That includes her privacy, her person, and her peace of mind. I thought it would be enough to have you see I have an interest in the charm of her company. This journey is a symbol of your failure to recognize the gravity of your actions. I am going to trust that won't happen again."

It was clear that Lord Fitch, like most bullies, had not expected to be confronted on his actions. "I've no interest in Lady Brewer," he finally managed to say weakly. "None at all."

"Ah . . . at last, exactly what I wanted to hear. If you do show an interest in the future, we won't have this discussion again, but will settle it in a much less civilized manner, man to man. That made clear, there's one more little matter to clear up before I leave you to your drink. How did you come into possession of the journal?"

"I never—" Fitch stopped in the middle of the denial then, and apparently thought better of it, his shaking hand on his glass. "I *found* it, Altea, damn you."

Years of war made one astute at reading men of all different walks of life, not just infantry soldiers and officers, but so-called gentlemen, Luke had learned since his return from Spain. "Where?" Luke asked flatly, sensing Fitch was telling the truth.

"At our club. It was lying on a table. I was one of the first in that day, and there it was. So I picked it up."

"How long ago?"

Fitch shrugged, but looked relieved that Luke seemed to believe him. "Three months, perhaps."

Poor Madeline had been putting up with this man's insinuations for *three* months?

"Did it never occur to you to return it to Lady Brewer?" Luke shoved himself to his feet in disgust. "Don't bother to fumble for an answer, since we both know what it is already."

He walked out without another word, pausing only

to hand the young barmaid a few coins in case the odious Fitch insisted he hadn't ordered the bottle and refused to pay for it. His purpose accomplished, Luke was headed back to London and it wasn't at all a short ride.

Someone had left Lord Brewer's journal in their club—on purpose? By accident? And how the devil had someone gotten hold of it in the first place?

At least Fitch seemed taken care of, but this new problem had surfaced.

Damnation.

The addition to their little party was not all that welcome. Not that Madeline actually disliked Alice, but they'd never managed to be close either, despite the family tie.

"You look well." Alice sank down onto a velvet-covered seat in the family box, where she was, theoretically, entitled to sit as a member of the May family. With Marta and her husband in the country, Madeline had invited her mother and Aunt Ida to accompany her to the opera, though she hadn't expected any other arrivals. Alice was the daughter of Colin's uncle, and also a young widow. "I think it has been too long since we've seen each other, Mad."

Colin's pet name for her had a different ring when said by anyone else.

Now it's Madge . . . Luke's way of annoying me, but I'm getting used to it . . .

Perhaps, Madeline had decided, she even liked it, especially when he said it in a certain deep, throaty tone as he held her close, their bodies moving in sensual communion. . . .

Not the time to think of *that* now.

"I'd heard you were traveling," she said neutrally, watching the other woman's friendly smile with a touch of wariness. Alice Stewart was a relative by marriage, but there was always a bit of distance between them and she'd never quite understood why.

"A bit, here and there." Alice acknowledged, inclining her head. She was a graceful beauty with dark hair and refined features, about the same age as Madeline. Her husband had died of a sudden illness, much like Colin, not long after they were married.

"It's good to have you back in London." Madeline's mother said warmly.

"It's good to be back, though it appears I have missed a bit of excitement. Where is Lord Altea?" There was just a hint of curious humor in Alice's voice.

"He's out of town," Madeline explained calmly, wondering if the twinge of annoyance she felt was because she was so sensitive on the subject. Was Alice judging her? "Though I admit I do not monitor his lordship's personal calendar. I have no idea where he went."

"Everyone is deliciously curious." Her mother waved her fan in a languid movement. "Note the prying stares."

Oh, Madeline had noticed them. Along with the raised opera glasses pointed her direction. "Maybe it is my gown," she observed dryly, referring to the new gold, raw-silk gown with tiny seed pearls bordering the short sleeves and neckline. It had been delivered just that morning and she was very pleased with it, for the material exactly matched the earrings Luke had given her. "But I confess I can't see why it would raise eyebrows when my décolletage is demure compared to Gabriella Fontaine's."

"Is that the standard against which you wish to be judged?"

Aunt Ida had an astute point. "Not really," Madeline admitted. "Though she is very beautiful, I suppose."

"We can certainly judge the full measure of her charms, for her bosom is all but hanging out." Ida's disapproving glanced raked the glittering crowd. "No doubt she dressed to make a sensation. Everyone is here. Except Altea, of course."

Hence the problem, Madeline supposed. This was the

first social event she'd attended without him in several weeks. As much attention as they drew together, she was drawing more for appearing alone. "No doubt everyone is twittering over whether or not he has already lost interest. Shall I take out an advertisement in the *Times* stating that he is merely out of London for a few days?"

"An engagement announcement would be even better," her mother said pointedly, flicking her fan shut. "Trevor is a darling, but he is only seven years old. A man in the family would be lovely."

Alice murmured, "That serious, is it?"

It was certainly best to keep speculation like *that* at bay.

"I am aware of your opinion on the matter, Mother, and you are aware of mine. The viscount and I are friends. Do not pin your hopes on anything more than that coming of it." Madeline spoke firmly, but inside she was not nearly as resolute. It was frightening to realize how his brief trip had affected her life. After Colin's death she'd been alone for years. How could Luke's absence for a few days have such a powerful impact?

Love, of course. It was exhilarating being in that state again. A sort of pleasure/pain combination quite different from what she had experienced with Colin, but exciting just the same.

The truth was, she couldn't wait for Luke to return.

"I do hope this evening is a reminder of what everyone is thinking, Madeline." Her mother's tone was prim.

"I already had a fair idea what everyone was thinking." She saw with relief the plush red curtain rising for the next act. "Can we drop the subject, please?"

"I think it is best we do." Alice said the words with understated amusement, her gaze fixed on the entrance to their private box. She added very softly, "Speak of the devil."

"Excuse me. I am late, but I see the second half is just starting. May I join you?"

At the sound of the deep voice a thrill shot through her, the drawling tone with just a hint of ironic amusement and sensual undertones familiar. *As if I've known him my entire life,* Madeline thought, glancing up to see Luke enter their private box, bend over a shocked Ida's hand first, and then greet her mother in a similar fashion.

"Lord Altea ... of course. Please join us," her mother said, obviously disconcerted, which was a contradiction, as she'd just been bemoaning his absence.

Or maybe she hadn't expected the larger-than-life topic of their conversation to suddenly arrive, as if magically summoned from thin air.

"My lord," Alice said in gracious greeting, inclining her head, her eyes bright.

The music precluded conversation, so Madeline merely smiled as Luke took the seat next to her, but if he had lifted her gloved hand at the moment, even through the satin fabric he would have felt her pulse pounding in her wrist.

The schoolgirl reaction to his sudden presence would have—should have—irritated her, but she was too happy, too aware of his rangy body as he sat in reserved elegance next to her in the seat that had always been Colin's, as if he belonged there—and, more telling, as if she had invited him.

Which she hadn't. Not with her mother and aunt in attendance. She'd had no idea Alice would join them, and that made matters even worse. Did he have any idea what he was *doing*? It was difficult enough to deflect all the avid interest in a romance that was merely sexual on his part, by his own declaration, but to come to the opera late and join them in the family box was ... well, just plain reckless.

Unless his intentions were honorable, which he'd said clearly they were not.

"What have I missed?" he asked, leaning toward her in outrageous proximity, close enough his breath brushed her cheek. "Let me guess. There's some sort of tragic debacle about to occur onstage."

"You don't like Italian drama, remember?" she whispered back, her opera glasses clenched in her fingers.

"I've made quite a few exceptions for you lately, my sweet."

The endearment rendered her speechless, though she quickly reminded herself it was just part of his charm, his easy, superficial charisma a facade.

How many people in attendance had noticed the arrival of Viscount Altea in her private box? Madeline steadfastly kept her gaze on the performers. Very quietly, she murmured, "I hope you count it worth it."

"I've seen an opera or two and survived."

"Do you often do so with unmarried ladies, their mothers, and matronly aunts?"

"Never, actually." His profile was clean and arrogantly aristocratic enough to match the half smile on his mouth.

"Then why are you here?"

"I'm not sure."

"That's cryptic enough. And in the meanwhile, you've caused a sensation."

"By attending the opera? However so?"

She adopted her best prim voice, imitating Aunt Ida. "Of course, I mean joining us so publicly."

"We've been together in public quite a few times now."

"This is different and you know it. My mother and aunt are here."

"Indeed, they are. Your point?"

"The attempt at innocence does not become you."

"Darling Madge, what *does* become me?" He was too close for propriety, his voice carrying a slight teasing edge.

God in heaven, he was wickedly handsome, the heavy promise in his stormy eyes enough to tempt any woman . . . much less one so besotted with him already.

They were whispering, and her mother was clearly trying to hear above the current aria, Ida was scowling in disapproval, and Alice was looking as bland as possible.

Madeline muttered, "What might become you is my glass of tepid champagne over your head if you don't stop feeding the gossip mill, Altea. Obviously it didn't work to keep Lord Fitch at bay, and so don't tell me being seeing together here will help my dilemma, because he still—"

"Fitch will never bother you again. We can discuss it later."

It stopped her midsentence because he sounded so quietly self-assured. And while she knew her reputation was suffering because of her association with the infinitely independent Lord Altea, she *did* trust him implicitly.

If she didn't, she wouldn't look so forward to sharing his bed. Or maybe the two issues were separate. . . . She found it difficult to think rationally in his presence.

The song swelled from the stage, the crystal-clear tones of the soprano riveting, but all she was aware of was the tall man at her side.

The exodus from the theater was going to be awkward, she knew, because both her mother and Aunt Ida had come in the same carriage, and if she made her excuses, it would be clear that there was a certain significance in allowing Luke to take her home.

They were skirting very close to outright scandal.

Chapter Twenty-one

It's only been four days, Luke reminded himself as he stood outside the opera house in the queue waiting for the carriages to be brought around. Worth the trip all the way to Somerset and back if it demonstrated to Fitch his seriousness. Madeline stood at his side, her graceful shoulders bare above the neckline of her fashionable gown, her shining, fair hair caught up with a few gold pins, the topaz earrings he'd given her the only adornment except, of course, for her dazzling, perfect beauty. He'd already decided four days apart from her was much, much too long.

"I don't suppose," Madeline said quietly, "the pretense of riding home with my mother and aunt will fool anyone."

"For myself, I don't care, but for you, I'll decorously hand you in to your own equipage and go my own way."

"Not too far away, I hope." She arched a brow and smiled at him.

As if I could.

"You might see me a bit later."

"I look forward to it." She glanced up at the velvety black sky spotted with diamond stars. "It's a beautiful night."

"I'll do what I can to live up to the stage set. It shouldn't be too difficult, when I will be inspired by a warm summer evening and the loveliest woman in England."

They were speaking in low tones, the chattering crowd around them actually helping to create a bit of privacy. Luckily, just because everyone was staring at them, it didn't mean they could make out what they were saying. Madeline's cheeks took on color at the compliment, but otherwise, if she was flustered, it didn't show. "How glib, my lord."

"How true, dear Madge."

The arrival of her carriage prevented her from saying anything else, and Luke politely helped in first her aunt, then her mother, and finally Madeline, with nothing more than a murmured "Good evening." The other occupant of the box when he arrived, introduced as the late Lord Brewer's cousin, Alice something—he hadn't quite caught it—had excused herself as soon as the curtain went down.

Now, he thought as he stepped back, all he had to do was count the hours until he could let himself into Madeline's town house and creep up to her bedroom. . . .

Appealing, but not appealing as it *could* be.

The clandestine nature of it bothered him more and more, hence his planned seduction at the inn. The next morning they'd drunk coffee and eaten scones while still in bed, comfortable with each other, both still naked, and he found he liked her sleepy and disheveled as much as he admired her cool, polished beauty . . . and, disconcertingly, maybe even more. When they'd made love that morning, it had been slow, sweet, and prolonged, and the pleasure exquisitely intense. Afterward, as they bathed, dressed, and prepared to leave the inn, Madeline had been very quiet.

No wonder. She had a son, and a respectable life up until he had entered it. Since he'd made his position on marriage clear, he shouldn't feel guilty for the repercussions their association might bring to her both personally and in society, but yet, somehow, he found it impossible to separate his feelings from their relationship.

Dangerous, that.

"My lord?"

He glanced up to see his driver holding the door of his carriage, and he shook himself out of the fit of conscience as best as possible and clambered into the vehicle. The club first, he decided as he gave his driver instructions, because he had questions to ask about the journal. If it had been left there, that meant whoever had it before Fitch was also a member, and that at least narrowed the list somewhat. How in the name of Hades he was supposed to find out who might have left a book on one of the tables months ago, he wasn't sure, but it wouldn't hurt to ask a few questions. If there was one truth about the elite masculine societies of the *haut ton*, it was that the stewards of the establishments they frequented knew their customers very well. They greeted the gentlemen by name, seated them at their usual tables, and always anticipated their favorite beverages before being asked.

Surely one of them might know something.

Not that sleuthing was his natural bent, but in this case, he had a vested interest in finding out the truth. To please Madeline and put her mind at rest, he would do anything. . . .

Almost anything. Short of proposing marriage.

It was unfair to her to not be able to offer her more, and not prompted by selfishness but experience, and God help him if the past did not weigh over him like a heavy stone, he might do it all differently. Tantalizingly it spread before him, a vision of Madeline holding his child, her lovely face aglow. . . .

No.

A child, of course, was possible.

No method to prevent pregnancy was infallible, and certainly the night they'd spent at the inn was an example. He wasn't normally so careless. . . . Actually he wasn't *ever* careless in such a fashion, for he had no desire to go around siring bastards, though it was a man's world and few of his class ever worried about illegitimate children. It tended to be the woman's responsibility, or, if she was married, her husband had to claim the child. Luke had in his circle of casual friends those with children that didn't even remotely resemble them, but personally, he didn't think he could ever look on such a situation with any degree of equanimity.

He had avoided thinking about what he'd do if Madeline conceived his child on the pretext—and he was only deluding himself—that worrying over an eventuality that might never happen was all but useless. Not true, of course, because bringing a child into the world was a weighty responsibility, and he knew himself well enough to understand he would never shirk it, nor would he abandon Madeline to handle the situation on her own.

He wanted to protect her, not ruin her life. What he *would* do was the real question.

So, he should stay away.

But he didn't think he could, and that knowledge was much more daunting than facing a column of French soldiers with glistening bayonets had ever been.

Sprawled in the seat of his carriage, moody, reflective, unsure, he stared at the empty seat opposite and took in a deep, calming breath. This wasn't a catastrophe; this was another milestone. Life was full of them, like reaching one's majority, or the first day at Eton, or, worse yet, that cold, clear morning when the sun touched the Spanish horizon and one knew there was going to be a battle—the first battle.

He'd endured those, and he could endure this.

When Maria had told him she was carrying his child, he'd been overwhelmed at first, then stricken with the weight of the responsibility, and, finally, overjoyed. The gamut of emotions had been run so quickly he had barely been able to reconcile his feelings before he'd dropped to his knees and begged her to marry him.

In the middle of a war-torn country. What a fool he'd been. But then again, what other course could he have taken? He'd been deeply in love for the first time in his life, and she'd carried his child.

Then he'd lost them both. . . .

Images of plump babies with dimpled smiles aside, he didn't believe in the *idea* of love any longer. Look at poor Miles, so besotted he hadn't truly looked at another woman besides Elizabeth all season. His unguarded expression every time he as much as glanced at her made Luke wonder how others saw him and Madeline, and provoked an unsettled consideration of how a man might perceive his emotions to be concealed when they were in plain view of anyone who was paying attention.

Shaking off the introspection, he alighted and went up the steps of White's. Solving the puzzle of the journal was infinitely preferable to trying to dissect the current unruly state of his unrest. He hoped the usual staff was available for a few questions.

That he had joined her so openly at the opera was unexpected. That Luke might not join her in her bedchamber was even more unexpected.

Had something happened? Madeline paced over to the window, jerked back the curtain, and stared outside. Surely she hadn't misunderstood. *You might see me a bit later.* That was clear enough, wasn't it?

Of course, he'd used the word *might*, and maybe she'd made too much of it, and . . .

The latch clicked and the door opened, and she froze. Her reflection in the glass was ghostly, the white of her nightdress and the pale length of her loose hair an ethereal image.

Luke came into view behind her, his faint smile familiar and his hands reaching out to cup her shoulders. "Watching for me?"

"Don't flatter yourself, my lord." She somehow managed to sound calm when his presence alone made her heart pound and the sound of his voice sent a telltale tingle up her spine.

He laughed, his breath stirring her hair. "I believe we've discussed my arrogance before."

"And no improvement has been made, I see." She shivered as he bent and pressed his warm mouth against the column of her neck.

"None," he murmured against her skin.

She had a weakness, she'd discovered in the past weeks, to his making love to her neck.

And the infernal man knew it too.

His lips traveled deliciously lower, to trace her collarbone above the neckline of her sleeping gown, the garment demure but lightweight enough for the summer heat. With typical audacity, he tugged the ribbon free with his teeth, the silken softness of his hair brushing her cheek.

A sigh escaped. She couldn't control it any more than she could stop the moon from ruling the ebb and flow of the tide.

A long-fingered hand skillfully slipped inside her bodice to cup a breast, fondling with gentle persuasion, bringing forth another involuntary sigh. Madeline turned in his arms then and kissed him, their lips clinging, her body pressing as close as possible. *If I could crawl inside you, I would*, she thought in hazy joy as his tongue brushed hers in delicious, sensual strokes.

Luke lifted her easily, not breaking the kiss, and she found the softness of the mattress at her back and his hand sliding up her calf and thigh with a possessiveness and confidence she might have found irritating if his touch wasn't so practiced and . . . perfect.

Absolutely perfect.

"Don't stop there," she murmured when he circled her hip in a teasing caress. "You're so close."

"Are you suggesting I do this?" His fingers slid between her legs.

She gasped as he cupped her mound and his middle finger slipped inside her. "Perhaps." Madeline arched into the intimate invasion. "Or something quite similar, but maybe with a part of you that's a bit . . . larger?"

"Show me what you want." His whisper was heated in her ear. "Touch me. Take me out. It doesn't always have to be on my initiative. I'm at your mercy."

Not so, not when she was mesmerized by the tantalizing glide of his fingers inside her, but to her disappointment, he removed his hand and instead smiled lazily down at her, the casualness of his pose at odds with the unmistakable bulge in the front of his fitted breeches. "Do with me as you like, my lady."

The challenge was venturing into precarious new territory. Madeline trusted Luke, and he inspired in her a daring she hadn't known existed even with Colin; she'd always assumed women were obedient in bed. "I . . . I don't know if I could."

"I'm telling you to do as you wish." His smile glimmered. "There is no embarrassment in bed, love."

He'd said it again. If only he meant it, but for now she was willing to accept the endearment as a small triumph, and it emboldened her. Actually, she found she rather liked the idea of being in command, especially when it was so obvious he wanted her.

"Stand up and don't move."

He straightened and his smile grew even more wicked. "I won't move a muscle unless ordered to do so."

Rising to her knees, first she pushed his fitted coat from his shoulders, the motion slow and deliberate. Then she ran her hands down his chest and across his taut stomach, and tugged his shirt free. The buttons were slipped loose one by one, and she was rewarded by the

increased cadence of his breathing, slight but noticeable as she worked. The garment fell to the floor, and
she busied herself with the fastenings on his breeches.
His arousal stretched the cloth, long and hard beneath
her fingers, and it wasn't the easiest task. She heard his
exhaled groan as the material parted, and his freed erection pressed her hands, hot and rigid.

She stroked him from ballocks to the flared tip and
watched his reaction from underneath the fringe of her
lashes. "Tell me how this feels."

"As close to heaven"—his exhale was audible—"as I
will ever come."

She leaned closer so her breasts brushed his chest.
"Would you prefer my mouth?" She delicately rubbed
the tip of his cock. "Here?"

"No." His muscles tensed.

"No?"

"If you do," he explained on a low growl, "our evening will be over very quickly."

"Well, we don't want that. Do we, Altea?" Her voice
was sultry, and she was *never* sultry, she thought with
emancipated delight. Or at least she'd never thought of
herself in that way. But with Luke it was . . . different.

They fit together, and not just in a sexual sense. The
insight stilled her hand, made her breath catch, and she
lifted her face to gaze at him. He wasn't perfect . . . no, far
from it. He was cynical, guarded, sexually experienced
but emotionally inaccessible. But he was also a warm,
kind man in many ways, though she doubted he'd ever
thought of himself that way. When she'd needed him,
he'd come to her without question, and she'd known—
and still knew—he'd protect her. If she was certain of
anything in the world, it was that she was safe with him.

I love you.

Almost. She almost said it out loud. It had been close,
and it shook her.

"I wouldn't dream of telling you what to do, but I
could join you on the bed." Long fingers caught her

chin and tilted her face up so he could brush his mouth against hers. "A suggestion only."

"Yes." The hushed word was rife with double meaning, and maybe he caught it, for he looked into her eyes for a single, long heartbeat.

Madeline licked her lips, her mouth suddenly dry. "Join me."

"A sound idea, I agree." He smiled.

He was too attractive, but she'd known her resistance to his aura of charismatic charm was nonexistent from the beginning. She was, in a word, outclassed by his experience. And if at the start she'd recognized it, she knew it now more than ever. Fighting the battle had simply ceased to be important to her. Even if it meant she would be hurt later, she didn't care, not now, not while she could hold him in her arms and taste his kiss, his passion.

"Undress." She didn't say *please*, but punctuated the directive by slowly pulling her nightdress above her head in a languid, seductive movement.

"My absolute pleasure." Luke sat down, seemingly oblivious to his erection, to tug off his boots and remove his breeches. Sleek, nude, and magnificently aroused, he stood before her and lifted a brow.

"Climb up and lie on your back," she instructed.

He did so, his eyes glittering beneath heavy lashes as he climbed onto the bed and lay on his back, his powerful body at odds with the submissive pose.

There were scars. She'd seen them before, of course, but never asked because she wasn't sure how much she dared. However, he'd said she was in charge and could ask anything. Madeline eased on top of him, skin to skin, his cock hard against her stomach, her finger tracing a pattern across his shoulder. "How did this happen?"

"I took a ball at Talavera."

A few inches over and he might have died. Madeline leaned forward and kissed the small, vivid mark, acutely aware of how grateful she was to have him in her life. "I'm sorry you were hurt."

"It happens in war." His fingers caressed her spine.

"And this one?" There was a jagged line across his ribs on the right side.

"Salamanca."

"You don't like talking about it."

"It's over. Besides, when a beautiful, naked woman is sitting astride my hips, I confess my thoughts are scattered to the winds. Madge, I know I promised you could be in charge, but could you possibly bring yourself to—"

She stopped his words with her mouth, leaning forward so her hair fell over her back and his shoulders, her tongue tracing the lower curve of his lip before provocatively dipping inside his mouth. It was as if a small detonation had taken place, with fire escalating along her nerve endings, and the kiss turned hot, wild, unrestrained. At his urging she rose, took his hard cock in her hand, poised herself above him, and lowered herself as he filled her, inch by slow inch.

True to his word, he gave her command, letting her ride his hips, the slick friction slow at first and then more urgent, their breathing increasing in rhythm with the rocking motion of pelvis to pelvis. She shuddered first, going tense and rigid as the pleasure took her. It wasn't until Madeline collapsed forward that Luke pulled her close and climaxed with a low, hoarse groan and convulsive arch of his spine.

The aftermath was always her favorite. Postcoital bliss was hearing the thud of his heart, feeling the clasp of his arms, inhaling the smell of clean sweat and sex. He rarely spoke after intercourse, and this was no exception, and she was content with the silence.

Soon she was going to tell him. She hadn't intended he ever know she loved him, but it was a secret no one should keep, she had come to realize. How many tortured lovers had held the precious knowledge and suffered for it? Luke could either walk away or he could choose to stay, but her feelings counted also and she *wanted* to tell him. If she never said it, she knew in her heart she would regret it—for herself, and, truly, for him also. He was a grown man. And what person did not benefit from knowing someone loved them?

She'd lost Colin, and thought the pain of it was too much to bear, and she'd come through it not unscathed, but wiser.

If she lost Luke simply because she loved him, he didn't deserve her.

"Tell me more about Spain."

He stiffened. It was almost imperceptible, but because they were so closely entwined, she felt his muscles tense and the lazy caress of his fingertips on the damp skin of her back stilled. "I'm not sure what it is you wish to know."

Maybe it was the contentment after a surfeit of pleasure; maybe it was their increasing intimacy that was no longer just sexual attraction, but she dared to think their connection had deepened to a point where she could probe at least a little.

Can you promise me you won't die . . .

Those words he'd said to her after the debacle with Lord Fitch still hung in her mind. There was substance behind them, but she was at a loss as to what had prompted it.

"You must have lost not just comrades, but friends." Madeline rested against his chest, speaking slowly. "I cannot compare your experiences with any of my own except Colin's death."

The man holding her didn't comment.

"I'm not prying," she explained softly, "but I admit I am trying to understand."

It was enlightening that he didn't pretend he didn't comprehend just what she was asking. Luke's fingers resumed the same gentle rhythm over her skin, but it took a moment. "Spain has nothing to do with my life now."

"Is that why you are still such good friends with Alex St. James and Lord Longhaven?"

"We knew each other before the war."

But something had happened. She could hear it in his voice.

She laid her palm flat against the spot where his heart beat. "You don't want to tell me."

"No, I don't."

Then, as if to soften the cold, clipped words, his arm circled her waist and drew her even closer, if that was possible. His voice was hoarse. "Please, Madge, don't ask me."

Chapter Twenty-two

Luke had returned from his trip early the evening before, abruptly changed his clothes, and gone out. Elizabeth knew this because he'd barely managed more than a swift greeting, and she wondered at his haste. He had not appeared at breakfast either, and when she asked later in the afternoon, he was ensconced in his study with his solicitor.

Miles, she hadn't seen at all in days.

For the past week, he'd been a veritable ghost in the house, leaving early and coming in when everyone else was abed. Still pointedly avoiding her, she knew. It was all worse than ever.

The kiss needed to be addressed. And she wasn't good at waiting, she'd discovered. So he was uncomfortable. Well, she was uncomfortable too, and damn Miles anyway for letting her brother intimidate him.

If *that* was the problem.

She'd thought about Miles and that telling kiss every waking second since it happened. Hence this visit, which was something she'd never done before. Her usual interaction with her half sister involved planned family gatherings, and those invitations were not accepted all that often. Regina liked to live an unfettered life, though Elizabeth did know that she and Luke saw each other fairly often.

The drawing room was fairly typical of most of London's upscale town houses, except, of course, the presence on the polished tables of chipped Greek statues, most of them missing some part of their anatomy, and a vast array of art in all different styles that was rather fascinating. She had to make a conscious effort not to stare and keep her attention on the conversation. This was the first time she'd been in her sister's home.

"Your mother would not like you stopping by like this."

Elizabeth thought Regina was probably right. "I don't see why. Luke does."

"Luke is the viscount and can do as he pleases." Today Regina was elegant in a dark green frock bordered with black ribbon, her rich hair loose about her shoulders. In contrast to her fashionable attire, she was barefoot. She looked beautiful, and characteristically unconventional.

"You are my sister," Elizabeth pointed out.

"Your illegitimate half sister from an affair our father had before he married." There was no trace of resentment in Regina's voice. "Your mother and I are polite to each other and maybe even a little fond of one another, but she doesn't approve of me for a variety of reasons, the least of which is my birth."

"That is her difficulty, not mine. I came for advice."

At that declaration, her older sister looked amused, cradling her porcelain teacup in one palm, her body relaxed in her chair. She swung her foot. "I see. And where do Luke and your mother think you are now?"

"My mother was out when I left, so she doesn't even know I'm gone. As for Luke, he's no longer paying much attention," Elizabeth muttered. "I suppose I should be grateful for it."

Regina laughed, and in her place, Elizabeth might have laughed too. Regina said tranquilly, "I don't suppose you have a prominent position in his thoughts at the moment. He's in love with Lady Brewer, and it is very hard for him to reconcile with his past."

Luke? In love? True, he'd been distracted lately, but . . . *love*?

"What past?" Elizabeth might not have asked, but there was something comfortable about Regina, something that invited confidences. Maybe it was how she'd never cared about proprieties. Her birth, of course, had precluded a proper entry into society, and it seemed to suit Regina very well. Elizabeth was never sure how to feel about having an older sister born on the wrong side of the blanket. It meant her beloved father had a mistress—though he hadn't yet met her mother, that was clear enough. But still, her half sister's existence said something about him as a man—albeit a young man, as their births were almost two decades apart.

"I don't know the specifics and I have never asked, but it has to do with a woman and the war." Regina looked into her cup and added softly, "He loved her, and she died."

Elizabeth was unaccountably shocked. Luke always seemed so collected, so invulnerable. "How do you know this? He's never said anything at all about it to me."

"Of course not, Liz. Nor has he told me. He isn't likely to either. Why recall the pain if there is a way to avoid it? Just the same, it is always there with him. He carries it around, and now he is going to have to make a decision of some kind about Lady Brewer, and it is occupying his thoughts constantly. But at least I notice he's sleeping."

"I wasn't aware he wasn't," Elizabeth muttered, brushing back a loose tendril from her chignon. "Apparently I'm not all that observant. How do you know? You live here."

"That is how I know. He hasn't come to see me in the middle of the night."

It was unreasonable to feel betrayed because she was younger, she wasn't his confidant, and yet a part of her was jealous of their easy relationship. "Luke doesn't tell me anything," Elizabeth admitted. "But I suppose that is no excuse for me not being more persistent in trying to understand why he stays so distant. I asked him, but he redirected the conversation."

"You are nineteen. When one is nineteen they are allowed to be self-absorbed." Regina smiled with her unique serenity. "I think that is probably why you never noticed Miles and his infatuation with you." She frowned. "Actually, I am not being fair to him, I suppose, by calling it that. It has been going on far too long for it to be a mere fascination of a sexual nature."

"It has?" She'd come to talk about Miles, but having Regina introduce the subject in such a way still startled her.

"Think about it. He's always been rather in your pocket, hasn't he?"

"We were children together," Elizabeth said loyally. "He is a little older, so naturally he watched out for me."

"Certainly, when you were younger. I'd say, though, that he *watches* you is more appropriate now."

If she didn't think that was exactly true, Elizabeth wouldn't be sitting in her sister's rather eclectic drawing room at this very moment. She got to her feet in a convulsive movement and walked over to stare blankly at what appeared to be a drawing of—of all things—an Indian elephant, long trunk, tusks, and all. It was actually a very striking piece. She confessed quietly, "He kissed me."

"Good for him. How was it?"

When she turned around, Elizabeth was blushing. "How do I know how it was? I've never been kissed before."

"I don't know if prior experience is a prerequisite for knowing if a kiss takes your breath away or not."

Surely Regina, with her lustrous dark hair and voluptuous figure, had attracted her share of men. Elizabeth had always been curious as to why her half sister never married. Legitimate or not, she was the daughter of a viscount.

"I might have been a bit breathless," she confessed. "It hardly helped that Luke saw us and came outside. He ordered me to go into the house. I have no idea what he said to Miles, but now Miles is staying away from me."

"And you miss him." It was put forth as a statement.

Did she? Yes, absolutely. She nodded. "So . . . what should I do?"

"You are assuming I'm not just older, but actually wiser." Regina's brow quirked upward. "I know I am one, but not sure of the other, not when it comes to men. However, I can offer an opinion, if you want it."

"That's why I'm here."

"It depends on what you want, Liz. What is most important? Titles? Money? Social standing?"

"None of that." She said it firmly, and it was true.

"Do you believe in your heart Miles can make you happy? He certainly seemed a perfect companion when you were children. No one could keep you apart. Friendship like that is different from romance, but if you could combine the two . . . I think it might be miraculous indeed."

Miraculous. She could still remember the feathering of his lips against hers, and the warm, possessive clasp of his hands.

"It might be." Her voice was barely a whisper. "But you still haven't told me what to do. I don't . . . well, I have no idea how to *approach* this."

"Darling," Regina drawled dryly, "you know him better than anyone. From what I understand just from this conversation, it will take very little to convince Miles that if he wishes to declare his ardent devotion, you would be receptive to his suit."

"He's hardly ardently devoted."

Or was he? Elizabeth knew she'd never forget his poignant expression when they broke apart.

"The only way to know for sure," Regina said with absolute conviction, "is to talk to him about it."

The last time she'd tried talking to him, it hadn't worked at all. Instead, he'd kissed her.

Actually, she realized, that was a good argument for trying it again.

Luke watched his sister adjust her ivory silk glove at the elbow, not sure whether to be amused or to rally at the side of his fellow male.

"All I ask," Elizabeth said succinctly, "is a few minutes alone with him."

"Most guardians," he said, cognizant that most guardians of innocent young ladies didn't have his reputation, "find it their designated duty to prevent their vulnerable charges from falling into the clutches of ill-intentioned suitors."

"Is Miles someone you'd ever think has ill intentions? Did he talk to you about it? What did you say to him? How—"

He held up a hand to halt the volley of eager questions. "Elizabeth, stop."

She did, but she looked very young, standing there by the side of his desk, dressed for the evening in a gown made of some shimmering silver material Luke was sure would bring Miles to his knees. As an older brother, Luke wanted to challenge his mother's judgment for approving something so revealing. Not that it was really less than demure, he had to grudgingly admit, but Elizabeth was his *sister*, and he'd have preferred a garment that buttoned up to her throat, and maybe even a veil tossed in to the ensemble.

It was somewhat different to be on the other side of the equation. He'd seen the looks Madeline's mother and aunt had given him when he joined them at the opera that fateful evening.

He'd have to consider his own situation later. Right now Elizabeth stood there, waiting.

His sister's expectant gaze made him think about Miles's similarly tortured expression and ask himself how relationships between men and women could be so confoundedly complicated. He was growing more and more aware of it by the moment. With effort he summoned a bland expression. "Why do you so urgently wish to talk to Miles?"

"Regina suggested I should."

"Did she, now?" How the devil had their older sister gotten dragged into this? Though come to think of it, he'd asked Regina's advice on the matter and she'd blithely admitted suspecting Miles's infatuation for quite some time. "I wasn't aware she'd called."

"She didn't. I went to see her." Elizabeth tilted up her chin just a fraction. "Mother doesn't know, though I can't see why it makes a difference when she is invited here quite often."

He privately agreed, but while their family—even their mother—accepted Regina, society wasn't quite as forgiving of her birth, and maybe even less so of her unconventional lifestyle. Besides, Elizabeth shouldn't be going out unchaperoned anywhere. "If you wish to call on her, I have no objection, but allow me to accompany you next time."

A rebellious glimmer flashed in her eyes, but after a moment she nodded. Elizabeth said, "Can we get back to my request, please? I've barely seen Miles since . . . well, *since*, and I agree with Regina: I think we need to talk to each other."

Since meant since that tender kiss he'd happened to glance up and witness from the open window of his study. She was right, of course. They definitely needed to talk to each other, but only once Luke knew for certain what Elizabeth wanted. He'd stood politely when she'd entered the room, and he indicated a chair. "Sit down, if you please. While I won't say exactly what he told me the other afternoon, I do promise I have the well-being of you both in mind."

"You sound so formal." Elizabeth sighed, but she did take one of the wing chairs, folding her hands in her lap. "This shouldn't be about well-being. It should be about . . . love."

There. She'd said it. Out loud. *Love.*

This was the point where he should ask her outright if she loved Miles, but he already knew the answer—he'd known it for some time. Still, his knowing it and *her* knowing it were two different aspects of the situation. "I don't pretend to be eloquent on the subject, but do you love Miles? Or is it possible you are confusing an old friendship with a new one?"

"Do you love Lady Brewer?"

The question took him aback and he sat silent, just looking at Elizabeth.

"It seems as fair as you asking me," she murmured, upright and poised in the chair, but her jaw jutted outward at just enough of an angle that he recognized a fight when he had one on his hands.

Besides, she, infernally, had a point.

"I'm in charge of your future," he countered, ruefully aware of how pompous that sounded. In his defense, he hadn't asked for the responsibility; it had just fallen to him. "It gives me the right to inquire about your feelings."

"And I am in charge of no one's future, not even my own?"

"You're wrong, Elizabeth. Please give me due credit for caring about not just your well-being, but also your happiness."

"I do." Her lashes fluttered down and she lowered her head to stare at her clasped hands for a moment. "And I suppose I don't know exactly how to answer you. About Miles, I mean. Isn't falling in love supposed to be accompanied by a great deal of heart pounding and flirtation and fanfare?"

"I don't know." That was frank and honest. What had happened with Maria had been quite different from his feelings for Madeline. He'd ceased trying to deny the latter, but still struggled to define it. "I think each experience is probably unique to the man and woman involved," he said quietly. "I also believe trying to analyze it is an exercise in futility. Poets have attempted since time out of mind, and I haven't noticed a true definition yet. The question you need to be asking yourself is how Miles fits into your life."

"Arrange for me to talk to him, and perhaps I *can* answer it."

"He has a modest living at best." Luke felt compelled to point it out.

"And no title." Her flippant tone told him she didn't care, and her gaze was now very direct.

Their mother might care, though. And unless Elizabeth was sure, maybe she would eventually wonder if she could have married better, though Luke was convinced Miles would make enough of a success of himself to invest in his venture.

He wouldn't mind seeing Elizabeth settled, and surely she could do worse than a young man with integrity and honor who adored her.

"How do you wish for me to arrange this meeting?"

"Short of creeping into his room in the middle of the night, I don't see how I can even snatch a few moments. He's deliberately staying away." Her glimmering look told Luke his sister had something in mind.

Poor Miles. He didn't stand a chance against such deliberate female determination.

"Creeping into his room in the wee hours isn't an option I approve of." Luke leaned back and crossed his arms. "What other venue do you have in mind?"

"Rather a thorny barrier, isn't it? Hence my presence here. If he can avoid me, he will, and I sense it is your fault."

"I never told him to stay away from you."

"Then you won't mind arranging for a chance for us to talk alone. As I said before, something private, please."

He registered the firmness in her tone and thought about Madeline, with her serene confidence yet yielding femininity. He wondered sometimes if males were as in command of the world as they thought they were. "I'll see what I can do," he agreed.

"Thank you." Elizabeth rose in a swirl of silken skirts. She hesitated and then came around his desk unexpectedly and hugged him. Her eyes were bright with tears. "I'm terribly nervous about this. Who would think? It's just Miles, after all."

When she left, Luke slumped in his chair, gazing at the empty hearth of the fireplace.

Are you in love with Lady Brewer?

The candid question had come out of nowhere, or perhaps it hadn't. Naturally his family would be curious. His mother had made no secret of it. Elizabeth, at nineteen, had a romantic view of the way it all worked, of course.

He'd naively thought he could keep the affair between himself and Madeline. He should have been more worldly. Lady Brewer was completely unlike his usual casual bed partners.

And there it was. As he sat there, he realized it *was* between them, but neither did it stand alone. She had a past. A son. *He* had a past.

A secret.

Chapter Twenty-three

He was doing it again. Not particularly well either, but as luck would have it, as far as he could tell, no one was paying any attention to him or his clandestine observation.

Certainly Elizabeth didn't seem to notice his covert surveillance.

Miles edged past the French doors on the terrace, pretended great interest in the drinks table when he hadn't had a drop in the past week, and surreptitiously shot a look at the dance floor. She whirled gracefully in a circle of silver silk that exactly matched her eyes, and he simply couldn't look away.

Even if she was in the arms of another man. It had been foolish, probably, to go ahead and attend the ball.

"Whiskey?"

Miles glanced up sharply, caught fairly in the act. Luke stood there, his smile bland.

"No, thanks," he muttered.

"I might like one," his cousin suggested, his tone dry.

"Oh." Miles glanced down and found a glass, picked up one of the bottles, and dashed some liquid in it.

"I haven't seen you much lately." Luke accepted the glass but didn't drink. "Your valet told me you had dressed for the evening. I hoped I'd see you here. You've been conspicuously absent lately."

It was true they lived in the same residence but hadn't crossed paths. The two of them currently had completely different schedules, though, ironically enough, for the same reason.

A woman. Luke spent his nights elsewhere, and Miles had made it a point to come in very late and leave again very early to avoid running into Elizabeth.

"I've kept my distance." He tried to not sound defensive, just conversational. "Not just for her sake either. You know how I feel. Can you blame me?"

"No, I can't say that I do, but is it how to deal with your dilemma? You cannot avoid her forever."

That was true, he supposed, but he was certainly trying. The music swirled, the dancers moved, and Miles wished more than ever that the season wasn't so far along and the weather so warm, because under his coat he was sweating. His gaze swung moodily back to the dance floor. "She looks lovely."

"She wants to talk to you."

Miles tore his attention away from Elizabeth's graceful form, his attention suddenly riveted. "Why?"

"Why? Devil take it, Miles, you know her. Naturally she wishes to discuss that kiss I witnessed by the fountain the other day, and I am going to guess a great deal more. Elizabeth has grown up, but she hasn't entirely abandoned the persona of that precocious companion you remember either. I think you recall very well that when she is bothered, she approaches the problem in a straightforward way."

Neither the words *bothered* or *problem* were very flattering. He swallowed and murmured, "I am not sure I wish to have that conversation."

"And I am just as sure you have very little choice. She's threatened to corner you in your bedchamber, a tactic I don't approve of, so why not save us both a great deal of worry and simply speak with her? This," Luke added impassively, "is your chance to make your case."

Miles felt something within him loosen. It wasn't true relief, because he still had to hear what Elizabeth had to say, but it was a release from the self-imposed distance he'd put between them. He could endure much, but not this separation. When she'd left after that soul-shattering kiss, he had agonized over what might happen next, and, yes, he'd known all along he was just putting off the reckoning. "She *can* be rather stubborn at times."

"You are telling that to her aggrieved guardian." Luke said dryly. "Perhaps you can relieve her current dance partner of his duties and take her outside to the garden for some fresh air. I think I can trust both of you to not surrender to a fit of passion in Lady Roteger's rose bed."

Miles wasn't sure she wanted to *ever* surrender to a fit of passion with him, and it was shredding his soul into tiny ribbons.

But maybe, since she'd asked her brother to approach him . . .

No, it wasn't prudent to hope. "Think of the possible scratches," he agreed with feigned calm. "I do believe we can be depended on to merely discuss matters as two adults might."

"Adults? Yes, please concentrate on that new slant to your relationship." Luke's gaze was watchful. "This is not child's play. Be prudent, and bring her back in before any whispers arise."

"I will," he vowed.

"The music is ending," Luke pointed out, "and I have a rather full evening, so if you don't mind, now would be an opportune time."

Miles knew a gift when he received one.

He went.

                         *   *   *

"You look flushed."

At the sound of the oh so familiar voice, Elizabeth took in a deep, calming breath. Miles stood only a few feet away, materializing out of the melee of dancers, tall and striking in his formal evening clothes. He went on in an ordinary tone, his expression neutral. "Not that it isn't becoming, but maybe a breath of fresh air wouldn't hurt, El."

Her partner, a young man whose exaggerated side whiskers and pomaded hair, coupled with diamond buckles on his shoes, gave him a dandified air, apparently caught the easy use of her nickname, and bowed a farewell.

Miles watched him go with an irritating air of amusement. Elizabeth said tartly, "He's actually very charming and waltzes beautifully."

"I am sure he is a veritable paragon of a fashionable gentleman." Miles transferred his gaze back to her. "Will you walk with me in the garden for a few moments?"

It happened again. One of those moments when her pulse quickened and she seemed to forget everything else in the world simply because he was looking at her.

Or maybe it was the *way* he was looking at her.

He lifted his brows, waiting.

After all, she was the one who wished to speak to him, to settle this between them, but she still didn't know what she was going to say, which was a very real problem. It would come to her, or she hoped it would, and all she knew was she couldn't bear a life with Miles avoiding her company.

She couldn't bear a life without *him*. Elizabeth nodded, and when he offered his arm she put her hand on his sleeve and let him escort her through the throng and out the open terrace doors. They weren't the only ones wanting a reprieve from the stuffy ballroom, and several other couples were outside, leaning against the balustrade or sitting on the stone benches. Miles chose to go down the steps and guide her toward the flagstone path, neither one of them saying a word.

It was cloudy and a bit close, the drifting cover above obscuring the moon, the light wind moving softly. In the shifting light, it was hard to read Miles's expression, and Elizabeth tried to emulate his composure by resisting the urge to start this conversation. As far as she was concerned, when he kissed her, he'd taken the initiative to change their lives.

Forever.

They stopped walking on one of the shadowed paths, his footsteps slowing until they halted, the breeze ruffling his hair. "Luke said you wished to speak to me."

The formal sound of his tone was irritating, but actually, she was grateful for it. Being irritated with Miles was nothing new, but her fluttering pulse in his presence now was disconcerting. Bolstering her courage she said, "I thought maybe we should discuss what happened."

"Happened?"

"Miles, don't be obtuse on purpose. You kissed me."

"Like this?" His hand cupped her cheek and he unexpectedly brought his mouth down to hers so quickly she gasped, his other hand running lightly down her bare arm as he kissed her . . . and kissed her . . . the nuances shifting like treacherous sands. First he was almost desperately tender, then forceful, and then sweetly giving again, twining their fingers together as he finally lifted his head. "You were saying?"

Had it not been for the slight unsteadiness of his voice, she would have been furious with him. After all, what she wanted was a calm, rational discussion of why on earth he'd kissed her in the first place, and now he'd gone and done it again.

Quite a thorough job of it too.

Leaving her incapable of coherent thought. "Yes, exactly like that. Well, no," she modified. "This time was a little different. . . . Oh, Miles, *why*?"

His grin was lopsided, the kind he used to wear when

he'd done something particularly annoying. "Would you believe me if I said it's because I adore you? That I think you are possibly the most beautiful woman in the world . . . Wait, did I just say *possibly*? *The* most beautiful woman on this earth, and that even back when you told me I was despicable and ill-mannered and wished me straight to perdition on a regular basis, I thought so then too."

Speechless, she could only stare at him, at those achingly familiar features—the slightly long nose, the lean shape of his jaw, the golden hue of his eyes, shadowed as they were by the insufficient light, and she realized this *was* heart pounding and flirtation and fanfare.

It was love. Good heavens, she loved Miles. Of course, a part of her knew she always had, but not in this way. There was affectionate love, and then there was *this*.

"When you went to university I . . . I was miserable over you leaving." The halting words were more for her own edification than his, as she looked back, remembering. "I couldn't believe it."

His fingers tightened around hers. "Think of me. I already knew I loved you. I was reluctant to go, knowing I wouldn't see you for months at a time, but Chas insisted and my mother agreed, and I suppose they knew even back then how I felt. You were too young anyway—they were right—but it was difficult. I thought it might get better."

As far as she could tell, everyone had known except her. "You should have told me."

"No." He shook his head, his hair brushing his collar. "Absolutely not. For many reasons, but the most important being that you needed your bow, and you needed to be courted and have flowers sent, and to decide for yourself if you ever wanted to settle for a man who hasn't an exalted place in society or a large fortune or anything in particular to offer except that he loves you."

Suddenly she was trembling, hot and cold at once, and she clung to his hand as if she would never let go. "I think you have a bit more than that," she murmured, her hold on her emotions a mere thread, her throat oddly tight. "You can climb a tree higher than anyone I know."

"The very stuff good husbands are made of." His mouth twitched.

Husband. She quivered. Was she really going to marry Miles?

Oh, yes.

"But you do have a lot of flaws," she pointed out, fascinated by the way he looked at her, as if maybe he truly did adore her . . . and how could she have been so blind anyway?

"Dozens," he confirmed, as his lashes lowered just a little and his gaze dropped to her mouth. "Perhaps even hundreds, but look at the positive aspects of our situation. You already know them all."

"I don't know if that's a point in your favor or not."

"Maybe this is." He pulled her closer and his mouth did something tantalizing to the spot under her ear. "I promise to satisfy all your curiosity, El. Every question I couldn't answer for you before. All the secrets your mother won't tell you about what happens between men and women. Are you interested?"

He knew she was, damn him, but he had yet to ask the real question. Her arms slid around his neck. "Perhaps you should clarify the offer. As it stands, I think you are more likely to find yourself at the end of Luke's dueling pistol."

"Will you consent to be my wife?" His whisper was sultry, seductive, and she shivered in response. "I vow to take you eel fishing, and for forbidden moonlit walks through the woods, and we can lie on the bank by the river on sunny afternoons and spin dreams. It isn't much, I know, but—"

She stopped him by pulling his head down so she could kiss him with lingering, eloquent pressure, still learning, still marveling over how such a simple contact could be so combustible. "Be quiet, Miles," she whispered against his lips. "You can be such a fool at times. It isn't much? It's everything, you dolt."

"Is that a yes?" He was laughing now, like she remembered, rich and mocking, and she *loved* the sound. "You can't accept a proposal and call your future husband a dolt in the same breath."

"Of course I can." She smiled at him mischievously. "I am very good at breaking the rules when I am with you, remember?"

So much for asking Miles to bring Elizabeth back before anyone noticed their prolonged absence. Luke pulled out his watch, looked at it again, and thought it was probably going quite well, considering the time passed.

"I thought I'd find you here."

At the sound of the cool, clear voice, Luke turned from his frowning appraisal of the open French doors to the terrace. "Michael."

"I received your note."

And correctly deduced his destination his evening, though it was hardly a secret, as he had to squire Elizabeth to all the most popular entertainments. This ball was certainly crowded to an uncomfortable extent, the hostess popular among the beau monde.

Madeline wasn't in attendance, sending word she was going to the country to stay a few days at her sister-in-law's estate before bringing Trevor back to London. It hadn't been welcome news. The restless ennui that had plagued him so severely during the past year was held at bay by her presence. He was, in short, going to miss her.

Very much so, he was afraid.

"I was merely curious as to if you had any ideas," Luke said slowly, wondering at his friend's sudden appearance. "Since you retrieved the journal for me, I thought you might find it an interesting new slant on the mystery. Is this important?"

He'd sent a brief missive describing Fitch's claim on how he came into possession of the journal, but he hardly thought his friend would find it so interesting he'd attend a ball just to discuss it. Michael wasn't much for social engagements, unless they were forced upon him.

"So Fitch says he *found* it?" Michael's hazel eyes held a speculative gleam. "That explains how it could wind up in the hands of such an unimaginative man, but tells us little else. Since the ghost of Lord Brewer is unlikely to pilfer the journal years after his death and haunt our club, only to carelessly leave the book of his most private thoughts behind, we can rule your beautiful lady's husband out as the careless culprit. No servant either could gain entrance to the club, and unless Fitch was lying to you, they would sell it anyway, if they'd bothered to steal it, or more likely, blackmail Lady Brewer."

"I quizzed the staff at the club to see if any of them remembered the incident, but it was months ago. No one had any helpful information."

"I might look into it myself."

Luke moved a little farther into the corner to avoid a group of young ladies who paraded past, twittering and whispering behind their gloved hands. Michael, as an unattached marquess, could well be the target of the calculated promenade, or it could be Luke—a viscount wasn't the same prize, but still significant. Either way, with resignation they inclined their heads politely before returning to their conversation. "I see you've thought about this. Why?"

"I have my reasons."

Of course he did. Michael always had reasons. He didn't blink an eye without just cause. "And they are?" Luke asked bluntly, puzzled over the journal and the course of events that had set about his world being knocked awry. Madeline was always the current focus of his thoughts.

"The journal is possibly tied to another investigation."

"How so?"

Michael looked at him directly, his eyes crystal clear and questioning. "You worked for Lord Wellington. Surely you've heard of Roget."

He had, but that had been back in Spain. It was incongruous to hear the infamous spy mentioned here, in a civilized London ballroom. Luke asked carefully, "What could a man like him have to do with Madeline's husband's journal?"

"I think he might have been involved in the original theft," Michael said with his usual lack of inflection, "and then he left it to be found. My question is . . . why? Tell me again about your conversation with Fitch. As close to word for word as possible."

Chapter Twenty-four

The rich green lawn echoed with delighted shrieks and a melee of running boys, two galloping puppies, and a wayward ball that seemed to find its way into the pond with unerring accuracy, causing someone to wade in after it. The end result was that all the children boasted a certain degree of mud, much, as far as Madeline could tell, to their delight.

Ah, if life were only that simple once again.

"Goodness, this has been a warm summer." Next to her, Marta sat languidly in her chair, watching the antics of her offspring with a motherly smile. "Lovely for the boys, though. They hate the rain keeping them inside."

Trevor certainly seemed to be enjoying himself, his dark curls in an unruly halo as he dashed after the ball again. The game being played was unclear, and Madeline suspected the rules were either made up as it went along or didn't exist at all. "This is good for Trevor. I don't use the country estate much because it so large and it is just the two of us, after all."

"Langley Hall is a bit less ostentatious."

"Maybe we'll spend more time out of the city next year."

"Trevor is always welcome here, of course." Her sister-in-law narrowed her eyes against the sun. "He looks more like Colin every day."

"I know." Madeline spoke with affectionate remembrance. The affair with Luke had given her that, among other gifts. The pain of her husband's loss wasn't gone—it never would be—but it was different. No longer a cause for loneliness and sorrow, but she could remember Colin, and see him in Trevor, with fondness and nostalgia, not acute pain. She was a woman who had loved and loved well, but was no longer the desolate widow.

"Tell me about the elusive but apparently now attainable Viscount Altea." Marta said it as naturally as she might request a second cup of tea. "Everyone is abuzz. Even David said something to me, and as you know, he notices absolutely nothing."

Madeline was very fond of Marta's genial but admittedly vague husband. She smiled, studying the tips of her slippers visible beneath the hem of her lemon muslin day gown, and then looked up. "Luke is rather hard to describe, actually. If pressed to do so, I suppose I would say that he is a complicated man who prefers to approach matters in an uncomplicated way."

"Meaning?"

All along, Madeline had known she would have to have this conversation at some point. She'd debated how to explain her decisions regarding Luke to her sister-in-law, but Marta had always been a dear friend and she was Trevor's aunt, after all, and honesty seemed to be the best course. "He's told me he isn't interested in a marriage between the two of us. So we are friends, but that is the extent of it."

Nonplussed, Marta gazed at her, a faint frown creasing her brow. "Friends? I do not think a man of Lord Altea's reputation has female friends in a strictly platonic sense."

If she hadn't blushed, perhaps she might have carried it off, but Madeline had no intention of lying to Marta. "I'm a widow," she said carefully. "The same strictures don't apply as when I was a young debutante. Now and then he escorts me to a function, and he joined us—my mother and Aunt Ida included—at the opera the other evening. Otherwise we are very discreet."

"I . . . see."

"Do you?" It was important that was true.

"He's extremely handsome, of course." The words held a certain hesitant tone, as if Marta was trying to excuse her sister-in-law's fall from grace.

Yes, he was, but his physical appeal aside, Luke was so much more than another titled gentleman with good looks and superficial charm.

To admit to a torrid affair with one of London's more notorious bachelors was not the easiest confession she'd ever made, especially since she valued Marta's opinion of her, but what she was about to say was even more difficult. Madeline looked out over the serene park, the sloping lawn with the playing children, the leafy elms fluttering verdant leaves in the summer breeze, and collected her emotions. "I'm very much in love with him."

The moment that followed was quiet, except for the splash as the ball careened into the water again. The young nanny in charge began to scold the offender, who stood obediently for the diatribe but had a suspiciously broad grin on his face.

"I'm glad to hear it." Marta's tone was soft. "But I know you well enough to have guessed that already, for you would not go lightly into such a relationship. Is a marriage truly out of the question?"

"He's adamant . . . or he was at the beginning." Madeline squared her shoulders. The realities were as they were. "I entered into this with full knowledge of his position on it ever being permanent. Do not blame him for deceiving me or seducing me, for that matter. It was freely my choice to enter into our arrangement. He was extremely honest beforehand."

"I doubt anyone would believe Altea forced you," Marta said dryly. "A man with his reputation always has options. Any number of beautiful ladies dangle after him at all times, I'm sure."

That was no doubt the truth, but Madeline preferred not to think about it. "I meant I knew you would hear the whispers, and I wanted to talk to you myself before you drew any conclusions. I am a lover, not a fiancée."

"What of Trevor?"

A simple three words that were not simple at all. "I considered him, of course," Madeline explained slowly, with emphasis. "But he's very young and Luke's interest in me will not last." She did her best to sound accepting of something that broke her heart each time she acknowledged it. "It can't last, by the very virtue of how we've chosen to conduct our relationship. Therefore any possible scandal will be so long in the past by the time Trevor is old enough to understand that I doubt it will matter. Perhaps he will hear of it, and perhaps he never will. I have no intention of embarking on a career as a merry widow, Marta. I won't say this is my way of finally putting Colin's death behind me. That isn't possible, and what is happening now is much too complex to define so easily, but it has freed me somehow. I feel like a woman again."

Even with their parasols the sun was warm and mellow, and the bucolic country setting, with the sedate stone country house behind them, incongruous to their somewhat scandalous conversation. The flagstone terrace reflected the heat, and Madeline brushed a damp lock of loose hair from her neck.

And waited.

Colin's sister's acceptance was so important to her. This was much harder than appearing with Luke in public for the first time and that had been hard enough. When she looked back on it, *he'd* been there, and it had somehow seemed quite natural, the two of them together. She cared also about her family's opinion, but knew that despite what she said about Luke, her mother and Ida both believed a wedding was in her future. Neither of them knew for certain there was a physical relationship either, but with Marta she felt compelled to tell the whole truth, partially because they were close friends, and partially because of their mutual love for Colin.

At last Marta, who had been silent for what felt like an eternity but was probably only a few moments, said, "I understand all of it but one part. Oh, I see why you'd be attracted to the viscount, and of course, why he'd seek you out . . . you are very beautiful, Madeline, and have much to offer any man. Wit, charm, style, and, most of all, a warm heart. Colin worshipped you. I believe he would have done so his whole life had he lived to be a hundred. While I am pleased you have found love again, should you ever settle for less than full measure back? Besides, there should be brothers and sisters for Trevor."

If she hadn't asked herself the same question, her smile would have been less tremulous. "Apparently I must settle for what he has to give."

As for brothers and sisters, there was the possibility she'd conceived, but it was difficult to feel joy over such an event when she was uncertain of Luke's reaction. He was an honorable man, and maybe he would offer marriage, but he had strong feelings on the subject, so it was hard to be sure. He wouldn't abandon her, that she knew, but even if he did agree to wed her for the sake of the child, it was not at all what she wanted. She wanted to be his wife, but only if he loved her.

"If he doesn't understand you are a treasure, then Lord Altea is a fool," Marta said stoutly, with a flash in her eyes.

On the contrary, Luke was both intelligent and honorable enough he would have left her alone. . . . He *had* left her alone for an entire year after that first night, but she had chosen to launch into their affair. "According to him, he isn't opposed to marriage, just marriage to me," Madeline murmured, wondering how she would bear it if he did marry some pretty young girl just to beget an heir.

"That makes absolutely no sense if you and he . . . that is . . . well, it makes no sense."

Unfortunately, Madeline was beginning to think it made a great deal of sense, at least to Luke. "He feels it too. The first time we met, it was there between us, not just the attraction, though that was very real. I don't know if I can explain it adequately, but we *know* each other. We are quite alike in many ways, and being together comes very naturally. I feel confident we would be happy if we wed."

Marta stared at her in perplexed inquiry. "If what you say is true, this discussion becomes more peculiar by the passing moment."

Quietly, she explained, "Marrying a woman he doesn't love means if he lost her, the pain would be bearable. I think he's very afraid he could love me."

What will happen, Madeline thought, *when he realizes he already does?*

She'd lose him, she feared. Immediately he'd distance himself.

Unless she could find a way to help him exorcise his demons, whatever they may be. She'd lost Colin because his illness had been a battle she could not fight. This— this was different. Nor was it just her happiness at stake. She loved Luke too much to let him settle for less than what she could give him.

What they could give each other.

"If you know you could make him happy, how can you possibly reconcile not insisting on a future together, Madeline?" Marta reached across the small table between their two chairs and clasped her hand, giving a gentle squeeze. "Not for your sake, but for his. *That* is love."

A very valid point.

*   *   *

At least his sister's future was settled.

Luke couldn't help but be amused at the difference in both Miles and Elizabeth, the air at the dinner table festive for the first time since his sister's debut in the spring. Even his mother, once he'd carefully explained that he was in favor of the match, had finally come around. He wasn't positive she entirely agreed the trappings of title and fortune were not linked to a contented marriage unless both parties were shallow and valued only the superficial, but he had pointed out Miles was hardly impoverished and likely, actually, to become affluent one day. There was also the irrefutable possibility that Elizabeth might stay stubbornly unmarried if she couldn't have her choice of husbands, and besides, no one in the family would be surprised they'd gone from unruly childhood friends to lovers.

He was glad for her, and a certain part of him he wasn't aware still existed envied their undeniable happiness.

"I'd like a winter wedding," Elizabeth said, spearing a small piece of chicken and daintily putting it in her mouth.

"Winter?" Miles looked entertainingly pained at the long wait.

Which, Luke had a feeling, was intentional on Elizabeth's part, for she immediately hid her expression by sipping her wine.

"It will take at least that long to plan," Luke heard his mother declare, her fork suspended near her mouth, her eyes narrowed. "One cannot rush a proper wedding, and Elizabeth is my only daughter."

The only problem was Luke had no confidence— after having seen that tempestuous kiss—that the two of them would wait half a year and not do something rash in the meantime, no matter what Elizabeth said. "The fall is nice," he suggested pleasantly. "Only a few months away, and the weather much more cooperative to travelers."

Miles looked grateful, his mother indignant, and Elizabeth took a moment, but then smiled with a mischievous glint across the candlelit table. "I suppose guests should be a consideration."

"Indeed," Luke said dryly.

"A few months?" His mother shot him a disbelieving look. "Obviously you know nothing about planning weddings."

She was right, of course. He knew very little about formal weddings, but he did know something about how an impatient groom might feel. Luke set aside his fork, doing his best not to react. "No," he agreed. "But this should be up to both Elizabeth *and* Miles."

The arrival of the dessert course stopped the argument, and when he and Miles retired for their port to his study, his stepcousin sat down with a rueful smile on his lips. "I appreciate the effort on my behalf."

"You'll have to stand firm if you don't want your wedding to be the grandest affair in the history of British society," Luke informed him ironically, sinking down into the comfortable chair behind his desk. "But I am going to guess you already know that, since you know my mother very well indeed."

"I do know." Miles stared at the beverage in his glass with moody humor. "But I can wait, if it is what Elizabeth wants."

"Humph." Luke had much less faith. "I think half a year is a bit optimistic."

"So do I," Miles admitted cheerfully, stretching out his legs.

A swift wedding was definitely in order from that cheeky smile, Luke decided then and there. And it wasn't Miles he was worried about, in truth. Elizabeth could always talk Miles into the most reckless behavior possible. "You'll need to quickly put a stop to the campaigning to make the wedding as grandiose an affair as possible."

"Aunt Suzette is no match for Elizabeth's tenacity."

"She's never married off a daughter before. Be careful."

"Or a son." Miles arched a brow jokingly.

"I've been married." The moment the words were out of his mouth, Luke wasn't sure why he'd said them. Perhaps it was Madeline's absence, which left him edgy and bereft. Maybe it was his sister's palpable happiness in the glow of first love that gave introspection a new meaning.

Maybe it was just time to hear the words said aloud.

There was no doubt Miles was astounded and speechless. He took a gulp of his port, choked and coughed, and sat up straighter in his chair. "What?"

"In Spain."

At least Miles had the good sense to stay quiet. Luke wasn't even sure why he'd mentioned it in such a casual manner. He never spoke of it, not even to Alex or Michael. They knew, or he was sure at least Michael knew part of it, but both were private enough individuals they had never asked questions.

"She was"—he smiled in memory that was bittersweet—"Spanish. A *senorita*. A true lady. Beautiful, courageous, and though the daughter of a don, also integral to the Spanish resistance in the area the British wanted to wrest from Bonaparte. We were allies."

"I see."

Miles didn't actually, Luke reflected. No one did. "I married her. She was killed by the French, along with the child she carried."

End of story.

No, not quite.

"Lord, Luke, I'm sorry." Miles's voice was strained.

"So was I." Luke refilled his glass, feigning a nonchalance he didn't feel.

"Elizabeth doesn't know this."

"No."

Miles nodded without hesitation. "Of course not. She would have told me."

That sort of conviction caused a twinge of envy. It was what made Elizabeth and Miles perfect for each other, because they were *friends*.

Was Madeline his friend?

Luke thought perhaps she was. Passionate lover, yes. Friendship was different. Even more intimate. That dangerous territory made him pour another glass of port. He'd never told Madeline what he'd just revealed to Miles.

He should.

Maybe.

"Why would I tell my sister?" Luke asked in a voice perfectly absent of any emotion—to his amazement, because his throat had tightened. "It was done, over, finished, by the time I came back to England."

"Why are you telling me now?"

"I have no idea."

"Don't you?" Miles was young and yet his expression held a certain venerable wisdom. "Might it have something to do with all this talk of weddings and a certain Lady Brewer?"

Chapter Twenty-five

Trevor had fallen asleep on the journey, and though normally he insisted he was too old for outward demonstrations of affection, he was tired enough he curled comfortably into her arms, and Madeline had the simple pleasure of holding him as they rocked along.

... brothers and sisters for Trevor ...

Madeline smoothed his hair from his brow and lightly traced the curve of his smooth cheek. He was so precious, a miniature of Colin, yet hers also, with his inquisitive mind and dark eyes. She was blessed, and Marta was right: she did want more children. She loved being a mother, experiencing the gift of her son's smile, the sound of his laughter, the joy of watching him grow.

If Luke and I had a child, she thought, leaning her head back on the seat and letting her imagination conjure the image of a smiling baby, *would he or she be blond, and perhaps have Luke's unusual gray eyes?*

No. She shut off the daydream abruptly, her eyes opening.

The weather had turned sullen, with low, ominous

clouds in charcoal banks across the sky, and the smell
of rain in the air. She had the curtain rolled up for ven-
tilation, for it was warm and humid, and she watched
the countryside roll by, the increased traffic on the roads
telling her they were approaching London.

And Luke.

Was she pinning false hope on an illusion? The night
after the opera, she'd caught sight of his reflected expression in the glass of the window when he'd entered
her room.

Not an illusion, she decided a quickened heartbeat
later, because she'd seen the unguarded vulnerability,
the stark look in his eyes he usually concealed so effortlessly. The real question was, should she allow him
to reach the conclusion that it wasn't passion alone that
brought them together on his own, or did he need her
help?

The latter, she decided firmly as the vehicle rumbled
along and it started to rain. A smile tilted her lips despite the dreary weather.

Michael had the list, the names of the staff, and a tentative timetable.

It was a start.

"The matter of motive," he said matter-of-factly, "is
still unclear. I'd like to talk to Lady Brewer if possible.
Or it might be better if you spoke with the lovely lady.
If any of the members had a special association with her
husband, it would help me immeasurably."

Luke walked his horse around a low-hanging tree
branch laden with droplets from the recent rain. "But
naturally, she is to know nothing of why I am inquiring
about her late husband's acquaintances?"

"Naturally." Michael's agreement was unruffled and
even, the sodden sound of his mount's hooves on the
muddy path muted. "Do you wish to inform her that her
husband's cousin could be an infamous traitor who will

hang the moment we can prove duplicity against the Crown?"

"No," Luke admitted, shaking droplets of moisture out of his hair. "But I doubt she is going to know anything that can help. Madeline isn't the kind of woman who would protect a traitor."

"We often know small, significant facts we have no idea are important."

"That us lesser mortals don't recognize the significance of, you mean." They splashed along, and Luke was happy to be out of doors despite the rain, physical activity an antidote to his restless spirit. "We all haven't your perceptive powers."

"We don't all need them."

"True," Luke agreed, remembering Michael's capture by the French. It was a miracle his friend wasn't dead, but both Alex St. James—then a colonel commanding a regiment—and he, an aide to Wellington, had moved heaven and earth to first find Michael and then free him.

"You have your uses," Luke drawled, glancing around, the park deserted in this weather. They were completely alone, most of the *haut ton* choosing the drier indoors on such an inclement afternoon. "So, did you read it?"

Michael didn't pretend to misunderstand. He could redirect and evade if he wished, but rarely did he pretend. "Yes."

So, Michael had read Lord Brewer's journal. "I see." Luke shot him a sideways look. "And?"

"And . . . nothing. I was looking for a book code or the like, not a peek in your lady's private life."

"But peek you did," Luke said bluntly as Michael drew up his horse by a small copse of dripping trees, bringing his own horse to a halt. "It's what you do, so I don't blame you. But tell me, did Brewer say anything that will humiliate Madeline, should Fitch choose to forfeit his life by speaking out?"

Michael looked startled, then amused. "A rather strong statement."

"I have rather strong feelings on the matter." No hesitation. "And he knows it. I made it quite clear in our little meeting in Bath."

"Unfortunately, he might not have been the one to send her the stockings and garters."

"How in the name of Hades did you know about—"

"I'm interested," Michael interrupted in explanation. "When I'm interested, I know—"

"Everything," Luke finished grimly. "I take it you have a spy in the house?"

"In a manner of speaking."

"Why?" Luke's hands tightened on the reins involuntarily.

"Just wait." Michael, as always, sounded absurdly calm. No doubt he'd sounded exactly the same way when pulled half dead from a squalid cell in a crumbling fortress after the French had done their best to extract the information they wanted.

Luke recalled clearly the account of how beneath the blood and filth his friend had been ashen white when rescued, and Alex, whose regiment had actually taken the fort, had reported Michael had been locked in a cell so small he couldn't stand without stooping. His condition was atrocious. Luke hadn't seen him until a few days later when he'd arrived at the camp. Michael had been only semiconscious, but at least washed and bandaged, and that had been bad enough.

Though it was said by the third day any man would reveal his secrets, by all accounts, Michael hadn't followed that rule. He'd had so many broken bones, however, the surgeons expected he'd be maimed for life, but one wouldn't know it now, looking at the well-dressed, urbane man so easily sitting his horse.

Needless to say, Lord Wellington had been extremely pleased his most valuable operative had been successfully retrieved at the time, but Luke had thought all of that intrigue behind them.

Not so, it seemed.

The tall figure that materialized from the misty afternoon rain turned out to be a young man in plain tradesman's garb, his slight slouch an affectation, at a guess. He pulled at the brim of his hat in exaggerated acknowledgment: "Milord."

"Don't be so deliberately obsequious, Lawrence," Michael said in greeting.

The new arrival straightened and gave a mocking bow. He had strong features, dark hair that curled beneath the hat, and an interesting jagged scar down half his face, starting above one brow. Lucky for him, the blade had somehow missed his eye. "I thought that's what you grand toffs wanted from us lesser folk."

Michael slid off his horse in a single lithe move. "Very amusing. Drop the cockney accent, if you will. What do you have?"

The businesslike tone of the conversation made Luke also dismount. Michael had invited him along for a purpose. The grass squished under his booted feet and his jacket grew more damp by the second, but this conversation was obviously worth a good soaking, at least to Michael and his colleague. The man called Lawrence eyed Luke, but then nodded briskly. "Lord Brewer apparently liquidated some funds before his death."

"Do we know why?" Michael didn't look surprised at all, seemingly oblivious to the sheen of moisture on his hair and the dripping trees.

"*We* can only guess. Nothing can be traced."

"Everything can be traced."

Luke followed the rapid exchange in some bemusement, not certain if he should be outraged on Madeline's behalf that Lord Brewer's financial records had somehow been investigated without her knowledge. "What does this have to with Madeline?"

"Her husband's cousin is a person of interest to me at this time."

"And you think Brewer gave the man money for illegal purposes?"

"Who said," Michael murmured, "that Lord Brewer's cousin was a man?"

Luke took a moment to digest this, moisture trickling down his neck. "You are investigating a woman?"

"Don't look so surprised. Do you think betrayal and political intrigue are limited by gender? You, of all people, know better."

How true that is, he thought grimly.

"No, of course not," Luke muttered. "I'm just having trouble ascertaining how this all ties together."

Lawrence lifted his puckered brow. "The lady might be the minnow that snags us the bigger fish. She's slippery enough on her own, though. Even the arrangements to watch her house haven't helped much. She must know we're there."

More mystified than ever, Luke looked at Michael.

"I asked Alex to arrange that his brother John very tactfully ask one of his former paramours, who happens to have the town house next to our quarry, if she would hire a footman on his recommendation with no questions asked. Disappointingly, so far our suspect is circumspect and observes every propriety. I didn't really expect Alice Stewart to be so careless, but one never knows."

Luke recognized the name of the dark-haired lady who'd been seated in the box at the opera the other night. She'd made a hasty exit, upon the conclusion of the performance, but it could have just been a desire to avoid the resulting crush of carriages waiting to depart. "Alice Stewart? I've seen her recently, conversing with Madeline."

"Not so surprising, since they are related by marriage." But Michael had subtly tensed, his gaze appraising. "Are they good friends? My informants say no."

Of course Michael had *informants*. "I have no idea. Shall I ask?"

"If you can be discreet and trust Lady Brewer to be the same."

He could, he realized. Absolutely. Madeline had the utmost discretion for a woman. Actually, males were just as bad when it came to gossip as women, so maybe he should qualify his trust and not attach it to her sex. "Yes." He smiled wryly, "better than most men I know, probably."

"Maybe you should introduce us," Lawrence murmured. "Beautiful *and* discreet?"

Luke eyed the man's shabby clothes, but readjusted his thinking. This was no minion. From his speech and demeanor, he was one of Michael's colleagues, and if not on equal footing, very close. He said curtly, "Sorry. She's unavailable."

"Pity." Lawrence looked at Michael, and his mouth twisted in the parody of a smile. "Since the topic has arisen, congratulations, my lord, on your betrothal. If you have new instructions, you know where to find me."

What?

Even as Luke absorbed the word, Michael nodded once in dismissal and Lawrence disappeared into the misty rain.

It took a moment, but Luke said incredulously, "Betrothal?"

"What?" Michael glanced over from apparently studying the spot where his associate had decamped into the middle of the park, his thoughts obviously elsewhere. "Oh, yes. I suppose the announcement will be in the paper in a day or two."

"You're engaged?" Had someone informed him he'd just been named successor to the throne of England, Luke could not have been more surprised.

Michael? Engaged to be married?

His friend's face was shuttered, his eyes unreadable. "My parents wish for me to fulfill the contracted marriage that was supposed to be Harry's responsibility. As we all know, when my brother died, his duties fell to me."

Do you wish this?

Luke almost . . . almost said it out loud, but managed to not ask the question he knew Michael would never want to answer. His friend didn't speak of his older brother's unexpected death often, and it was unlikely he'd start now. Plus, the three of them—Alex, Michael, and him—had not just years of friendship between them but had survived a hellish war by giving each other the ultimate courtesy of staying out of each other's business.

Only, at this point, it seemed his business and Michael's had collided.

Luke looped the reins in one hand, preparing to mount. It was raining harder and a bit wet for his tastes, and he had a feeling Michael might want to finish his ride alone. "I'll talk to Madeline, if you wish."

"Among other things, I imagine." Michael grinned, but he didn't quite pull off the lighthearted expression. "In the throes of passion, perhaps the beauteous Lady Brewer will reveal all her secrets."

Or maybe Luke would reveal his. It was a sobering realization.

"If she has anything to say I feel is significant, I'll send word."

"Luke." Michael hesitated. "Four years ago we knew there was an Englishwoman with ties to the aristocracy who was acting as a courier and spy for the French. Our intelligence here suspected Alice Stewart because she was seen more than once in the company of other known agents, but it was always in a social context, so it was difficult to find solid evidence, especially given her family connections. One of our men following her ended up dead. It looked to be an accident, but I don't believe in accidents when one is trailing a spy who would be hanged if caught."

Luke didn't either. He ground out, "I thought the damned war was over."

"Wars are never over." It was just a flash, but Michael looked weary for a moment. "I think she's dangerous. I saw nothing in the journal, but obviously she worried there might be. If she realizes we have someone watching her house, she could decide her cousin possibly confided in his wife. Trust me—when you are in a risky occupation, you do not take chances."

"Madeline is in danger?"

"It's possible."

Luke set his heel to his horse and galloped off.

Luke was entirely wrong about Lord Fitch. He'd struck again.

Or at least she was fairly sure it was him.

Who else could it be?

Madeline gazed at the drawing and wondered how something used as a calculating weapon to disturb could be so hauntingly beautiful. The background was a vague, shadowy setting of moonlit draperies and walls. The only truly clear object, except the single figure in the foreground, was an open window, the illusion of the curtains lifted by the breeze perfectly captured with simple elegance that was probably not simple at all to execute.

A woman. Still, half turned away, her graceful, nude silhouette executed with such skill it took the breath away. The slight lift of the subject's face bore a curiously dignified and serene opposition to the fact that the outline of breast and hip and every other curve exposed by the created iridescent lighting was both shocking and—Madeline had to admit—ethereally striking in an artistic way. It was not a nude in the style of the old masters, but different. Erotic. Modern and evocative.

The woman in the drawing had long, pale hair.

The woman in the drawing was *her*.

"There is a lady here to see you, madam." Hubert, solemn and staid, stood in the doorway. "She refuses to give her name or a card because she says"—he stopped, obviously pained—"the British aristocracy is stifled by archaic social customs that might indicate too much inbreeding."

She stared at him for a moment, not at all sure how to respond, but his expression was so comical—maybe the burst of laughter was genuine mirth, maybe it was a reaction to nervous tension, but Madeline clapped a hand over her mouth to stifle the potential outburst. Hubert had said *lady*. If the caller in question didn't qualify, he would have said *person*. "I'm sorry. I suppose you should show her into the blue drawing room," she murmured. "I'm curious, if nothing else."

"Very well, madam." His response was a little stiff.

Carefully, she turned the drawing upside down on Colin's desk so no one else could see it. She reached up to straighten her hair, decided that any visitor who announced herself in such a way probably wouldn't care about the state of her hostess's coiffure, and rose to go greet her mysterious guest.

Two steps into the drawing room, she stopped, arrested, her gaze fastened on a tall woman with hair an interesting shade between chestnut and auburn, scrutinizing the portrait above the mantel, which happened to be of Colin's great-grandfather, complete with a cavalier's plume in his hand and a rakish smile on his face.

Hesitantly, because her visitor seemed familiar but she couldn't come up with the name, Madeline said, "Good afternoon."

"The face is good," the woman said by way of greeting, still studying the picture, "but the body all wrong. Do you see how his neck is too elongated despite the ruff, and the way his hand sits on his sword is awkward?"

"I've never thought about it," Madeline told her truthfully.

That made her guest turn around, and with a small shock, she realized though they'd never met, it was easy enough to know why the woman was so recognizable. The distinct features of high cheekbones and straight nose aside, those silver eyes were unmistakable. Maybe they were shaded by dark, feminine lashes, but those were Luke's eyes, and whoever she was, they were very closely related. She wasn't in the first bloom of youth, but still very beautiful.

"I'm Regina. And you are Madeline."

Informal to say the least. Madeline cleared her throat and then managed to say evenly, "It is a pleasure to meet you."

"Did you get my gift?" Elegant and interestingly attired in half boots and a watered silk gown in a shade of dark green that complemented her hair, the woman smiled.

"Gift?" Madeline had to admit to being off balance.

Without being asked, Regina chose a settee and sank down in a graceful, feline movement. "The sketch. I thought it quite good. You have lovely bones. Up close, I now think I did you justice even though I merely studied you from some distance."

"Studied me?"

"Opera glasses have their uses."

This was by far the most bizarre conversation ever had in this drawing room. Madeline, however, was so relieved to realize Fitch hadn't sent the drawing, she smiled. "You drew it?"

"Of course. I'm an artist."

"Yes, indeed, you are, if you sketched that picture. It's . . . remarkable." Madeline took an opposite chair and gazed at her unusual caller. "Thank you. I'm just not sure how you . . ."

"Imagined you nude?" Regina laughed, her gray eyes full of humor. "I saw you with Luke at the opera. Clothes are just trappings."

Luke. Said so easily. If it wasn't for the remarkable resemblance, Madeline would be jealous.

"You should have joined us."

"I don't think so." Regina's mouth twitched. "Your mother might have fainted. I am not received, usually.

It's more by choice than birth, but that is part of it, of course. Do you know who I am?"

"No." It was a relief to be able to admit it.

"Luke's older sister. Half sister, actually. Born well before the marriage and the heir, but not under the best of circumstances. I am not precisely an embarrassment, but very close. If I were a little less outré, I might fit in better with the Daudet family, but as it is, I am like the eccentric aunt you never want to sit next to at the dinner table."

Madeline blinked at the frank declaration. It was true; their coloring was very different, but she believed the claim. And it made sense. "I see."

"I believe the general view is that I might say or do anything. Like"—one auburn brow quirked up— "drawing a nude of my brother's paramour. Do you mind me coming for an impromptu visit?"

"Of course not."

"Are you being polite and politic, or truthful?"

"Truthful." Madeline meant it. This was a fascinating glimpse into a part of Luke's life she didn't know existed. "Please stay. Shall I ring for tea, or would you prefer sherry?"

"You are admirably difficult to shock, Lady Brewer. I like that."

"My life isn't exactly following a conservative and acceptable course at this time," Madeline murmured, meaning every word. "I am in no position to cast askance glances at anyone. I take it Luke did not send you here."

"Of course not. He might even be furious with me." Regina relaxed back on the settee and grinned. The lighthearted expression granted her already beautiful features an undeniable charm. "Luckily, as much as he hates interference in his life, he gets over being angry very quickly. Did you know that?"

It was impossible to not laugh. "No. What else don't I know?"

"Plenty, I am sure. My brother has his secrets, but I doubt by saying that I am giving away anything you haven't guessed already about him."

"He reveals only what he wants you to know and that isn't much, I admit."

"Yes." Regina leveled an approving look at her. "I think we will get along. Tell me, are you in love with him?"

This time she *was* rendered incapable of speech at the deeply personal nature of the question upon such brief acquaintance. She wasn't sure she would answer her mother if asked so directly. Madeline just sat helpless.

"You must be," Regina Daudet said in a philosophical tone. "I've thought about it. This isn't typical behavior for you any more than it is for him, so you have to possess an underlying reason to risk your reputation this way. Oh, it is hardly likely society will ostracize you, since you are a widow, but still, you have carefully preserved that status for quite a long time. Luke is different, and, I agree, worth a risk or two."

"I haven't told him." The words were stilted, but still they came out as a clear admission.

She wasn't sure why she confided it so easily, but it was . . . liberating.

"No?" Regina raised a brow. "Still, you've been good for him. It's just getting him to admit to himself you are not just another passing fancy that will be difficult. But you must be. The nightmares are better, or at least he hasn't visited me in the hours before dawn since he met you."

"He has trouble sleeping?" True enough, Madeline had always fallen asleep first, even that night at the inn. She didn't know, and it bothered her instantly because she wanted to know *everything* about him. With a frown she thought back over their nights together. There actually weren't all that many to consider, but she did realize she'd never seen him asleep.

His sister nodded, her gray eyes somber and distant.

"He lost the woman he loved in Spain, and she still haunts his dreams."

Frozen, shocked, Madeline sat very still. The clock in the corner sounded loud.

It explained so much.

And yet didn't explain nearly enough.

"Can you tell me about her?"

Regina shook her head, her silver eyes sympathetic. "No. For two reasons. Firstly, I don't know enough to help you, and secondly, because he needs to be the one." She stopped, and then added softly, "Luke needs to tell *someone,* and I think you are the perfect choice."

Chapter Twenty-six

It was the sense of disquiet before the battle.

Luke recognized it. A certain quality of sensation that crawled along the skin and left marks in its wake, like a poisonous creature with tiny claws. Not necessarily impending doom—that was far too dramatic—but an inherent unease when you knew something was wrong.

Alice Stewart was both cousin to Lord Brewer and possibly the recipient of a significant amount of funds just before his death. The proximity of his death and the gift of the money bothered Luke, and he tugged on a dry shirt and picked up a clean cravat, his mind moving swiftly as he reviewed the brief facts he knew.

Madeline's husband had withdrawn money from his bankers and given it to someone—possibly Mrs. Stewart, and then he had suddenly died. Hopefully those two events weren't connected, but it made him wonder. Colin May had given the woman a considerable amount of coin—or Michael apparently thought so—and then he had perished from an unexpected ailment.

Luke didn't like the sound of it.

Then, five long years later, the journal turned up. Why? Subsequently, it was left in a place where it would be found, and, if so, that made Fitch merely a prop in the drama. Would anyone else deliberately want to humiliate Madeline?

At a guess, Alice Stewart would have access to the house as a guest. She could have taken the journal at any time in those five years after her cousin's death. Having it put where it would be found was a petty act, and, quite frankly, seemed directed purposely at Madeline. He'd thought so the minute he found out how Fitch came to have it. Sending the stockings and garters also seemed malicious, but not actively dangerous. In retrospect, perhaps it was more an action a vindictive female might take.

Michael wanted him to talk to Madeline. Luke was beginning to think perhaps he shouldn't wait.

Hastily he finished dressing, yanked on his boots, and ordered his carriage brought around in the unfriendly drizzle. Not fifteen minutes later he clambered out of the vehicle, and heedless of the late-afternoon hour and that anyone might see him, swiftly took the steps and used the brass knocker on the door.

Madeline's butler, Hubert, opened the door and stepped back in resignation with a formal bow. "My Lord Altea. Please come in or you'll get a soaking. I will announce you."

Luke stepped into the polished foyer, an amused part of him reading the expression on the butler's face. Were any of the servants ignorant of the fact he was Madeline's lover? Probably not.

"Thank you." Why did he think this visit so urgent? He wasn't sure, but it felt in his gut like it might be. Michael was never involved in small intrigues. His interest alone was alarming enough to warrant an interview as soon as possible.

"Just a moment, sir."

Luke waited impatiently, not certain what he was

even going to say when he had a chance to question her about all this, his mind forming and discarding theories on why, suddenly, she was linked to possible espionage, deceit, and maybe even murder.

She could be in danger.

It wasn't Hubert who came down the hall, but, to his amazement, his older sister, who took one look at his face and laughed, the sound light and musical. "I sketched her," Regina said in explanation as a footman hurried to retrieve a light cloak.

What the devil was going on? "Regina, what are you doing here?" he asked, and without thought reached forward to take the garment and settle it around her shoulders.

"As I said, I sketched her." She smoothed back her hair and smiled at him, a knowing look in her eye. "I wanted to stop by and see if she liked the gift."

"I've never interfered in *your* life," he said dryly, not that it ever did any good whatsoever to chide his older sister on her sometimes impulsive actions.

"I've never needed it," she declared blithely, oblivious to the footman and Hubert, who had returned and now stood waiting. "You, on the other hand, have foibles that have to be addressed."

She swept out into the dreary, late-afternoon rain, the smile on her expression causing him severe misgivings. Was there anything more dangerous than two women in a man's life talking about him without his presence?

He doubted it.

This was all becoming very complicated.

But that aside, not nearly as complicated as the mess with the journal. Luke followed Hubert down the hall to a formal drawing room, where Madeline still sat in a delicate chair upholstered in dark blue velvet, a half smile on her soft mouth. "Good afternoon, my lord. I am rather surprised to see you, but this is a day for surprises, apparently."

He could really only imagine what she and Regina

had to say to each other. "Why would you be surprised to see me?"

Hubert withdrew and tactfully pulled the doors closed without being asked.

Yes, all the servants know. Probably all of London knows.

"Because you have never called in the afternoon."

No, he hadn't. He was usually forced to sneak through the back door in the shelter of the night. "I need to talk to you," he said, trying to ignore the irritation he felt— irrationally, of course—over not being able to stroll through her front door like any other caller.

Well, he *could.* If he wished.

Did he wish?

He was afraid he did. That he wanted to call in the daylight, send flowers, buy her a magnificent necklace to match the earrings, to wake up in her arms . . .

"About?" Madeline wore a simple blue gown that matched the surroundings. Her gaze was direct, her body seemingly relaxed, yet somehow he knew she wasn't.

"About what?" he asked, riveted in the moment, just gazing at her. Was this love? The first time it had happened to him it had been different. Blazing, combustible, part of the drama of war and danger and forbidden longing . . . He'd been younger, too, and more idealistic, and Maria, with her fiery temper and dark, dramatic beauty, such a contrast to his cool English demeanor. This was different, like drifting down a serene river, warm and contented, with the sun shining above and the whisper of a breeze in the green leaves of the trees on the bank. . . .

It held at bay the past. Nothing would ever erase it, but maybe for the first time he knew it could be set aside. The pain, the guilt, the horror . . .

"You said you need to talk to me."

The interruption to his reverie was welcome, because he didn't want to travel down that dark path of painful memories. "Tell me about Alice Stewart," he ordered more abruptly than he'd intended.

"Alice?" Madeline stared at him, wide-eyed, obviously bewildered. "What do you wish to know?"

"Everything."

"Why?" She blinked.

"I'll explain, but first, just tell me what you know about her."

Madeline considered his request, her smooth brow furrowing. "She's been out of the country for years and just recently returned. We aren't close acquaintances, despite her relationship with Colin. I doubt I can tell you anything of significance at all."

"Would she have known about the journal?"

Madeline sat back, her fine brows drawing together in a quizzical frown. "Colin's journal? I . . . I don't know. She called, of course, upon her return to England. We did, naturally, speak about Colin. Perhaps I mentioned his journal. She knew of his tendency to write down his thoughts; all of his family did. Why?"

"Where was she when she was out of the country?"

"I'm not sure. Is this an interrogation?"

"France, possibly?"

"Of course not. We were at war."

He ignored that indignant denial, starting to form a clearer picture of what might have happened if Roget was really involved. "Did you know she'd asked for a large sum of money from your husband before she embarked on her trip out of the country that lasted so many years?"

The question made her straighten in her chair. Her eyes were dark and liquid in the muted afternoon light. Slowly she replied, "That was where it went? When the solicitor was going through Colin's affairs, he asked me about it. I was too devastated in my grief to even venture a guess, but later I did wonder. My husband didn't normally discuss his business affairs, but it was quite a sum, and I was surprised he didn't tell me what he'd done with it."

Luke stared at a small statue on a side table for a moment, not seeing it, his mind elsewhere. It was coming together, but they were still missing quite a few pieces. "So she might have received money from your husband right before he died, it is undisputed she disappeared for years, and the moment she comes back to England the journal is stolen and subsequently left for Fitch—or anyone else—to find. Have I got the right of it so far?"

"I suppose." Madeline gazed at him, her expression troubled. "Whatever made you think of all of this in such a light? I've never cared for Alice all that much, but then again, I don't dislike her either. Colin was fond of her, and that was enough for me."

"Why would he have given her money? Can you venture a guess?"

"No." She shook her head. "Though if she needed it, I would guess he would have helped her. That was his generous nature."

In light of that declaration, and to spare her, he didn't want to suggest the possibility of murder. All loss was difficult, but he knew firsthand that dealing with the vagaries of fate was one matter, and human viciousness quite another. If Lord Brewer had succumbed to a swift but deadly illness, it had not been preventable. If he had been killed to keep him silent, that was a different kind of grief.

What could he have known? What could he have written in his journal?

Michael had looked him in the eye. *She's dangerous.*

At all costs, Luke needed to protect Madeline.

"You are coming home with me."

She wasn't sure what made her catch her breath more, that he'd issued an ultimatum as if he had the slightest control over her life or that he'd said *home*.

"You and Trevor both," Luke elaborated, looking grim and shaken, his hair damp and wavy. "Have your maid pack enough for several days at least. We can send for more clothing if you need it."

"Luke." Madeline couldn't think of anything else to say, the protest coming out as a mere shocked whisper of his name. His expression spoke volumes.

"I am uninterested in discovering later I didn't take the proper precautions. Some mistakes should not be repeated."

Mistakes? Did he blame himself for what happened to the woman in Spain, the one his sister said he'd loved?

"You aren't making a great deal of sense," she managed to say coherently. "What can possibly be so alarming?"

"I'll explain later. If I even *can* explain." He swallowed, his throat working. "Lord, Madge, please. Don't argue with me. Suffice it to say I don't feel comfortable with you here alone. Come with me and stay with my family for a few days—or at least until I think it is safe."

"I'm hardly alone." Not with a houseful of servants.

"You aren't with *me*. I want you in my home. In my arms."

Held in the moment, Madeline looked at him and knew that while it was not precisely a declaration of love, it was very, very close, and her heart soared. She still didn't quite understand what any of this current drama had to do with Colin's journal and Alice, but the man she loved wanted to keep her close to him. No—he demanded her presence in his house, no less.

A less autocratic order would have been better, but then again, his vehemence was moving.

He'd said *please*. Lord Altea, the jaded sophisticate who moved so casually among the exalted circles of the *ton*, had looked at her and said *please*.

"Do you really think this is that urgent?"

"If I didn't, would I be here?"

No, of course not. If she knew anything at all, it was he would never ask this of her easily. She nodded and stood, reaching over to the bellpull. Hubert appeared moments later and she gave instructions to have her maid ready the necessities for a short trip for both she and Trevor, and to have his governess pack also to accompany them.

"Is your family prepared for you to move in your mistress and her child?" she asked, half joking, but also half serious.

Maybe more than half.

"You aren't my mistress." A muscle in his jaw tightened.

"What am I, then?"

"Don't make me look at it too closely right now." If he'd made an effort at his usual easy charm, it failed, for his smile did not reach his eyes. "All I know is if I walk out of here without you, I will worry all night. This isn't a game. I understand games. I understand lies, deceptions, even reckless wagers. But there are parts of my life I am not willing to risk."

She was one of them? Madeline declined to ask. He'd said more than he intended already, if she was to judge.

"I trust you this is important." She stood with her arms at her sides, resolute and hopeful, and wondered if she should trust either emotion.

"So you should," he said softly. "If anything happened to you . . ." He stopped, his voice dropping low.

The moment flared between them, poignant, meaningful, and yet Madeline wasn't certain just what meaning it held. She was not the one who had declared marriage an impossibility—he had.

She loved him and she wanted to be his wife, bear his children, and sleep in his arms for the rest of her life. Was she greedy, yearning for a second chance at a happy life with a man she adored? Maybe, but fate had cruelly robbed her the first time, and now she'd been given love again. Surely she should be able to keep it.

Whatever she might have said next was interrupted by the return of Hubert, his face creased in the usual anxious frown, but the lines perhaps a bit deeper. "Madam,

I have given the instructions you requested, but I am afraid it appears Lord Brewer is not at home."

She hadn't quite gotten used to Trevor being referred to in that way yet, but he had inherited the title despite his young age. "I wasn't told Miss Chaucer was taking him to the park. The weather is hardly suitable."

"Miss Chaucer is here, my lady. The young master left with Mrs. Stewart several hours ago when you were out."

Madeline knew the blood left her face, for she went cold all over. *"What?"*

"Mrs. Stewart is family, madam. I am sure that—"

It was Luke who interrupted in a staccato delivery of questions. "When? How did they leave? Did Alice Stewart say where they were going? Was she alone?"

"I'm not—not sure I know, my lord." Hubert stammered, his fleshy face betraying dismay.

"Please get the governess down here at once."

"Yes, my lord."

A moment later, Madeline's shaking body was pulled into a comforting embrace. Even without Luke's disturbing visit she would have been unhappy over Alice taking her son out without her permission. It had certainly never happened before. The most Colin's cousin had ever done was politely ask about Trevor's health.

Which meant, a terrified part of her realized, this was not a logical event. A small sob escaped her throat.

Luke's mouth was against her hair, his arms strong and supportive. "It will be fine. Don't look so stricken, my love. Michael has someone watching her house. We'll find her and Trevor and bring him back."

Michael Hepburn, the Marquess of Longhaven? What did he have to do with all this? He was watching Alice? "Why would she take Trevor?" Her voice was merely a wisp. Madeline was surprised Luke could hear it at all.

"I don't know." His arms tightened. "But I promise you, I will find out."

*   *   *

There might be two puzzles, both with many parts.

Michael listened to the rain against the glass of the long windows and contemplated what he knew.

He knew, for instance, that Roget had an English accomplice that was female. Decoded communiqués had mentioned her, and Mrs. Stewart fit the profile. She was young, pretty, and on the fringes of society but not actually a prominent figure, with connections but not enough prestige or wealth she couldn't be tempted into betrayal. Lord Brewer had given her money; Michael had become convinced now that she was the recipient, for she'd paid all her debts and booked passage for the Continent the day after Colin May's funeral.

It was quite likely the woman had killed her generous cousin. The timing was suspicious, at the least.

And then she'd been gone for the worst of the war, those grueling last four years, and not returned to England until all the dust had settled. Not only had she come back, but she'd come back wealthy enough to rent a town house in a fashionable neighborhood and begin to edge back into society. Right after she'd stolen the journal.

That too, seemed likely. If Michael had to speculate, she'd not known it existed before she left, but discovered it was a danger upon her return, and so she'd easily enough gotten the information of its whereabouts and taken it, checked for the damning evidence that apparently wasn't there, and left it to be found.

Only she couldn't have left it in the club, as women were not allowed. There was an accomplice somewhere.

Messy, that. An accomplice could talk.

Unless he was dead, of course. Michael's inquiries had unearthed that a young waiter had been stricken only three months ago with a mysterious illness that sounded remarkably like what killed Lord Brewer.

Supposition, all of it, but as it collected, a bit damning.

Puzzle one: was Alice Stewart a traitor? If so, why did she kill her cousin? He'd given her money, so it wasn't for gain. Obviously he knew something she was afraid he'd written down. Why she'd come back to England wasn't as much of a mystery. The war was over, her mission was accomplished, and France was not such a desirable place to be in the aftermath of defeat.

Puzzle two: if she stole the journal and it was harmless, why not quietly put it back? It rang true that it resonated of female vindictiveness to try to expose the intimate secrets of Madeline May's marriage in such an oblique way . . . most males would not think of it, in Michael's opinion. The gift of the stockings was also particularly disturbing and malicious.

So, if he was going to come to conclusions, he knew two things: Alice Stewart was capable of treachery and murder and she hated Lady Brewer.

It was not a good combination.

"We have an interesting development."

Michael glanced over at the doorway, unsurprised. "I *almost* didn't hear you come in."

Lawrence leaned against the doorjamb, his expression bland. "Don't be too smug. I wasn't being particularly careful. We have a problem. A new game is afoot."

Chapter Twenty-seven

The governess, a young, thin woman with curly red hair, knew nothing, her expression going from bewildered to frightened as Luke questioned her.

Hours. Alice Stewart had kidnapped the boy hours ago. Luke knelt by Madeline's chair and took her shaking hand.

He needed to do something *now*.

"I think the next logical step is to go visit your husband's cousin before we panic. I'll be back or send word right away." His mind raced forward. . . . Was this about blackmail? More money? Revenge of some sort?

Madeline lifted an ashen face and spoke the words he wasn't surprised to hear. "I'm coming with you."

"Darling, someone needs to be here in case we are alarmed for no reason and Alice brings him back."

Neither of them thought it a possibility, though. The words didn't have to be said.

"I'll send for my mother." She'd begun to cry when he was talking to her son's governess, but silently, a glistening trail of tears streaking down the porcelain curves of her cheeks, her eyes huge. "She can wait here. I can't, Luke. I cannot sit here and merely wait."

Luke debated lifting her in his arms, carrying her out to his carriage, and taking her to the sprawling Mayfair mansion that was a tribute to the Daudet fortune, upstairs to his suite of rooms and ordering her to stay there under the threat of several burly footmen keeping guard. He wanted her safe, but also declined being so high-handed. The guards would be for him—to keep her protected for his peace of mind and sanity—and that wasn't fair.

"Whatever makes you feel better." He reached for her and gently tipped her chin up, so their eyes met. Hers were wet, and he didn't in the least blame her for crying. It was rather hard to believe, but she looked even more beautiful to him with a reddened nose and damp cheeks.

"I'll write the note." She nodded, the movement mechanical.

"Fine," he said, and bent his head to lightly kiss her, regardless of Hubert hovering in the doorway. It was a dispassionate contact of comfort and reassurance, her trembling lips cool against his. When he lifted his head all he said was, "Tell your maid you'd like a light cloak. It's damp this evening."

She nodded, the muscles in her slender throat rippling as she swallowed.

Moments later they were climbing into his carriage.

He fully understood what it was like to be a helpless bystander when someone you loved was in grave danger. In his case, he hadn't been able to prevent the tragedy. This, though, *this* would be different.

Mrs. Stewart lived on a fashionable street a short drive away, but when the door was answered by a middle-aged maid, she shook her head when asked if her mistress was home.

Luke didn't often use his title to intimidate or persuade, but he said curtly, "I am Lord Altea, and this is

Lady Brewer, Mrs. Stewart's cousin. Where did she go?"

"Packed up." The woman wiped her hands on an already soiled apron. "I'm the last one left, milord. Just finishing cleaning up the house."

Madeline made an inarticulate sound of distress next to him.

"Where?" he demanded.

"Don't rightly know," the servant squeaked in response to his lethal tone. "I swear it, sir. Sailing off is me guess. I heard her tell her personal maid to leave out her heavier walking dress, for the sea breezes can be cold. We was all given our notice and a full week's wages."

Even if they had to search every ship readied for departure, he vowed, handing Madeline into the carriage without ceremony, they'd find her son.

"The pier," he told his driver, and clambered inside as the vehicle started rolling forward.

She didn't understand. Not any of it. Not why Alice would ever take Trevor, not why she was leaving England again so soon, not why Luke had arrived in a flurry of concern earlier. He clearly knew something she didn't, and it was supported by what had just happened.

If he hadn't been there, she wouldn't have known what to do.

Actually, Madeline still didn't. Paralyzed by fear, her hands wound together so tightly her fingers ached, the swaying of the racing vehicle almost toppled her to the floor once or twice, she held herself so stiffly.

Oddly enough, she was grateful Luke wasn't trying to tell her all would be well. He was worried. She could see it in the tension in his broad shoulders and the grim set of his mouth. Nor was he feeding her platitudes or false hopes, and despite the chasm in her soul at the moment at the idea of Trevor, perhaps frightened and alone, needing her, it was calming to not be told to stop worrying.

As if she could. She was petrified.

But it was clear she wasn't alone. Luke sat across from her, his long legs extended, his eyes somber and concerned.

"Why is Lord Longhaven having Alice watched?"

"I am not sure. Michael is"—his mouth twisted a bit—"not all that he appears. Yes, he is the son of the Duke of Southbrook, glib when he chooses, charming occasionally, and women pursue him, but they don't know him by half. Quite frankly, I've never been so glad in my life that he is what he is."

A nonanswer if there ever was one, but Madeline felt she understood nonetheless. She nodded. There was something he wasn't saying, but if she needed to know it, he would have told her. It mattered, or it wouldn't be a secret, but it didn't pertain to retrieving her son. "He'll help us?"

"No one can help us better than Michael," he confirmed tersely.

And that was *all* that mattered.

When they came to a lurching halt, Luke climbed out in one lithe movement and reached for her, swinging her out without ceremony. "We'll find out if she's booked a passage."

But thirty minutes later they hadn't. They'd only managed to talk to the captains of three different ships, and it was getting later. . . .

Misty, cold, dreary with the smell of fish in the air and sailors passing by . . . Madeline was far colder inside than out, though her cloak was soaked by now.

Trevor.

At the fourth ship they struck gold. Not in the form of an informative ship's officer, but of the same man she'd seen once before—the one who had delivered the journal back into her hands, scar and all, his smile ironic as he emerged from the growing shadows, his boots loud on the slick, wet surface of the dock. "Lord Altea, I've been looking for you. I think we are at cross-purposes at the moment."

Luke nodded and squeezed Madeline's hand. "Alice Stewart?"

"We have her. Longhaven had an agent following the lady, and he nabbed her trying to board yon ship." He pointed into the shadows at a hulking vessel still bobbing at her moorings. "It would have sailed in the morning for France."

Perhaps, just perhaps, her heart began to beat again. Madeline wanted to weep with joy.

"Did she have a child with her? A young boy?"

The scarred man's gaze slid briefly to Madeline's face and then back to Luke. "No. She wishes to negotiate."

The joy vanished. *Negotiate?*

Luke asked hoarsely, "How so?"

"Safe passage for the location of the child."

Though she'd never fainted in her life, Madeline swayed, the change from fear to relief to fear again so acute she wasn't sure she could breathe. "You don't have Trevor?"

"We had only one man following her, my lady." The scarred man's voice was gentle and surprisingly cultured, considering he wore old breeches and a shabby coat, not to mention a dilapidated hat with a worn brim. "After she left your residence with the young viscount, she met up with someone else and he left with the boy. Our operative had to make a choice of whom to follow. His orders were to keep on Mrs. Stewart's trail and he followed his instructions, but he did send a note as soon as he realized she was going to board a ship."

Luke said a word under his breath Madeline had never heard before, but she was fairly sure it wasn't flattering to Alice. "Where is she?" he asked in a voice much colder than the spitting rain. More like slick, black ice on a midwinter country road in a frozen landscape. It chilled Madeline, and she wasn't sure she could get much colder.

"I'll take you." The scarred man nodded once. "Follow me."

Michael had the lady, her trunks, and a young man with a very businesslike pistol ensconced in a small, abandoned office in one of the warehouses just off the main docks. It was a dismal enough space, lit now by several lanterns, with only a few chairs and a desk that hadn't been used in years, judging from the layer of dust on it. Looking unsurprised at their arrival, Alice Stewart sat composed in a rickety chair, her dark hair drawn back in a neat chignon, her smile slight and perhaps even a shade condescending.

"Where's my son?" Madeline, Luke observed, lost no time crossing the filthy floor, under the arc of the old sagging ceiling above, her slender hands drawn into small fists, her pale hair gleaming with moisture. "Where is Trevor?" she asked fiercely.

For such a normally genteel and elegant woman, she looked positively ready to attack her husband's cousin.

"Safe for now," Alice said with remarkable coolness, considering Madeline's outrage, Michael's brooding regard, and Luke's no doubt visible anger, not to mention the gun still pointed her way. "I'm so glad you arrived so soon, Mad. I was afraid it would take much longer. The ship I will be on draws up anchor at dawn."

"How could you do this?" Madeline asked, spots of angry red on her otherwise colorless cheeks. "He is Colin's son."

"The heir. Yes, I know." Alice's laugh was mirthless and her eyes glittered. "The beautiful child you dutifully produced like a little paragon of a wife. Such the nauseatingly perfect life you had before Colin decided to turn up his toes."

The patent dislike shocked Madeline. Luke could see the effect almost as if she'd been slapped. She stared at the woman in the chair as if she'd never seen her before.

And perhaps she hadn't, he thought, noting the thin sneer on Alice's mouth. Mrs. Stewart said, "And if you'd like the precious little viscount back, let's bargain."

Luke stepped forward, doing his best to insulate Madeline from such overt venom. "What the devil do you want?"

"Lord Altea." The woman's hostile gaze transferred to him. "How unlike you to be so attentive to one lady. Madeline must be everything my cousin found her to be and perhaps more, yes? His journal was . . . fascinating. She looks like such a lady, but apparently has the inhibitions of a whore. Has she worn the garters and black stockings for you yet?"

He'd never actively contemplated violence against a woman, but perhaps he could reconsider. Through his teeth he said, "Money?"

For the first time, Michael spoke, his tone perfectly polite, as if they weren't in some seedy, abandoned dockside building, interrogating a kidnapper. "I take it you wish funds and clemency?"

Alice Stewart sat up a little straighter, but her voice was still cool and silky. "In exchange for the child. That was my purpose for taking him. Trust me, I wouldn't want him otherwise."

Luke caught Madeline's arm.

Michael, however, simply looked thoughtful. "You'd think I would put more than one agent to following you, Mrs. Stewart. I suppose I could be forgiven for not doing so; I was suspicious, yes, but there wasn't much to indicate you were worth such an investment of the time of what humble staff the Crown provides me. I must say you are quite crafty. If the agent followed you after you gave Lady Brewer's son to your colleague, you had the leverage of a hostage. If the agent followed Lady Brewer's son and your accomplice, then you could get clean away and we wouldn't know where you'd gone. A rather inventive plan."

"She must have seen me watching her," the young man with the pistol muttered. "I swear, sir, I—"

"We'll discuss it later," Michael interrupted smoothly. "For now the matter at hand is apparently a small impasse. Trust is always an issue in a case like this. For instance, should I agree to let you go, Mrs. Stewart, how can I be sure you'll give me the correct location of Lady Brewer's son? On the other side of the coin, if I promise you safe passage, how can you be sure I won't change my mind when I have what I want? Always such a devilish dilemma."

"Roget told me about you, my lord." Alice Stewart leveled a stare in Michael's direction. "I will only negotiate with Madeline. I assume, since her lover is one of your best friends, you will not want his harlot to lose her only child? You can have Trevor when the tide goes out tomorrow, but not before. My friend has his instructions. If you try to take the boy before that, it could be *unfortunate*."

"Colin was good to you!" Madeline looked again as if she might hurl herself at her husband's cousin—so much so that Luke reached out and pulled her into his embrace. "Your fathers were brothers."

"Twins, no less, and all I had to show for that few minutes' difference in their births was a modest dowry my husband promptly spent on wine and willing women. Oddly enough, the fool died quite young." Her laugh was both mocking and chilling. "I wonder how *that* happened."

Luke could tell from Madeline's aghast expression not only that she had no idea the simmering resentment ever existed, but that she never entertained the idea Alice was a murderess. After a moment, she said quietly, "My husband gave you money before he died. Why?"

"I was under suspicion here and decided it was prudent to leave England. I informed my dear cousin I was with child and the father wasn't interested in taking responsibility. It wasn't true, but the very idea of such a situation made him immediately put sufficient funds at my disposal for a swift exit from the country." Alice Stewart's features twisted. "He was most scandalized. Tell me,

Mad,"—her voice held idle malice—"how would Colin feel about your casual liaison with Lord Altea?"

"It isn't casual. I love him. Now where is my son?"

Said so matter-of-factly, it was a startling declaration, especially under the circumstances. Madeline loved him. Luke found he wasn't surprised either. He'd looked into her eyes and tasted her kiss, and he had enough experience to know the difference between desire and something altogether different.

What they had together was the latter.

"How . . . quaint," Alice murmured, but her eyes narrowed.

To her credit, though Luke could feel her trembling under his restraining hold, Madeline didn't even blink an eye at the bitter sarcasm. "Where is my son?"

"Where is my promise of freedom?"

"How much?" Luke asked, the money nothing to him, but Madeline's happiness everything. "Name your price."

"You are reckless, aren't you, my lord? Let's say . . . twenty thousand, for you are fond of that sum."

"Done." He would rouse his banker from bed if need be, considering the circumstances.

Alice went on, "But it will do me no good unless you convince Lord Longhaven to release me tomorrow morning so I can board my ship."

That Michael said nothing was telling. Luke had been in enough life-or-death situations that he understood the power of timing. "I'll give you the money, but I have a feeling Michael needs a concession, as well, Mrs. Stewart. In the spirit of the game, of course. Roget might be a good place to start."

Her lips curled. "And sign my life away? I don't think so. I couldn't run far enough. There isn't enough world to evade Roget if he decided I was worth the effort to find."

As if it mattered not at all, Michael murmured, "If you are on a ship bound for an unknown destination with twenty thousand pounds and he is under arrest and facing a hangman's noose, surely you could effectively disappear."

Alice's laugh was mirthless. "I thought you knew him. I'd be dead soon enough. Obviously you aren't as clever as you are reputed to be."

"No?"

Luke should have known when Michael smiled a certain way that the situation was about to change. He'd seen that mannerism before, but undoubtedly it was new to Mrs. Stewart.

"In that case, surely you can offer me something . . . a small tidbit about Roget to tempt me into the bargain you seek?" Michael was, as usual, unruffled, urbane, his hazel eyes veiled by his lashes, his pose nonchalant. "If, in your opinion, I am not clever enough to catch him, that is."

"You'll grant me my bargain for Altea's sake without any input on my part already."

"Will I?" Michael's voice held a distinctive edge of uncompromising rigidity. "Don't be so sure."

Madeline tensed, and Luke pulled her closer in the guise of comfort. "Shh," he whispered in her ear. "Trust him."

"Fine." Alice's chin lifted above the proper collar of her traveling costume. "Roget is in England."

"Tsk, tsk, you must do better. That isn't news."

"London, then." Her gaze wandered across the audience, resting briefly on the young man with the gun, flitting past Lawrence, ignoring Luke and Madeline with disdain, and then back to where Longhaven stood.

Michael looked unimpressed. He glanced at Lawrence and nodded. The other man slipped out the door only to step back in a moment later holding the hand of a dark-haired young boy, who took one look at Madeline and said joyfully, "Mama."

Madeline yanked herself out of Luke's arms in an instant, and he watched as she ran across the room in a rustle of silken skirts, then fell on her knees despite the

filthy floor, holding her son tightly to her, whispering his
name over and over, stroking his dark curls.

The intensity of his relief made Luke shove his hand
through his hair and exhale raggedly, his gaze fixed on
the poignant picture of mother and child. Something in
his chest eased, and not for the first time he pictured a
younger brother or sister for Trevor . . . a family.

His family.

If he could bring himself to risk it.

He was starting to think it was too late already. The
risk had been taken even with his best efforts at resistance. He couldn't replace what he'd lost; neither could
he give Madeline back what *she* had lost, but the idea
of building a new life together was coming sharply into
focus, as if his existence had been a blurred image these
past few years, the future an abstract concept he'd refused to think about until now.

Until Madeline.

"Perhaps you'd like to see Lady Brewer and her son
home," Michael said pleasantly, meeting Luke's eyes. "It
seems Mrs. Stewart isn't in need of funds after all. The
Crown will take care of her living expenses until her trial.
Unless, of course, she wishes to answer some questions of
a somewhat sensitive nature not for everyone's ears."

Luke said wryly, "I don't even want to know. Thank
you for your help."

"On the contrary," Michael murmured. "I think *you*
helped *me*. This unfortunate incident has been quite . . .
fortuitous."

Alice Stewart said nothing, her composure belied by
the sudden ashen pallor of her cheeks and the cornered
look in her eyes. Luke went to take Madeline's arm. "I
am sure you have no objection to us taking our leave,
my love."

"No," she agreed fervently, not bothering to even
look at the woman who had betrayed her and her husband's trust and endangered her child.

Trevor was clearly unharmed and seemed to sense

he'd been on an adventure, for he chattered on about
the docks as they left the old building and walked along
the wharf, sending curious, sidelong looks at Luke all the
way to the carriage and on the ride back to Madeline's
town house.

As they alighted, Luke let his hands linger at Madeline's waist for a moment. "I'm staying tonight," he informed her. "I want to be with you."

"That's an arrogant assumption, Altea," she responded, but her smile was soft and hopeful.

"You and Trevor might need me."

Her gaze went to her son as he dashed up the steps
of the house, being welcomed by an obviously relieved
and delighted Hubert and what looked like the entire
household of servants hovering behind him. "He seems
quite remarkably unscathed by what happened. Thank
goodness for the resilience of children."

"Nonetheless, I think I should be available, just in
case you *do* ever need me."

Madeline must have caught the singular inflection in
his voice, for her eyes widened.

"I was rather thinking the next fifty years or so,"
Luke went on calmly, as if he wasn't proposing marriage
outside on the wet street. "If you are willing to take the
chance. My first wife died."

"I'm so sorry. I didn't know."

"My family doesn't even know. She was Spanish . . .
we met after Talavera. I was still wounded and on light
duty, assigned to meet with our allies." He stopped, took
a breath, and then went on as unemotionally as possible.
"Our paths crossed again after Badajoz. When she told
me she was pregnant with my child, we married. But it
was war, and she was passionate about the resistance . . .
and she was killed. I thought I would never recover." It
was a simple explanation, and one day he would tell her
the whole story, but not now. He wanted to think about
the future, not the past.

Now Madeline's beautiful eyes were filled with tears

again. The rain touched her hair with a jeweled mist of moisture. She whispered, "Oh, Luke."

"You petrified me," he said honestly, his voice slightly hoarse. "I told myself after that one night we spent together it was too big a risk to even allow myself near you. Kneeling by Maria's grave, I swore I would never take that chance again."

"Colin died." She took in a breath. "And I thought *I* would never recover. The idea of it frightens me, too. We have far too much in common." Her voice was low, with a quiver he loved.

Because he loved *her*.

"I agree, my darling Madge. Especially this."

He kissed her then, regardless of the neighbors, the passing carriages, the thin mist of rain, and no doubt all of her staff gathered in the doorway. "I love you," he murmured against her lips. "I love you."

"I love you too. I even love it when you call me Madge." She withdrew from his embrace, blushing. "But don't you feel we have far too many meaningful and personal conversations on the street?"

He leaned forward then and whispered in her ear exactly how, where, and when he wished to continue the discussion, and if she had been flushed before, she turned positively scarlet now.

With a grin, he escorted her up the steps.

Epilogue

Three months later

The sun was setting in a brilliant display of magenta with splashes of indigo, and the shadows were thickening under the trees.

"Do you mind telling me just where we are going?"

Elizabeth grinned and looked over her shoulder at her husband. He was particularly handsome today in charcoal gray, a beautiful red rose tucked into a buttonhole in his lapel. "It's a secret."

"El, we have guests." The protest was halfhearted, though; she knew him well enough to interpret the tone of his voice. There was an underlying laugh and a bit of curiosity.

Good. She wanted him intrigued.

On her wedding day, wasn't she allowed to be a bit spontaneous? And, as she'd been waiting for Miles her whole life, maybe to be a little impatient as well? "Those are mostly my mother's guests," she told him, her slippers light on the long grass, her ice blue skirts brushing the foliage as they left the formal gardens. "They are dancing and drinking and having a lovely time. They won't even miss us."

The path wasn't nearly as clear as she remembered it, but she could have found her way blindfolded. Past the wild honeysuckle bushes in overgrown disarray, as this was no longer part of the formal gardens, near the hovering elms on the outskirts of the park . . .

"The riverbank?" Miles, holding her hand and easily keeping up with her hurried footsteps with his long strides, guessed with unerring accuracy.

"Our secret spot."

It probably wasn't as much of a secret as she thought, but truly it was a very secluded portion of the estate and not tended by the gardening staff, so they could be relatively alone. The sight of the river when it came into view, the shimmering water moving lazily in a quiet flow between the banks, and the scent of early autumn in the air brought back poignant memories and emphasized her euphoria. Elizabeth whirled around in the small clearing they had once as children christened as their very own and asked, "Do you want to go swimming?"

Miles tugged her toward him. "Maybe later."

"Later?"

"After," he equivocated, his gaze intent. "Since you lured me down here, abandoning our guests—"

"My mother's guests," she corrected with a breathless laugh, as his arms closed around her.

"Whatever you say, my lovely wife."

Wife. She was his wife. She'd married *Miles*.

And who would think it would make her the happiest woman in the world?

Well, perhaps anyone who has experienced the intoxication of his kiss, she decided a few moments later as his mouth claimed hers. His hands too seemed to leave a trail of tingling sensation as he brushed her skin in his quest to remove her dress. Then there was the way he whispered in her ear that he wanted her, and he untied the ribbon to her chemise and pushed the garment off her shoulders.

Then, somehow, he was undressed also, shedding his clothes in haphazard disregard, his cravat actually landing in the water and floating away.

The grass was cool at her back as he lowered her down and nuzzled her neck, making her shiver. "You were right," he murmured against her skin. "This should be done here, where we have shared so many adventures."

It *was* another of their reckless escapades, she discovered with each touch, each heated kiss, every forbidden caress. When he stroked her breasts, she gasped at the sensation, her nipples tightening in a way she'd never expected, an unknown excitement coiling in a tight ball in her belly. At the moment when he gently coaxed her knees apart and settled between her thighs, his erection nudging her feminine opening, she was already so far gone she merely whispered his name and clung to him.

And she and Miles embarked on another wild adventure.

Together.

"What a beautiful wedding."

Luke made a small sound that Madeline interpreted as male derision. He sat down on the edge of the bed to tug off his boots and muttered, "I am just grateful it is over."

"Elizabeth was radiant." Madeline bent to lift her skirts and untie her garters. "And Miles was so handsome."

"Nice of them to so conveniently disappear." Her husband sounded disgruntled.

As she actually thought it was very romantic, Madeline just smiled. She'd seen them stealing through the gardens hand in hand. "On such a day, I think they can be granted a little latitude."

"I preferred our wedding, to be honest. No crush of guests, no lengthy ceremony." Luke's cravat went next, tossed carelessly on the floor, his gaze suddenly fastened on her bared legs as she rolled down her silk stockings. "Just a spectacular honeymoon."

"We stayed in London and didn't leave our suite," she pointed out with a laugh.

"As I said, it was perfect." His smile was wolfish and unrepentant. "Let me help you with your gown."

"Undress yourself, Altea."

"I'd rather undress *you*, my darling Madge. Turn around."

Autocrat, she thought with an inner smile, but obeyed so her husband could unfasten her gown. His long fingers were skillful and efficient, and in moments she found herself on the bed, his lean body balanced on top of hers, his mouth doing sinfully wonderful things to her neck.

Later, drowning in sensual joy, she ran her fingers down Luke's bare back and her sigh stirred his hair. He rolled off her carefully and his hand trailed down to rest on the swell of her stomach. "I hope I wasn't too demanding. Are you exhausted after all the festivities?"

In truth, she felt wonderful, fertile, happy in her current state of conception, and yet she reveled in his concern. For such a notorious gentleman, he was a very considerate husband and was going to be a wonderful father. Already he and Trevor were forming a special bond. "I'm fine," she assured him, smiling. Then her smile faded. "What did Michael take you aside to tell you at the wedding dinner?"

A shrug lifted her husband's muscular shoulders. "He said the entire affair was 'satisfactorily concluded.'"

Relaxed in the curve of Luke's arm, Madeline frowned. "What does that mean? There hasn't been a whisper about Alice since we left her there that evening in the old warehouse."

"I have no idea what it means, but I trust Michael."

She did as well, but a few facts were still unclear in

her mind. "Whatever do you suppose she thought might be in Colin's journal?"

In the lamplight Luke's austere features were outlined by shadowy definition. He said slowly, "I've thought about it myself. My theory is Colin must have seen her with the wrong person. Maybe it was as simple as running into her on the street, or an unexpected visit to her house. He would have probably thought nothing of it, but it was significant enough she worried later he might note it in his writings."

"Roget?" She had no idea what that name meant or who the man was, but she did know it meant *something*.

"That would be my guess," Luke admitted. "So she stole the journal, found she had worried for nothing, and then made a fatal mistake by not simply returning it as quietly as she took it. Leaving it to be found so you would be humiliated was a grave error in judgment."

It bothered her she hadn't realized Alice's animosity. Yes, there had been an underlying dislike she couldn't quite put her finger on, but she hadn't known there was active, malicious emotion. "I had no idea she hated me."

Luke lifted her hand and tenderly kissed a fingertip. "Not you, darling, for that would be impossible. You are infinitely lovable. She hated what you represented. A happily married woman with a doting husband and a healthy, beautiful son, who was also prominent in society. Envy is one of the worst sins. From what little I heard, I suspect your father-in-law's twin brother resented not inheriting the title. Alice took the legacy of bitterness just a bit too far."

"If she hadn't been so vindictive . . ."

"You wouldn't have had to conk Lord Fitch with a poker and send for me. I might even still be convincing myself that the night we spent together that first time was a mistake," he finished for her, his silver eyes holding a gleam.

A rather wicked gleam, she recognized with a small thrill. Really, the man was insatiable. But then again, when in his arms, so was she.

"But you've changed your mind?" Madeline asked suggestively, moving a little closer, her hand straying low between their bodies, touching and caressing.

"*You* changed my mind," he answered hoarsely. "Shall I demonstrate again?"

"By all means."

Read on for a preview of Emma Wildes's
enthralling historical romance

My Lord Scandal

first in the Notorious Bachelors series
Available now from Signet Eclipse

The alley below was filthy and smelled rank, and if he fell off the ledge, Lord Alexander St. James was fairly certain he would land on a good-sized rat. Since squashing scurrying rodents was not on his list of favorite pastimes, he tightened his grip and gauged the distance to the next roof. It looked to be roughly about the distance between London and Edinburgh, but in reality was probably only a few feet.

"What the devil is the matter with you?" a voice hissed out of the darkness. "Hop on over. After all, this was your idea."

"I do not *hop*," he shot back, unwilling to confess that heights bothered him. They had ever since that fateful night when he'd breached the towering wall of the citadel at Badajoz with forlorn hope. He still remembered the pounding rain, the ladders swarming with men, and that great, black drop below. . . .

"I know perfectly well this was my idea," he muttered.

"Then I'm sure, unless you have an inclination for a

personal tour of Newgate Prison, which, by the by, I do not, you'll agree we need to proceed. It gets closer to dawn by the minute."

Newgate Prison. Alex didn't like confined spaces any more than he liked heights. The story his grandmother had told him just a few days ago made him wish his imagination was a little less vivid. Incarceration in a squalid cell was the last thing he wanted. But for the ones you love, he thought philosophically as he eyed the gap, and he had to admit he adored his grandmother, risks had to be taken.

That thought proved inspiration enough for him to leap the distance and land with a dull thud but, thankfully, keep his balance on the sooty shingles. His companion beckoned with a wave of his hand and in a crouched position began to make a slow pilgrimage toward the next house.

The moon was a wafer obscured by clouds. Good for stealth, but not quite so wonderful for visibility. Two more alleys and harrowing jumps and they were there, easing down onto a balcony that overlooked a small walled garden.

Michael Hepburn, Marquess of Longhaven, dropped down first, light on his feet, balanced like a dancer. Alex wondered, not for the first time, just what his friend did for the War Office. He landed next to him and said, "What did your operative tell you about the layout of the town house?"

Michael peered through the glass of the French doors into the darkened room. "I could be at our club at this very moment, enjoying a stiff brandy."

"Stop grumbling," Alex muttered. "You live for this kind of intrigue. Lucky for us, the lock is simple. I'll have this open in no time."

True to his word, a moment later one of the doors creaked open, the sound loud to Alex's ears. He led the way, slipping into the darkened bedroom, taking in with a quick glance the shrouded forms of a large canopied bed and armoire. Something white was laid out on the bed, and on closer inspection he saw it was a nightdress edged with delicate lace, and that the coverlet was already turned back. The virginal gown made him feel very much an interloper—which, bloody hell, he was. But all in a good cause, he told himself firmly.

Michael spoke succinctly. "This is Lord Hathaway's daughter's bedroom. We'll need to search his study and his suite across the hall. Since his lordship's rooms face the street and his study is downstairs, this is a much more discreet method of entry. It is likely enough they'll be gone for several more hours, giving us time to search for your precious item. At this hour, the servants should all be abed."

"I'll take the study. It's more likely to be there."

"Alex, you do realize you are going to have to finally tell me just what we are looking for if I am going to ransack his lordship's bedroom on your behalf."

"I hope you plan on being more subtle than that."

"He'll never know I was there," Michael said with convincing confidence. "But what the devil am I looking for?"

"A key. Ornate, made of silver, so it'll be tarnished to black, I suspect. About so long." Alex spread open his hand, indicating the tip of his smallest finger to his thumb. "It'll be in a small case, also silver. There should be an engraved *S* on the cover."

"A key to *what*, dare I ask, since I am risking my neck to find it?"

Alex paused, reluctant to reveal more. But Michael had a point, and moreover, could keep a secret better than anyone of Alex's acquaintance. "I'm not sure," he admitted quietly.

Michael's hazel eyes gleamed with interest even in the dim light. "Yet here we are, breaking into a man's house."

"It's . . . complicated."

"Things with you usually are."

"I'm not at liberty to explain to anyone, even you, my reasons for being here. Therefore my request for your assistance. In the past you have proven to not only think fast on your feet and stay cool under fire, but you also have the unique ability to keep your mouth firmly shut, which is a very valuable trait in a friend. In short, I trust you."

Michael gave a noncommittal grunt. "All right, fine."

"If it makes you feel better, I'm not going to steal anything," Alex informed him in a whisper, as he cracked open the bedroom door and peered down the hall. "What I want doesn't belong to Lord Hathaway, if he has it. Where's his study?"

"Second hallway past the bottom of the stairs. Third door on the right."

The house smelled vaguely of beeswax and smoke from the fires that kept the place warm in the late-spring weather. Alex crept—there was no other word for it—down the hall, sending a silent prayer upward to enlist heavenly aid for their little adventure to be both successful and undetected. Though he wasn't sure, with his somewhat dissolute past—or Michael's, for that matter—if he was at all in a position to ask for benevolence.

The hallway was deserted but also damned dark. Michael clearly knew the exact location of Hathaway's personal set of rooms, for he went directly to one door to the left and cracked it open to disappear inside.

Alex stood at a vantage point where he could see the top of the staircase rising from the main floor, feeling an amused disbelief that he was a deliberate intruder in someone else's house, and had enlisted Michael's aid to help him with the infiltration. He'd known Michael since Eton, and when it came down to it, no one was more reliable or loyal. He'd go with him to hell and back, and quite frankly, they *had* accompanied each other to hell in Spain.

They'd survived the fires of Hades, but had not come back to England unscathed.

Time passed in silence, and Alex relaxed a little as he made his way down the stairs into the darkened hallway, barking his shin only once on a piece of furniture that seemed to materialize out of nowhere. He stifled a very colorful curse and moved on, making a mental note not to take up burglary as a profession.

The study was redolent of old tobacco and the ghosts of a thousand glasses of brandy. Alex moved slowly, pulling the borrowed set of picklocks again from his pocket, rummaging through the drawers he could open first, and then setting to work on the two locked ones.

Nothing. No silver case. No blasted key.

Damn.

The first sound of trouble was a low, sharp, excited bark. Then he heard a woman speaking in modulated tones—audible in the silent house—and alarm flooded through him. The voice sounded close, but that might have been a trick of the acoustics of the town house. At least it didn't sound like a big dog, he told himself, feeling in a drawer for a false back before replacing the contents and quietly sliding it shut.

A servant? Perhaps, but it was unlikely, for it was truly the dead of night, with dawn a few good hours away. As early as most of the staff rose, he doubted one of them would be up and about unless summoned by his employer.

The voice spoke again, a low murmur, and the lack of a reply probably meant she was talking to the dog. He eased into the hallway to peer out and saw that at the foot of the stairs a woman was bent over, scratching the ears of what appeared to be a small bundle of active fur, just a puppy, hence the lack of alarm over their presence in the house.

She was blond, slender, clad in a fashionable gown of a light color. . . .

Several more hours, his arse. One of Lord Hathaway's family had returned early.

It was a stroke of luck when she set down her lamp

and lifted the squirming bundle of fur in her arms, and instead of heading upstairs, carried her delighted burden through a door on the opposite side of the main hall, probably back toward the kitchen.

Alex stole across the room and went quickly up the stairs to where Michael had disappeared, trying to be as light-footed as possible. He opened the door a crack and whispered, "Someone just came home. A young woman, though I couldn't see her clearly."

"Damnation." Michael could move quietly as a cat, and he was there instantly. "I'm only half done. We might need to leave and come back a second time."

Alex pictured launching himself again across more questionable, stinking, yawning crevasses of London's rooftop landscape. "I'd rather we finished it now."

"If Lady Amelia has returned alone, it should be fine," Michael murmured. "She's unlikely to come into her father's bedroom, and I just need a few more minutes. I'd ask you to help me, but you don't know where I've already searched, and the two of us whispering to each other and moving about is more of a risk. Go out the way we came in. Wait for her to go to bed, and keep an eye on her. If she looks to leave her room because she might have heard something, you're going to have to come up with a distraction. Otherwise, I'll take my chances going out this way and meet you on the roof."

With that, he was gone again and the door closed softly.

Alex uttered a stifled curse. He'd fought battles, crawled through ditches, endured soaking rains and freezing nights, marched for miles on end with his battalion, but he wasn't a damned spy. But a moment of indecision could be disastrous with Miss Patton no doubt heading for her bedroom. And what if she also woke her maid?

As a soldier, he'd learned to make swift judgments, and in this case, he trusted Michael knew what the hell he was doing and quickly slipped back into the lady's bedroom and headed for the balcony. They'd chosen that entry into the house for the discreet venue of the quiet, private garden, and the assurance that no one on the street would see them and possibly recognize them in this fashionable neighborhood.

No had Alex managed to close the French doors behind him than the door to the bedroom opened. He froze, hoping the shadows hid his presence, but worried that movement might attract the attention of the young woman who had entered the room. If she raised an alarm, Michael could be in a bad spot, even if Alex got away. Luckily, she carried the small lamp, which she set on the polished table by the bed. He assumed his presence on the balcony would be harder to detect.

It was at that moment he realized how very beautiful she was.

Lord Hathaway's daughter. Had he met her? No, he hadn't, but when he thought about it, he'd heard her name mentioned quite often lately. Now he knew why.

Hair a shimmering gold caught the light as she reached up and loosened the pins, dropping them one by one by the lamp and letting the cascade of curls tumble down her back. In profile her face was defined and feminine, with a dainty nose and delicate chin. Though he couldn't see the color of her eyes, they were framed by lashes long enough they cast slight shadows across her elegant cheekbones as she bent over to lift her skirts, kick off her slippers, and begin to unfasten her garters. He caught the pale gleam of slender calves and smooth thighs, and the graceful curve of her bottom.

There was something innately sensual about watching a woman undress, though usually when it was done in his presence, it was as a prelude to one of his favorite pastimes. Slim fingers worked the fastenings of her gown and in a whisper of silk, it slid off her pale shoulders. She stepped free of the pooled fabric wearing only a thin, lacy chemise, all gold and ivory in the flickering illumination.

As a gentleman, he reminded himself, *I should politely look away.*

*   *   *

The ball had been more nightmare than entertainment, and Lady Amelia Patton had ducked out as soon as possible, using her usual—and not deceptive—excuse. She picked up her silk gown, shook it out, and draped it over a carved chair by the fireplace. When her carriage had dropped her home, she'd declined to wake her maid, instead enjoying a few rare moments of privacy before bed. No one would think it amiss, as she had done the same before.

It was a crime, was it not, to kill one's father?

Not that she *really* wanted to strangle him in any way but a metaphorical one, but this evening, when he had thrust her almost literally into the arms of the Earl of Westhope, she had nearly done the unthinkable and refused to dance with his lordship in public, thereby humiliating the man and defying her father in front of all of society.

Instead, she had gritted her teeth and waltzed with the most handsome, rich, incredibly *boring* eligible bachelor of the *haut ton*.

It had encouraged him, and that was the last thing she had wanted to happen.

The earl had even had the nerve—or maybe it was just stupidity—to misquote Rabelais when he brought her a glass of champagne, saying with a flourish as he handed over the flute, "Thirst comes with eating . . . but the appetite goes away with drinking."

It had really been all she could do not to correct him, since he'd got it completely backward. She had a sinking feeling that he didn't mean to be boorish; he just wasn't very bright. Still, there was nothing on earth that could have prevented her from asking him, in her most proper voice, if that meant he was bringing her champagne because he felt, perhaps, she was too plump. Her response had so flustered him that he'd excused himself hurriedly—so perhaps the entire evening hadn't been a loss after all.

Clad only in her chemise, she went to the balcony doors and opened them, glad of the fresh air, even if it was a bit cool. Loosening the ribbon on her shift, she let the material drift partway down her shoulders, her nipples tightening against the chill. The ballroom had been unbearably close and she'd had some problems breathing, an affliction that had plagued her since childhood. Being able to fill her lungs felt like heaven and she stood there, letting her eyes close. The light wheezing had stopped, and the anxiety that came with it had lessened as well, but she was still a little dizzy. Her father was insistent that she kept this particular flaw a secret. He seemed convinced no man would wish to marry a female who might now and again become inexplicably out of breath.

Slowly she inhaled and then let it out. Yes, it was passing. . . .

It wasn't a movement or noise that sent a flicker of unease through her, but a sudden, instinctive sense of being watched. Then a strong, masculine hand cupped her elbow. "Are you quite all right?"

Her eyes flew open and she saw a tall figure looming over her. With a gasp she jerked her chemise back up to cover her partially bared breasts. To her surprise, the shadowy figure spoke again in a cultured, modulated voice. "I'm sorry to startle you, my lady. I beg a thousand pardons, but I thought you might faint."

Amelia stared upward, as taken aback by his polite speech and appearance as she was by finding a man lurking on her balcony. The stranger had ebony hair, glossy in the inadequate moonlight, and his face was shadowed by hollows and fine planes, eyes dark as midnight staring down at her. "I . . . I . . ." she stammered. *You should scream,* an inner voice suggested, but she was so paralyzed by alarm and surprise, she wasn't sure she was capable of it.

"You swayed," her mysterious visitor pointed out, as if that explained everything, a small frown drawing dark, arched brows together. "Are you ill?"

Finally, she found her voice, albeit not at all her regular one, but a high, thin whisper. "No, just a bit dizzy. Sir, what are you doing here?"

"Maybe you should lie down."

To her utter shock, he lifted her into his arms as easily as if she were a child, and actually carried her inside to deposit her carefully on the bed.

Perhaps this is a bizarre dream. . . .

"What are you doing here? Who are you?" she demanded. It wasn't very effective, since she still couldn't manage more than a half mumble, though fright was being replaced rapidly by outraged curiosity. Even in the insubstantial light she could tell he was well dressed, and before he straightened, she caught the subtle drift of expensive cologne. Though he wore no cravat, his dark coat was fashionably cut, and his fitted breeches and Hessians not something she imagined an ordinary footpad would wear. His face was classically handsome, with a nice, straight nose and lean jaw, and she'd never seen eyes so dark.

Was he really that tall or did he just seem so because she was sprawled on the bed and he was standing?

"I mean you no harm. Do not worry."

Easy for him to say. For heaven's sake, he was in her bedroom, no less. "You are trespassing."

"Indeed," he agreed, inclining his head.

Was he a thief? He didn't look like one. Confused, Amelia sat up, feeling very vulnerable lying there in dishabille with her tumbled hair. "My father keeps very little money in his strongbox here in the house."

"A wise man. I follow that same rule myself. If it puts your mind at ease, I do not need his money." The stranger's teeth flashed white in a quick smile.

She recognized him, she realized suddenly, the situation taking on an even greater sense of the surreal. Not a close acquaintance, no. Not one of the many gentlemen she'd danced with since the beginning of her season, but she'd seen him, nevertheless.

And he certainly had seen *her*. She was sitting there gawping at him in only her thin, lacy chemise with the bodice held together in her trembling hand. The flush of embarrassment swept upward, making her neck and cheeks hot. She could feel the rush of blood warm her knuckles when they pressed against her chest. "I . . . I'm undressed," she said, unnecessarily.

"Most delightfully so," he responded with an unmistakable note of sophisticated amusement in his soft tone. "But I am not here to ravish you any more than to rob you. Though," he added with a truly wicked smile, "perhaps, in the spirit of being an effective burglar, I should steal *something*. A kiss comes to mind, for at least then I would not leave empty-handed."

A kiss? Was the man insane?

"You . . . wouldn't," she managed to object in disbelief. He still stood by the side of the bed, so close if she reached out a hand, she could touch him.

"I might." His dark brows lifted a fraction, and his gaze flickered over her inadequately clad body before returning to her face. He added softly, "I have a weakness for lovely, half-dressed ladies, I'm afraid."

And no doubt they had the same weakness for him, for he exuded a flagrant masculinity and confidence that was even more compelling than his good looks.

Her breath fluttered in her throat and it had nothing to do with her affliction. She might be an ingenue, but she understood in an instant the power of that devastating, entirely masculine, husky tone. Like a bird stunned by smoke, she didn't move, even when he leaned down and his long fingers caught her chin, tipping her face up just a fraction. He lowered his head, brushed his mouth against hers for a moment, a mere tantalizing touch of his lips. Then, instead of kissing her, his hand slid into her hair and he gently licked the hollow of her throat. Through her dazed astonishment at his audacity, the feel of his warm lips and the teasing caress caused an odd sensation in the pit of her stomach.

This was where she should have imperiously ordered him to stop, or at least push him away.

But she didn't. She'd never been kissed, and though, admittedly, her girlish fantasies about this moment in her life hadn't included a mysterious stranger stealing uninvited into her bedroom, she *was* curious.

The trail of his breath made her quiver, moving upward along her jaw, the curve of her cheek, until he finally claimed her mouth, shocking her to her very core as he brushed his tongue against hers in small, sinful strokes.

She trembled, and though it wasn't a conscious act, somehow one of her hands settled on his shoulder.

It was intimate.

It was beguiling.

Then it was over.

God help her, to her *disappointment* it was over.

He straightened and looked more amused than ever at whatever expression had appeared on her face. "A virgin kiss. A coup indeed."

He obviously knew that had been her first. It wasn't so surprising, for like most unmarried young ladies, she was constantly chaperoned. She summoned some affront, though, strangely, she really wasn't affronted. "You, sir, are no gentleman."

"Oh, I am, if a somewhat jaded one. If I wasn't, I wouldn't be taking my leave, lest your reputation be tarnished by our meeting, because it would be, believe me. My advice is to keep my presence here this evening to yourself."

True to his word, in a moment he was through the balcony doors, climbing up on the balustrade, and bracing himself for balance on the side of the house. Then he caught the edge of the roof, swung up in one graceful, athletic motion, and was gone into the darkness.

Read on for a preview of Emma Wildes's
next enthralling historical romance

His Sinful Secret

third in the Notorious Bachelors series
Coming from Signet Eclipse in November
2010

"This should have been stitched together." Fitzhugh tossed aside the crusty bandage and sent him a level glare of disapproval. "I say you should damn the questions and summon a physician to look at it, sir. It's a right nasty one."

Michael returned the look with a small smile, though the injury was sore as hell and the removal of the wrapping had caused a light sweat to sheen his skin. "I am uninterested in having a physician perhaps reveal to someone he treated the Marquess of Longhaven for a knife wound. I've been hurt worse, and you've seen to it. Stop fussing and just get on with it."

The older man shook his head but obeyed, cleaning the wound and placing clean linen on it before wrapping strips of cloth to keep the pad in place. Stocky, weathered, and trustworthy, he played valet with as much efficiency as he'd performed his duties when they had served together under Wellington's command. A few moments later Michael eased into his shirt and surveyed his appearance in the mirror. Clean-shaven and dressed, he looked perfectly normal, except maybe for the faint shadows under his eyes. He hadn't slept well, partly due to the wound itself, and partly due to its cause.

Two murder attempts, a volatile matter to handle for his superiors, and now a problematic wedding night.

No wonder he hadn't managed more than a half doze for a few hours.

His former sergeant had an uncanny ability to read his mind. "What are you going to tell her, if I might ask, my lord?" The form of address still came awkwardly. Fitzhugh was used to calling him *Colonel* and frequently lapsed out of sheer habit.

"I'm not sure." He finished tying his cravat and turned around. "I thought of saying I fell from my horse, but I fear, even to an inexperienced eye, it looks like what it is—a knife wound. Eventually the bandage will come off and the scar would prove me a liar. Not an auspicious way to start a marriage."

There was a small, inelegant snort. "The lovely young lady had better get used to half-truths, with the business you dabble your toes in."

He ignored the comment. "I have to come up with something else."

Fitzhugh picked up his discarded robe and bustled off to the dressing room to hang it up. It was a warm morning and brilliant sunshine lit the bedroom with golden light. Michael hadn't taken Harry's suite of rooms—it felt like the worst kind of betrayal to take anything more that had once belonged to his brother. He'd already inherited his title, his fortune, and his fiancée, so moving into his apartments was out of the question. The furnishings in his suite were a bit austere, the same as before he left for Spain. Plain dark blue hangings on the carved bed, a simple cream rug on the polished floor, matching curtains at the long windows. He'd been twenty-one when he'd boarded the ship to sail away to war, and decorating had hardly been a top priority in his life at that time. It still wasn't. Maybe Julianne would care to redo their portion of the Mayfair mansion, but then again, maybe she wouldn't. He knew very little about her, really.

Too little. And the distance was deliberate and entirely his fault.

It doesn't matter what she might be like, he reminded himself. He was going to marry her regardless, for his parents mourned his brother with acute grief.

He'd been startled and off guard when they had asked him to please honor the arranged marriage and take Harry's place. Though he wasn't at all sure that years of war and intrigue hadn't hardened him to a frightening degree, there still must have been some vestige of sentiment left, for he hadn't been able to refuse. He'd come home, assumed his brother's position as the heir, and now was going to appropriate the young woman destined to be his wife.

It would make him feel much less guilty if Harry hadn't been so enamored of her and looking forward to the union.

The dutiful letters from home had, at first, only hinted of it. His older brother had mentioned how beautiful she was becoming as she matured, how intelligent and good-humored, how charming and gracious. The final letter, which hadn't reached Michael until Harry was gone and in his grave, had explained how fortunate he was to be pledged to a woman who would not only grace his arm in public and his bed in private, but also enrich his life.

Did Michael feel undeserving?

A resounding affirmative to that question, he thought as he sighed and ran his hand through his neatly combed hair, ruffling the thick strands. He was nothing like Harry. There wasn't an easygoing bone in his body and his mind worked in circles, rather than in straight lines. He'd seen enough horror that he'd come to understand it, and that was frightening in itself, and all the scars he bore were not just skin deep. He told his valet, "My marriage will be a matter of convenience."

"Yours or hers?" Fitzhugh was as blunt as always. "You conveniently go about your business and she conveniently doesn't notice stab wounds, long absences, and late-night comings and goings. Is that how it will work?"

"How the devil do I know how it will work? I have never been married before, but most aristocratic unions—especially those arranged by parents—involve a certain level of detachment. Besides, she's very young. Not even twenty."

"What does that have to do with it?" Fitzhugh furrowed his brow. "She's got eyes, hasn't she? A very pretty pair of them, at that. Now, I say you'd better come up with a good excuse for your current state of incapacitation, Colonel, or there will be all hell to pay from the beginning. I'm guessing, from the looks of that wicked gash, you're not going to be in top form tomorrow night to claim your husbandly rights. Young or not, that bonny lass will wonder why you didn't enjoy taking her, or worse yet, why *she* didn't enjoy it."

"I can't imagine she'd know the difference between a good performance or a poor one on a sexual level," he said dryly. "And thanks for your confidence in my masculine prowess."

A flicker of humor washed over the other man's broad face. "I imagine you'll get the job done."

"Thank you. Ah, at last, some flicker of faith."

"My faith is in her allure doing the trick, Colonel." Fitzhugh grinned. "There's no denying she's a beautiful girl. It wouldn't be like you not to notice."

"I've noticed." Michael turned and restlessly moved across the room.

Yes, he had. The unusual rich color of her glossy hair, like mahogany silk, warm and soft, framed a face that was fine-boned and elegant. Her figure was slender yet nicely shaped in the strategic places. And Fitzhugh was right: the long-lashed beauty of her dark blue eyes was striking. Julianne was a little quiet for his tastes, but then again, he hadn't really ever attempted much conversation with her either.

In his mind, she still belonged to Harry. Unfortunately, he got the sense she also held the same preconception.

It seemed like the worst treachery ever to contemplate bedding the woman his brother had wanted for himself. On the other side of the coin, his parents had set aside their acute grief in celebration of this marriage. His mother, especially, had thrown herself into the preparations for the wedding with almost frantic joy, and it was hardly a secret that in her opinion the sooner a grandchild arrived, the better.

Michael was in one devil of a dilemma because of the murderous assault, and that was discounting the mystery of just who had bloodthirsty designs on his person.

"I suppose I could just tell her the truth. That on my way home from an appointment, someone attacked me. I have no idea why, or who he was, but I managed to defend myself, and he ran off. I kept it secret so as not to put a damper on the celebration or worry my mother in her current state of happiness. What do you think?"

"The truth usually isn't your first choice." Fitzhugh looked both dubious and amused.

"It usually isn't an *option* at all," Michael pointed out cynically. "As for my mother, that is true enough. She has had little joy since my brother's death. Julianne might understand my motivation in keeping such an event to myself to protect my parents. I'm sure she still mourns Harry also and knows how important this wedding is to them."

" 'Tis natural she would. So you do mourn him, sir, or you wouldn't be marrying the girl."

Did he? Maybe. He'd never given himself time to think about it. Sometimes Fitzhugh was too damned insightful for comfort.

Michael gave a philosophical shrug, and then grimaced as pain shot through his side. "I would have to marry someday, so why not her? It's expected."

"Not what *you* expected, sir. You usually go your own way."

That was true. He said neutrally, "She's lovely and seems even tempered and not as spoiled as some of the petulant young society ladies I've had the misfortune to meet. At least now I won't be besieged by eager mamas parading their daughters in front of me at every event. All my good friends have married."

For love. Both Alex St. James and Luke Daudet, his comrades and brothers-in-arms, had found the women who completed them—the women they had to have despite familial and social obstacles.

Not everyone was so lucky. So he would wed out of duty. As he'd just said, Julianne was perfectly acceptable.

He added succinctly, "It's time, and there's freedom in being a married man."

His valet chuckled, the sound rumbling out into the sunny room. "Freedom? Let me know if you still feel that way in a few months, Colonel."

Also Available

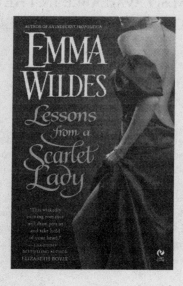

Also Available

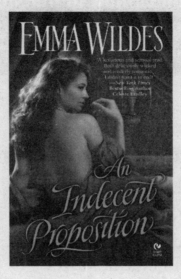

It's the talk of the town. London's two most notorious rakes
have placed a public wager on which of them is the greater
lover. But what woman of beauty, intelligence, and discernment
would consent to judge such a contest? Lady Carolyn Wynn is
the last woman anyone would expect to step forward. But if the
men keep her identity a secret, she'll decide who has the most
finesse between the sheets. To everyone's surprise, however, what
begins as an immoral proposition turns into a shocking lesson
in everlasting love...

**"A spectacular and skillfully handled story that stands head
and shoulders above the average historical romance."**
—*Publishers Weekly* (starred review)

S0126

Penguin Group (USA) Online

What will you be reading tomorrow?

Tom Clancy, Patricia Cornwell, W.E.B. Griffin,
Nora Roberts, William Gibson, Robin Cook,
Brian Jacques, Catherine Coulter, Stephen King,
Dean Koontz, Ken Follett, Clive Cussler,
Eric Jerome Dickey, John Sandford,
Terry McMillan, Sue Monk Kidd, Amy Tan,
J. R. Ward, Laurell K. Hamilton,
Charlaine Harris, Christine Feehan...

You'll find them all at
penguin.com

*Read excerpts and newsletters,
find tour schedules and reading group guides,
and enter contests.*

Subscribe to Penguin Group (USA) newsletters
and get an exclusive inside look
at exciting new titles and the authors you love
long before everyone else does.

PENGUIN GROUP (USA)
us.penguingroup.com